D0931374

John S. Sargent
august 1896

SIEGFRIED SASSOON

Meredith

CONSTABLE · *Publishers* · LONDON

LONDON

PUBLISHED BY
Constable and Company Ltd.
10–12 Orange Street, W.C.2

INDIA
Longmans, Green and Company Ltd.
BOMBAY CALCUTTA MADRAS

CANADA
Longmans, Green and Company
TORONTO

First published . . . 1948

*,8238
M559xs*

Printed in Great Britain by
RICHARD CLAY AND COMPANY, LTD.
BUNGAY
Suffolk
FRONTISPIECE PRINTED IN COLLOGRAVURE BY HARRISON AND SONS LTD.
PRINTERS TO HIS MAJESTY THE KING, LONDON, HAYES (MIDDX) AND HIGH WYCOMBE

To

G. M. TREVELYAN

12-14-66 Colonial 4.50

My grateful acknowledgments are due to Mr. Desmond MacCarthy and to Messrs. Putnam & Co., Ltd., for permission to quote a long passage from the essay on Meredith which appeared in his volume of *Portraits*, and to Mr. Orlo Williams for an extract from the essay on *The Egoist*, included in his volume *Some Great English Novels*; also to Messrs. John Murray for permission to print extracts from *Works and Days* by Michael Field.

S. S.

CONTENTS

Contents

The frontispiece is reproduced, by courtesy of the Syndics of the Fitzwilliam Museum, Cambridge, from J. S. Sargent's drawing of George Meredith. This drawing was made in August, 1896, and is now in the possession of the Fitzwilliam Museum.

CHAPTER ONE

1

GEORGE MEREDITH was born on February 12th, 1828, at 73 High
Street, Portsmouth. He was an only child, and his mother died
when he was five years old. His father, born in 1797, was the
son of Melchizidec Meredith, who died in 1814 at the age of
fifty-one.

For thirty years Melchizidec had been a tailor and naval
outfitter at 73 High Street. To this business, which had become
the leading one of its kind in Portsmouth, his son succeeded,
capably assisted by his mother, who died in November, 1828.

Such is the bare outline of a family who were by no means
ordinary provincial tradespeople. It might even be claimed
that Melchizidec was extraordinary; he was undoubtedly
remarkable. To begin with, he was a fine figure of a man, tall,
good looking, and agreeable. He had qualities of character
which enabled him to be on friendly terms with many of his
customers and patrons, among whom must have been most of
the distinguished naval officers of the time and many of the
country squires of the locality. With some of the latter he
became so popular that he was a welcome guest at their dinner-
tables, and extremely well liked by their ladies. He kept
horses and hunted, and was an officer in the Portsmouth
Yeomanry Cavalry during the threat of Napoleonic invasion.
In fact, he was a very passable imitation of a swell gentleman,
and there is no need to disbelieve the story of his being mistaken
for a Marquis during a visit to Bath.

His social aspirations, of course, were a handicap to the
business. He lived beyond his means, seldom sent in a bill,
and left large debts when he died. Of his five beautiful daughters
four married well; one to a brewer; one to a prosperous grocer
and banker who was Mayor of Portsmouth in 1833; one to a
Lieutenant in the Marines who subsequently rose to be General
Sir S. B. Ellis, K.C.B.; and one to a purser in the Royal Navy

I

who became Consul-General in the Azores. Two of these daughters died in 1812 and 1813. The other three figure conspicuously in the pages of *Evan Harrington*, along with the pervading personality of their defunct parent, ' the Great Mel '. Their brother Augustus can only be described as ineffective and insignificant. At the time of his father's death he was intending to be a doctor, but in obedience to the masterful ' Mrs. Mel ' gave up this ambition and did his best to train himself for the distasteful profession which circumstances imposed on him. Good looking and gentlemanly, he evidently lacked ability and initiative. He was careless in money matters and fond of entertaining his friends, and after ' Mrs. Mel's ' death the business steadily declined.

In 1841 he married his housekeeper, sold the business, and moved to London, where he is known to have carried on a tailor's shop in St. James's Street from 1846 to 1849. This should have been profitable, but his inaptitude caused it to be a failure. He then emigrated to South Africa, establishing himself as a tailor in Cape Town, where he remained until 1860.

Returning to England, he lived in retirement until 1876. Someone who knew him in Cape Town described him as ' a smart, dapper little man, very quiet and reserved, a good sample of a self-respecting and courteous shop keeper '. There is other evidence that he was a cultured, generous type of man, a great chess player and fond of reading. Like his son, he was a strong walker; it is recorded that when over sixty he climbed Table Mountain without fatigue. Towards the end of his own life, Meredith pronounced a crushing and melancholy epitaph upon him. ' He was a muddler and a fool.' This, no doubt, referred to his incompetence in money matters, which his son had reason to resent. Nevertheless, though unable to win the confidence and affection of his son, poor Augustus did all he could to give him a good education.

The mother of George Meredith was the daughter of Michael Macnamara, who kept a tavern, ' The Vine ', a short distance from 73 High Street. The choice of Augustus seems to have been a sensible one. Despite her origin, Jane Macnamara was refined, talented, and witty. Her brother became a clergyman, but nothing is known of him except that ' he lived for some time at Southsea at a later period '. It can be assumed that Meredith derived some of his qualities from her. He claimed that his mother was of Irish origin, but it has been proved that for several generations her family had lived in Hampshire. According to his own statements, his child-hood was not a happy one, but it is certain that he was loved and cared for by both his parents and allowed the privileges of an only child. From an early age, however, he was dis-satisfied with his environment, and, as always, acutely sensitive in temperament. At nine years old he was sent as a day boy to St. Paul's School, Southsea, where he had the reputation of being proud and reserved with his contemporaries, which can hardly be wondered at. When his father left Portsmouth he spent a year at a boarding-school near Petersfield, an experience which he has described in *Harry Richmond*. His mother's small fortune had been left in the hands of trustees for him. (Later he became a ward in Chancery, most of the trust-money having disappeared.)

It has been stated that he chose his next school for himself. The selection was a surprising one—the Moravian School at Neuwied, on the Rhine, near Cologne. He went there in August, 1842, and remained for nearly two years, without any break for holidays. At that time a great many English boys were at the school.

It had been founded in 1756 for a sect which can be sum-marised as having affinities with the Quakers. The educational aim of the Moravian brothers was to practise what you preach, and to do as you would be done by, without insisting on dogmatic doctrine. Their liberal teaching had begun in an age of religious unrest and intolerance. Lutherans, Calvinists, Catholics, Moravians, Jews, were allowed full liberty of thought and worship in Neuwied in the mid-18th Century, under the enlightened rule of their Prince, who started the school. The influence of the place upon Meredith's youthful mind must have been profound. ' There cannot be any goodness unless it is practised goodness ' was always part of his philosophy.

The conditions were austere. Fifty beds in the dormitory were so close together as to leave no room for moving between them. A master slept by the bay window, which was never opened. But here Meredith began to be educated, for, according to his own account, he had learned very little at his previous

3

schools, and among his favourite reading had been *The Arabian Nights*, which, he said, ' doubtless fed an imagination which took shape in *The Shaving of Shagpat* '.

The moral training of the Moravians was a fine thing for him; it gave him an outlook which over-rode narrow religious prejudices and taught him the value of liberalism and good manners. Neuwied also benefited him by providing a needed antidote to the provincialism of his family background at Portsmouth. It enabled him to begin his career, at sixteen, with an invincible resolve to rise above that background—and we shall see how strongly he was influenced by the peaceful old Germany of that period, when Goethe had been dead only ten years. The romantic and poetical associations of it filled his mind with a wealth of absorbed experience which found fruition in *Farina, Harry Richmond*, and elsewhere. He loved the hills and vineyards, the ' tumbled, dark and light green country of swelling forest-land and slopes of meadow ', the feudal gleams of ruined turrets above the river, and the distant village roofs of blue and white. In long, Nature-worshipping walks he learnt to know the Rhineland well. His main studies were in German and French literature, but he acquired something equally valuable from the kindliness, simplicity, and good sense of his teachers. In fact, without going into the details of his intellectual and emotional development, one can say that he gained more at Neuwied than he would have done had he shared the experience of Shelley and Swinburne at Eton.

2

From the time he left Neuwied until February, 1846, nothing is known of Meredith's doings. Possibly he was with his father, helping with the account work of the business in St. James's Street.

Shortly before his eighteenth birthday he began his duties as an articled clerk with R. S. Charnock, a solicitor in Paternoster Row.

Being a ward in Chancery, he was probably told that the law was the most suitable profession for a young man with literary aspirations; so what remained of his money after the mismanagement of trustees was unprofitably employed in binding him for five years of legal tutelage to a person who, as he afterwards said, ' had neither business nor morals '. He had no inclination, of course, for the career of an attorney, but no alternative presented itself to him.

Charnock, however, was much more advantageous to his literary beginnings than a competent and successful lawyer would have been; and I suspect that the self-reliant young George may have had a hand in the selection of him. For he was not only an odd and interesting character but also by no means negligible as an author and philologist.

> Tall, dark and thin, sometimes untidy, often dirty, with something goat-like in his bearded face, he was not interested in his profession. He preferred to smoke, to take long walks, to pour out robust or cynical jokes, to idle away a day fishing, to hunt out the meaning of place-names, or to plan a walking tour in the Harz or the Tyrol.

(Thus he is described by one of Meredith's biographers.) Born in 1820, his name was one of the earliest on the books of the British Museum Library, he having been admitted a reader in 1838. He was a Fellow of the Society of Antiquaries, and belonged to the Arundel Club, whose members included Dickens, R. H. Horne, and Lord John Manners—afterwards Duke of Rutland, and at that time ardently associated with the ' Young England ' movement which figured in Disraeli's *Coningsby*. Charnock, who lived, lonely and unmarried, to the age of eighty-four, seems to have abandoned the law after he was thirty. An old book of reference describes him, in 1899, as having travelled through the whole of Europe.

> He has also visited the North of Africa and Asia Minor, and has devoted much time to the study of anthropology, archaeology, and the Celtic and Oriental languages. He is a Ph.D. of the University of Göttingen.

He published several books, among them *Patronymica Cornu-Britannica*, or the *Etymology of Cornish Surnames*, of which I have seen, in a bookseller's catalogue, a copy presented by him to Meredith.

Meanwhile he gave significant help in starting his pupil on his non-legal career by introducing him to his own set of intimates, mainly writers and artists, among whom the handsome youth, with his red-brown hair, splendid physique, and exuberant energy of mind, must have caused more than a flutter of excitement. In 1848 he stimulated his literary coterie by starting a manuscript magazine, *The Monthly Observer*, which each contributor edited and criticised in turn. The quarto sheets were bound and circulated among them, Charnock himself supplying an account of his tour in the Harz. In 1910, five numbers of the magazine, sold at Sotheby's for £80, were acquired for the Widener library, two of these numbers being edited by Meredith. He inserted several of his translations from the German poets, and a poem on Saint Theresa which was probably echoed from Tennyson's St. Agnes—

> Around her gloried form the air
>   Is starred with falling snows
> That cover all the convent bare
>   With symboll'd pure repose.
> Above her halo'ed head the sky
>   Is studded thick with spheres
> All swimming to one blissful eye
>   Whose beam is bright with tears.

His first printed poem (also in the magazine) appeared in *Chambers's Journal*, July 7th, 1849. It was inspired by a battle, one of the most sanguinary of the Sikh wars, which had been fought early in that year. Each of the six stanzas begins with the name of the battle, duplicated. To Meredith's young mind the name was ' natural music and a dirge above the dead, sad and strange like a breeze through midnight harpstrings '.

> Chillianwallah, Chillianwallah!
>   'Tis a village dark and low,
> By the bloody Jhelum river
>   Bridged by the foreboding foe;
> And across the wintry water
>   He is ready to retreat,
> When the carnage and the slaughter
>   Shall have paid for his defeat.

When sending the poem to the editor, he wrote that ' it was written immediately on receipt of the intelligence which it chaunts, and will, I think, even now find many an echo in hearts akin to the subject and the name which christens it '.

It is possible, however, that he over-estimated the natural magic of the name; and the poem can safely be classified as the worst he ever published.

By this time he was living in lodgings—a single room—in Ebury Street, Pimlico. He had no money except the small remnant of his mother's property, but the journalistic legend, that he started his career as a writer with one guinea, which he invested in a sack of oatmeal, has long since been confuted as nonsense.

From Pimlico he went long walks into the country—in those days easily accessible—and thus began his lifelong devotion to the hills and heaths of Surrey. His chief companion on these excursions was Edward Peacock, a friend of Charnock's, three or four years older than himself, and a son of Thomas Love Peacock. Edward was an athlete—a champion sculler and, like Meredith, fond of boxing. He was a clerk in the East India House, where his father held the post of Chief Examiner for twenty years until his retirement in 1856. Early in life he had been to sea, which probably accounts for his sister Mary having married a naval officer, Lieutenant Edward Nicolls, who was drowned within three months of the wedding. This was in 1844; and Mrs. Nicolls was now staying, most of her time, with her brother, who had rooms in Devonshire Street, near the British Museum. There, in 1847 or 1848, she met Meredith, who fell in love with her. From what is known of her, this must have been quite easy to do. She was beautiful, witty, literary minded, and an amateur poetess. She had the liveliness and social sophistication of one who had mixed with the world that rode in Rotten Row, and a nature susceptible to the attraction of men of genius or talent. Unquestionably, she was a bewitching apparition for young Meredith, and her charms have been immortalised by him in prose and verse seldom, if ever, surpassed as illuminations of the rapture of first love. Enthralled by the strong enchantment of her physical attraction, he also saw in her an intellectual brilliance fit to mate with his own. For this was the daughter of one who had been a friend of Shelley, whose graceful songs and satiric novels had charmed the chosen spirits of his time, and whose social background was rich in literary associations and intimacies. Alluring and exciting must that brother and sister have seemed to his inexperience, unwarned of their instability of temperament, oblivious to everything but Mary's fascinating qualities. She was six and a half years older than he was; she was sentimental and sarcastic by turns; she was argumentative and unacquiescent. He had no premonition that any of these facts would be to his disadvantage. Several times she refused him, for he had nothing to offer her but genius and good looks. But she was in love with him, and on August 9th, 1849, they were married in St. George's Church, Hanover Square. The register was signed by T. L. Peacock, who disapproved of the match, for obvious reasons, but cannot have failed to realise that he was acquiring a son-in-law whose mental abilities gave promise of high achievements.

CHAPTER TWO

1

WHEN charting an outline of the next eight years, one finds recorded details fragmentary and disconnected. To begin with, we have been given three variant accounts of the duration of his honeymoon period. An editorial note in the *Letters* stated that ' the next few years were spent chiefly on the Continent '. The *Dictionary of National Biography* reduced this to ' a year or more abroad '. Later on, S. M. Ellis wrote that ' soon after the marriage, the Merediths went to the Continent on the proceeds of a legacy which had come to George from a relative in Portsmouth; but they were back in London by November, when they stayed with T. L. Peacock at his house in London '. This can be accepted as the accurate version. Evidence of their visit to the Rhineland survives in the six immature sonnets, *Pictures of the Rhine*, which Meredith must have written while abroad.

During the next three and a half years, according to Ellis, ' they passed their time between Peacock's homes and various lodgings and boarding-houses by the seaside (particularly at Felixstowe and Seaford) and in Surrey '.

Peacock's country house was at Lower Halliford, two miles from Weybridge, which was where the Merediths mainly lived in these unsettled years.

They boarded with Mrs. Macirone at The Limes, a pleasant house with a large garden. Mrs. Macirone, a woman of culture and charm, was the widow of a Colonel who had been A.D.C. to Murat, King of Naples. She knew many interesting people, and it was here that Meredith met Tom Taylor (1817–1880), from then onwards one of his best friends. Taylor was a prolific and successful playwright, and for the last six years of his life was editor of *Punch*. In the summer of 1850 he introduced Meredith to Sir Alexander Duff Gordon and his wife, who were living in Weybridge, of whom (with their

9

daughter Janet, then aged eight) there will be much to relate in connection with *Evan Harrington.*

Another guest of Mrs. Macirone's was Samuel Lucas (1818–1868). He was on the staff of *The Times,* and subsequently became editor of *Once a Week,* the magazine in which *Evan Harrington* appeared as a serial.

For biographical purposes, 1851 and 1852 are lost years. All we know is that by the middle of 1853 the Merediths had taken up their abode with T. L. Peacock at Lower Halliford. Peacock's wife had died in the previous year; and the young couple, desperately short of money, needed all the help he could give them. On June 13th their son and only child, Arthur, was born.

Having traced their existence thus far, we must go back to 1851, where some much-needed material awaits inspection. This, of course, is the volume of *Poems* with which Meredith made his first bid for literary reputation. Dedicated to Peacock 'with the profound admiration and affectionate respect of his son-in-law', it appeared on June 30th, published by J. W. Parker, who was a friend of Peacock's. Five hundred copies were printed, of which only a hundred were bound. As Meredith subsequently destroyed three hundred, the small octavo book, in its faded green binding, has since been a rarity, and most of the survivors are presentation copies from the author (who lost sixty pounds on the publication). Significant among these is one inscribed ' To R. H. Horne Esqre by whose generous appreciation and trusty criticism these " Poems " were chiefly fostered '. On the title-page is printed a quotation from Horne's *Orion.*

Shortly before his marriage, Meredith had been in touch with Horne, who was a friend of Charnock's. Their association did not last long, for Horne went to Australia in 1852 and remained there seventeen years. He is remembered as a well-known figure in the literary world of the '40s, partly through a voluminous correspondence with Mrs. Browning and his editorship of *The New Spirit of the Age,* to which she contributed an essay, but mainly by the epic *Orion,* which he brought out in 1843 at the price of a farthing, containing his only ' familiar quotation '—' 'Tis always morning somewhere in the world '—(a line that somehow suggests Meredith and his attitude to life). He was an extraordinary and absurdly eccentric personage, an expert swimmer, and very vain of his physical strength and accomplishments.

As a writer his talent was fugitive; for a few years he was quite a good poet and enjoyed a considerable reputation, which had dwindled to nothing when he died in 1884. That *Orion* evoked Meredith's young enthusiasm is not surprising. The verse is dignified and melodious and the philosophy contained in it is recognisably Meredithian, in an embryonic way. Horne explained the hero of his epic as ' a type of the contest between the intellect and the senses . . . a dreamer of noble dreams tending to healthy thought or to practical action, with a heart expanding toward the largeness and warmth of Nature '. But his influence ended with the 1851 *Poems*, which are no more than competent and promising Juvenilia, showing no sign of the later style, though every kind of poem he was afterwards to write is represented in the volume. That he himself regarded the book as a mere indication of what he hoped to accomplish is shown in two contemporary letters, in one of which he said, ' It all reads too young'. The other was to Charles Ollier, who had written to him with appreciation and encouragement. Ollier had published for Keats and Shelley, was the friend of Lamb, Leigh Hunt, Peacock, and many other writers, and acted as literary adviser to Edward Moxon. Meredith replied, with gratitude, that the poems were all the work of extreme youth, and that the strictest criticism could scarcely be more unsparing than himself on the faults that were freely to be found in them.

Before the end of the year, however, the book was favourably reviewed by W. M. Rossetti, who assigned its author to the Keatsian school and found an amiable and engaging quality in the poems, though complaining of an undue hankering after novelty of metre. This was followed by Charles Kingsley's gracious and sympathetic critique in *Fraser's Magazine*, praising the Pastorals for their sweet and wholesome writing and the love poems for their depth of thought and feeling. Both reviews singled out *Love in the Valley* as showing promise, Rossetti quoting it in full. These eleven crude and lovable stanzas were the first version of the great lyric which, in riper years, he rewrote, amplified, and perfected. Even in its earliest form it evoked the admiration of Tennyson, who was sent an advance copy and at once wrote to Meredith saying how much it charmed him and that he went about the house repeating its cadences to himself. In later life Meredith dismissed the poems as rubbish and discouraged all reference to them. In 1908 he wrote of them as ' worthless, immature stuff of a youth in his teens, who had not found his hand '. They were reprinted in 1898, in the edition de luxe of his complete works.

2

Peacock was a reclusive, comfort-loving, and studious man, whose writings were little known, though the suffrage of the fit and few had already established him as a minor classic. In 1853 he was sixty-eight. Naturally, he found the Meredith ménage too great a strain on him. His son-in-law was restless and unamenable to the ceremonious household routine. Also he was a perpetual smoker, and Peacock had a vehement antipathy to the habit. The cause of his dislike for tobacco was partly an intense dread of fire. He would never allow more than a few matches in the house at a time. Edith Nicolls, at the end of her long life, remembered Meredith as ' the most wonderful of playmates ' ; but she added that her grandfather ' could not stand him '. The arrival of the baby was the climax to Peacock's discomforts and by the end of the year he had rented a cottage for them on the other side of Lower Halliford Green. From this place Meredith went his customary long walks through the rural countryside which became the background of at least two of his earlier novels. Here he lived for the next two years, and the only definite things known about his existence are that he wrote *The Shaving of Shagpat*, and that in 1855 he gave a reading from it at the house of a friend in London. It was an astonishing achievement, utterly unpredictable as the successor of the *Poems*.

Primarily an outburst of youthful vitality and intellectual high spirits, it revealed its author as already a master of imaginative narration, sumptuously descriptive prose, and richly triumphant humour. Yet it was begun and carried through as a burlesque of *The Arabian Nights*, and was in essence a *jeu d'esprit*, though expanded to a book of well over

100,000 words. In old age he told someone that it was 'written with duns at the door'. It can be assumed that he believed it likely to earn him a good sum of money, for he must have put an immense amount of work into the writing, which is elaborate and highly finished. In boyhood *The Arabian Nights* had been among his favourite reading, but he is said to have been stimulated to begin the book after listening to a marvellous Oriental fantasy told by an old gentleman at the Duff Gordons' house. Published at the end of 1855, it was immediately reviewed by George Eliot, who hailed it as 'a work of genius, and of poetical genius'.

> Mr. Meredith [she wrote] has not simply imitated Arabian pictures, he has been inspired by them. In one particular he differs widely from his models, but that difference is a high merit: it lies in the exquisite delicacy of his love incidents and love scenes. In every other characteristic—in exuberance of imagery, in picturesque wildness of incident, in significant humour, in aphoristic wisdom, *The Shaving of Shagpat* is a new Arabian Night.

She confesses, however, to 'having felt rather a languishing interest towards the end of the work; the details of the action became too complicated, and our imagination was rather wearied by following them'. The present writer has felt the same. In fact it is possible to find *Shagpat* somewhat boring, in spite of the superb passages in which it abounds. This opinion was not held by Edmund Gosse, who wrote, in a graceful essay, published in 1891:

> Delicious in this harsh world of reality to fold a mist around us, and out of it to evolve the yellow domes and black cypresses, the silver fountains and marble pillars, of the fabulous city of Shagpat. . . . The variety of scenes and images, the untiring evolution of plot, the kaleidoscopic shifting of harmonious colours, all these seem of the very essence of Arabia, and to coil directly from some bottle of a genie.

The general public, however, oblivious to George Eliot's recommendations, gave the extravaganza little support, and the first edition was sold off as a remainder. From the first, Meredith was expecting too much of his readers, crediting them with more intelligence and appetite for originality than they possessed.

One other biographical detail is extant for this period. In July, 1855, Meredith wrote as follows to J. W. Parker:

I have ready for publication, a volume of Songs, which I purpose to call ' British Songs ', as under that title they come best. In consideration of our association together in my first attempt, I offer it to you. I need scarcely say that I am quite conscious of not proposing in this, any remarkable advantage to you. You will, probably, comprehend my motive, and that it springs neither from a feeling of conceit, nor from any considerations of self-interest. But, knowing your appreciation of the poetical market just now, it is very improbable you will entertain my proposal when I add, that I must sell the book, having spent on it, latterly, valuable time. Should you, under these circumstances, not decide till you have seen the book, and care to see it, I will forward it to you.

Of this volume nothing else is known except that, in 1890, Meredith wrote to John Lane (who was then publishing Richard Le Gallienne's book on him), ' I destroyed the " British Songs " on being told of the small chance that they would be read.' It seems possible that the proposal was a desperate effort to earn money. Had Meredith thought well of their quality he would not have destroyed the poems. It can be added that his only recorded earnings up to the appearance of *Shagpat* were derived from *Household Words*, which had printed twenty-three poems, for which, according to the contributor's book of that magazine, he received £31 12s. Until 1852 Horne was assistant editor. In 1911 Meredith's son disclaimed the authenticity of all but three of them. It may be inferred that some of them were written in collaboration with Mrs. Meredith, and that none were included among the vanished ' British Songs '.

3

No explanation has been given as to why the Merediths gave up the cottage at Halliford about the end of 1855. We are merely told, by S. M. Ellis, that ' during 1856 and 1857 they were living mostly at Seaford '. Once again, it seems, the inquiring biographer is to be denied his ingredients for a re-creation of the domestic scene. We do, however, get a glimpse of what they did and why they went to what was then a dull and stagnant little place, made tolerable for Meredith by the Sussex Downs, whereon he could stride his huge quota of wind-blown miles.

They were induced to go to Seaford by Maurice FitzGerald, who owned property there and had got to know them at Weybridge about three years before. FitzGerald was now twenty-one and had just left Cambridge. He was a nephew of Edward FitzGerald and a first-rate classical scholar. (In 1867 he published a volume of translations from Euripides and Theocritus, of which his incomparable uncle writes approvingly in one of his letters.) Maurice was also a connoisseur of fine cooking and an avoider of any form of violent exercise. Gastronomy, whist, and literature comprised his main interests in life. He was, unquestionably, the original of the Wise Youth in *The Ordeal of Richard Feverel*. A drawing by Samuel Laurence shows him as almost nobly handsome—a face not unrelated to the gods of ancient Greece. Noting the finely elongated eye-setting and the primly sensual mouth, one at once exclaims ' Adrian Harley to the life! '

The Merediths shared the lodgings at Marine Terrace where he and his brother lived with a carpenter and his wife, Ockenden by name. Mrs. Ockenden was an exceptionally good cook and a full-flavoured character. She can be identified as Richard Feverel's ' Mrs. Berry ', and also figures prominently in *The House on the Beach*, an amusing little story for which Meredith took Seaford as the background. Anyhow, Meredith was in good spirits when he wrote, in the summer of 1856, to Eyre Crowe:

> Come and stay a week. The weather is lovely. The heat quite sweltering. Mrs. Meredith joins in kind regards. She says you must come under pain of her displeasure. Come, O Crowe! Here is fishing, bathing, rowing, sailing, lounging, running, pic-nicing, and a cook who builds a basis of strength to make us equal to all these superhuman efforts.

Crowe was another friend acquired from Mrs. Macirone's circle at Weybridge. He was an A.R.A. and a painter of some

15

distinction. In the early '50s he acted as Thackeray's secretary and amanuensis, accompanying him to the United States on his lecturing tour.

I have said that no reason has been given for the Meredith's departure from Lower Halliford. It occurs to me, however, that an explanation can be inferred. All was not well in the married life of the Merediths through causes which will in due course be disclosed. Alleviation of their strained relationship was thus provided by Maurice FitzGerald, who was an artist in avoiding unpleasantness and making daily life diverting. He acted as a buffer between the highly-strung, disputatious couple, and Meredith always found him the best of company, both then and thereafter. Often he may have resorted to him as ally and protector when his wife was in a difficult mood and the tragi-comedy of domestic disagreement showed signs of involving him in yet another nerve-devastating scene. And often must the half-Irish humour and mellow cynicism of the wise youth have intervened between their temperamental discords.

During 1856 Meredith completed *Farina : A Legend of Cologne*. Little more than a third the length of *Shagpat*, this was a burlesque of the mediaeval romanticism which had been the fashion since *The Castle of Otranto*, and a subtly ironical comment on such writers as M. G. Lewis and Mrs. Radcliffe. It is the sort of thing which only a young man would have bothered to write, and is justifiably the least admired of Meredith's prose works. Nevertheless, there is much beautiful writing in it, and as a whole it is a highly finished and spirited narrative. At times he evidently forgot that he was indulging in literary antics, and allowed his poetic imagination full play. Some of the scenic descriptions are in his best style. In a few passages, too, Meredithian mannerisms are already distinctly observable. George Eliot, admittedly disappointed, gave it a short review (in an article which also discussed *Barchester Towers* and *Madame Bovary*). She did her best, by calling it original and entertaining, but it found few readers, though Smith, Elder & Co. reissued it in a shilling edition eight years afterwards.

For his next novel Meredith was returning to Chapman & Hall, who had published *The Shaving of Shagpat*. In December, 1856, we find him writing about it, from Seaford, to Edward

16

Chapman, with whom he was on very friendly terms. In the previous summer he and his little son Arthur had spent a holiday at Folkestone with the Chapman family. (It is significant that Mrs. Meredith and her twelve-year-old daughter Edith Nicolls were not with him there.)

Will you send me, this week, the £25 for which I made application, to sum the £70 requested in advance, and so doing oblige your faithful poet. I remain here, as I can work better than elsewhere, though, engaged as I am, the DULNESS is something frightful, and bangs on my shoulders like Sinbad's Old Man of the Sea. I dream of Boltons. [Chapman's house at Tunbridge Wells.] I promise myself a visit there at Christmas just for a beguilement; but it is doubtful if I shall quit hard work for a day, till the book is finished. I will come Manuscript in hand. The name of the novel is to be *The Fair Frankincense*. Tell me what you think of it. There are to be two Prophets in the book, and altogether a new kind of villain,—being Humbug active—a great gun likely to make a noise, if I prime him properly. Have you, or do any of your people know of, a book of Hampshire dialect? I have a Sussex. Ballads, or Songs, with the provincialisms will serve. Perhaps Mr. Frederic Chapman may know of such a thing. Also a Slang Dictionary, or book of the same with Gloss. And if you have, or can get these, will you forward them by post?

Mrs. Meredith is staying at Blackheath. [With Lady Nicolls, and the two children.] Don't wait to send by her, as I am anxious she should spend Xmas in town. Dulness will put out the wax lights, increase the weight of the pudding, toughen the turkey, make lead of the beef, turn the entire feast into a nightmare down here, to one not head and heels at work.

Thuswise we discover that he was at work on *Richard Feverel*. And how strange it seems that but for the survival of this letter we should know nothing whatever about the process by which that famous novel was written. Here he was, receiving a £70 advance on it. Two and a half years elapsed before it was published. What else do we know? One biographer asserts that it was conceived in 1852! The only other information came from Meredith when, as an old man, he told Edward Clodd, 'Feverel was written at 7, Hobury Street, Chelsea; it took me a year to write.' That, we know, was in 1858.

We can only conjecture some serious interruption which thwarted his intention to ' come Manuscript in hand ' on his next visit to Chapman at Tunbridge Wells. For 1857 is another blank year for the biographer. *The Fair Frankincense*, as the first provisional title, evidently suggested the sacrifice of Lucy. One cannot regret its disappearance. It is a classic example of an author's first thoughts not being the best. The request for dialect books is of interest as showing that the dialogue of his rustic characters was rather artificially contrived. And, compared with Hardy's, they do sometimes give an impression of being not quite natural.

From these literary considerations we turn to the final paragraph of the letter. ' Mrs. Meredith is staying at Blackheath.' The words are more than ominous. For it was not the urgency of his creative activity which made him choose to spend his Christmas alone. Seven years earlier he had written, after their marriage—

> No longer, severing our embrace,
>   Was night a sword between us;
> But richest mystery, robed in grace,
>   To wrap us close and screen us.

She had been the inspiration of *Love in the Valley*. With her he had lived, in himself, the idyll of first love which would irradiate the pages of *Richard Feverel* for future generations. And now he was sitting at dull Seaford, with the fire dying in the grate, ' anxious she should spend Xmas in town '.

' Wishing for the sword that severs all ' would probably have been nearer the truth, had he revealed his inmost thoughts to Edward Chapman. The scene was set for *Modern Love*, wherein he wrote the testament of his unhappiness, awarding the woman he had loved the cold comfort of immortality in a poetic masterpiece.

5

In *Modern Love* there is no revelation of the disharmony which caused this miserable break-up. Only the disillusionment and its climax are anatomised and described, and the actions which accompanied them are altered beyond recognition.

All that we know of the climax is that, some time in 1858, Mrs. Meredith went to Capri with Henry Wallis, and that she returned to England in the following year with a baby. Wallis was a gifted painter who had already made a name by exhibiting at the Royal Academy. *The Death of Chatterton*, which can be seen in the Tate Gallery, ranks with the best Pre-Raphaelite pictures of the '50s. It was painted in the Gray's Inn chambers of Austin Daniel, one of the contributors to *The Monthly Observer*. Meredith was the model, and it can certainly be regarded as a portrait of him in 1855, though it is probable that by then he had grown a beard. In January, 1858, Wallis painted the head of Peacock which is in the National Portrait Gallery. He lived to be eighty-six, having ceased to exhibit at the Royal Academy after 1877, becoming a landscape painter, and an authority on the Ceramic Art of the Near East, where he lived for many years. Abandoned by him, Mrs. Meredith is said to have sought a reconciliation with her husband, but he had warned her of the irreparable consequences of her action before she left him. There is no evidence that he ever saw her again.

What were the causes of the calamity?

Two highly-strung temperaments—man and wife—each imaginative, emotional, quick to anger, cuttingly satirical in dispute, each an incomparable wielder of the rapier of ridicule, could not find content within the narrow bounds of poverty and lodgings.

Thus, in an editorial note to the *Letters*, his son W. M. Meredith summed up the situation. In the following lines from *Modern Love* he himself epitomised the tragedy of ' the union of this ever-diverse pair '.

> These two were rapid falcons in a snare
> Condemned to do the flitting of the bat.
> Lovers beneath the singing sky of May,
> They wandered once; clear as the dew on flowers:
> But they fed not on the advancing hours:
> Their hearts held cravings for the buried day.
> Then each applied to each that fatal knife,
> Deep questioning, which probes to endless dole.
> Ah, what a dusty answer gets the soul
> When hot for certainties in this our life!

Meanwhile we have seen him sitting at Seaford writing the first chapters of *Richard Feverel*. It can be assumed that by then he was aware that he could not continue his work as a writer while living with his wife. Separation was inevitable, though he must, at that time, have contemplated some compromise arrangement.

It had been a union of physical passion, but it had long been apparent that he was married to the wrong woman. As Peacock's daughter she had brought him a cultivated, witty, sophisticated mind worthy to match with his. At her best she must indeed have been delightful. Holman Hunt described her to someone as 'a dashing horsewoman who attracted much notice from the " bloods " of the day'. Others who knew her said that she was charming, with intellectual gifts above the average.

During their early years together Meredith had outlined her qualities in some lines, which, by the way, are very much in the manner of Peacock's light verse.

> She can be as wise as we,
> And wiser when she wishes;
> She can knit with cunning wit,
> And dress the homely dishes.
> She can flourish staff or pen,
> And deal a wound that lingers;
> She can talk the talk of men,
> And touch with thrilling fingers . . .
>
> Soft and loving is her soul,
> Swift and lofty soaring;
> Mixing with its dove-like dole
> Passionate adoring . . .
>
> She is steadfast as a star,
> And yet the maddest maiden:
> She can wage a gallant war,
> And give the peace of Eden.

In other words, she could ' get on well with men ', was an amateur writer, incalculably feminine, indulged in emotional uplift, was fatiguingly argumentative, and was adept in the arts and allurements of love-making. ' Only mark the

rich light striking out from her on him!' he exclaims in
Modern Love, supplementing this, later on, by remarking that
' Madam's faulty feature is a glazed and inaccessible eye, that
has soft fire, wide gates, at love-time only '. Wedded to such
a woman, he needed two lives, one for her fine feelings and
nerve-tension relievings, and another to do his work in. And
no one knew better than he did that he wasn't an easy man to
live with. All his life he had a sharp tongue which served a
mind that delighted in exhibition flights of irony.

It remains to ask what he gained from these years of domestic
attrition and spiritual discomfort. He had married her as an
ambitious youth with no family or social background of his
own. She had provided an excellent one in the Peacock *milieu*,
with its distinguished literary associations and the presiding
presence of T. L. Peacock himself. In the words of Desmond
MacCarthy:

> Meredith's nature was clearly one to take a strong infusion of
> Peacock's personality. That robust scholar, with his preference
> for the vanished England of the Regency, his intellectual high
> spirits and dry exaggerative wit, was certain to call out those
> propensities in the younger man. . . . You may search the novels
> through without finding trace of a debt more authentic than that
> they owe to the author of *Maid Marian* and *Gryll Grange*.

In their personal relations the admiration seems to have been
mainly on Meredith's side, but the ' clever old man '—as he
called him—evidently influenced and encouraged his brilliant
son-in-law to the best of his ability, imbuing his mind with
the vintage flavour of a highly civilised conception of the
refinements and humanities of existence. This having been so,
it would be unfair to assert that the marriage was an un-
mitigated disaster. But a writer's workshop is his head; his
head has to do its work at home; and the craft of authorship
demands of him an immense nervous output. The conditions
imposed upon Meredith by his first wife must, surely, have
been excruciating. To what extent his productiveness was
impeded can only be conjectured. The fact remains that by
the end of 1857 he had completed only two prose works, one
of them short and comparatively trivial. The sequel to his
separation speaks for itself. During his first three years of what

can only be called liberation, he wrote the greater part of *Richard Feverel* and the whole of *Evan Harrington*, to say nothing of *Modern Love* and the other fine poems in the 1862 volume. More must be said about the ill-starred union when we arrive at that volume. Meanwhile it is certain that he emergèd from the ordeal disillusioned and grievously stricken in his proud spirit, but having won a philosophy of courage in adversity. Henceforward, courage was for him the most necessary of the virtues, and that the brave are repaid by what they have suffered is a theme which continually appears in his writings.

6

During 1858, as already stated, Meredith was living in lodgings at 7, Hobury Street, Chelsea. The only other detail I can ascertain for that year is that his son Arthur was taken charge of by Lady Nicolls, the mother of Mrs. Meredith's first husband. This arrangement ended sometime early in 1859, when he moved to Esher, where, with Arthur as his inseparable companion, he remained until the autumn, staying in a pleasant old house which had formerly been a coaching inn.

The Ordeal of Richard Feverel was published on June 20th, and was reviewed on July 9th in *The Athenaeum, The Saturday Review*, and *The Spectator*. Of these *The Athenaeum* is worth quoting—

This 'Ordeal' is about as painful a book as any reader ever felt himself compelled to read through, in spite of his own protests to the contrary—for read it through he must, if once he begins it, for the sole purpose of knowing what comes of it all. The book is very clever, with a fresh, vigorous vitality in the style; but it is not true to real life or human nature; only true to an abstract and arbitrary idea.

Thus it leads off, and, after a disparaging analysis of the plot, the critic concludes by remarking that ' the only comfort the reader can find on closing the book is—that it is not true. We hope the author will use his great ability to produce something pleasanter next time.' (*The Athenaeum*, by the way, ignored *Evan Harrington*.) *The Saturday Review* devoted twice as many words to being portentously stupid, and was only a little less discouraging in its verdict.

If this is all that Mr. Meredith can do, it is a failure; but it gives us hopes that it may prove the prelude to a work that will place him high in the list of living novelists.

And *The Spectator* accused the book of ' low ethical tone '— whereupon Mudie's Library, having bought three hundred copies, refused to circulate them to subscribers. Its reception seems to have been much the same as that of *Tess of the D'Urbervilles* thirty years later; but it fell dead, whereas *Tess* immediately became a best-seller. In October *The Times*, prompted, one assumes, by Tom Taylor and Samuel Lucas, who were on the staff, gave it a three-column review, amplified by long excerpts. This article, while indicating the book's defects, strongly defended it against the denunciations of Mrs. Grundy, and found it ' powerful, penetrative in its depth of insight, and rich in its variety of experience '. Nearly twenty years passed before the second and much-revised edition was published.

The Ordeal of Richard Feverel has been the most widely known and read of Meredith's novels. It is by no means his best written book, and is in some ways his saddest, though presented as a romantic comedy. Yet it has been enjoyed by a multitude of non-Meredithians, the majority of whom, one infers, have regarded *The Egoist* as beyond their intellectual capacities. There is one elementary reason for this popularity. With the general run of readers the title of a book makes a big difference; and the public of fifty or sixty years ago found this one attractive, whereas *The Fair Frankincense* would probably have fallen on unheeding ears. When it became known that *The Ordeal* was also a moving love-story, success was assured. Thus prosaically I arrive at my declaration—and how often it has been made before—that the love-story of Richard and Lucy is immortal. Immortality was achieved in the matchless chapters which describe how these two shared the rapt experience of youth's first love—innocent, amazeful, and unreasoning. Safeguarded from sentimentality by the mastering astringency of Meredith's mind, the episode is an Elysian enchantment. All his emotion went to the making of it, and all the early freshness of his art. With the first sentence, we surrender to the spell and lyrical intensity of a ' once in a lifetime ' piece of writing:

' Above green-flashing plunges of a weir, and shaken by the

thunder below, lilies, golden and white, were swaying at anchor among the weeds.' (Was he conscious, when writing those words, of the symbolism which contrasts the resistless onflow of passion with the anchored lily that was Lucy?) Once again in his life he recaptured the magic of this first meeting, when he re-wrote *Love in the Valley*. The poem is what Richard felt, but could only express in a lover's monosyllables—Meredith said it for him—' She is what my heart first awaking whispered the world was; morning light is she.' And again—' Could I find a place to be alone with heaven, I would speak my heart out: heaven is my need.'

It has been pointed out that in *The Ordeal* there is all of Meredith, though not fully developed. We are also told that it was the originator of the modern novel, bringing into existence a new method of telling a story. And Arnold Bennett described it as a weak book, full of episodic power and overloaded with wit, but the first entirely honest novel since Fielding.

Respectfully accepting these opinions, I must add that for me *The Ordeal* has meant something quite different. Reading it in my youth, I vaguely realised that it was a young man's book, that there was something in it which gave me delicious thrills of romance and regretfulness. Possibly I would have preferred a happy ending; but the last words of the book were poignantly unforgettable, and always will be. ' He lies there silent in his bed—striving to image her on his brain.' Thirty-five years later I feel the same, and am conscious of those qualities which make the book abidingly lovable, atoning for its defects of inconsistency, artificiality, and uneven style. Even now I cannot confidently put my finger on those qualities; the only explanation which I can formulate is that Meredith was using material from his most impressionable period with a sense of delight in producing his effects for the first time. Much of it came from his heart, and from his memories of the countryside where he had been in love with Mary Peacock. Also it was completed during what must have been the darkest year of his life, and therefore imbued with pathos and emotional subjectivity which he did not afterwards allow himself. With all its failings, *The Ordeal* contains those elements which give a book survival power, immune from the hungry generations of pundits and their critical opinions. Through them I now transmit the information that the style of *Richard Feverel* was influenced by Sterne, Carlyle, and Jean Paul Richter. It has also been suggested that the publication in 1858 of Herbert Spencer's famous essay on the place of natural reactions in education acted as a stimulus to Meredith's satirisation of Sir Austin Feverel's despotic parental system. (If this was so, I must confess that it is a bit of enlightenment which I could have done without.) Jean Paul Richter is only a name to me; but I can recognise the influence of Carlyle as a potent one. From boyhood Meredith had absorbed his philosophy admiringly, and his phraseology is apparent in many passages of *The Ordeal*. Carlyle read it in 1859, and wrote to the publishers, asking about the author. Meredith went to see him and was advised to turn to history as the repository of facts. Nearly fifty years later he described the occasion to a visiting journalist.

> I said to him, with all deference, I thought there were greater things in the world than facts. He turned on me and said, ' But facts are truth, and truth is facts.' I said, ' No, pardon me; if I may say so, truth I take to be the broad heaven above the petty doings of mankind which we call Facts.' He gave me a smile of pity for my youth, as I suppose, and then said, ' Ah weel, if ye like to talk in that poetic way, ye may; but ye'll find it in your best interest, young man, to stick to Fahcts.'

In *Beauchamp's Career* he introduced the well-known paragraph in which he refers to Carlyle's ' wind-in-the-orchard style '. After his death he wrote, in a letter, that ' he was one who stood constantly in the presence of those " Eternal verities " of which he speaks. . . . He was the greatest of the Britons of his time; Titanic, not Olympian: a heaver of rocks, not a shaper.'

Turning to the unavoidable subject of the autobiographical ingredients in *The Ordeal*, one can only conclude that Meredith drew on himself for much of the character of Richard, and that in Lucy—the first of his matchless gallery of noble dames—he found imaginative compensation for what he had endured with his wife. For Lucy was not clever; she was sensible: loving, gentle, and submissive, she passes through the story in a subdued radiance of ill-used loveliness. She is the antithesis of the tragic wife in *Modern Love*, a shadowy presentment of whom appears in Lady Feverel, unfaithful, banished, and forlorn.

25

It has been assumed that, while narrating the disastrous consequences of Sir Austin's System, Meredith had his own parental responsibilities much in mind. But Arthur was only five when the book was being finished, and it seems obvious that in any case his devoted father would have been deeply concerned with the problem of his upbringing.

In a letter to Samuel Lucas, Meredith explained his main design and moral purpose as follows.

> The System does succeed through the young fellow's luck in finding so charming a girl. The strength of his pure love for a women is a success—till the father strikes down his fabric. The System, you see, had its origin not so much in love for his son as in wrath at his wife, and so carries its own Nemesis. . . . The moral is that no System of the sort succeeds with human nature, unless the originator has conceived it purely independent of personal passion. That was Sir Austin's way of wreaking his revenge.

CHAPTER THREE

1

WHEN Meredith took Arthur to Esher he had already, in the previous year, begun what proved to be the deepest and most enduring friendship of his life. Born in 1833, Frederick Maxse was a naval officer who had served with gallantry and distinction in the Crimean War as aide-de-camp to Lord Raglan. A hard rider to hounds, a quixotic Liberal in politics, and an ardent disciple of Carlyle, he is now known to us as the hero of *Beauchamp's Career*. ' A naval man loose upon society ', Meredith called him in 1861, adding that he was ' a very nice fellow with strong literary tastes '. His mother, a daughter of the Earl of Berkeley, was also an admired and valued friend to Meredith until her death, more than twenty-five years later, when he wrote of her, ' so strong a spirit is not of the dead '. Maxse's home was at Effingham Hill, about twelve miles from Esher, which may have had something to do with his going there to live. But the two had yet to become intimate; at the end of 1859 he began a letter ' Dear Captain Maxse ' and signed himself ' yours faithfully '.

In the meantime Esher bestowed on him one of those happy experiences which are so opportune that they seem predestined rather than fortuitous. This is how it happened, as related by Janet Duff Gordon when writing her memoirs at the age of seventy. (Through a slip of memory, she antedated the occurrence by a year, a mistake which has been overlooked by previous biographers.)

> In the early spring of 1858 [sic] I was riding down to the station to meet my father, as I did every day, when a small boy fell in the road just in front of my horse. I jumped off, picked him up, and he made heroic efforts not to cry. ' Papa says little men ought not to cry,' he said, stifling his sobs. I asked him where his father lived, and he pointed to a house with a garden in front, where I knew lodgings were to be had. Telling the groom to ride on, I

led my horse with one hand and the little boy with the other, and rang. A gentleman came out, kissed the child, and then looked hard at me. ' Are you not Lady Duff Gordon's daughter? ' he asked; and before the answer was out of my mouth he clasped me in his arms, exclaiming: ' Oh, my Janet! Don't you know me? I'm your Poet.' Meredith had left Weybridge before we moved from London to Esher (in 1851), and though all his friends, particularly Tom Taylor, had tried to find out where he and his baby boy were, he seemed to have vanished into space. He did not know we were at Esher, and at once declared he would come and live near us. I was obliged to ride off to the station to meet my father, but on our way home we stopped and told him to come to dinner. Great was the joy at having found our friend again. Next morning I joined him in searching for a cottage, and we found one, fit retreat for a poet, standing alone on Copsham Common, near the fir woods behind Claremont Park. There Meredith installed himself; and when he went to London twice a week, being reader to Chapman and Hall, he brought his little son Arthur to me, and I taught him German. We used to take long walks together. The Black Pool in the fir woods was one of our favourite haunts. My Poet would recite poetry or talk about his novels. I made him write down some of the verses he improvised as we sat among the heather, and still have the faded scraps of paper with his characteristic writing in the well-known blue ink. *Evan Harrington* was *my* novel, because Rose Jocelyn was myself. (Sir Frank and Lady Jocelyn were my father and mother, and Miss Current was Miss Louisa Courtenay, a very old friend of my parents, who often stayed with us at Esher.) With the magnificent impertinence of sixteen I would interrupt Meredith, exclaiming: ' No, I should never have said it like that '; or ' I should not have done so.'

This lively girl, whose doings were thus remembered by an autocratic old lady sitting in her villa overlooking Florence, had already known many of the eminent people of the Early Victorian period. As a child she had been made much of by Dickens, Thackeray, Macaulay, and A. W. Kinglake. She had breakfasted with Samuel Rogers; Richard Doyle had drawn pictures for her as she sat on his knee; G. F. Watts had drawn her head while she listened to the youthful Joachim playing the violin in his studio. She had rebuked Carlyle for being rude to her mama; and it was while she was riding with him in

Rotten Row that his wideawake blew off and was picked up by a working man, to whom the sage—instead of giving him sixpence—remarked, ' Thank ye, my man; ye can just say ye've picked up the hat of Thomas Carlyle.'

To all this she would now be able to add her final claim to distinction, ' I am Rose Jocelyn.' To Meredith she brought delightful companionship at a time when he most needed it. When she was eight years old he had carried her on his shoulder and told her fairy tales. And now, until her marriage at the end of 1860, she filled him with a romantic enthusiasm. Re-reading his letters towards the end of her life, she was heard to exclaim, ' Good God! my poet must have been in love with me! ' In love with her he was, and one marvels that he succeeded in keeping her unaware of it, though the following verses, given to her in 1859, made his feelings plain enough.

> We sat beneath the humming pines:
>   We knew that we must part.
> I might not even speak by signs
>   The motions of my heart.
>
> And as I took your hand, and gazed
>   Subdued into your eyes,
> I saw the arm of Fate upraised,—
>   And stilled the inward cries.
>
> I saw that this could never be
>   Which I had dared to pray:
> And in the tear that fell from me,
>   There fell my life that day!

As a family, the Duff Gordons suited him perfectly for friendly intimacy. Socially, they were ' swells '; but they were unaffluent and unconventional swells. Sir Alexander was a permanent official at the Treasury, and afterwards became private secretary to his cousin, Sir George Cornewall Lewis, when Chancellor of the Exchequer. He was extremely popular for his charming manners and witty conversation. Lady Duff Gordon was one of the most remarkable women of her time. Her father was John Austin (1790–1859), the celebrated jurist, of whom Macaulay said that he had never known his superior as a talker. As a girl, Lucie Austin listened to Carlyle, Sydney Smith, John Stuart Mill, and other famous men who were her father's friends. As Lucie Duff Gordon she drew to her circle those celebrities who have already been mentioned as the early associates of Janet. But she was consumptive, and her death in 1869 at the age of forty-eight left them saying that they would never know her like again. Writing in 1902, Meredith commemorated her qualities as follows.

Her humour was a mouthpiece of nature. She inherited from her father the authority and composure of a judicial mind. Hers was the charity which is perceptive and embracing—a singular union of the balanced intellect with the lively heart. Her aim was at practical measures for help; she doubted the uses of sentimentality, and had an innate bent for exactitude. It was known to all intimate with her that she could not speak falsely in praise nor unkindly in depreciation. In her youth she was radiantly beautiful, with dark features of Grecian line, save for the classic Greek wall of the nose off the forehead. Women, inclined rather to criticise so independent a member of their sex, have said that her entry into a ballroom took the breath. She preferred the society of men, on the plain ground that they discuss matters of weight, and are—the pick of them—of open speech, more liberal, more genial, better comrades. Was it wonderful to hear them, knowing her as they did, unite in calling her *coeur d'or*?

Tennyson took her as the prototype of his ' Princess '. And Kinglake wrote of ' the classical form of her features, the noble poise of her head and neck, her stately height, her uncoloured yet pure complexion. . . . She was so intellectual, so keen, so autocratic, sometimes even so impassioned in speech, that nobody feeling her powers, could feebly compare her to a mere Queen or Empress '.

2

By the autumn of 1859, Meredith had settled at Copsham Cottage, which was to be his home for the next five years. A contemporary photograph shows it as a plain, four-windowed little house with a white double-gate in the hedge dividing it from the four crossways that met there. Though only two miles from Esher, it was at that time surrounded by lovely heaths and commons, gorse and heather, and those woods of larch, fir, and pine which he was to make his own in poetry and prose. Close to the cottage there was a sandy burial-mound, rising half the height of the firs, bounded by a green-grown fosse. Here he often sat, and the place was described in *Sandra Belloni* and *Juggling Jerry*. Copsham Common was a great resort for gipsies and tinkers, with whom he enjoyed conversing, thereby acquiring much first-hand knowledge of which he was to make good use. ' My cottage has very much the appearance of a natural product of the common on which it stands,' he explained in a letter. He had, in fact, found an ideal habitation, after a ten years pilgrimage from one set of lodgings to another. And one is glad to know that he and Arthur were made comfortable by a good housekeeper, Miss Grange, from whose father he rented his rooms. He has described her as an invaluable person: excellent temper, spotless principles, indefatigable worker, no sex: thoughtful, prudent, and sensible. Written at that time, the fine poem *Autumn Evensong* expresses his sense of thankfulness in its final stanza.

> Pale the rain-rutted roadways shine
>   In the green light
> Behind the cedar and the pine:
>   Come thundering night!
> Blacken broad earth with hoards of storm:
> For me yon valley-cottage beckons warm.

Obviously, this was one of the turning points in his career. Things had begun to look better for him, in spite of the failure of *Richard Feverel* to gain approval from Mudie's Library, and the novel-reading public.

Befriended and stimulated by the Duff Gordons, he was compensated for the harassments of his ruined marriage (which continued until the end of 1861) by a delightful relationship with his adored Janet. And this had that humanly sustaining element, the interest of a spirited girl in the little boy of a man whom she admires for his character and achievements. Meanwhile he was making such good progress with *Evan Harrington* that by the beginning of December he was writing to Samuel

Lucas, the editor of *Once a Week*, about its serialisation in that magazine, which had been started in 1859 as a rival to *Household Words* and *All the Year Round*. Most people find *Evan Harrington* the easiest of Meredith's novels to read (though some might say the same of *Harry Richmond*). It is therefore significant that the conditions under which he wrote the weekly numbers allowed no time for over-elaborating the manuscript.

In his letters to Lucas we see him actively at work, developing the story as he goes along, and still undecided what to call it. On December 20th he thinks the title should be *Evan Harrington*, but within the next two weeks he had lapsed into suggesting the following disastrous alternatives: *The Substantial and the Essential*, *Shams and Realities*, *All but a Gentleman*, *The Tailor's Family*, *Gentle and Genteel*, *The Gentleman-Tailor's Family*, and *Gentility and a Gentleman*.

The first number appeared on February 11th. During January he was doing his best to get well ahead of his future weekly instalments, and evidently feeling the strain of this hitherto unexperienced method of production, as well such a literary artist might. On New Year's Day he wrote:

> Copy you shall have shortly. But try and spur me on without giving me the sense that I am absolutely due; for then I shall feel hunted, and may take strange leaps. I am in a sort of a knot just now. The endings of the numbers bother me. I can work out my idea; but shall I lead on the reader? That's my difficulty, till I get into the thick of it.
>
> *January 12th.* Proofs of chapters 1. 2. 3. returned herewith. The later the day, the better the work. I can say no more. I shall have that amount, or more, ready when you start. I will, as far as a man may say, keep up, and give you no anxiety.

Meanwhile illustrations were being prepared by Charles Keene, and the journalism-fiction game was in full swing. Strange to think of the Olympian Meredith in this vortex of improvisation, temperately asking his taskmaster, 'Are you sure you're not thinking of the quantity of matter as suitable for your editorial requirements, rather than the quality of the chapter in question?' Nevertheless, Samuel Lucas saw where the danger lay when he urged the serialist to simplify his narrative. Meredith's reply is significant.

Your advice is good. This cursed desire I have haunting me to show the reason for things is a perpetual obstruction to movement. I *do* want the dash of Smollett and know it.

Had he but kept that ' cursed desire ' under control during the rest of his career as a novelist, how much easier it would have been for posterity to enjoy him! But he decided otherwise, and in the final sentence of his final novel he prays our patience ' while philosophy and exposure of character block the course along a road inviting to traffic of the most animated kind '.

In the case of *Evan Harrington*, there is no doubt that it owes its freshness and spontaneity to the haphazard conditions under which it was composed. It seems worth pointing out that when the serial was in its sixth number, less than a third of the whole was in manuscript. It was written ' as it went along '. The final number appeared on October 13th, and the conclusion was sent in on September 27th, with the comment—' It is finished as an actor finishes under hisses.' The serial had been accused of dullness, and it has been said that it damaged the circulation of the magazine. Yet Dickens was reading it, and admired it greatly! Its predecessor in *Once a Week*, by the way, had been Charles Reade's *The Cloister and the Hearth*.

Quite early in 1860, Meredith was arranging with Bradbury & Evans, the proprietors of *Once a Week*, that they should offer the book to Harper's, of New York, who published an edition in one volume toward the end of the year. The English edition was published by Bradbury & Evans in January, 1861. *The Saturday Review* was quite kind about it.

It is not a great work, but it is a remarkable one, and deserves a front place in the literature that is ranked as avowedly not destined to endure.

3

There is much in *Evan Harrington* that appertains to Meredith's personal and family history. But before looking into that, let me consider its qualities as a novel and its relation to those that he afterwards wrote. I say ' me ', rather than ' us ', because the only critical method I feel capable of adopting is to describe my own experience when re-reading the book after an interval of more than twenty years. In the past I had found it enjoyable, but my judgment was immature, even had I troubled to exercise it. I now approached it with an eye for defects, devoutly hoping that I should not be disappointed, yet resolved to behave as a stern and unbending biographer. My sense of relief was immediate.

> Long after the hours when tradesmen are in the habit of commencing business, the shutters of a certain shop in the town of Lymport-on-the-Sea remained significantly closed, and it became known that death had taken Mr. Melchisidec Harrington, and struck one off the list of living tailors.

Thus the book begins, with that indefinable note of assurance which causes the reader to settle into his chair, knowing that he is in for a comfortable journey. Masterpieces have a way of winning one's confidence with the opening sentence. Effortless, memorable, and ordinary, the words dispel our doubts. And, if the years have taught us to make the most of a good thing, we say to ourselves, ' This must be perused with the deliberation which it deserves.'

After reading the first seven chapters in this delectable manner, I decided that, so far, it was a classic performance; clear narration in ripe and sound English; rich material; the characters introduced with precision and controlled gusto; and a sense of being conducted by admirably unhastening stages toward the development of events. The preliminaries of the story are presented with a firm hand; there are no blurred outlines; no obtrusive explanations.

At the end of the twelfth chapter I was feeling as comfortable as ever. Now and again I had noticed that Meredith was writing a little over the heads of the insipid subscribers to *Once a Week*; but the story continued lively, and his occasional asides about life and character were sensible, and not too elaborate in phrase and metaphor. For instance:

> When we have cast off the scales of hope and fancy, and surrender our claims on mad chance, it is given us to see that some plan is working out: that the heavens, icy as they are to the pangs of our blood, have been throughout speaking to our souls; and, according to the strength there existing, we learn to comprehend them. But their language is an element of Time, whom primarily we have to know.

And by now I was once more delighting in the superb high comedy of the Countess de Saldar, of whom one might almost say that she is the backbone of the book.

At this point I remembered that I had read somewhere a stringent criticism of Meredith as a constructor of stories. Looking it up, I found the following remarks:

> He must be regarded as one of the worst narrators in the history of the English Novel. This lack not merely of the born story-teller's gift but even of any ordinary skill in planning and setting out a narrative is undoubtedly a serious defect . . . for the Novel, no matter what new purpose it may serve, must always remain a tale.

This being the considered opinion of an able and eminent 20th-Century novelist, I began to wonder about my own qualifications as an unprofessional appreciator of romantic comedy, although the convictions I have just expressed were unshaken.

Anxious to avoid involving my mind in a one-sided wrangle with an invisible opponent, I told myself that the subject of Meredith's novels as a whole would probably be investigated by me in some future chapter, and that in the meantime I proposed to go on enjoying the story in my amateurish way. It might be true that, as this clever critic boldly asserted, ' the involved action of *Evan Harrington* will not stand the slightest examination, and the whole business of the Cogglesby brothers is preposterous.' Nevertheless, I was finding the involved action quite clear and credible (allowing for the quickened eventfulness and condensation of a work of fiction), and I had rejoiced in the chapter where the Cogglesby brothers meet at ' the Aurora—one of those rare antiquated taverns, smelling of comfortable time and solid English fare '. I had rejoiced in the idiosyncrasies of old Tom Cogglesby and the humanity of his humdrum brother Andrew, and I knew that I should continue to do so. In fact as far as I was concerned there was nothing wrong with the entertainment provided. This novel of the Regency Period had, for me, a vintage flavour and the mellowness of an Old Master. Above all, it seemed to prove that, when he chose to submit himself to the standards of conventional novel-writing, Meredith could do it every bit as well as his competitors of the Victorian Age. Admittedly he lacked the cosy middle-mindedness of Trollope and the ingenuity of Wilkie Collins as an elaborator of plots. (Higher comparisons—with Dickens, George Eliot, and Hardy—must be evaded as redundant.) My point is that his later habit of careless construction and wilful neglect of persuasiveness was caused by impatience with the stereotyped and plot-ridden method of story-telling and resentment of the ungrateful reception given to his earlier novels. His temperament was that of a poet and intellectual experimenter. He was always an unwilling novelist, and he became contemptuous of the task of writing fiction for a middle-minded public.

4

Having offered sufficient recommendation of the story, I will only add that its interest is sustained to the end. We must now turn to the inner history of the book and its biographical revelations. The well-known facts are as follows. He adapted the situation in which his father found himself when, at the age of seventeen, he inherited the debt-encumbered family business —tailor and naval outfitter—at Portsmouth. He made full-length portraits of his grandfather, the immortal ' Old Mel ', and his grandmother, a strong-minded, sensible woman with a genius for plain speaking. He made full use of his father's three sisters, evolving from one of them the Countess de Saldar, an adventurous schemer and sentimentalist who would have ranked high among Thackeray's characters had she been one of them. Evan Harrington himself appears to be, in the main, a made-up hero, though to some extent a composite of Meredith and his father. (Like so many young men heroes in novels, he does not always impress one as convincingly alive.)

Another detail of this family reunion in fiction is that one of the three sisters married a brewer, who evidently suggested one of the Cogglesbys. Finally, Sir Frank and Lady Jocelyn and their daughter Rose were the Duff Gordons, drawn to the life.

No alteration was made in the Portsmouth background; even the publican, the butcher, and the confectioner who figure in the first chapter were recognisable as tradesmen known to Meredith in his boyhood. The local topography is identifiable

—the house described as Beckley Court being, as in the book, five miles from Petersfield. All this brings us to the slightly wearisome problem, how it was that Meredith gave away the whole story of his family history in 1860, and thereafter covered up his tracks so assiduously. I call it wearisome because I have found it so while reading all the comments on it which appeared when S. M. Ellis's *Life* was published, in 1919. He was accused of insincerity and snobbishness; the arch-enemy of Humbug was admonished for having been ashamed of the tailor's shop connection and for encouraging the picturesque rumours which were current about his birth. Making allowance for the immense prestige of his reputation at the time of his death, and the startling effect caused by the announcement of his real parentage, I formulated the following simple explanation of Meredith's behaviour. Throughout early manhood and onward to middle-age he naturally disliked it to be known that he was the son of a tailor (though FitzGerald, Maxse, and other intimate friends were apparently cognisant of it). When, in the '80s, he became a considerable celebrity, he disliked it still more. Finally, as the laurelled and Olympian sage of Box Hill, he realised that there was nothing for it but to maintain secrecy. For instance, Edward Clodd was staying with him, in March, 1901, when the census papers had to be filled in. Clodd did this for him, but when asked where he was born he asked, ' Is that necessary? . . . Well, say near Petersfield.' He declined to give his occupation as ' author ', telling Clodd to put ' has private means '! Which reminds me that on a similar occasion, many years later, Elgar refused to describe himself as a composer, merely writing ' gentleman '. Such are the foibles of great men. In Meredith's case, reticence was justified. Rightly regarded by the world as a supremely dignified and distinguished person, he had no intention of what would now be called ' letting the show down '. He did not wish the tailor's shop to be talked about. Ordinary common sense dictated his decision. It is possible that he saw in the situation the workings of the Comic Spirit. He also knew that the armchair he sat in was to many of us the throne of English Letters.

After he was dead, people could say what they liked. Meredith was genuinely unconcerned about the opinions of posterity.

His creed was to make good use of life and meet old age and death with fortitude.

Much more interesting for speculation is his state of mind when producing *Evan Harrington*. ' What made him put down this monumental record of so many people and facts about which he never wanted a word to be said? ' inquired *The Manchester Guardian*, in 1919. Well, my present business is to provide an answer, with which anyone who likes is at liberty to disagree.

The first—and fairly obvious—solution is that he was an ambitious novelist in urgent need of a story; and here were the elements of a lively and amusing one. The situation was there, and ' Old Mel ' alone was a mine of rich material. He had been dead forty-five years; Augustus Meredith was well out of the way, in Cape Town, and not worth bothering about, anyhow. Moreover, the greater part of the plot would be entirely invented. Family history merely provided the basic ingredients. One imagines Meredith turning it over in his mind while finishing *Richard Feverel*, sketching in the early chapters while lodging at Esher, realising that he was writing with enjoyment, talking his ideas out to Janet Duff Gordon in the summer of '59, and realising that in her he had discovered the perfect model for his heroine. The book was the thing that mattered. For the time being he ceased to care about his own inheritance of the stigma of the shears. His mentality became detached, controlled by the spirit of romantic comedy.

In addition to this, there was the compensation of making a tailor's son victorious over county-family arrogance, making him a finer gentleman than any of them. But I do not think that he dreamed himself into the experiences of Evan. He wasn't that sort of man, though he may have relished the idea of winning the hand of Rose Jocelyn-Duff Gordon. I believe that he was hard-headed about the whole affair. It has been suggested that he was taking the opportunity of criticising the attitude of society toward gentility, expressing resentment against snobbery, and vindicating his own claim to be—as he knew himself to be—one of nature's thoroughbreds. In support of this a passage can be quoted.

He considered himself as good a gentleman as any man living, and was in absolute hostility with the prejudices of society.

And again—

However boldly antagonism may storm the ranks of society, it will certainly be repelled, whereas affinity cannot be resisted; and they who, against obstacles of birth, claim and keep their position among the educated and refined, have that affinity.

Also there is the Countess de Saldar's significant remark in one of her letters to her sister, Mrs. Cogglesby. ' As to *hands* and *feet*, comparing him with the Jocelyn men, Evan has every mark of better blood. As Papa would say—"We have Nature's proofs ".' There, indeed, Meredith spoke from personal feeling. For some strain of ' better blood ' was evidently in him. He went through life—physically—' a nobleman in disguise '; and this outwardness had been endowed by Nature with the daemon of a masterful and magnificent intellectual genius.

My explanation, therefore, amounts to no more than this: that once the creator in him was active, the personal dilemma of his origin was transformed into a grand opportunity for a serio-comic extravaganza. Let it also be conceded that while writing the book he worked out of his system the lurking resentment he had felt at not having been born a gentleman. Naturally, he had found it a nuisance to be ' the son of a snip '. But he was now taking advantage of that situation, and doing so with relish.

As to his relations, there is no evidence that he wished to bury them all in oblivion. He told one of his friends that he owed much to one of his aunts who had lived in Portugal, and that to her he was indebted for his manners and courteous bearing toward women. He always spoke of her with respect and admiration. This was his aunt Louisa, from whose behaviour his imagination created the Countess de Saldar. No doubt she talked much of courts and foreign nobilities, for her husband had been a friend of Pedro, Emperor of Brazil and sometime King of Portugal, and her daughter married a Portuguese Marquis and Minister of State who was subsequently appointed Ambassador to the Vatican.

As for his grandfather, ' Old Mel ', those who knew him well late in life have said that he gloried in him. And there is further evidence of this in the fact that he used ' Old Mel ' a second time in *Harry Richmond*. The character of Richmond

Roy, though an altogether different creation, can have germinated from no one else.

Looked at from this point of view, *Evan Harrington* offers no support to any suppositions that Meredith used it to ventilate a grievance against society. He was essentially robust-minded and humorous, and by 1860 he had been toughened by experience. Circumstances compelled him to adopt a severely practical attitude to his profession as a writer. In the best interpretation of the word, he was highly sensitive, as all men of genius must be. But in *Evan Harrington* he gave proof that when doomed to go in company with a sartorial ancestry he could ' turn his necessity to glorious gain '.

5

In October, 1860, Janet became engaged to Henry Ross. They were married early in December. Twenty years older than her, he was a banker in Alexandria. She had met him when staying with A. H. Layard, the excavator of Nineveh, whom he had assisted during that remarkable operation on remote history.

> Mr. Ross sat next to me at dinner [she wrote in her *Reminiscences*] and told me stories about pig-sticking. How once when his horse put his foot in a hole and rolled over with him, the wild boar turned upon him, and would perhaps have killed him, had not Layard galloped up and drawn the beast's attention off; about the excavations they had done together; and the wild life among the Yezidis. So wonderfully vivid a raconteur I had never met, and longing to hear more, I asked him to come to Esher. . . . Soon afterwards Mr. Ross came, and I took him out with the Duc d'Aumale's harriers, and was much impressed by his admirable riding, his pleasant conversation, and his kindly ways. The result was that I promised to marry him, to the dismay of many of my friends who did not at all approve of my going to live in Egypt.

To Meredith, who had no pig-sticking adventures to recount, the news must have been a blow. His comradeship with the hard-headed and practical, but impulsive girl had been opportune, and he cannot have expected it to end so abruptly. However, he made the best of it, with

God bless you, my dear girl. If you don't make a good wife, I've never read a page of woman. He's a lucky fellow to get you, and the best thing he can do is to pray that he may always know his luck. . . . How do you feel? Do write down half a page of your sensations, and hand them to me, under seal, with directions that I may read them a year hence and compare with results. Not that you're romantic, and I don't suppose you flutter vastly just when you are caught, but still, dear Orange Blossom, you're a bit of a bird, like the rest. . . . I pray fervently you may be happy.

The marriage was a successful one, though Mr. Ross lost his fortune through being involved in Egyptian finance, after which they lived in Italy in great contentment until he died in 1902. For the next few years Meredith's devotion to her continued, though he saw her seldom. After that they became old friends divided by circumstance. In 1889, when she wrote asking his permission to include him in her first book of recollections, he replied ' No one knows better than I, that you are the most faithful of souls to old acquaintanceship.' They met for the last time at Box Hill in 1904. After his death she sold his letters and manuscript verses addressed to her, for the excellent reason that she needed the money for the maintenance of her Florentine farm. Her great-nephew has described her in old age as ' white-haired and erect, stern and eagle-eyed '. A determined old lady, who had once been the Amazonian and imperious inspirer of him whom she still called ' my poet '. To visitors who made the pilgrimage to her villa, she would say, ' I am Rose Jocelyn.' Some of them may have vaguely confused her with ' Rose Aylmer ' !

CHAPTER FOUR

1

In May, 1861, a long letter to Janet Ross told her, ' My experiences are all mental—I see nothing of the world, and what I have to say goes into books.' He was, however, able to report that he had seen the Royal Academy Exhibition, and had been taken by Maxse to a House of Commons Debate, where ' Gladstone swallowed the whole Conservative body with his prodigious yawn and eloquence alternately.' He had begun two novels, but was making little progress with them, being at that time in rather a bad state of health. And he had ' made friends with a nice fellow lately: a son of the Ambassador at Athens, Sir Thomas Wyse, whom your mother knew. He married a Bonaparte—a daughter of Lucien.' Bonaparte Wyse (1826–1892) was a bit of a poet; he had made a special study of Provençal metres and was intimate with Frederick Mistral, of whom Meredith wrote that his poetry combined the pastoral richness of Theocritus with the rough vigour of Homer.

Wyse was living at Guildford; in the spring of 1861 the two went long walks together, and Meredith's letters to him are full of gaiety and high spirits. He begins one of them with a ditty, ending—

> We laughed at jests profane to quote,
> I and my Bonaparte Wyse.
> We cracked our joke improper to quote,
> I and my Bonaparte Wyse——

and continues:

> Yesterday, being fair, I marched me to the Vale of Mickleham. An English *Tempe*! Was ever such delicious greenery? The nightingale saluted me entering and departing. The walk has made me a new man. I am now bathed anew in the Pierian Fount. I cannot prose. I took Keats with me to read the last lines of *Endymion* in the spot of composition.

Now, listen: come here by the afternoon train on Thursday, and I will return with you for a day through Mickleham, and over the hills. Perhaps Maxse will join us. The cuckoo has been heard. And through the gates of his twin notes we enter the heart of spring. We will have rare poetizing, no laughter, no base cynical scorn, but all honest uplifting of the body and soul of us to the calm-flowing central Fire of things. Even so, my friend.

At the end of May, Wyse went to France and Italy. Meanwhile Meredith's doctor had prohibited work and tobacco and advised him to take two months holiday, preferably where he could get tonic glacier air.

In his next letters to Wyse he is planning to meet him in Belgium or Switzerland, though leaving Arthur was a problem that bothered him. This problem he solved by taking ' the dear little man ' with him, disregarding the fatigue and anxiety thus incurred. For in those years Arthur was his sustaining happiness—more so than ever since Janet had married and gone to Alexandria. With deep and undeviating devotion he made Arthur the purpose of his existence and his money-earning endeavours, concentrating on him the parental love which is fathomless and immeasurable in terms of emotion, being decreed by Nature. Father and child travelled to Zürich in July, and then on to Innsbrück and Meran. While Arthur made a collection of beetles and butterflies, and was looked after by Mrs. Wyse, Meredith walked thirty miles a day. Wyse, who had done well enough as a walker in Surrey, proved less adequate for his strenuous companion in the Tyrol.

We walked from Innsbrück to Landeck in three days [wrote Meredith to Maxse on July 26th]. Wyse does not walk in rain, or when it's to be apprehended; nor when there's a chance of nightfall; nor does he like it in the heat; and he's not the best hand in the world at getting up in the morning, and he's rather excitable. But still thoroughly kindly and good.

But although he complained of him as ' half Prince, half Paddy, with little pluck, a great deal of desultory reading, and no control over his nerves ', their friendship continued. That Meredith found him sympathetic is shown by letters which are as intimate as any that have been printed, though never so memorable as those he wrote to Maxse, to whom he now records his impressions in two fine passages.

> Nothing can be grander than the colossal mountains of porphyry and dolomite shining purple and rosy, snow-capped here and there, with some tumultuous river noising below, and that eternal stillness overhead, save when some great peak gathers the thunders and bellows for a time. Then to see the white sulphurous masks curl and cover round it, and drip moisture on the hanging meadows, would task your powers of description! . . .
>
> My first sight of the Alps has raised odd feelings. Here at last seems something more than earth, and visible, if not tangible. They have the whiteness, the silence, the beauty and mystery of thoughts seldom unveiled within us, but which conquer Earth when once they are. In fact they have made my creed tremble.—Only for a time. They have merely dazzled me with a group of symbols. Our great error has been (the error of all religion, as I fancy) to raise a spiritual system in antagonism to Nature. What though yonder Alp does touch the Heavens? Is it a rebuke to us below? In you and me there may be lofty virgin points, pure from what we call fleshliness. . . .

From Milan, on August 16th, he wrote that he had been alone with Arthur in Venice, where he ' had to watch the dear boy like tutor, governess, courier, in one '. They went to the Lido every morning to bathe in the tepid Adriatic under enormous straw-hats, and floated through the streets at night in a gondola—Arthur exclaiming, ' Papa, what a dear old place this is! We won't go, will we? ' He had been able to get only one week's walking; the rest of the time the little fellow had been on his hands.

> But what a jolly boy and capital companion he is! Full of fun and observation, good temper and endurance. As for me, I am much better in health, and believe I shall now be in condition for labour of the remunerative kind. Could I but afford to rest and look on man for one year! . . .

Unforgettable is the paragraph where he describes how he had been following in Byron's and Shelley's footsteps.

> Do you remember in ' Julian and Maddalo ', where the two, looking toward the Euganean hills, see the great bell of the Insane Asylum swing in the sunset? I found the exact spot.

I have seldom felt melancholy so strongly as when standing there. You know I despise melancholy, but the feeling came. I love both those poets; and with my heart given to them I felt as if I stood in a dead and useless time. So we are played with sometimes! . . .

While in Milan he went to see Wyse at Como, where he was staying with his mother.

She received me affably [he wrote to Janet Ross]. Madame la Princesse desires that she should hear it, as I quickly discovered. I grew in favour. She has no difficulty in swallowing a compliment. Quantity is all she asks for. This is entre nous, for she entertained me, and indeed I was vastly entertained. Look for it all in a future chapter. A good gross compliment, fluently delivered, I find to be best adapted to a Frenchwoman's taste. If you hesitate, the flavour evaporates for them. Be glib, and you may say what you please. . . . Thence over the Mont Cenis to Paris. The little man was in raptures at the thought of crossing the Alps. He would barely close his eyes. I had him in my arms in the coupé of the diligence, and then he was starting up every instant, shouting, and crowing till dawn; when I had no chance of getting him to sleep. When we reached Macon at night I put him to bed, and gave him a little weak coffee. He slept like a top till morning. He was impatient to be home, and cared little for Paris. Under the circumstances, with a remonstrating little man, there was nothing for it but to return hastily. Thank Heaven! I got him home safe.

From Copsham, Arthur sent an engaging description of his travels to Janet, and a very good letter it is, for a boy of eight, as the following extracts will show.

About three months ago I went on the continent with my papa. I started from Dover to Ostend and going in the harbour I saw some Belgian peasants picking perywinkles; they laughed at us and had such rosy cheeks and I thought them very funny. Then I had a long day in the train from Ostend to Coblentz. In the morning I saw a steamer going to Mainz and so we dressed and got in it. . . . The waiter at Mainz took me upstairs to a high place and showed me a stork's nest in a chimney. I went to Zurich, where the lake was so clear that you could see to the bottom of it. The next day I went up part of a mountain and dined, and I saw the Alps at a distance; there was a crow which came hopping

45

along and was quite tame, but another boy teased it, and so it flew away. . . . I stopped at Munich a day and at twelve oclock I heard a nice band . . . I went to Venice where I was very happy. At the Liedo the water is so hot that you can stopp in a long while. I dine at tables d'hote and had my own bottle of wine, lots of grapes; and lemonade on the place St. Mark. At Paris I had breakfast at cafés I went to the Champs Elysees I saw the monument of Napoleon on which were the battles he fought. Then I went home.

This was dated September 25th, and with it went a note from Meredith, in which he says:

I have been going to write you an account of the Travels; but I am now so torn to pieces and hard at work that I can't sit down to anything . . . Arthur is now at Weybridge seeing his mother daily.

He had returned to find trouble awaiting him. After two years of tragic loneliness, his wife was dying. Ever restless, she had wandered from place to place, harrowed by separation from Arthur, and continually indulging in uncontrollable emotion. She used to meet him for a short time occasionally, but he was not allowed to go to her house. It has been stated that in those last years of her life she was always sad and constantly in tears. Her father, apparently, never saw her again after 1858.

She had now sent a message begging Meredith to come and see her. He did not go. For this he has been condemned; but it is a case where the truth cannot be known. Through the mediation of a friend, he relented to the extent of allowing Arthur to go to her when she was dying, as has already been indicated. She died in October. Meredith was in Suffolk at the time. His only recorded comment is in a letter to William Hardman.

When I entered the world again I found that one had quitted it who bore my name: and this filled my mind with melancholy recollections which I rarely give way to. My dear boy, fortunately, will not feel the blow, as he might have under different circumstances.

He never blamed her, and it can be assumed that he realised his own share in their mistakes and misunderstandings. In this connection, the following passage from Lady Butcher's *Memories* can fitly be quoted.

At Flint Cottage I constantly met Mr. X, one of his very oldest friends. One evening as Mr. X and I travelled back to London, he told me the early history of Mr. Meredith's first marriage, upon which he had accurate and trustworthy contemporary information. It was a very moving story, and every detail remains in my memory. All that I can say here is that the history of his relations with his first wife was very different from that suggested in a recent publication.

Mr. X was probably Lionel Robinson. The ' recent publication ' was S. M. Ellis's biography, which gave a somewhat unfavourable impression of Meredith's behaviour. In old age, he remarked to Edward Clodd, ' No sun warmed my roof-tree; the marriage was a blunder; she was seven years my senior. Peacock's wife became mad, and so there was a family taint.' With his brother-in-law, Edward Peacock, who died in 1869, Meredith always remained on good terms. One of his letters mentions him staying at Copsham in the summer of 1862.

2

Another biographer of Meredith has written, of his treatment of his first wife, that ' he showed himself somewhat cold and implacable in the face of suffering and sorrow that reduced his own injuries to mere trifles: his pride would not allow him to speak the forgiving word and make the generous gesture '. This may have been so. But those who knew and understood him never doubted that the failure of his youthful marriage was—and remained—a profound shock to his proud and sensitive nature. We have seen that he was outwardly reticent about it. Let us now examine the poetic masterpiece in which he strove to put the tragic experience behind him.

There are two aspects of *Modern Love* to be considered—its revelation of his private history, and the circumstances in which it was written. They are closely connected and equally interesting. (The ' story ' in the poem is, of course, altered—the wife's suicide being substituted for elopement with her lover.)

I began my investigation of these aspects with a preconceived notion that the poem took him about three years to write. I imagined him outlining it in 1859, after his wife's elopement, and even speculated that some of the sonnets might have been written during his spiritual discomfort before the climax. Here were fifty sixteen-line sonnets of highly perfected workmanship, constructed as a finely-woven monodrama, and abounding in memorable passages and variety of mood. The vigour and spontaneity of sustained movement were there; but could so much indestructible art have been put into the sequence by a single creative effort? I was thinking of the performance in terms of a poet's technique—the intermittent periods of inspiration, the subconscious incubation of ideas, and the labour of the file. I assumed that in the autumn of 1861 he must have taken the manuscript up again and finished it at a high pressure of transfused emotion. But there was much in it which, to my mind, appeared to have been written while the drama of discord and estrangement was being enacted.

In all this I was entirely wrong. I had forgotten that Meredith was also a novelist! The poem was begun immediately after his wife's death and completed in little more than three months.

The history of this astonishing achievement is as follows. During the earlier part of 1861 he had found himself unable to make headway with novel-writing and had turned to poetry, stimulated, no doubt, by his association with Wyse. By the autumn he had several ' poems of the English Roadside ' and other pieces, but hardly enough for a volume. At the end of November we get the first announcement of *Modern Love*.

Writing to congratulate Maxse on his engagement, he ends the letter thus. ' I have done a great deal of the " Love-Match " —Rossetti says it is my best. I contrast it mentally with yours, which is so very much better! ' About ten days earlier he had written to Janet Ross that he was busy on Poems. ' I think it possible I shall publish a small volume in the winter, after Christmas.' . . . He mentions ' A Love-Match ' as one of his recent pieces. At the beginning of January he writes to Maxse again. ' I send you a portion of proofs of The Tragedy of Modern Love. There are wanting to complete it, 13 more sonnets. Please read, and let me have the honest judgment.

When done with, return. The poem will come in the middle of the book.' Here was not only quick work but notably professional literary procedure! His wife's death had released in him the power to conceive this subtly introspective poem, this disinterment of an unhappy past, in which—unsparing of himself—he forgives and is reconciled to the dead woman who had wronged him. Never again would he lay bare his soul as he was now doing, or express his intimate thoughts with such passion and directness. Yet, before it is half finished, he has shown the manuscript to his friend D. G. Rossetti, and can be almost facetious about it to Maxse. This, surely, is an interesting case for the psychologists.

My own explanation is, that his ordeal had been lived through while he was writing *Richard Feverel*. We have seen how, during those eighteen months with Janet, he had recovered, and shown it by writing *Evan Harrington*, the happiest of all his books. His wife's death had come as a relief, causing him no disintegrating emotion. Hence his ability to produce *Modern Love*, refashioning his own love tragedy with the control of art, intellect, and irony to a human drama from which, in his creative capacity, he could stand aside. Hence, also, his manifestly matter-of-fact attitude about it. He knew that he was writing a fine poem, and delighted in it, fortified by Rossetti's favourable opinion, the significance of which he realised. And one is, perhaps, justified in assuming his awareness that the poem was just what was needed to strengthen the volume with which he was about to break his ten years silence. Not many months after it was published, he described it as a dissection of the sentimental passion of these days which could only be apprehended by the few who would read it many times. ' I hold the man who gives us a plain wall of fact higher in esteem than one who is constantly shuffling the cards and dealing with airy delicate sentimentalities.' Naturally, he insisted on the work being judged apart from its personal significances; but one cannot quite classify it among his condemnations of senti-mentality. It was an exercise in self-scrutiny and a rejection of self-pity and sensitiveness. But there is more in it than that. It remains, and will endure, as a great and original poem, an artistic construction of perfect unity.

Examining it with the biographical material in mind, I have

discovered very little that can be identified in connexion with
the actual background of his married life. There are scenes
evidently derived from memories of Lower Halliford and its
village green. In one of the finest sonnets he pictures the
autumnal Thames there, with swallows gathering by the osier-
isle. And the conclusion is enacted at Seaford (where he had
his final meeting with Mary).

> Here is a fitting spot to dig Love's grave;
> Here where the ponderous breakers plunge and strike,
> And dart their hissing tongues high up the sand.

Throughout the sequence the essential revelations of private
history are to be found in the monodrama of self-examination
and realistic remembrance.

> I claim a star whose light is overcast:
> I claim a phantom-woman in the Past

he cries. And again—

> In this unholy battle I grow base:
> If the same soul be under the same face,
> Speak, and a taste of that old time restore!

And yet again—

> My crime is, that the puppet of a dream,
> I plotted to be worthy of the world.

He bleeds, but her who wounds he will not blame. He dreams
a banished angel to him crept, but no morning could restore
what they have forfeited.

> I see no sin:
> The wrong is mixed. In tragic life, God wot,
> No villain need be! Passions spin the plot:
> We are betrayed by what is false within.

Thus, in many a memorable line, he unlocks his heart, until
the magnificent close where he uplifts the mismarriage of two
minds to a plane of pity and understanding.

Modern Love and Poems of the English Roadside was published
at the end of April. Meredith informed a friend that it had
' subscribed wonderfully well '. Nevertheless, it attracted so
little attention that for many years a number of copies remained
unbound. The sonnet sequence was not reprinted until

1892. Small indeed is the literary world that welcomes a work of genius. Yet Meredith had won the approval of his peers. Writing to Maxse on June 9th, he says, ' I saw Robert Browning the other day, and he expressed himself astounded at the originality, delighted with the naturalness and beauty.' As well he might; for he was the only man alive whose mind could have produced anything comparable in analytic power and penetration (and whose experience of delayed public recognition as a poet was similar to Meredith's). It is also worth recording that the *Modern Love* volume was a perennial favourite of T. H. Huxley's. Meanwhile, *The Spectator* had made what one can only call an exhibition of itself, and had done it to an extent which must be read to be believed.

> Mr. George Meredith is a clever man, without literary genius, taste, or judgment. The effect of the book on us is that of clever, meretricious, turbid pictures by a man of some vigour, jaunty manners, quick observation, and some putonal skill, who likes writing about naked human passions, but does not bring either original imaginative power or true sentiment to the task. . . . [Putonal, by the way, is an obsolete word cognate to putrid.] Meddling causelessly, and somewhat pruriently, with a deep and painful subject on which he has no convictions to express, he sometimes treats serious themes with a flippant levity that is exceedingly vulgar and unpleasant.

It is difficult to understand how these ludicrously unjust remarks were sanctioned by *The Spectator's* literary editor, who was none other than R. H. Hutton, a man of distinguished mind and sympathetic character. Moreover, when criticising *Harry Richmond* ten years later, he began, ' This book shows originality, wealth of conception, genius, and not a little detailed knowledge of the world.' Anyhow, he made honourable amends by printing a long ' Letter to the Editor ' which really amounted to a second review of the book, cancelling the first. In printing this defence of Meredith he described the writer of it as one ' whose opinion of any poetical question should be worth more than most men's '. This is interesting, because the writer was Swinburne, who was then only just twenty-five and had hitherto put his name to no prose production.

After a preliminary protest against the tone of the article, in which he refers to Meredith as one of the leaders of English literature who has fought his way to a foremost place among the men of his time, he makes this declaration.

Praise or blame should be thoughtful, serious, careful, when applied to a work of such subtle strength, such depth of delicate power, such passionate and various beauty, as the leading poem of Mr. Meredith's volume : in some points, as it seems to me (and in this opinion I know that I have weightier judgments than my own to back me) a poem above the aim and beyond the reach of any but its author. Mr. Meredith is one of the three or four poets now alive whose work, perfect or imperfect, is always as noble in design as it is often faultless in result.

(A few months later, Hutton gave further proof of editorial vitality by allowing Swinburne to startle *The Spectator's* sub-scribers with a long essay on Baudelaire's *Les Fleurs du Mal.*)

As far as I can ascertain, it was twenty-five years before *Modern Love* received any further critical recognition. Arthur Symons, in a survey of Meredith's poetry, then wrote that ' the poem stands alone, not merely in its author's work, but in all antecedent literature. It is altogether a new thing; we venture to call it the most " modern " poem we have '. I am tempted to rank it second to the Sonnets of Shakespeare. But Meredith would have deplored the comparison. So I will content myself with pointing out that it contains many lines which might be mistaken for familiar quotations from Shakespeare's plays.

CHAPTER FIVE

1

IT seems probable that Meredith's association with Rossetti dates from the end of 1859, or soon after. One can assume that they were brought together by Millais, who had illustrated two of Meredith's poems in *Once a Week*. Rossetti admired *Evan Harrington*, and by 1861 the friendship had ripened. We have seen that in November of that year Meredith showed him *Modern Love* in its half-finished state. Rossetti responded by letting him see his own unpublished poems (which he buried in his wife's coffin three months later). Meredith wrote as follows to Maxse.

He sent me a book of M.S.S. original poetry the other day, and very fine are some of the things in it. He is a poet, without doubt. He would please you more than I do, or can, for he deals with essential poetry, and is not wild, and bluff, and coarse; but rich, refined, royal-robed!

The sonnet *A Later Alexandrian*, written when Rossetti died, gives his final estimate.

An inspiration caught from dubious hues
Filled him, and mystic wrynesses he chased. . . .
The moon of cloud discoloured was his Muse,
His pipe the reed of the old moaning waste.
Love was to him with anguish fast enlaced,
And Beauty where she walked blood-shot the dews.

In the same letter he makes an acute comment on Swinburne.

He is not subtle; and I don't see any internal centre from which springs anything that he does. He will make a great name, but whether he is to distinguish himself solidly as an Artist, I would not willingly prognosticate.

The Swinburne association had begun in the previous year, for in October he told R. M. Milnes that his friend George Meredith had asked him to contribute poems to *Once a Week*.

Anyhow, there they were, this wonderful trio, and one laments that the surviving records of their intimacy are so scanty. There is, however, the historic episode which occurred at Copsham in July, 1862, when Swinburne came to stay with him. In a letter to *The Times* after the death of Swinburne, Meredith gave an account of it.

It happened that he was expected one day on a visit to me, and he being rather late I went along the road to meet him. At last he appeared waving the white sheet of what seemed to be a pamphlet. He greeted me with a triumphant shout of a stanza new to my ears. This was FitzGerald's Omar Khayyám, and we lay on a heathery knoll beside my cottage reading a stanza alternately, indifferent to the dinner-bell, until a prolonged summons reminded us of appetite. After dinner we took to the paper-covered treasure again. Suddenly Swinburne ran upstairs, and I had my anticipations. He returned with feather pen, blue folio-sheet, and a dwarf bottle of red ink. In an hour he had finished 13 stanzas of his *Laus Veneris*.

One smiles in thinking of ' good Miss Grange ', with her spotless principles, sounding that dinner-bell while Swinburne chanted Omar's creed from the Mound. Still more does one smile to think of her washing up the dinner-things while that feather pen squeaked across the blue foolscap sheet.

> Behold, my Venus, my soul's body, lies
> With my love laid upon her garment-wise,
> Feeling my love in all her limbs and hair
> And shed between her eyelids through her eyes.

Little did she suspect that there was, on that evening, ' the langour in her ears of many lyres ', or that the red-haired young gentleman who couldn't keep his hands and feet still was loosening ' over sea and land the thunder and the trumpets of the night '. One assumes that her thoughts were confined to feeling glad that Mr. Meredith was enjoying himself with his friend, and hoping that they weren't keeping little Arthur awake with their noise.

The famous ' discovery ' of FitzGerald's quatrains has been variously related. The date has been given as 1860, but this can only have been a legendary assumption. Lady Burne-Jones recorded that Swinburne gave her husband a copy early in 1862. It is certain that after the publisher, Quaritch, had failed to sell the pamphlet at five shillings, about 200 of the 250 copies were on sale for a penny each on a stall in St. Martin's Lane, where Rossetti and Swinburne bought half a dozen each, and on returning next day for more found the price raised to twopence. (In 1929 a copy was sold in New York for 8000 dollars.) In later life Swinburne asserted that the 1859 version was the only one worth having, but has found few to agree with him. It may be added that an abridged version had been offered to *Fraser's Magazine*, which kept it two years, until FitzGerald withdrew it. In a letter to Quaritch he instructs him ' to advertize in the Athenaeum and any other Paper you think good: sending copies of course to the Spectator &c.'. No review of it appeared. He took forty copies for himself, having paid all expenses of publication and given the unsold copies to Quaritch, to whom he wrote, ' I wish Omar to do you as little harm as possible, if he does no good '.

To return to Rossetti, it was in the summer of 1862 that he took the lease of the house in Cheyne Walk which he occupied for the rest of his life. Meredith described it to Maxse as ' a strange, quaint, grand old place, with an immense garden, magnificent panelled staircases and rooms,—a palace. I am to have a bedroom for my once-a-week visits '. This was in June. Meredith's tenancy began in October, and will in due course be discussed.

It seems odd that Meredith had not heard about the *Rubáiyát* from Maurice FitzGerald, who often stayed at Esher. It was on one of these occasions in 1860 that FitzGerald introduced F. C. Burnand to him. More than forty years afterwards, Burnand, then famous as the humorous author of *Happy Thoughts* and a knighted editor of *Punch*, described the meeting in the jaunty journalese of his *Reminiscences*. Meredith was standing at the gate of his cottage and strode toward them.

> He never merely walked, never lounged; he strode, he took giant strides. He had on a soft, shapeless wideawake, a sad-coloured flannel shirt, with low open collar turned over a brilliant scarlet neckerchief tied in loose sailor's knot; no waist-coat, knickerbockers, grey stockings, and the most serviceable laced boots, which evidently meant business in pedestrianism;

crisp, curly, brownish hair, ignorant of parting; a fine brow, quick observant eyes, greyish—if I remember rightly—beard and moustache, a trifle lighter than the hair. A splendid head; a memorable personality. Then his sense of humour, his cynicism, and his absolutely boyish enjoyment of mere fun, of any pure and simple absurdity. His laugh was something to hear; it was of short duration, but it was a roar; it set you off,—nay, he himself, when much tickled, would laugh till he cried, and then would struggle with himself, hand to open mouth, to prevent another outburst.

Here—allowing for the boisterous manner of the ' born raconteur '—we have a sketch from the life which confirms the less detailed descriptions of Meredith as a genial companion and the man of physical strength and energy who felled trees and sawed up logs to promote circulation and improve his digestion. I had always fancied that this impression was balanced by the head of Christ by Rossetti in his drawing *Mary Magdalene at the door of Simon the Pharisee*, for which, traditionally, Meredith was the model in 1860. In this, the features are sensitive, serious, and almost feminine. So, I thought, the poet must have looked to Rossetti; and although it now seems certain that it was Burne-Jones and not Meredith who sat for this head, I am reluctant to abandon my belief that the ' memorable personality ' observed by Burnand was only one of the several emanations of a many-sided character. Alone with Lady Duff Gordon or her daughter, he would not have been as he was while entertaining Burnand, even though he was wearing his country clothes. Alone with Rossetti, his face, I still believe, would have expressed a profound awareness that he was with one who was not only a ' dear fellow ' (as he always continued to call him), but one of the most interesting and remarkable men he was ever likely to know. In their way of life, the two had nothing whatever in common. In their poetry, sumptuous nocturnal Italian atmosphere and imagery are contrasted with hill-top oxygen and displays of muscular intellect. Prolonged intimacy was impossible; but for a few years Meredith battled against the incompatibility and submitted to the spell. For, as Max Beerbohm has written, ' In London, in the great days of a deep, smug, thick, rich, drab, industrial complacency, Rossetti shone, for the men and women who knew him, with the ambiguous light of a red torch some-where in a dense fog.' To which he added a drawing which remains the most satisfactory divination of their relationship. Rossetti sits dour, sallow, and engrossed at his easel; Meredith, red-tied and ruddy, gesticulating as was his wont, is exhorting him to ' come forth into the glorious sun and wind for a walk '.

In the autumn of 1861 Meredith had acquired a friend perfectly suited to his outdoor self, with whom he could be exuberantly jolly. William Hardman was a burly Lancashire man, a barrister, who in 1872 became editor of *The Morning Post*. He was a cracker of hearty jokes, widely read, who enjoyed interrupting Meredith's poetical rhapsodies with Cobbett-like common-sense, requesting him to define his terms and pointing out discrepancies in the enthusiastic views expressed by him. Their relationship was epitomised in the fact that they were known to one another as ' Tuck ' and ' Robin '. Their friendship, which flourished until Hardman's death in 1890, was a perennial festivity, aided by Mrs. Hard-man's personal charm and musical talent. To Meredith he was ' one Tuck, a jovial soul, a man after my own heart '. In April, 1862, he writes to him as follows.

> Oh, what a glorious day ! I have done lots of Emilia, and am now off to Ripley, carolling. I snap my fingers at you. And yet, dear Tuck, what would I give to have you here. The gorse is all ablaze, the meadows are glorious—green, humming all day. Heaven, blessed blue amorous Heaven, is hard at work upon our fair, wanton, darling old naughty Mother Earth. Come, dear Tuck, and quickly, or I must love a woman, and be ruined. Answer me, grievous man! In thine ear!—Asparagus is ripe at Ripley. In haste.—Your constantly loving friend, George M.

There are many letters written in a similar strain of facetious hyperbole, pleasant in themselves, and showing the immense liveliness which was part of Meredith's make-up. Hardman, with his solid enjoyment of the good things of life, was obviously a blessing to him, and, better still, a friend to be relied on in all weathers. From Hardman's journals we get a well-detailed account of Meredith as he knew him, though inevitably some-what over-infused with the personality of the writer. In 1868, by the way, he sat to W. P. Frith for a picture of Henry the Eighth. There is a photograph of him in this dress in which the resemblance is quite remarkable. (Meredith referred to it when he drew him as Blackburn Tuckham in *Beauchamp's Career*.)

Meanwhile, in August, 1862, he writes to Tuck from Ryde to tell him that he is off to the Channel Islands on a yachting cruise. 'I have got a Pea-jacket and such a nautical hat, and such a roll of the legs already.' The yacht belonged to James Cotter Morison, another immensely valued friend of that period and after. Morison, though a recurrent figure in Meredith's life-history for the next twenty-five years, is an unobtrusive one, partly because very few of his letters to him were preserved. He was a literary man of some distinction, mainly known for his *Life of St. Bernard*, which caused him to be named ' St. Bernard ' by his friends. He was also prominent on the staff of *The Saturday Review* when, under the editorship of J. D. Cook, it was the leading weekly paper. He is described as a man of versatile tastes and singular social charm, the multiplicity of whose interests prevented him from doing justice to his powers. In an epitaph, Meredith called him ' a fountain of our sweetest, quick to spring in fellowship abounding '. He seems to have been one of those people who are indirectly creative through influencing others by generous encouragement and sympathy. He was the son of a Scotch West Indies merchant who at the age of fifty-two .invented a vegetable pill, the principal ingredient of which was said to be gamboge. With this he cured himself of life-long ill-health, and it became widely popular as ' Morison's Pills ', earning him a large fortune. I mention this as an oddity in conjunction with one whose *St. Bernard* was admired by Matthew Arnold and who was an intimate friend and literary associate of John Morley.

2

Toward the end of 1861 Meredith had received a letter of remonstrance and eulogy from a clergyman, the Headmaster of Norwich Grammar School. This was Augustus Jessopp, then a stranger to him, but who soon became one of his most helpful and trusted friends. Jessopp was an active and stimulating headmaster, and at this time he was transforming his school from a decayed institution to a flourishing modern one. On his retirement in 1879, he was a country parson for thirty-two

years, acquiring a distinguished reputation as a learned anti-
quarian and attractive writer on mediaeval England. Vigorous,
kindly, and unconventional, he was evidently the sort of man
to get on well with Meredith, who at once invited him to stay
at Copsham. Jessopp had told him that parts of *Richard
Feverel* had shocked him, but that he and his Cambridge friends
ranked him next to Tennyson in poetic power (though they had
only read the 1851 *Poems* and a few magazine contributions).
Some years later, Meredith thanked him for the noble bouncing
quality of his praise, which he found so generous and refreshing.
By September, 1862, he had reluctantly decided that Arthur
must go to a boarding-school, and his natural choice was
Jessopp, to whom he wrote:

> I would trust him, who is my only blessing on earth, to you with
> full confidence. . . . This is Arthur's character. It is based upon
> sensitiveness, I am sorry to say. He reflects and he has real
> brains and just ideas. He is obedient: brave: ,sensible. His
> brain is fine and subtle, not capacious.

After taking Arthur to Norwich and staying a few days, he
wrote to Hardman praising Mrs. Jessopp. ' She unites worth
and sweetness of nature and capacity.' Everything at the
school pleased him. There were only twenty-five boarders, so
Arthur had individual attention and he made a happy
beginning. One can be sure that the hearts of the Jessopps
were touched by Meredith's devoted dependence on his child,
as well as being delighted by his confidence in them. This
was indeed a very special parent. They recognised his genius
as a writer, and must have felt the high privilege that was
theirs in being able to help him as the simple being, poor and
overworked, who afterwards wrote—in a rhymed letter to
Mrs. Jessopp—' Pray tell me (with the door shut) do you find
him such a darling 'tis no wonder that I dote?' To be—as
Swinburne had proclaimed—one of the leaders of English
literature was cold comfort when compared with this love
which sustained him in the depths of his being. In his friendships he could share the joy and adventure of living. Arthur
alone could fill his eyes with light. Unless we take the reference
to sensitiveness as significant, he felt no forebodings.
Various apocryphal and unauthentic accounts have been

given of Meredith's attempt at domestic intimacy with Rossetti and Swinburne, and of its abrupt termination. Meredith had to spend one day a week at Chapman & Hall's in connexion with his work as their reader of manuscripts, so it seemed a good arrangement for him to stay the night at 16 Cheyne Walk. He rented a bedroom and had the use of a sitting-room, Swinburne and W. M. Rossetti being the other sub-tenants. This arrangement began in October, 1862. We have seen that he had known Rossetti for about three years, and that Swinburne was his loyal admirer. He had spent convivial evenings with them, and had taken Hardman to Rossetti's studio in the previous April. (Hardman described ' the celebrated Pre-Raphaelite painter ' as a very jolly fellow, and gave a return dinner at his Club, where, he wrote, ' I flatter myself they never sat down to a better selected meal in their lives.')

But the realities of Rossetti's home life were more than Bohemian. His habits were excessively unwholesome, and some of his associates must have been undesirable to Meredith, who was fastidious in his unconventionality. Swinburne, too, was entering on a period of irregular living which included much imbibing of brandy, and was a most tempestuous person to be with. He got on Meredith's nerves. And Rossetti told Edmund Gosse, ' Algernon used to drive me crazy by dancing all over the studio like a wild cat.' The blameless W. M. Rossetti has given a guarded account of the situation. His brother, he wrote, had seen Mr. Meredith increasingly for some time past, and his talents and work he seriously, though not uncritically, admired.

> Mr. Meredith and Rossetti entertained a solid mutual regard, and got on together amicably, yet without that thorough cordiality of give-and-take which oils the hinges of daily intercourse. . . . In the matter of household routine he (Meredith) found that Rossetti's arrangements, though ample for comfort of a more or less off-hand kind, were not conformable to his standard. Thus it soon became apparent that Mr. Meredith's sub-tenancy was not likely to stand much wear and tear, or to outlast the temporary convenience which had prompted it.

In other words, Meredith found the goings on at Queen's House altogether too much for him. Swinburne may—or may not—have thrown a poached egg at him because he spoke disrespectfully of Victor Hugo. It is certain that he said, long afterwards, that 'the household was too disorderly for him and his work'. In 1868 he gave Hardman some retrospective details.

> Poor Dante Rossetti seems to be losing his eyesight, owing entirely to bad habits—a matter I foretold long ago: Eleven a.m. plates of small-shop ham, thick cut, grisly with brine: four smashed eggs on it: work till dusk: dead tired on sofa till 10 p.m. Then dines off raw meat and stout. So on for years. Can Nature endure these things? The poor fellow never sleeps at night. His nervous system is knocked to pieces. It's melancholy.

It is impossible to say how often Meredith used his rooms, but there is reason for believing that he went there very seldom, and it is certain that the arrangement ended with some sort of row with Rossetti. But the break was temporary, for in January, 1864, he wrote to Hardman that he was bringing Arthur to 'have his face taken' by Rossetti, who did a sketch of him with a dog in the background. And he was still paying rent in June, 1863, when he wrote cordially to W. M. Rossetti—

> I will bring you the money on Monday, and pray say to Gabriel everything in my excuse. I can conceive now that my recent absence from the house must look odd to him.

With Swinburne he remained on amicable terms, though their incompatibility of temper had become obvious. In 1866, when the publication of *Poems and Ballads* caused a storm of reprobation and abuse, he supported Swinburne wisely and faithfully. 'As for the hubbub,' he wrote to him, 'it will do you no harm, and you have partly deserved it; and it has done the critical world good by making men look boldly at the restrictions imposed upon art by our dominating damnable bourgeoisie.' About five years later he received a violent letter in which Swinburne complained that his society was baneful to him. Meredith's reply was dignified and forbearing. He hoped that, by seeing little of one another for a few years, they might come together again naturally. 'And if not, you will know I am glad of the old time, am always proud of you, always heart in heart with you on all the great issues of our life, and in all that concerns your health and fortunes.' It was the end of their intimacy.

c

Meredith was offended by Swinburne's inability to admire his later novels. But in 1873 he described him as ' by far the finest poet of the young lot '. And at his death he paid a noble tribute:

> He was the greatest of our lyrical poets—of the world, I could say, considering what a language he had to wield. Song was his natural voice.

CHAPTER SIX

1

THE importance of Arthur in Meredith's existence at this period compels me to record that during his holidays in April, 1863, he developed measles, and was kept at home for four months. And at the end of July he had a nasty accident through the carelessness of someone who was giving him a ride on a horse, being dragged by the foot and badly bruised about the head. Meredith wrote to Hardman in a state of distress; but Arthur soon recovered from the mishap, though it was evidently an alarming one.

In July the two had spent ten days at Seaford with Maurice FitzGerald and his brother. The painful associations of the place must have been in Meredith's mind before he arrived there; but he was allowed no opportunities for bitter retrospection, which would in any case have been uncharacteristic of him. For the FitzGeralds had collected a party and revelry was in progress. Burnand was there, ' reeking puns from every pore ', Samuel Laurence, the painter, and several others, including H. M. Hyndman, then a Cambridge undergraduate. Meredith called it the Champagne-Loo party, and went to Goodwood Races with them, where he lost £5. ' Wise grows the loser, merely happy the winner. A great pastime! We elbowed dukes: jostled lords: were in a flower-garden of countesses.' Fifty years afterwards, Hyndman—then one of the veterans of the Socialist Movement—wrote a chapter of his *Reminiscences* on Meredith and the FitzGeralds. He recalled an occasion when they were all sitting on the beach at Seaford tossing stones lazily into the sea. Meredith was discoursing with even more than ordinary vivacity and charm when Burnand suddenly came out with ' Damn you, George, why won't you write as you talk? '—a remark which has been much quoted. Hyndman goes on to lament that Meredith, with such a wonderful gift of clear, forcible language, should have deliberately cultivated artificiality.

He had a marvellous flow of literary high spirits throughout his life, and his unaffected natural talk was altogether delightful. But his writing showed even then, to my inexperienced eye, little trace of this unforced outpouring of wisdom and wit; while his conversation was almost equally artificial, not to say stilted, except with men and women he had known well for years.

Hyndman himself, judged by the fustian phraseology which pervades his reminiscences, had very little sense of words. One cannot help wondering what Meredith's novels would have been like had he adapted himself to his requirements—and those of Burnand, the hard-boiled professional humorist, who wrote long afterwards that ' his work was killed by his conceit '. With certain reservations, however, Hyndman admired and venerated him. And it must be admitted that the artificiality of which he complained was Meredith's failing. As W. E. Henley pointed out, he was the master and the victim of a monstrous cleverness which would not permit him to do things as an honest, simple person of genius would. But he also said that his capacity for unsatisfactory writing was equalled by capacities for writing that is satisfactory in the highest degree.

In May, 1864, he stayed for a fortnight at Cambridge with Hyndman, who was a Trinity man and could show him University life at its best. The little glimpse we get of him there is valuable, as it is one of the few accounts of what he was like when in his thirties.

Though no judge of games, he took pleasure in looking on at rowing, cricket, racquets and sport of all kinds, being himself always in training and very much stronger muscularly than he looked. In fact he was all wire and whipcord without a spare ounce of flesh on him, and his endurance, as I found out in more than one long walk and vigorous playful tussles, was unwearying. . . . I had become accustomed to his incisive methods of expression, and the strange way in which he would of a sudden turn into ridicule about half what he had said seriously just before. But my undergraduate friends did not know what to make of him, and I dare say the same would have been the case had I not had the previous experience. That Meredith was witty, powerful,

active, good-humoured and a very keen observer of all that was
going on around him they recognised clearly enough. Yet he
never seemed to be conversing on the same plane as themselves,
clever fellows as some of them were. I felt this myself, and I am
confident that the lack of sympathy arose from the artificiality I
have noted.

What is the picture to be derived from this? I see him as
the visiting stranger, a non-'Varsity man, young enough to
want to behave almost like one of them, anxious to be brilliant
in conversation, and conscious that no reputation had preceded
him as a person of any great importance. I hear them saying
to one another, 'Who on earth *is* this fellow Meredith, and
where did Hyndman pick him up? Has he really written anything worth reading? Jolly clever, of course; but what on
earth did he mean by saying that St. Simeon saw the Hog in
Nature, and took Nature for the Hog? Hyndman says his
books are full of things like that!'

I see Meredith enjoying it all, in spite of being on show.
But I also see him being made uneasy by a sense of inferiority—
social inferiority—while talking over the head of some patrician
athlete who just fails to conceal his bored mystification. It
was then, perhaps, that he let fall some unguarded opinion
which caused the undergraduate to wonder whether he was
quite a gentleman, so that he instinctively knew it, hesitated,
and then conversed more audaciously than ever. All his life
he had been experiencing moments like that, when the tailoring
ancestry brandished its shears in the back-shop of his mind,
making him more than ever defiantly aware of his natural
high-breeding and intellectual distinction. And—as he might
have said to himself—it is the privilege of the young to apply
the dart of deflation to the bladder of a sensitive man's good
opinion of himself. Among the Trinity 'bloods', I expect,
Meredith felt a bit of an outsider. Forty years later he was
the smartest bit of intellectual finery a Cambridge man could
sport, and it was utterly *infra dig* not to admire him.

2

When Meredith wrote that no slavery was comparable to
the chains of hired journalism he was, doubtless, referring to

those eight years during which he contributed, to *The Ipswich Journal*, a weekly leading article and a column summarising the week's news from London and abroad. For this he is said to have received about £200 a year. He obtained the employment in 1860, through the owner of the paper, T. E. Foakes, who was a neighbour of his at Weybridge. Every Thursday he went to London to transact business and complete his ' copy ', and ' Foakes' Day ', as he called it, was a black one in his calendar. *The Ipswich Journal* was a strong Conservative paper, and Meredith's views were Radical, though less stalwart then than in later years. In 1893 someone obligingly ferreted out his articles and gave extracts to the world in a magazine, thereby providing ammunition for those who enjoyed the opportunity of using it. It was, indeed, somewhat disconcerting to Meredith's admirers when they learnt that he had written in support of political principles he did not accept. To me, I must admit, it was unfortunate rather than incriminating that he should have attacked Bright, Lincoln, and the Northern States in the American Civil War when his private convictions were on their side. Does it matter that he justified the ways of Disraeli to Suffolk farmers and disagreed with the Parliamentary reforms of Gladstone? Years afterwards he expressed admiration for ' Dizzy's ' intellectual agility and picturesque wit. And when, in 1887, he met Gladstone at the Eighty Club, he ' heard a speech from him enough to make a cock robin droop his head despondently. This valiant, prodigiously gifted, in many respects admirable old man, is, I fear me, very much an actor.' Anyhow, Meredith made no secret of his Tory journalism to his friends, and it is worth mentioning that at least one of his articles was written for him by that paragon of Liberalism John Morley. In 1860 he needed money badly. *Evan Harrington* brought him in little, and his next novel was not finished until 1864. At this time and for many years afterwards he added to his income by reading to a blind lady, Mrs. Wood, at Eltham (a sister of Parnell's Mrs. O'Shea and aunt to Field-Marshal Sir Evelyn Wood). He combined this with his weekly expedition to London, returning to the Garrick Club to dine after the reading. Mrs. Wood was a woman of considerable intelligence, with whom he often discussed contemporary topics. The newspaper work had to be undertaken to pay for Arthur's education, and he went on with it for years because he could not afford to give it up. Let those with lofty moral principles blame him, leaving the rest of us to imagine what the real Meredith must have felt like with that awful partisan stuff to be pumped out every Thursday. The wonder was that he continued to do it at all and did it so cheerfully.

Few realised [wrote Frederic Harrison in 1911] what passionate senses of right and wrong, what a high heart, he could keep in all his early struggles to be recognised for what he was, what determination burned within him never to yield one jot of his own ideas and methods to any public demand, to any pecuniary effort.

Quoted in this context, those words may seem ironic. I do not intend them as such. They are essentially true. *The Ipswich Journal* episode was merely an expedient which enabled him to pay tradesmen's bills.

It was in the autumn of 1860 that he became literary adviser and reader of manuscripts to Chapman & Hall, succeeding John Forster, who for nearly twenty-five years had acted as negotiator with them on behalf of Dickens. His salary was £250 a year, and until 1894 this was the basis of his income. During these years he read almost all the manuscripts sent in to the firm. One day a week he went to the office, where he interviewed those authors whom he thought worth advising. Once again we see him as a thoroughbred horse pulling a four-wheeled cab. He was condemned to examine with patience heaven knows how many thousand pages of trash per annum, seldom rewarded by anything of merit, a fine example of the discipline to which a strong nature will subject itself in the obligation to earn a living. For it was a more trying task than reviewing. A printed book can be skimmed through fairly comfortably, and the reviewer is not responsible for deciding whether it ought to have been published. Also it must be remembered that Meredith's drudgery was done before typescripts were in existence, which would add appreciably to the demands on mind and eye. My own opinion is that all this reading of commonplace writing was to some extent answerable for the exaggerated mannerisms of his style. The perennial perusal of mediocre performances must have made him more contemptuous than ever of bourgeois taste, and more than ever determined to be fervid and fantastic and exceptional.

Soon after his death there appeared an account of his work as publisher's reader by a member of the firm who admired him greatly. The intention of the article was to show what a conscientious reader he was, and to give extracts of his opinions of the works submitted to him. Interest, however, was mainly aroused by the revelations of certain books rejected by him. He was blamed for over-fastidiousness and for turning down books which afterwards became best-sellers. Certainly, from the commercial standpoint, he began and ended badly. Within six months of his appointment *East Lynne* arrived at the office. His judgment was ' Opinion emphatically against it. In the worst style of the present taste.' The fact that he was right did not prevent it selling a million copies when published by Bentley. It must be added that Edward Chapman, the senior partner, agreed with Meredith. He ' considered that the tone of the book was not good for the general public '. About the same time Meredith decided against Whyte Melville's *Market Harborough*, which was merely a mistake. In 1892 he was unable to recommend *The Heavenly Twins*, the meteoric success of which is now very difficult to understand. He advised the authoress to put the MS. aside until she had learnt to ' drive a story '. ' She has ability enough, and a glimpse of humour here and there and promises well for the future.' He had also dismissed one of Ouida's early novels. And Samuel Butler's *Erewhon* was told that it would not do. (Butler wrote afterwards that if he had been the publisher's reader he would have advised them to the same effect.)

Records of Meredith's critical judgments have been preserved in the ' catalogue ' volume which he kept for the purpose. Here are a few of his laconic comments on rejected rubbish.

' Weak wild stuff—M.S. looking as a survival of a dozen shipwrecks.'

' The dulness of vapid liveliness marks the style of this work. It has no quality.'

' A provincial maiden aunt of the old time had about the same notions of humour and horror. A similar manner of narrating.'

' Would seem to be written in sighs of languor.'

The Autobiography of a Donkey. ' Faithful only to the donkey's dulness.'

There is a valuable chapter on Meredith in Arthur Waugh's

A Hundred Years of Publishing, which is not only the story of
Chapman & Hall but a history of the book trade in the last
century. He pays him the following tribute.

> As against a few emphatic refusals of books, some of which after-
> wards attained success, there is to be set a long array of early
> appreciations, encouragements, corrections, and advices, which
> prove him to have shown extraordinary versatility in the post
> which he so long and so patiently occupied. . . . He was bound to
> support the claims of literature, and to reject what was illiterate.
> If he missed a few successes by the way, he at least preserved his
> own self-respect, and the firm's as well. Too little has been said
> about the shining integrity of his literary ideals, and the consistent
> encouragement which he gave to the promise which he himself
> was often the very first to perceive.

The same writer records that—

> his punctilious attire attracted the attention of many visitors,
> especially women: one remembered his lavender gloves, another
> his crisp hair; and all were impressed by his gracious courtesy,
> and by the sudden access of shyness with which he always declined
> to give his name. 'You must excuse me,' he would say, and
> bow the visitor into the passage. By the clerk at the desk he was
> always referred to as ' the reader.'

In 1869 there was an interview which has since become
historic. About a month before, a young man had called
at the office in Piccadilly with the manuscript of his first
novel under his arm. An aged figure in an Inverness cape and
slouched hat was leaning on one elbow at the clerk's desk.
One of the Chapmans was in the back part of the shop, and
he remarked with nonchalance, ' You see that old man talking
to my clerk? He's Thomas Carlyle. Have a good look at him.
You'll be glad I pointed him out to you some day.' The
young man was Thomas Hardy. His second visit was in
response to an invitation to call on the publishers and ' meet
the gentleman who has read your manuscript '. He was shown
into a back room, dusty, untidy, and piled with books and
papers. Nearly sixty years later he reticently recalled Meredith
as ' a handsome man with hair and beard not at all grey, and
wearing a frock coat buttoned at the waist and loose above, his
somewhat dramatic manner lending him a striking appearance

to the younger man's eye, who even then did not know his name. Unfortunately I made no notes of our conversation: in those days people did not usually write down everything as they do now for the concoction of reminiscences, the only words of his that I remember being, " Don't nail your colours to the mast just yet." ' Meredith had found the novel too sweeping a satire on social conditions for conventional taste. He advised him to soften it down considerably, but preferably to put it away and attempt a novel with a purely artistic purpose, giving it a more complicated plot. This advice resulted in the highly melodramatic *Desperate Remedies*, but it may also have led to the ' purely artistic purpose ' of *Under the Greenwood Tree : A Rural Painting of the Dutch School.* Anyhow, there is no doubt that Meredith saw promise in the crude and immature manuscript, and that he gave Hardy all the encouragement he could. Hardy's own view of Meredith, written at his centenary, was that—

> after some years have passed, what was best in his achievement—
> at present partly submerged by its other characteristics—will rise
> more distinctly to the surface than it has done already. Then he
> will be regarded as a writer who said finest and profoundest
> things often in a tantalising way, but as one whose work remains
> as an essential portion of the vast universal volume which en-
> shrines as contributors all those who have adequately recorded
> their reading of life.

CHAPTER SEVEN

1

EVAN HARRINGTON, as we have seen, was finished in September, 1860. The first we hear of his next books is about eight months later, when he writes as follows to Janet Ross.

> I have three works in hand. The most advanced is ' Emilia Belloni ', of which I have read some chapters to your mother, and gained her strong approval. Emilia is a feminine musical genius. I gave you once, sitting on the mound over Copsham, an outline of the real story it is taken from. Of course one does not follow out real stories; and this has simply suggested Emilia to me.— Then my next novel is called ' A Woman's Battle '. Qy.—good title? I think it will be my best book as yet. The third is weaker in breadth of design. It is called ' Van Diemen Smith '—is interesting as a story.

(This was *The House on the Beach*, which was laid aside and completed fifteen years later.)

' Emilia ' and ' A Woman's Battle ' occupied him alternately for the next four years; the latter being *Rhoda Fleming*. In July, 1861, he mentioned on three occasions, in letters to F. M. Evans, of Bradbury and Evans, a story called ' The Dyke Farm ', which was evidently yet another name for *Rhoda Fleming*. In these letters he asks whether Lucas wants the story for *Once a Week*, so he must have been planning it as a serial. For in June he had sent some chapters to Lucas, telling him— ' Say that you want to begin it and I'll sit down and finish it.' But *Once a Week* was in a precarious condition, and Lucas must have decided that another story by Meredith would hasten its end, which occurred a year or so afterwards. Nothing more is heard of the story until January, 1863, when he begins a letter to Maxse—' Rhoda now rushes to an end. I don't at all know what to think of the work.' Six months later he again refers to it as ' an English novel of the real story-telling order '. Another fifteen months elapse, and then he writes to Hardman,

' I really trust to have a one volume novel for January, ripe and ready. " Rhoda Fleming, a Plain Story ". . . . If I compress it into one volume I shall bring it back complete.' In the same October he writes to Jessopp, ' I have, during the last month, written 250 pages of " A Plain Story " of 600 pages (2 vols).' And again to Jessopp, at the end of another three months, that he had put aside Vittoria (the sequel to ' Emilia ', which had been published in April, 1864), ' to finish off Rhoda Fleming in one volume, now swollen to two—and oh! will it be three?—But this is my Dd. Dd. Dd. uncertain workmanship '. Yet another three months, and it ' is just completed (all but the last two chapters). It is three vols, six months work. Tinsley offers £400 for it. I don't quite like to sell it for that sum.'

For some inexplicable reason, Chapman & Hall wanted to delay publication for six months, so the book went to Tinsley, appeared in October, 1865, and had a very poor sale. Tinsley Bros. were a new and enterprising firm which aimed at providing the libraries with popular novels. They also published Hardy's *Desperate Remedies* (at the author's risk and expense). I have given all these rather fussy details as a necessary preliminary to my remarks about *Rhoda Fleming*, because I regard them as contributing significant elucidation of its imperfections. I see these details as the grievous chronicle of a fine tale bedevilled by the writer's inability to stick to his conception of ' A Plain Story ', and enfeebled by the artistic error of plot elaboration.

Let me say at once that there have been notable opinions to the contrary. R. L. Stevenson called it ' the strongest thing in English letters since Shakespeare died ', and Arnold Bennett ranked it, with *The Egoist*, as the best of the novels. Why, then, should it leave on my mind the impression of being a mismanaged masterpiece? Let us take the ' Plain Story ' as first conceived by Meredith. It can have amounted to no more than this: he thought of a stolid yeoman-farmer, a man of narrow mind and inflexible principles, with two daughters; dark-haired, heroic Rhoda, and Dahlia, golden, beautiful, and sweet-natured. Dahlia is seduced by a nephew of the local squire. The ' Woman's Battle ' of Rhoda is to rescue her. Rhoda must have a faithful admirer, and one was devised in Robert, the farmer's assistant. There are also two excellent creations of country folk in Mrs. Sumfit and Master Gammon. Of the essential and living characters of the story, W. E. Henley wrote:—

> They have the unity of effect, the vigorous simplicity of life, that belong to great creative art; and at their highest stress of emotion, the culmination of their passion, they affect us with force and directness by the expression of human feeling in the coil of a tragic situation.

We have seen that Meredith originally planned it as a one-volume novel, which I take to mean seventy or eighty thousand words, or possibly less. He intended a powerful, homespun tragedy, written round the characters of two country girls, innocent and romantic in their social aspirations, and involved in calamity through Dahlia's deception by a man of good family. My reason for complaint is that, with all its excrescences and mishandling, *Rhoda Fleming* leaves an after-effect of singular intensity; the Flemings and their story remain in one's mind as something poignant and permanent. The book gives one a curious impression of having been written in collaboration with Hardy, and also has an air of what used to be called ' a novel with a purpose '. I suggest that the after-effect I have mentioned is the essence of the story as it first took shape in Meredith's mind, when he believed that it would be ' his best book as yet '. But a plot had to be contrived for the working out of the Fleming misfortunes, and there the trouble began. Where noble simplification of design should have served the purpose, a series of side issues began to encumber the original outline. Subsidiary and unconvincing characters were contrived, with stories of their own which got out of control; the dreadful business of intricate plot-weaving bred disproportion and redundance; the protagonists, in their flesh-and-blood reality, became entangled in a muddle of interest-sustaining episodes which have no valid connexion with the story. Throughout the book one observes a deliberate effort at straightforward narration. There are no interludes where the author lectures his audience from in front of the curtain, and almost every chapter begins with an onward movement of the events in progress.

But how one wishes that the novel had been commissioned for *Once a Week*, thereby escaping its four years process of laborious amplification. Meredith himself did not think very highly of it. When revising it for the collected edition of his works he made only a few minor alterations, and in 1883 he wrote to one of his admirers that it was not worth reading. I need only add that my own adverse criticisms are the outcome of a reluctant conviction that, though containing the elements of a great novel, it fails because at least half of it is a disfigurement of the original design. For this we must blame the accursed Victorian convention of plot contriving. But it also showed that Meredith lacked the sense of construction which should have warned him that he was going wrong.

2

Emilia in England (renamed *Sandra Belloni* when reprinted in 1886) is a hundred pages longer than *Rhoda Fleming* and planned on a bigger scale. It took him three years to write, and his letters contain several references to the difficulties he had to overcome. At the end of 1862 he wrote that he had cut to pieces four printed chapters and was totally dissatisfied. In March, 1863, he was 'overwhelmed with disgust at Emilia', and nine months later 'Emilia is not all right. She has worried me beyond measure.'

He had packed an immensity of work and thought into the book, but the effort it cost him is apparent in many places. Judged as a whole, it is not a good novel; there are chapters, especially toward the end, which are wearisome to get through, and once again one asks why he should have imposed this clumsy and unwieldy mechanism of 'full-length fiction' on his mercurial imagination. One sees him struggling with the octopus of his plot, becoming strained and artificial through fatigue, and desperately resorting to a filling in of the background with material that suggests bad Dickens. And the forty-fourth chapter is ominously invaded by 'The Philosopher' who demands the pulpit and addresses us in the peremptory manner which we know so well in the later novels. He now informs us that to be madly in love is, for the sentimentalist, to be ON THE HIPPOGRIFF, ' by which it is clear to me that my fantastic Philosopher means to indicate the lover mounted in this wise, as a creature bestriding an extraneous power ',

This leads to an ironic disquisition on the disadvantages of the novelist who cannot be content to provide the usual unphilosophic fare.

Right loath am I to continue my partnership with a fellow who will not see things on the surface, and is blind to the fact that the public detest him. I mean, this garrulous, super-subtle, so-called Philosopher, who first set me upon the building of THE THREE VOLUMES, it is true, but whose stipulation that he should occupy so large a portion of them has made them rock top-heavy, to the forfeit of their stability. He maintains that a story should not always flow, or, at least, not to a given measure. When we are knapsack on back, he says, we come to eminences where a survey of our journey past and in advance is desirable. He points proudly to the fact that our people in this comedy move themselves,—are moved from their own impulsion,—and that no arbitrary hand has posted them to bring about any event and heap the catastrophe. In vain I tell him that he is meantime making tatters of the puppets' golden robe-illusion: that he is sucking the blood of their warm humanity out of them.

Here, anyhow, we have illuminating evidence of Meredith's awareness that he was imperilling his success as a story-teller by being too clever. He was reminding himself of what his detractors have been saying ever since. The story-teller, even when he is ' widening the scope of the Novel ', must not indulge in obtrusive opinions and explanations, or introduce qualities of thought and poetry that are incompatible with well-behaved fiction. In the fifty-first chapter he again confers with The Philosopher, who denies ' the critical dictum that a novel is to give us copious sugar and no cane '.

Such is the construction of my story [he concludes] that to entirely deny the Philosopher the privilege he stipulated for when with his assistance I conceived it, would render our performance unintelligible to that acute and honourable minority which consents to be thwacked with aphorisms and sentences and a fantastic delivery of the verities. While my Play goes on, I must permit him to come forward occasionally. We are indeed in a sort of partnership, and it is useless for me to tell him that he is not popular and destroys my chance.

The Philosopher, however, makes but one brief reappearance, when ' up to this point rigidly excluded, he rushes forward to the footlights to explain ' that one of the characters symbolises the vice of Sentimentalism.

These passages seem to me strongly significant of the attitude which Meredith was already tending to adopt toward his public —a tendency to write for his own satisfaction and let them make what they could of it. He was rebelling against the convention which refused to sanction the free play of ideas in a novel and rejected penetrative analysis of motives. As he wrote in a letter a few years afterwards, ' The English public will not let me probe deeply into humanity. You must not paint either woman or man: a surface view of the species flat as a wafer is acceptable.' Being what he was, it could not have been otherwise. ' My method ', he claimed, ' has been to prepare my readers for a crucial exhibition of the personae, and then to give the scene in the fullest of their blood and brain under stress of a fierce situation.' His claim is often justified by results. But The Philosopher was always at his elbow, while he strove to adulterate his vivid and uneasy genius with the quietude of traditional style, to conform to the demands for a more pedestrian psychology, and to discipline his naturally flamboyant humour. Above all, The Philosopher was the experimentalist in him, the Pegasus that mounted up into the sky, contemptuous of dear old Trollope bowling safely along the country roads in his brougham.

I have said that I do not consider *Sandra Belloni* a good novel, for the reason that it contains tracts of heavy, unvitalised writing and other faults of construction and character-drawing. (Meredith himself said that it had good points and some of his worst ones.) But all this is balanced by the many fine things in it, and the whole is dominated by the superb figure of Emilia (or Sandra), the half-Italian girl whose truth and simplicity are made the touchstone of all she comes in contact with.

As with all his great women characters, in creating Emilia, Meredith could not go wrong; she was real to him; he believed in her, and wrote from his heart. Speaking through The Philosopher he outlined her as follows:—

Passion, he says, is *noble strength on fire*, and points to Emilia as a representation of passion. She asks for what she thinks she may have; she claims what she imagines to be her own. She has no shame, and thus, believing in, she never violates, nature, and offends no law, wild as she may seem. Passion does not turn on her and rend her when it is thwarted. She was never carried out of the limit of her own intelligent force, seeing that it directed her always, with the simple mandate to seek that which belonged to her.

It might be said that she overbalances the book, for she is so adorably unreserved, so natural, so true to the instincts of her loving and passionate being, that she makes the people around her seem invented and unreal. She is like living music, and her humanity is expressed by the magnificent voice which is to make her career. She is a soul harmonious with nature, and when she sings among the nightingales on a night of frost in May, she is one with them and the moonlight. ' Emilia had gained in force and fulness. She sang with a stately fervour, letting the notes flow from her breast, while both her arms hung loose, and not a gesture escaped her.' That scene is at the end of the book. In an earlier chapter we see her in love. The passage must be quoted, for the mastery of its descriptive writing.

A half-circle of high-banked greensward, studded with old park-trees, hung round the roar of the water; distant enough from the white-twisting fall to be mirrored on a smooth-heaved surface, while its outpushing brushwood below drooped under burdens of drowned reed-flags that caught the foam. Keen scent of hay, crossing the dark air, met Emilia as she entered the river-meadow. A little more, and she saw the white weir-piles shining, and the grey roller just beginning to glisten to the moon. Eastward on her left, behind a cedar, the moon had cast off a thick cloud, and shone through the cedar-bars with a yellowish hazy softness, making rosy gold of the first passion of the tide, which, writhing and straining on through many lights, grew wide upon the wonderful velvet darkness underlying the wooded banks. With the full force of a young soul that leaps from beauty seen to unimagined beauty, Emilia stood and watched the picture. Then she sat down, hushed, awaiting her lover.

The structure of the book, therefore, is dependent on the presentation of this glorious creature; without her, it would be a failure, though it is full of lively humour and social satire, and was the first of his novels in which incident was subordinated to development of character. The main aim of it appears to have been a subtly devastating dissection of Sentimentalism, which is represented by the three Miss Poles and their half-hearted brother Wilfrid. Arabella, Cornelia and Adela were the daughters of a city merchant. Cultured, snobbish, complacent, and socially ambitious, ' their susceptibilities demanded that they should escape from a city circle. They supposed that they enjoyed exclusive possession of the Nice Feelings, and exclusively comprehended the Fine Shades.' They are comedy bordering on burlesque. Their patronage of Emilia causes much confusion in their minds and behaviour, while they seek to win social credit from her musical genius. They were the sort of ladies who exchange meaning looks and indulge in hazy emotions and elaborate introspections. In the circle which they designed to establish at their country house, Celebrities, London residents, and County notables were to meet, mix, and revolve.

In the case of Tracy Runningbrook they had furnished a signal instance of their discernment. They had eyes and ears for a certain tone and style about him, before they learnt that he was of the blood of dukes, and would be a famous poet.

Here, with his hair red as blown flame, we find a somewhat diluted portrait of Swinburne, who does, however, become fully recognisable in a letter to Wilfrid Pole, who has sent him a review of his last book.

Why the deuce do you write me such infernal trash about the opinions of a villainous dog who can't even pen a decent sentence? Let the fellow bark till he froths at the mouth, and scatters the virus of the beast among his filthy friends.

One suspects this to have been a quotation from the original source. Of the other persons in the book, it is enough to mention Mr. Pericles, the millionaire impresario whose only religion is music, and Mrs. Chump, a broadly depicted vulgarian and figure of 'fun, neither of whom is convincingly successful, and of whom one could do with less. There is much of Meredith's peculiar recklessness in it, and in places he seems not to have cared how fantastically improbable the story was becoming. One feels, as I have already suggested, that at times he was losing patience with regulation novel-writing. The good things in *Sandra Belloni* are very good indeed. The bad things are the contrivings of a brain taxed to desperation. If that brain could have been scientifically examined, it might have been found to be unfitted for the drudgery imposed on it by these enormous works of fiction. It was the substance for a mind which rose to great opportunities, throve on high-pitched emotional effects, and could not adapt itself to the ponderous mechanism which inferior writers managed by appropriately pedestrian methods.

3

Toward the end of August, 1863, he went abroad for a month's holiday. After spending three days in Paris with Hardman, who 'could not get him past the more modern pictures of battles at Versailles', he joined his faithful friend Lionel Robinson at Grenoble. (He had got to know Robinson through Hardman, who lived next door to him in London.) They walked through Dauphiné, doing ten hours a day; crossed Mont Genèvre into Italy to Turin and Lago Maggiore; then over mountains and valleys into Switzerland to Geneva; thence to Dijon. In December we find him writing to Mrs. Jessopp of Arthur's return home from school:—

> How could I have stopped away from my living heart so long? But I have him and won't moan that it's only six weeks. More than ever do I thank the blessed chance that inspired you to make yourselves known to me and render me the most indebted of men. For, I see not only that every care is taken of my darling under your roof, but that happiness is his vital air there. He breathes it. Shall he not be robust in spirit? At least I have faith in the experiment. . . .
>
> Thackeray's death startled and grieved me. And I, who think that I should be capable of eyeing the pitch-black King if he knocked for me in the night! Alas for those who do not throw the beetle!

He ends the letter with one of his grumbles about 'Emilia': 'She grieves me. I have never so cut about a created thing. There's good work in her: but the work?' I can discover no actual mention of his having met Thackeray, though he probably did so through Peacock or Eyre Crowe. He wrote of him afterwards as 'a great modern writer, of clearest eye and head, capable in activity of presenting thoughtful women, thinking men, who groaned over his puppetry—that he dared not animate them, flesh though they were, with the fires of positive brainstuff. He could have done it, and he is of the departed! Had he dared he would (for he was Titan enough) have raised the art in dignity on a level with history '—words in which he spoke, not only of Thackeray, but of his own aspirations as a novelist. The ' beetle ' was the implement he used for exercising himself. His first reference to it is in a letter to Maxse in February, 1863. ' My best solitary exercise is throwing the beetle—a huge mallet weighing 18 or 19 pounds— and catching the handle, performing wondrous tricks therewith.' He continued this performance for many years, and the violent exertion was believed to have contributed to the spinal weakness which ultimately incapacitated him.

Emilia in England was published in April, 1864, at the author's risk and for his profit—what would now be called ' on a commission basis '. The profits cannot have been large; but he was making a fairly good income, and was entering on a period of comparative prosperity. In May he was elected to the Garrick Club.

Meanwhile, the supremacy of Arthur in his thoughts and devotion was drawing to its close. In the previous autumn he had become acquainted with Mr. Justin Vulliamy, a widower with four daughters, three of them unmarried. They lived at Mickleham, a few miles from Esher, having settled there in 1857, when Mr. Vulliamy retired from his wool-manufacturing business in Normandy.

In April, Meredith became engaged to the youngest daughter, Marie, who was twenty-four. From the first he was aware that she lacked vitality, but found it ' compensated by so very much sweetness '. To Maxse he wrote:—

> She is intensely emotional, but without expression for it, save in music. I call her my dumb poet. But when she is at the piano, she is not dumb. She has a divine touch on the notes. She is very fond of the boy. Not at all in a gushing way, but fond of him as a good little fellow, whom she trusts to make her friend.

The shadows of the future now lie across those words. For with all her merits as a wife, she was not an interesting woman, and Meredith's loyalty to her could not disguise the fact. That is but the shadow of a passing cloud. The dark omen is upon the words about Arthur, for the ' good little fellow ' was never able to accept the situation of being super-seded by a step-mother, admirable though her intentions may have been. All was well with the world, however, when the rapturous lover exclaimed in this same letter :—

My friend, I have written of love and never felt it till now.— I have much to pass through [he had to overcome Mr. Vulliamy's opposition] in raking up my history with the first woman that held me. But I would pass through fire for my darling, and all that I have to endure seems little for the immense gain I hope to get. When her hand rests in mine, the world seems to hold its breath, and the sun is moveless, I take hold of Eternity.

On the following day he wrote, to Hardman :—

I never touched so pure and so conscience-clear a heart. My own is almost abashed to think itself beloved by such a creature. The day when she is to be mine blinds me.

To Wyse, in July, he described her, in more sober style, as ' a very handsome person, fair, with a noble pose, and full figure, and a naturally high-bred style and manner such as one meets but rarely. I trust I may have strength, as I have honest will, to make her happy.' But a month later, he was again ecstatic to Maxse :—

I write with my beloved beside me; my thrice darling—of my body, my soul, my song! I have never loved a woman and felt love grow in me. This clear and lovely nature doubles mine. And she has humour, my friend. She is a charming companion, as well as the staunchest heart and fairest mistress.

They were married on September 20th, 1864, at Mickleham, by Mr. Jessopp. Janet Ross attended the ceremony, but did not mention it in her memoirs. One imagines that she regarded the chosen of her Poet with a somewhat critical eye. He wrote to someone that the wedding passed like smooth music. ' The whole business now presents itself to me as if I had been blown through a tube and landed in Matrimony by Pneumatic Despatch.'

4

After a fortnight at Southampton, they stayed for a month with Maxse at Bursledon. Meredith wrote joyously to Hardman of the comfortable house where life was so jolly.

> I rise, bathe, run, and come blooming to breakfast. . . . Fancy a salt river, crystal clear, winding under full-bosomed woods, to a Clovelly-like village, house upon house, with ships, and trawlers, and yachts moored under the windows, and away the flat stream, shining to the Southern sun till it reaches Southampton Water, with the New Forest over it, shadowy, and beyond to the left, the Solent and the Island. This is possible from our window. The air makes athletes. All round are rolling woods, or healthy hills.

The accommodation at Copsham being inadequate, they spent the winter in lodgings, first at Esher and then in Kingston, where in the spring they took a three-years lease of Kingston Lodge, a pleasant little house with a good garden, chosen because it was close to Norbiton Hall, where the Hardmans lived. Here he finished *Rhoda Fleming*, and wrote most of *Vittoria* and a great part of *Harry Richmond*. On July 27th, 1865, his son, William Maxse Meredith, was born. 'What he weighs I know not,' remarked Hardman in his Journal, ' for Meredith is very superstitious, and would not do anything that ancient crones regard as unlucky.'

In April he had visited Monckton Milnes (Lord Houghton) at Fryston, which he described as the dullest house with the driest company in the dismallest country he had ever visited. Swinburne was also staying there, but the dry company complained of may have been provided by Connop Thirlwall, the historian and Bishop of St. Davids, and J. H. Bridges, the positivist philosopher. And Lord Houghton, though abundant in social friendliness, was too much of a literary dilettante for Meredith. (Swinburne called him ' a good-natured old fellow whose title might have been " Baron Tattle of Scandal ".')

It was at Fryston, by the way, in 1862, that Swinburne one Sunday evening after dinner was asked to read some of his poems to an audience which included the Archbishop of York, Thackeray, and his two young daughters. He read *Les Noyades*, at which the Archbishop made so shocked a face, and the young ladies giggled so loud in their excitement, that Lady Houghton was obliged to exclaim, 'Well, Mr. Swinburne, if you will read such extraordinary things, you must expect us to laugh.' *Les Noyades* was then proceeding on its amazing course, and the Archbishop was looking more and more horrified, when suddenly the butler threw open the door and announced, 'Prayers, my Lord!'

At this time Meredith's letters to Maxse contain some interesting passages of literary comment. Of Hawthorne he says:—

> His deliberate analysis, his undramatic representations, the sentience rather than the drawings which he gives of his characters, and the luscious, morbid tone, are all effective. But I think his delineations untrue: their power lies in the intensity of his egotistical perceptions, and are not the perfect view of men and women . . . I strive by study of humanity to represent it: not its morbid action. I have a tendency to do that, which I repress: for, in delineating it, there is no gain. In all my, truly, very faulty works, there is this aim. Much of my strength lies in painting morbid emotion and exceptional positions; but my conscience will not let me so waste my time. Hitherto consequently I have done nothing of mark. But I shall, and 'Vittoria' will be the first indication (if not fruit) of it. My love is for epical subjects— not for cobwebs in a putrid corner; though I know the fascination of unravelling them.

With this one can appropriately compare Henry James's definition of Hawthorne's romantic morbidity.

> Nothing is more curious and interesting than this almost exclusively *imported* character of the sense of sin in Hawthorne's mind; it seems to exist there merely for an artistic or literary purpose.

But Meredith must surely have been aware of the beautiful quality of the prose in which the classic novelist expressed himself, and might well have imitated its lucidity in 'Vittoria'. Of Carlyle he says:—

> Bear in mind that he is a humourist. The insolence offensive to you, is part of his humour. He means what he says, but only as far as a humourist can mean what he says. See the difference

between him and Emerson, who is on the contrary a philosopher. The humourist, notwithstanding, has much truth to back him. Swim on his pages, take his poetry and fine grisly laughter, his manliness, together with some splendid teaching. I don't agree with Carlyle a bit, but I do enjoy him.

Tennyson, on the other hand, he was no longer able to admire.

I'm a little sick of Tennysonian green Tea . . . limp, lackadaisical fishermen, and panderings to the depraved sentimentalism of our drawing-rooms. I tell you that ' Enoch Arden ' is ill done, and that in twenty years time it will be denounced as villainous weak, in spite of the fine (but too conscious) verse, and the rich insertions of tropical scenery.

In another letter he refers to the ' bar of Michael Angelo ' line in *In Memoriam,* and indulges in a little grumbling.

I can't attempt to explain it. Great poets attain a superior lustre by these obscurities. If I had written such a line, what vehement reprobation of me! what cunning efforts to construe! and finally what a lecture on my wilfulness! In Tennyson it is interesting. In Browning you are accustomed to gnaw a bone and would be surprised to find him simple. But G. M. who is not known, not acknowledged, he shall be trounced if he offers us a difficulty—we insist upon his thinking in our style.

It must be added that this was written in east wind and a frost, and distaste for his surroundings at Kingston, which was already becoming suburban.

This was toward the end of 1865, and *Vittoria* was near enough to completion for it to have been accepted by *The Fortnightly Review* for serial publication, which began in January, and continued until December, 1866. For this he received £250. *The Fortnightly* had been started in May, 1865, as a politically independent rival to the heavy quarterlies, and the first English periodical to adopt as a rule the plan of signed articles. Published by Chapman & Hall, it was edited by G. H. Lewes. Trollope was chairman of the Board of proprietors, and had subscribed £1200 to the original capital of £9000. His novel *The Belton Estate* appeared in the first numbers, Walter Bagehot was a contributor, and the quality and vigour of the magazine were immediately recognised among the judicious. It seems probable that Meredith had been suggested as sub-editor; about nine months before, he wrote that there was a chance of his getting an under Editorship of a new Review. But nothing more came of it, though he acted as editor during the last months of 1867 (during the absence in America of John Morley, who had succeeded Lewes at the end of the previous year), and contributed many poems and several long articles and reviews subsequently.

The outbreak of hostilities between Italy and Austria brought him experience as a war correspondent. He went on behalf of *The Morning Post*, and on June 22nd wrote the first of a dozen despatches, from Ferrara, where Cialdini had his army corps ready to force the passage of the River Po. The last one was from Venice, on July 20th. He accompanied the Italian army, driving and camping with the troops, but did not see much of the actual fighting. His letters are competent journalism, but do not make interesting reading. He was back in England before the end of July, but returned to Austria and Italy in August. In Vienna he met Leslie Stephen for the first time, an event of profound significance for both of them.

Going on to Milan, he found Hyndman, who was describing the campaign for *The Pall Mall Gazette*. Also G. A. Henty, of *The Standard*, and G. A. Sala, of *The Daily Telegraph*. In Venice, where he witnessed the triumphal entry of Victor Emanuel, he had encountered Janet Ross, with whom he made several excursions, talked of ' the dear old Esher days ', and decided that he loved Carpaccio only a little less than Titian and Giorgione. He also fell out rather badly with Sala, an episode which Hyndman has described in detail.

His keen and at that period rather sardonic and satirical intelligence grated on Sala's ebullience, and there was continual friction below the surface from the first time they met, though none would have thought so who saw all of us cheerfully chatting on the Piazza San Marco. The quarrel arose out of a very petty matter, which only amounted to the fact that Meredith, though just in all his dealings and hospitable in his way, was by no means liberal, while Sala, though extremely liberal, and hospitable as well, was by no means always just. Anyway, there arose a tremendous storm on Sala's part, and he insulted Meredith grossly at the hotel table. Meredith could easily have killed Sala in any

85

personal encounter, but he kept a strong restraint on himself and simply went away.

George Augustus Sala's personality being what it was, this climax of incompatibility need not be wondered at. For one thing, Meredith was a conversationalist. He enjoyed a good story, but did not care for conversation which consisted of nothing else. Sala, according to an ' illustrated interview ' which I have been looking at, was ' one of the merriest men of the nineteenth century, literally loaded with fun and good humour. Touch him on his anecdotal trigger and you will receive a volley. Ask him a question and his answer is—an anecdote.' Famous in his day as a paragon among reporters and leader-writers, he was also one of the biggest bounders who ever boasted himself the best judge of a Havana in Clubland. Beside him, F. C. Burnand must have been almost Walter Pater-like in refinement and reticence. One interprets Hyndman's ' very petty matter ' as concerned with the ordering of wine. Sala, though his father was an Italian, was every inch a Fleet Street Bohemian, and his convivial suggestion may be assumed to have been ' What about a bottle of the boy? ' Meredith, always obliged to be mindful of family expenses, would rightly have preferred a cheap and delectable wine of the country, and it is not unlikely that he indicated that, in Venice, champagne was only drunk by vulgarians. Anyhow, two more incongruous Georges could not easily have been discovered,—an assertion which is supported in the *Dictionary of National Biography* by the following sentence:—

> The facility with which Sala drew upon his varied stores of half-digested knowledge, the self-confidence with which he approached every manner of topic, the egotism and the bombastic circumlocutions which rapid production encouraged in him, hit the taste of a large section of the public.

Obviously an antithesis to the poet who wrote:—

> Our life is but a little holding, lent
> To do a mighty labour: we are one
> With heaven and the stars when it is spent
> To serve God's aim: else die we with the sun.

5

Vittoria was published at the end of the year, but Meredith had returned from Italy in time to enlarge and improve the serialised version by the knowledge and observation he had acquired in Italy. It had no success, either with the critics or the public, and two months after its appearance he wrote to Swinburne that it had passed to the limbo where his other works reposed.

> I see the illustrious Hutton of *The Spectator* laughs insanely at my futile efforts to produce an impression on his public. I suppose I shall have to give it up and take to journalism, as I am now partly doing.

For the adventures of Emilia in Italy he had taken the period of the unsuccessful revolt under Mazzini in 1848–9. Begun as a sequel, it is altogether different from *Sandra Belloni*. His object was to enter action with his people, and to represent the revolt, with the passions animating both sides. Written when the cause of Italian freedom was generally regarded as momentous, the book was an affirmation of the enthusiasm for progress and humanity which he shared with Swinburne, who was at that time producing *A Song of Italy*, wherein he hailed the rose of resurrection in nearly a thousand lines of rapturous rhetoric.

> Italia! by the passion of the pain
> That bent and rent thy chain;
> Italia! by the breaking of the bands,
>   The shaking of the lands;
> Beloved, O men's mother, O men's queen,
> Arise, appear, be seen!

One evening, when Mazzini came to his lodgings, Swinburne read the whole of this poem aloud to him, an exhausting experience for both of them, but particularly for Mazzini, since *A Song of Italy* is vociferous, and sometimes scarcely intelligible. It is always rather unsafe for poets to address a nation in fraternal or filial terms, or to call down retribution on Monarchies and Republics.

87

The fine fervour of those days has departed, and the honoured memory of Mazzini no longer stimulates us to idealism. The late unlamented Mussolini has unavoidably altered our outlook on the Italy which Swinburne celebrated as

> . . . hallowing with stretched hands
> The limitless free lands,
> Where all men's heads for love, not fear, bow down
> To thy sole royal crown,
> As thou to freedom.

The attitude of Meredith was controlled, aiming at impartiality, though his heart was given to Italia and her unification against Austrian oppression. In *Vittoria* he set out to write a historical romance, with Emilia and her magnificent voice as a central figure, precipitating the insurrection. A primer to the novels recommends that ' the story should be read alongside of a plain historical summary of the period '; but I doubt whether this will make things any easier for most of us. The fact is that *Vittoria* is extremely difficult to get through. In the opening chapter we are given one of his grandest Alpine descriptions, and the book contains many passages of comparable power and beauty. But he so overcrowded his panoramic canvas with a confusion of incidents and characters that Emilia, who should dominate the whole, is often submerged and eliminated. The narrative is tortuous, and has no large lines of construction.

It is evident that I am not alone in finding *Vittoria* a perplexing subject, for I notice that the critical appreciators of Meredith's novels say very little about it. He himself described it as ' a field of action, of battles and conspiracies, nerve and muscle, where life fights for plain issues . . . in the day when Italy reddens the sky with the banners of a land revived '.

The defects of technique are due to the fact that he had several stories to tell, and that the exigencies of the historical background forced him to tell them all together, with the result that the masses of detail overlap and cumbrousness ensues. There are supreme moments and episodes, such as the Mazzini scenes and the opera chapters. But as a whole the writing shows too much conscious artistry and effort to be suitable for a narrative which aimed at sustained impetus and excitement. Meredith was incapable of writing slackly, but a little less effort would have made *Vittoria* easier to read. Moreover, in his determination to keep the story vivid and forcible, he rarely allowed it to be reposeful. This overstrained abruptness of style is one of the main defects of the book. It makes too continuous a demand on our attention. The voice is too high-pitched and voluble.

CHAPTER EIGHT

1

A GAP in Meredith's published *Letters* reduces me to biographical beggardom in the chronicling of his minor activities. From March, 1867, to December, 1869, there are only seven letters, three of them written in five days at the end of January, 1868. At that time he was acting as editor of *The Fortnightly* during John Morley's absence in America, and we find Swinburne indignantly complaining of being inadequately paid for a poem. Meredith had reminded him that he himself had received only £5 for his *Phaéthón*. (One cannot help feeling that he put a considerable strain on *The Fortnightly*'s subscribers when inviting them to surmount 150 lines of galliambics. He himself admitted that ' a perfect conquest of the measure is not possible in our tongue '; and *Phaéthón*, fine though it is, can only be scanned by experts in prosody.)

It is not known how much Swinburne received for his 160 lines, *The Halt Before Rome*. The finances of *The Fortnightly* were at a low ebb; and the acting editor might well have replied by quoting a stanza of *The Halt*, in which Liberty exhorted her Italian supporters to

> Serve not for any man's wages,
> Pleasure nor glory nor gold;
> I give but the love of all ages;
> Silver and gold have I none.

As it was, he pointed out that Morley might have to pay the extra amount out of his own pocket, and concluded his letter with ' My wife and Willie hope to greet you in the warm Spring days.' But I can find no evidence that they ever met again, though there is an unauthenticated story of a meeting at the Garrick Club, in 1871, which only made things worse between them.

He was now settled at Flint Cottage, which was to be his

home for the rest of his life. On January 31st he wrote his first letter from there, to Hardman, expressing exuberant relief at escaping from Kingston Lodge, which had been much invaded by the bricks and mortar of speculative builders.

I am every morning on the top of Box Hill—as its flower, its bird, its prophet. I drop down the moon on one side, I draw up the sun on t'other. I breathe fine air. I shout ha ha to the gates of the world. Then I descend and know myself a donkey for doing it.

In his *Recollections*, Morley has delineated the matutinal Meredith as he was at Copsham in the early '60s.

He came to the morning meal after a long hour's stride in the tonic air and fresh loveliness of cool woods and green slopes, with the brightness of sunrise on his brow, responsive penetration in his glance, the turn of radiant irony in his lips and peaked beard, his fine poetic head bright with crisp brown hair, Phoebus Apollo descending upon us from Olympus. His voice was strong, full, resonant, harmonious, his laugh quick and loud. . . . Loud and constant was his exhortation. Live with the world. Play your part. Fill the day. Ponder well and loiter not. Let laughter brace you. Exist in everyday communion with Nature. Nature bids you take all, only be sure you learn how to do without. . . . He lived at every hour of the day and night with all the sounds and shades of nature open to his sensitive perception. To love this deep companionship of the large refreshing natural world brought unspeakable fulness of being to him, as it was one of his most priceless lessons to men of disposition more prosaic than his own.

Thus Lord Morley of Blackburn, in his eightieth year, gave forth what one might call the authorised version of Meredith as he knew him. One might also call it a Royal Academy portrait. Dignified, authentic, and valuable, these prose cadences are recognisably akin to an obituary notice in *The Times*. Some brief notes that Morley made while Meredith was still alive are more incisive—less framed and varnished—as will be seen when I have occasion to quote them.

Meanwhile, a refreshing contrast is available in Lady Butcher's artless account of her first meeting with him. It was in June, 1868. She was thirteen, and staying with her relations, the Gordons, near Box Hill. Her cousin, an Eton boy of sixteen, suggested that they should walk up Box Hill to see the sun rise. She gladly agreed, hardly sleeping all night for excitement.

We started long before it was light and as we went along the Leatherhead road, Jim Gordon said, ' I know a man who lives on Box Hill. He's quite mad, but very amusing; he likes walks and sunrises. Let's go and shout him up! ' So we trudged up the little drive to Flint Cottage, and began to throw stones at the window of his bedroom. It was quickly thrown up, and a loud, cheerful voice asked what we meant by trying to break his window. We explained that we wanted him to climb up Box Hill with us and see the sun rise. In a miraculously short time he joined us, his nightshirt thrust into brown trousers, and his bare feet into leather slippers, no hat on his head, twisting his stick, and summoning his brown retriever dog. He started to walk very fast up the steep grass incline, easy for him to climb in those vigorous days, and for my country-bred cousin, but pantingly difficult to my town-bred lungs and muscles. ' Come on, London-pated girl,' he shouted, and up I struggled, to sink exhausted on the top, and then we sat and watched the sun rise and glorify the valley and the hills. If we had overstrained the powers of the body climbing so fast up the hill, he certainly strained the powers of our minds as he poured forth the most wonderful prose hymn to Nature, Life, and what he called *obligation*, by which I understood he meant Duty. I was weary in mind and body when I returned home, but I knew that I had watched the sun rise beside a Poet and a Thinker, his enthusiasm, his personality, one with Nature, the summer, and the morning. And thus began a friendship that never diminished during the forty-one years that it lasted.

This was Alice Brandreth, who grew up to become the successor of Janet Ross in youthful evocation of Meredith's affection. In 1878 she married Jim Gordon. By then she had been made the model for Cecilia Halkett in *Beauchamp's Career*. There she is described as ' the handsomest girl, English style, of her time. . . . One can't call her a girl, and it won't do to say Goddess, and queen and charmer are out of the question, though she's both, and angel into the bargain.' Elsewhere, she ' seemed to offer everything the world could offer of cultivated purity, intelligent beauty and attractiveness , , , an ideal English lady, and a trustworthy woman for mate ',

She was, in fact, one of Meredith's well-bred, open-air heroines
—' a radiant landscape, where the tall ripe wheat flashes
between shadow and shine in the stately march of Summer '.—
She loved riding and yachting, and was musical and literary in
an unassuming way, a delightful girl who matured to a woman
of true metal, sensible, warm-hearted, and well endowed with
fortitude. Her friendship with Meredith is one of the
pleasantest things in his middle and later life. But most I
like to think of that midsummer dawn when he came down in
his slippers and hurried her up the hill; for then he was still
in the opulence of bodily powers, rejoicing in new surroundings,
and as yet unimpaired by endless output of brain-work and
nervous energy. And, as always, he was his most ardent and
natural self when with young people, eager to learn from them,
and, in return, to give them the best that was in his mind.
One boy, afterwards a distinguished general, went for a walk
with him in the early '80s, and was taught the different sorts
of heather on the Surrey hills. Writing home, the boy
described him as ' a ripper '.

2

The new life which began for Meredith with his second
marriage had been happy in all ways, but for a single disappointment. And that was a deeply disturbing one. Soon
after the marriage he had written to Jessopp that his little man
would now have a mother. Three months later he ends a
letter to the same friend, ' Marie has, I believe, written fully
anent the Son. We mourn and howl over him.' Well might
they mourn, for Arthur had returned from school to take his
diminished status very badly. His step-mother, one can be
certain, behaved admirably toward him, in her common-
sense way; she was kind, patient, and unfailingly dutiful,
though, perhaps, lacking the tact and understanding which
the case required of her. But his character, as Meredith had
told Jessopp when entrusting him to his care, was based on
sensitiveness. Possibly he had inherited his mother's nerves.
Handsome, clever, and reserved, he had been over-indulged
by the solicitude of his adoring father. One can imagine what
the poor boy felt like. Everyone being so nice to him; and

yet—all his previous supremacy subtly superseded, all the intimacies and confidences of the Copsham days gone for ever, leaving him with a sense of being only half wanted, only half admitted to his father's heart.

It was an agonising situation, in which no one could help him; and how could he sustain himself by being philosophic, at eleven years old? He was proud and rather unresponsive by nature, and one doubts whether his affection for his father had been strong. It can be conjectured that he now withdrew into an obdurate hostility to his step-mother, blamed his father for letting him down, and felt that to be treated like that was more than he could bear. He had no other relatives except his devoted half-sister, Edith Nicolls, and a Peacock great-aunt, of whom nothing is known except that she left him some money after he was grown up.

At the age of fourteen he was sent to a school near Berne, conducted on the system of Pestalozzi, which had for its basis graduated object teaching—whatever that may be! There, apparently, he remained for two years. In August, 1869, Meredith went with Lionel Robinson to see him, and they spent some weeks in the Alps. He found Arthur a good swimmer, with plenty of fun in him, with good wind, and with an eye clear and honest; he was popular in the school. But away from the school, he found that the boy had ceased to be responsive. He had a reserve which his father was never again to pierce. He liked walks alone and did not often speak. If one wanted speech from him, the subject to choose must be philology. Then he moved a little in his chrysalis, but only a little. He was then taken to Stuttgart, where he completed his education, living with a Professor Zeller, and remaining there until July, 1873. I have no evidence that he had come home to Flint Cottage during the previous five years. There is an indication in one of Meredith's letters to him that he refused to do so. Mrs. Meredith was probably thankful, but arranged for him to stay with her elder sister in Savoy for two of his summer holidays. Up to April, 1872, there are seven longish letters to him from his father. They are lifeless letters, written with a strong sense of duty, which leave an impression of someone knocking on a door without expecting to be admitted. He offers serious advice about health, and about the Franco-

Prussian War (Arthur disliked the Germans, and Meredith—though sympathetic to the French as a nation—considered that their Emperor was 'the knave of the pack', and that the Germans 'reaped the reward of a persistently honourable career in civic virtue'.)

> I lay stress on physical condition for the reason that it is the index to the moral condition in young men. If not physically healthy, a lad will not be of much value. The day comes when we are put to the test, and it is for this day we should prepare with a cheerful heart. Don't imagine me to be lecturing you. I have favourable reports of you, and I merely repeat simple words of advice that it will be well for you to keep in mind. . . . I admire and respect the Germans, and God knows my heart bleeds for the French. But my aim, and I trust it will be yours, is never to take counsel of my sensations, but of my intelligence. I let the former have free play, but deny them the right to bring me to a decision. You are younger, and have a harder task in doing that; you have indeed a task in discerning the difference between what your senses suggest and what your mind. . . . Train your eyes to observe, and while they are at that work keep the action of your mind in abeyance. Young men can observe shrewdly, but the opinions of young men are not quite so important.

All this was sound enough; but if it wasn't lecturing, what was it? One pictures Arthur's irritation on receiving these paternal admonitions. Yet, since he preserved his father's letters, he must have set some value on them, didactic though they were. A couple of months later 'the fine moral qualities of the Germans' are again being dinned into him, and again it is

> Don't think I preach too much. I am naturally anxious about you. I have passed through the wood, and know which paths to take, which to avoid. . . . The Professor says you do not consort with Germans at all. I am grieved at this. . . . Look around you, and try to be accessible to your German associates. Consider whether you are not yielding to your immediate sympathies and luxurious predispositions in your marked preference for English ones.

It is noticeable that these letters very seldom reply to anything written by Arthur. All the letters contain expressions of affection and signs of solicitude for the well-being of his son. But between the lines one reads their failure to get on together, and in them one sees Meredith, with pathetic efforts to bridge the gulf, progressively alienating Arthur and making their incompatibility obvious.

In the last one, however, there is an answer to some adverse comment on Christianity.

> What you say of our religion is what thoughtful men feel: and that you at the same time can recognize its moral value, is a matter of rejoicing to me. The Christian teaching is sound and good: the ecclesiastical dogma is an instance of the poverty of humanity's mind hitherto, and has often in its hideous fangs and claws shown whence we draw our descent. . . . Belief in the religion does this good to the young; it floats them through the perilous sensual period when the animal appetites most need control and transmutation. If you have not the belief, set yourself to love virtue by understanding that it is your best guide both as to what is due to others and what is for your positive personal good. . . . We grow to good as surely as the plant grows to the light. Do not lose the habit of praying to the unseen Divinity. Prayer for worldly goods is worse than fruitless, but prayer for strength of soul is that passion of the soul which catches the gift it seeks.

It was an example of the maxim that to give good advice is absolutely fatal. Yet the advice was good, though not so finely worded as when he wrote, elsewhere, that ' in our prayers we dedicate the world to God, not calling him great for a title, no—showing him we know him great in a limitless world, lord of a truth we tend to, have not grasped '.

To all Meredith's suggestions for his future, Arthur proved intractable. When he was seventeen and a half, Jessopp proposed that he should try for a Scholarship in modern languages at Oxford, his father being scarcely able to afford the full expense of sending him there. Nothing came of it, though he was told, for his encouragement, that ' Mr. Swinburne gained the Scholarship through his consummate knowledge of French '. A year and a half later Maxse found a possible opening for him which sounds more like a bad practical joke. It was an examination in the Foreign Office for the post of Chinese interpreter.

If successful, you go out to China with a salary of £200 per annum and learn the Chinese tongue of li-ro and fo-ki. I declined it: I hope I was right. I felt sure that it would be repugnant to you to spend your life in China, where the climate is hard, society horrid, life (to my thought) scarcely endurable.

For once, Arthur must have found himself in fullest agreement with his parent!

Several months after I had written this chapter I discovered the existence of six long letters from Arthur to his father. The first is dated January, 1870; the last, July, 1873. There is nothing in them to indicate misunderstandings or resentments. He provides meticulous details of his expenditure, describes his holidays, and discusses his studies, his health, and such ideas as he has formed of his future career. They are dutiful, self-centred, and dull. One imagines Meredith reading them with a sigh. Three of them were written in the summer of 1873, and by then the young man was giving evidence of being extremely long-winded and pedantic. In the last and longest, he explains how his historical studies have brought him to a system of philosophical ideas, and treats his father to a tedious essay, quite in the heavy Teutonic style, which must have caused the sigh to become a groan of boredom. To me these turgid and didactic pages are incontestable proof of that incompatibility of mind which they afterwards found impossible to overcome. The penultimate letter is mainly concerned with Arthur's arrangements for returning to England. From this it can be inferred that he was at Flint Cottage that autumn. After that he seems to have gone to Havre where a post had been obtained for him with a commercial firm.

In the autumn of 1871, Jessopp was sent the following account of his former pupil. Meredith had returned from a six weeks holiday on the Continent, and had spent eight days with Arthur.

He is a short man, slightly moustached, having a tuft of whisker; a good walker, a middling clear thinker, sensible, brilliant in nothing, tending in no direction, very near to what I predicted of him as a combatant in life, but with certain reserve qualities of mental vigour which may develop; and though he seems never likely to be intellectually an athlete, one may hope he will be manful. In a competitive examination of fifty he would be about the twenty-fifth; but in an aside conversation the penetrative professor would haply discover stores in his mind. He is always grateful to you.

Up to a point, this can be considered satisfactory as a dispassionate specification of Arthur's appearance and aptitudes. Nevertheless, remembering ' God bless my dear little man, prays his loving Papa ', and ' How could I have stopped away from my living heart so long? '—the only footnote one can add is a line of William Morris—

> O Death in life, O sure pursuer, Change.

The failure of their relationship has been brought forward in criticism of Meredith's character, with his father and his first wife as further proofs of his inhumanity in family life. There seems no doubt that he was not an easy man to live with. But against this we have the manifestation of his actions, the testimony of his friends, and the self-revelation of his writings. Meredith was a good man. Possessed by the turbulence of his genius, he strove to subdue himself to a philosophy of noble endeavour and service of that Comic Spirit which he called the Sword of Common Sense, through which he sought to know ' the music of the meaning of Accord ', and to ' speak from the deep springs of life '. Arthur was a bad mixer, pedantic-minded, a being of small stature, to whom his father's emotional and intellectual gestures were incomprehensible and unlikeable. And so, for eight years after 1873, all communication between them appears to have ceased.

3

In 1868, at the age of forty, he entered on the meridian of those productive powers which culminated, seventeen years later, in the publication of *Diana of the Crossways*. The early years of this period were, one assumes, as full of contentment as any he experienced. Happy in his married life, he had found a home which suited him. . . . Thus might a bland biographer continue to the close of his chapter. But some inward prompting warns me that this sort of thing won't do at all. In imagination I am confronted by the protesting presence of Meredith as he was in his prime. He reminds me that although I have been thinking about him for many months with concentrated industry while exploring a mass of printed material concerning his career, I am still far from justified in generalising about what he was like and how full of contentment were his first few years at Flint Cottage. He asks me to consider the remoteness and unreality of the mid-Victorian Age, and the impossibility of unshrouding an author who, unlike Dickens, preferred his personality to be private. (Not, he adds, that his compatriots had hitherto shown any inclination to illumine his obscurity with the gas-light glare of popularity.) He goes on to say, in most kindly and forbearing tones, that a man cannot be re-created from a few printed letters which happened to be preserved, and were never intended to be used for the purpose of propping him up like a ventriloquist's dummy.

What I was in my early forties [he concludes] can never be known to you or anyone else. You can see *through* me, but you will never see *into* me. The best of me is in my books, such as they are. Make what you can of them, particularly the poems, but beware of suppositions about my everyday life. The evidence is inadequate. Meanwhile I extend cordial condolences to you in your contest with the posthumous opacity which I have phantasmally interrupted.

Bowing with a sort of elaborate courtesy, he vanishes. His career, however, remains. My bookshelves are crowded with it, and portfolios of press-cuttings are piled intimidatingly on a table. Squaring my elbows, I return to my task. The interview has been a wholesome incentive to mental alertness.

Resuming my conscientious scrutiny of the letters, I find him writing, in October, 1868, to Jessopp, from Holly Hill, Southampton.

I am staying with my friend Capt. Maxse to see him through his election, a dismal business, but I take to it as to whatever comes. . . . At present I am tied to the pecuniary pen and am not a bright galley-slave. I write almost every week in *The Pall Mall Gazette*.

And to Arthur, early in the following year :—

My time is occupied with work, and I am, or rather have been, much distracted by affairs. My two months down with Captain

Maxse was a dead loss of time to me. I never regret anything I am able to help him in, as you will believe, but that's another matter. We were badly beaten at Southampton, but I think it will be proved that bribery was done there. . . . I fancy Captain Maxse had to pay about £2000 for the attempt. He acted simply in a spirit of duty, that he might enter Parliament to plead the cause of the poor.

The electioneering experience was to provide material for *Beauchamp's Career*, so nothing need be said about it at this point. His work for *The Pall Mall Gazette* was the beginning of a valuable friendship with Frederick Greenwood, who edited this evening newspaper until 1880. The paper had been started in 1865 by George Smith, the head of Smith, Elder & Co., a man who is notable as the inaugurator of the *Dictionary of National Biography* and one of the most admirable personalities in 19th-Century publishing. Greenwood, one of the ablest editors and journalists of his time, is remembered in connexion with the purchase of the Suez Canal shares by the British Government in 1875. Having obtained early information that the Khedive Ismail was intending to sell them, he at once communicated with the Foreign Secretary and Lord Beaconsfield, who acted on his advice. Thirty-five years later the market value of the shares had increased by 20 million pounds, but Greenwood never made a penny out of the transaction, and died a poor man in 1909, when his daughters were granted a civil list pension of £100 a year. Meredith was also writing occasional articles for *The Morning Post*. As I have previously stated, in 1868 he gave up the *Ipswich Journal* drudgery.

One of his associates who might have been mentioned before this was Frederick Sandys, who in 1865 had drawn a very queer frontispiece for the second edition of *Shagpat*. He was one of the group of notable artists assembled by Samuel Lucas in the first years of *Once a Week*, a group which included all the best men of that unique period in the history of black and white illustration, with the exception of Rossetti, who held aloof from the enterprise. This led to his knowing Meredith, and in 1862 he did a Dürer-like drawing for *The Old Chartist*. Two years later he stayed for a month at Copsham while painting the background of his picture *Gentle Spring*. Soon afterwards he made a superb crayon portrait of Mrs. Meredith, which commemorates her good looks and gentleness while suggesting her mental limitations. Sandys was a convivial character; his thriftless bohemianism was the undoing of his career. But he was good company, and Meredith delighted in him, and managed to remain on friendly terms with him to the end. There is a letter, beginning 'My dear old boy', dated May, 1863, in which Meredith waxes frolicsome about the Garrick Club Sweepstakes on the Derby, for which he had drawn the darkest of dark horses, while Sandys had backed Pretender at 2 to 1. At that moment, Sandys's *Medea* was the picture of the year in the Academy; but a Jewish bailiff was occupying his lodgings in Leicester Square. Six years later he drew the winner, Galopin, with a ticket Meredith gave him. 'It is evident,' he wrote, 'that you now have an Income for life in the Garrick Sweepstakes. I expect a dinner. But let me order it. There's a dry still Champagne I know of.' Rossetti had called Sandys 'the greatest living draughtsman', and Millais said he was 'worth two Academicians rolled into one'. But although he lived until 1904, his powers had long since declined. In appearance he was tall and distinguished, and not unlike Don Quixote. Whatever his circumstances, he always wore a spotless white waistcoat with gold buttons and patent leather boots. His personal charm and lively talk reconciled his friends to his embarrassing habit of borrowing. One who knew them both has described to me a memorable occasion in the '90s when Sandys, at Flint Cottage, tried to persuade Meredith to sit to him for a portrait. Meredith apostrophised him thus: 'When you were young, my dear Sandys, the winged words of wisdom I poured into your ears would have penetrated the skull of a bullock, but you would not listen. Ah, Sandys, Sandys, if you had but listened, what a different Sandys it would have been!' One hears that voice, slow, resonant, and regretful.

4

For several years after the *Modern Love* volume of 1862 Meredith's output of poetry almost ceased. It was a luxury he could not afford to indulge in. The impulse returned to him at the time of his marriage, but *Rhoda Fleming* and *Vittoria* had to be finished and money collected by journalism. In 1867, as we have seen, the massive verse exercise *Phaéthôn* appeared in *The Fortnightly*, preceded by the *Lines to a Friend Visiting America*, an animated epistle addressed to Morley. Early in 1868, *Macmillan's Magazine* printed *The Orchard and the Heath*, from which twenty of the thirty-one stanzas were omitted when the poem was reprinted in 1883. This belongs to the category of what he had called his ' Roadside ' poems, though it indicates an advance toward his matured style of expression. (In most of these ' Roadside' poems the influence of Browning is perceptible.) It was followed by *Aneurin's Harp*, a ballad wherein he ridicules ' the Norman nose ' as the type of England's aristocracy. The main interest of the poem is that he speaks as a Welshman, his claim to an unauthenticated Celtic extraction being always a source of pride to him.

The shock of the Franco-Prussian War stimulated him to produce a long Ode, which appeared in *The Fortnightly* of January, 1871. Written at the crisis of the catastrophe, it was the biggest sustained effort in verse that he had yet attempted, and the theme was monumental. *France—December 1870* ranks among his greatest achievements. It is an impassioned lament for the downfall that she had brought upon herself, ending with an avowal of faith in her resurrection as the Mother of Reason, ' making of calamity her aureole ', and is doubly significant in its appropriateness to the tragedy of 1940.

> We look for her that sunlike stood
> Upon the forehead of our day,
> An orb of nations, radiating food
> For body and for mind alway.
> Where is the Shape of glad array;
> The nervous hands, the front of steel,
> The clarion tongue? Where is the bold proud face?
> We see a vacant place;
> We hear an iron heel.

Thus it begins; and the declamatory passages follow in wave upon wave of surging eloquence and striving thought. It is a formidable poem; but when studied carefully there are few obscurities, and the abundance of metaphor is typically Meredithian. It was an act of fiery faith, emotion, and imagination.

His attitude to the War was stated in one of his letters.

I am neither German nor French. I am European and Cosmopolitan—for humanity! The nation which shows most worth, is the nation I love and reverence. The French have conducted themselves like mere children throughout. The Germans have behaved as the very sternest of men, caring more for their Fatherland than for the well-being of men in the mass. I am susceptible of admiration of their sterling qualities, holding nevertheless that they will repent of the present selfish restriction of their views.

He could not forget that militaristic France had always been the perturbation of Europe. ' The Germans may be. That is to be seen. They at least are what they pretend to be.'

France was enduring retribution for Napoleon, ' whose eagles, angrier than their oriflamme, flush the vext earth with blood '. But, while green earth forgets,

> the Gods alone
> Remember everlastingly : they strike
> Remorselessly, and ever like for like.
> By their great memories the Gods are known.

Thus he unconsciously foretold the doom of Germany in 1945.

In this great Ode he emerged as an impressive figure among the poets of the period. To the discredit of that period it awarded him no increased recognition of his powers. The Ode remained hidden in the files of *The Fortnightly* until 1887, when it was reprinted in *Ballads and Poems of Tragic Life*, where it again fell on unheeding ears.

To please the public taste he should have been more mellifluous—there should have been more Tennyson and less Carlyle in the compressed and craggy utterances of his didactic philosophy. Carlyle, he wrote, had ' called for power in his mountain prose ', and he loved him for it. Of Tennyson's ' Holy Grail ' he had complained to Maxse that

. . . the lines are satin lengths, the figures Sèvres china. . . . The foremost poet of the country goes on fluting of creatures that have not a breath of vital humanity in them, and doles us out his regular five-feet with the old trick of the vowel endings. The Euphuist's tongue, the Exquisite's leg, the Curate's moral sentiments, the British matron and her daughter's purity of tone : so he talks, so he walks, so he snuffles, so he appears divine.

Why, this stuff is not the Muse, it's Musery. The man has got hold of the Muse's clothes-line and hung it with jewelry. But the ' Lucretius ' is grand. I can't say how much I admire it and hate the Sir Pandarus public which has corrupted this fine (natural) singer. In his degraded state I really believe he is useful, for he reflects as much as our Society chooses to show of itself. The English notion of passion, virtue, valour, is in his pages: and the air and the dress we assume are seen there. . . . Isn't there a scent of damned hypocrisy in all this lisping and vowelled purity of the Idylls? . . . Tennyson has many spiritual indications, but no philosophy, and philosophy is the palace of thought.

In a similar strain he wrote to Morley of the mild fluency and dandiacal fluting, the praises of which shut him away from his fellows. His impatience is understandable; it was one with his crusade against the sentimentalist who is

> . . . housed in the drop of dew
> That hangs on the cheek of the rose,
> And lives the life of a twinkle.

But for him the lesson of the Gods was

> The lesson writ in red since first Time ran,
> A hunter hunting down the beast in man :
> That till the chasing out of its last vice,
> The flesh was fashioned but for sacrifice.

Nevertheless, I must admit that for me ' The Holy Grail ' is full of lovely lines, and the exquisite artistry of Tennyson an abiding delight. I am one with the Victorians in surrendering to the charm of

> —they sat
> Beneath a world-old yew-tree, darkening half
> The cloisters, on a gustful April morn
> That puffed the swaying branches into smoke—

and I confess to sharing the curate's thrill when

> . . . Stream'd through my cell a cold and silver beam,
> And down the long beam stole the Holy Grail,
> Rose-red with beatings in it, as if alive—

Moreover, it cannot be denied that Meredith's *Ode* is an oration which only just avoids tub-thumping in its magniloquent urgency. The event demanded that he should be at the top of his form. He was. But he also spoke at the top of his voice, and a sensitive hearer is liable to find the effect somewhat overwhelming.

It is, in fact, a relief to go back to *The Fortnightly* of six months earlier, to which he contributed a sequence of nine short lyrics entitled *In the Woods*. They are unequal in quality, but in two of them, *Dirge in Woods* and *Woodland Peace*, we find the quintessence of Meredith as a nature poet. The almost strident tones of the invocation to France are subdued to the meditative soliloquy of the poet footing on pine-wood paths where the voice of the woodland is slow, grave, and still, like Time, Life, and Death. Therein, the lover of life, whose vivid and turbulent spirit had waved it ' like a brand, for an ensign of pride ', is at peace. In deep woods, between the two twilights of the towering trees, he is acquiescent and absolved. He accepts the lesson of the trees which ' question not, nor ask the hidden to unmask, the distant to draw near '.

> Sweet as Eden is the air,
> And Eden-sweet the ray.
> No Paradise is lost for them
> That foot by branching root and stem,
> And lightly with the woodland share
> The change of night and day.

In these two poems there is a profound simplicity which defies analysis. Against the background of Meredith's harlequinade of intellectual activity, they seem a final manifestation of the strength of reticence and serenity. Both will hold their place in English poetry when *The Egoist* (as, with all its merits, it may) has joined Lyly's *Euphues* as a museum piece of literary ingenuity. For, as he tells us,

> —we drop like the fruits of the tree,
> Even we,
> Even so.

CHAPTER NINE

DURING his first two years at Flint Cottage he finished *The Adventures of Harry Richmond*, which had been begun and laid aside in 1864, when he mentioned it to Jessopp as ' a spanking bid for popularity '. His next reference to it is in January, 1870, to Morley.

' As to ' Harry Richmond ', I fear I am evolving his personality too closely for the public, but a man must work by the light of his conscience if he's to do anything worth reading.'

The bid for popularity prospered. It was accepted by *The Cornhill*, and appeared from September, 1870, to November, 1871, with illustrations by du Maurier. This was the best thing he could have hoped for. At that time, to be serialised in *The Cornhill* meant success for a novelist. He was paid £500. (George Eliot had received £7000 for *Romola*, which few of us now find easy to peruse.) It is probable that Leslie Stephen helped to obtain him this plum of his profession, for he had much influence with the proprietor, George Smith, though not appointed editor until six months later.

The book was published by Smith, Elder & Co. in October, 1871, and achieved a second edition before the end of the year. This unprecedented event in Meredith's career was undoubtedly due to *The Cornhill*, for the reviewers gave him very little assistance. *The Athenaeum* recommended it as ' quite worth reading, as a good romance '. *The Spectator* waited three months, and then devoted three columns of its small print to damning the book with faint praise.

It would be truer to say that it has the stuff for half-a-dozen first-rate novels in it, than that it is a first-rate novel itself. . . . A grand plot is developed which, though full of cleverness, becomes utterly wearisome before the close. . . . There are plenty of illustrations of affectation in the style, and still more of an apparently affected obscurity of manner, which tend to spoil a novel containing the evidence of really great powers.

' The illustrious Hutton ' was at it again. (He had described
Vittoria as ' worth reading once, but written in such a falsetto
key, that, apart from the crowd of uninteresting and dim
figures on the canvas, no one would wish to read it again '.)

Hutton, it seems, was a prime example of those minds in
which Meredith creates antipathy while they are compelled
to admit his great gifts. And when people dislike Meredith
it is useless to argue with them. All his obvious faults rise up
and become the allies of their animosity. Hutton was one of
those fair-minded and able literary men who can be relied on
to write admirably about anyone who has been canonised as a
classic. Such men should avoid taking risks with contemporary
talents. Professional verdicts sometimes look silly afterwards.
And—as Goethe remarked—

> Grey, friend, is Theory—true though Theory be,—
> And green the foliage of Life's golden tree.

Hutton complained that, while reading *Harry Richmond*, he
had met with manifold retardations, caused by its want of
narrative-flow and simplicity of style, and the lack of clear
relation between the different parts of the tale. He found the
hero radically uninteresting, and the two heroines with whom
he fell in love deficient in fascination. Let us now listen to
what—sixty years later—Leslie Stephen's daughter, Virginia
Woolf, had to say about the book.

> The story bowls smoothly along the road which Dickens has
> already trodden of autobiographical narrative. It is a boy
> speaking, a boy thinking, a boy adventuring. For that reason,
> no doubt, the author has curbed his redundance and pruned his
> speech. The style is the most rapid possible. It runs smooth,
> without a kink in it. Stevenson, one feels, must have learnt much
> from this supple narrative, with its precise adroit phrases, its
> exact quick glance at visible things.

Mrs. Woolf, whose critical perceptions were as superfine as
her literary art, was not altogether satisfied with the earlier
chapters; but when the plot develops—

> . . . we sink [she says] into the world of fantasy and romance,
> where all holds together and we are able to put our imagination
> at the writer's service without reserve. That such surrender is
> above all things delightful: that it adds spring-heels to our boots:

that it fires the cold scepticism out of us and makes the world glow in lucid transparency before our eyes, needs no showing, as it certainly submits to no analysis. That Meredith can induce such moments proves him possessed of an extraordinary power.

Bowing gratefully to the gifted lady, I pursue my brain-conserving method of allowing other people to say for me what I cannot say so well myself. This time it is a Frenchman, M. Photiadès, whose admirable book on Meredith appeared in 1912. This is how he begins his summary of the story.

Although this book does not surpass the others in depth of thought, it is the one which many eminent men prefer, because nowhere has Meredith's fancy found such freedom. Uncurbed by philosophical reservations, he has been able to allow his imagination free scope; and happy in feeling free, it has displayed for the first time the extent of its power. . . . Harry Richmond pretends to be nothing more than a fine story. This is evident at the beginning. Contrary to the other novels, it does not begin with a tortuous preface, but with a prologue which has the boldness and the precision of a tale, the brightness of a fairy-story, and the pathos of a little one-act drama. This prologue gives the novel an unforgettable frontispiece. It testifies to the superior essence of an imagination which is ever displaying greater strength in later chapters. And forthwith the writer leads us into strange paths, and fairy lands, where a commonplace novelist would never venture.

Inwardly exclaiming ' Vive Photiadès ! ' I leave the reader to decide whether Richard Holt Hutton and his ' famous review ' have been put in their proper place. M. Photiadès uses *Harry Richmond* to demonstrate the genius of Meredith, devoting two-fifths of his book to it. His motive was to be persuasive. He did not wish to discourage his French audience, so he recommended what they would find easiest to enjoy. It must, however, be admitted that *Harry Richmond* is not a characteristic specimen of Meredith's novels, partly because it is the only one written in the first person, and narrated by a young man who, like most heroes in fiction, is not particularly interesting or original. First planned as a picaresque story of the 18th-Century type, it ultimately grew into a romance intermixed with comedy.

These opposing elements, we are told by certain critics,

have not been successfully united. This may be so; but, like M. Photiadès, I am making it my business to encourage new readers to explore my admired author, and the test I apply to this book—and to any novel of repute—is to ask what remains in my mind after I have read it. I consider this to be an effective test. For, among all the books we read, how few there are which leave any strong impression on us. And how little we retain, even of a masterpiece, can be discovered by anyone who re-reads it after a period of years. We learn so little and forget so much; and what we remember is often some trivial detail of human behaviour, memorable through its simplicity, such as Mr. Harding, in *The Warden*, playing on an imaginary 'cello when mentally perplexed. Meredith, with his vitality of imagination, could light up his big scenes with a sudden splendour. The power is intermittent; whole chapters are laboured and without momentum; but illumination arrives, and we remember. There are many such revelations in *Harry Richmond*, as M. Photiadès ably indicated. But the unforgettable figure is Harry's father, Richmond Roy, without whom the story would be like Hamlet with the Prince left out. He is the hero of the book and the backbone of its organism.

In one constructive element it resembles *The Ordeal of Richard Feverel*. It is a study in the relations of father and son, with the essential difference that the father wins the confidence of his son, and fails to destroy his happiness in spite of his errors. Both fathers went wrong through misguided affection—Sir Austin Feverel by his ' system ', Roy by his pride in ancestral dignity, for which he conceives it his duty to train Harry as though he were a prince of royal blood. And Harry, throughout, is fascinated, influenced, and overshadowed by the flamboyant adventurer, though altogether unlike him in temperament.

When first thinking of Richmond Roy, Meredith must have had ' the Great Mel ' at the back of his mind—' a robust Brummel, and the Regent of low life ' certainly suggests it. But Roy, though a florid charlatan, possessed many qualities of a grand gentleman; he was a mixture of nobleness and vulgarity, of superb social genius and scheming effrontery. He has been aptly described as ' moving in an atmosphere where wit and farce are fired by poetic imagination '. Apart from this, the idea of him must have been based on the Royal Dukes of the Regency period, whom he resembles in the description of his physical appearance.

When considering Richmond Roy, I have wondered about the hypothetic psychological chemistry which enabled Meredith to invent this figure of magnificent proportions who took such complete charge of the story. Hypothetic psychological chemistry. . . . My pen ceases to crawl across the paper, as though protesting against the sledge-hammer jargon which I have caused it to perpetrate! Nevertheless I can think of no other words to introduce my notion that, while creating the career and character of Richmond Roy, Meredith was indirectly indulging his repressed conception of himself as ' a nobleman in disguise '. Laughing himself out of it also—with his unfailing good sense—' When Harry Richmond's father first met me, when I heard him tell me in his pompous style about the son of a duke of blood royal and an actress of seventeen years of age, I simply roared with laughter ! ' This was said by him to Marcel Schwob in 1894. It confirms the reports of his characters being so real to him that he talked aloud to them when alone in his study.

The enigma of his ancestry must have been with him all his life. Often he must have wondered where he came from and whence he derived his thoroughbred points and the almost angelic refinement of the upper part of his face. Not for nothing had Peacock's friend T. J. Hogg, the biographer of Shelley, named him ' son of the morning '. Racial heredity and atavism were subjects of recurrent speculation for him. Anyhow, I am prepared to maintain that from the start he decided to be an aristocrat in literature, since the world denied him the hall-mark of patrician birth. And in *Evan Harrington* and *Harry Richmond* I see him playing with an idea which could set his mind alight because it belonged to his psychologic inwardness rather than his intellect. Absurd though it sounds, I am inclined to believe that in the nonsense world of dreams Meredith sometimes became a Marquis. For in dreams we remain adolescent, and our fantasies are foolish. Not that he attached any importance to titles. It was the idea of fine breeding which appealed to him. For him, lineage meant a tradition of civilised manners and intelligence.

Harry Richmond is the longest of Meredith's novels, and the amount of good work he put into it was prodigious. Considered merely as an output of highly finished writing, it commands the respect of all who have ever tried to produce a page of decent prose. Personally, I marvel at the vitality and determination of the man who did it, under conditions by no means easy. There are one hundred and sixty-nine characters in the book, and all are carefully drawn. And again I marvel—at his depth and richness of resource. Next to Richmond Roy, the dominant figure is Squire Beltham, Harry's grandfather—a likeable old autocrat, fated to spend his last years in an obdurate and exasperated struggle with his preposterously extravagant son-in-law, culminating in the tremendous scene where he finally defeats him. ' He was a curious study to me,' says Harry, ' of the Tory mind, in its attachment to solidity, fixity, certainty, its unmatched generosity within a limit, its devotion to the family, and its family eye for the country.'

And here is Richmond Roy as first seen in the book:—

A largely-built man, dressed in a high-collared great-coat and fashionable hat of the time, stood clearly defined to view. He carried a light cane, with the point of the silver handle against his under lip. There was nothing formidable in his appearance, and his manner was affectedly affable. He lifted his hat as soon as he found himself face to face with the squire, disclosing a partially bald head, though his whiskering was luxuriant, and a robust condition of manhood was indicated by his erect attitude and the immense swell of his furred great-coat at the chest. His features were exceedingly frank and cheerful. From his superior height he was enabled to look down quite royally on the man whose repose he had disturbed.

He had called, one February midnight, at Riversley Grange, to take away his five-year-old son, and was standing at the great hall-doors. Twenty years later, the Squire has the last word with the music-master who had married his daughter and squandered his son's fortune:—

For nine-and-twenty years you've sucked the veins of my family, and struck through my house like a rotting-disease. Nine-and-twenty years ago you gave a singing-lesson in my house: the pest has been in it ever since! You breed vermin in

the brain, to think of you! Your wife, your son, your dupes,
every soul that touches you, mildews from a blight! You were
born of ropery, and you go to it straight, like a webfoot to water.
What's your boast?—your mother's disgrace? You shame your
mother. Your whole life's a ballad of bastardy—You cry up the
woman's infamy to hook at a father. You swell and strut on her
pickings. You're a cock forced from the smoke of the dunghill!
You shame your mother, damned adventurer! You train your
boy for a swindler after your own pattern; you twirl him in
your curst harlequinade to a damnation as sure as your own.
The day you crossed my threshold the devils danced on their
flooring. I've never seen the sun shine fair on me after it.

As a result of this eloquent 18th-Century diatribe ' a dreadful
gape of stupefaction had usurped the smiles on my father's
countenance; his eyes rolled over, he tried to articulate, and
was indeed a spectacle for an enemy '. No wonder, poor man,
for all his schemes had been shattered, through the information
dealt him by the Squire, and his attempt to prove that he was
the legitimate son of a Royal Duke could no longer be
maintained.

There are three backgrounds to the narrative—Hampshire;
London; Germany. It is the Hampshire of *Evan Harrington*,
adjoining Sussex and south of Petersfield. Riversley Grange
can be identified as a few miles from Harting, where, while
the boy was carried away by his father, ' the breeze smelt fresh
of roots and heath in the half-dark stillness of quiet hill-lines
and larch and fir-tree tops, until they were beyond the park,
among the hollows that run dipping for miles beside the great
high-road for London '. In this heath country Harry has his
adventures among the gipsies, one of whom, the girl Kiomi, is a
superb achievement, ranking with Borrow's Isopel Berners.
The original of this character was the gipsy model whom Sandys
painted several times, notably in his ' Judith '. To the Hampshire background belongs Janet Ilchester, chosen by Squire
Beltham as a suitable wife for the heir to Riversley and his great
estates—' a bold, plump girl, fond of male society ' who
develops into the shrewd and self-reliant woman ' as firm as a
rock and as sweet as a flower on it ', who, when united to
Harry, brings his story to a happy and hopeful ending. In
London, after the delightful chapter describing their life in

lodgings, he shares his father's ostentatious grandeurs for a few years, until sent to a school (evidently remembered autobiographically). These early London chapters are comparable to the beginning of *David Copperfield* in their quality of imaginative recollection. They have a sensitive perfection and pictorial distinctness which puts them apart from anything else he ever wrote. It is strange that the perceptiveness of Virginia Woolf failed to appreciate this. But her objection was to the experiences of Harry and his schoolboy friends, whom she found unauthentic—' novelist's specimens, altogether too pat, and the adventures which befall them altogether too slick'. I can only say that I disagree with her. They are period schoolboys of pre-railway times and have quite as much reality as those in the works of Marryat. Rippinger's, which occupies only a brief episode, was one of those ill-organised academies that preceded the evolution of the modern preparatory school.

In the fifteenth chapter we are taken to a Germany which, though not the Rhineland of Meredith's Neuwied years, is felt and presented with invigorating freshness and romantic action. Eppenwelzen-Sarkeld is somewhere in Hanover, and there, at the Court of the ruling Prince, Richmond Roy has found a temporary anchorage wherein to disport himself. Harry arrives just in time to witness a scene which is one of the most brilliantly contrived things in the book. An equestrian statue is being unveiled.

> The statue was superb—horse and rider in new bronze polished by sunlight. The Marshal was acknowledging the salute of his army. He sat upright, bending his head in harmony with the curve of his horse's neck, and his baton swept the air low in proud submission to the honours cast on him by his acclaiming soldiery. His three-cornered lace hat, curled wig, heavy-trimmed surcoat, and high boots, reminded me of Prince Eugene.

But it was Richmond Roy who, for a prank to please the sister of the Prince, was impersonating his warrior ancestor. And when the boy approaches it, shouting something in English, the statue turns its head with a cry of recognition. The man of metal dismounts and embraces him. The crowd is stupefied; the Prince rides away in a fury at the trick played on him. Roy, while being relieved of his ponderous shell, compares himself to a lobster. The boy, who for several years has been separated from his father, now realises that the gay companion of his childhood is a mountebank and almost a madman. But in spite of this he is soon won over by the affability and charm of his plausible parent, whose career is a charade of audacious effrontery and his mind conveniently oblivious to the debts and misdoings of yesteryear—and even yesterday. He is absorbed in the present, and for him the future is a carnival of roseate illusions. All his talents are wasted in the pursuit of things of no worth. Already he is scheming to marry his son to the Prince of Eppenwelzen's daughter Ottilia, and a few years later, when they meet her by chance at Ostend —Harry being now of age—the plan begins to materialise. Princess Ottilia, in contrast to staunch and sensible Janet Ilchester (who has affinities with Janet Duff Gordon), is romantic and sentimental. She idealises Harry, while behaving in accordance with her high-minded principles. She is a fine creature, though not one of the most vital of Meredith's women. Compared with Sandra Belloni she is—as he somewhere describes her—' like a statue of Twilight '. In their attachment to one another they are always the victims of Roy's skilful designs for Harry's social advancement. The plot of their love-story is spun by him, and not by their passions.

I have now, I hope, done enough to indicate some of the elements of the book; more than enough, indeed, for those readers who prefer the first chapter of a romance to be the gateway into an unknown region of art and imagination. It remains, however, for me to suggest that the actual adventures of Harry Richmond provide us with most of our enjoyment, though the serious theme of his narrative is the development of his matured manhood after it has taken arms against a sea of troubles. To all this Meredith devoted an immense amount of thought and labour, but somehow he failed to make it impressively interesting. In fact, toward the end, he got into one of his tangles when bringing Harry and Janet together again, though he improved the mismanagement by omitting two unsatisfactory chapters of *The Cornhill* version when revising for the definitive edition.

In the facetious history—or tragi-comedy—of Richmond

Roy he is supremely successful, and one continually pauses to exclaim—

> . . . that was music! good alike at grave and gay!
> I can always leave off talking when I hear a master play!

And when Harry is on the open road we get a sense of heightened experience and share the physical glory of youth. For Meredith was always at his best when describing life at its fullest. When feeling and intellect were fused to poetic power he became a matchless and memorable writer. He can make us remember what it felt like to be young, can recover for us the rapture and dizzying uncertainty of first love, can make us breathe the air of early morning, and bring back the forgotten strangeness of mountains looked on long ago. To middle-aged minds he can be a magician. In this book there are—for constructive reasons—few passages of sustained landscape description. But in one of the concluding chapters the voice of Meredith takes control of Harry and we hear him in a characteristic and strenuous exordium.

> Carry your fever to the Alps, you of minds diseased: not to sit down in sight of them ruminating, for bodily ease and comfort will trick the soul and set you measuring our lean humanity against yonder sublime and infinite; but mount, rack the limbs, wrestle it out among the peaks; taste danger, sweat, earn rest: learn to discover ungrudgingly that haggard fatigue is the fair vision you have run to earth, and that rest is your uttermost reward. Would you know what it is to hope again, and have all your hopes at hand?—hang upon the crags at a gradient that makes your next step a debate between the thing you are and the thing you may become. There the merry little hopes grow for the climber like flowers and food, prompt to prove their uses, sufficient if just within the grasp, as mortal hopes should be. How the old lax life closes in about you there! You are the man of your faculties, nothing more. Why should a man pretend to more? We ask it wonderingly when we are healthy. Poetic rhapsodists in the vales below may tell you of the joy and grandeur of the upper regions, they cannot pluck you the medical herb. He gets that for himself who wanders the marshy ledge at nightfall to behold the distant Sennhüttchen twinkle, who leaps the green-eyed crevasses, and in the solitude of an emerald alp stretches a salt hand to the mountain kine.

Meredith

A prose poem, which must have owed something to that famous mountaineer Leslie Stephen, who was the first to climb the Schreckhorn, and of whom Hardy wrote that his personality had a semblance to its ' quaint glooms, keen lights, and rugged trim ', imagining, in a magnificent sonnet, that after death, the eternal essence of his mind would

> Enter this silent adamantine shape,
> And his low voicing haunt its slipping snows
> When dawn that calls the climber dyes them rose.

Anyhow, here was Meredith bursting out of Harry Richmond, while he sat in his room at Flint Cottage, with a sudden longing to be in the mountain-lands he loved. All through the book he had been subduing and excluding that self of his, with its tendency to an almost strident philosophising, its insistence on a morning minded attitude to life. Never again would he succeed in doing so. And it occurs to me as an afterthought that his obvious imperfections as a story teller were caused by the irrepressible energy and obtrusiveness of his nature. His novels were vehicles propelled by an engine which was too highly powered for the passengers whom he invites to travel in them. One cannot accuse him of being a reckless driver; but the running of the machine is boisterous and unequal; and he has an uncomfortable habit of turning his head to shout something at us just when he is approaching a sharp corner.

CHAPTER TEN

1

Having conducted Meredith to his forty-fourth year in a somewhat meticulous manner, I now feel at liberty to relax my method and allow him to travel toward his fifties under less strict supervision.

He has reached the point in his career when one can take a wider view of his doings in everyday existence. He is settled at Box Hill for the rest of his life. He has a family to support. And for the next twenty years or more he will be writing his novels and poems, reading manuscripts for Chapman & Hall, increasing his circle of friends, and gradually winning his way to acceptance by an intelligent public, and Olympian fame with a multitude who abstained from reading him.

The life of a literary man, once he has ceased to be young and enterprising, is always likely to be uneventful outwardly. He just sits there and writes his books. Uneventfulness is what he needs, and to be drawn into public life—for poet-novelists like Meredith and Hardy—would have been disastrous. As Hardy remarked in old age—

> When my contemporaries were driving
> Their coach through Life with strain and striving. . . .
> I lived in quiet, screened, unknown,
> Pondering upon some stick or stone,
> Or news of some rare book or bird
> Latterly bought, or seen, or heard,
> Not wishing ever to set eyes on
> The surging crowd beyond the horizon.

Meredith was more social than Hardy, being a talker, whereas Hardy was a listener, though a delightfully sociable one. Both preferred to be in the country as much as possible. In 1875 Meredith wrote to R. H. Horne that his hatred of London kept him out of it, except under compulsion to go there on business. But this may have been an evasion of an old acquaintance with whose eccentricities he felt unable to become involved. For about that time he often went to the Brandreth's at Elvaston Place to take part in a series of Shakespeare Readings, in which he was Benedick to Alice Brandreth's Beatrice, Petruchio to her Katharine, and Orlando to her Rosalind. After the latter occasion he wrote to her as follows.

> Young Orlando, reared as hind,
> Was fit mate for Rosalind.
> He had youth like Rosalind.
> Shall a man in grey declined
> Seem the same for Rosalind?
> Yea, though merely aged in rind
> Is he worthy Rosalind?

Nevertheless, though ' a man with wrinkles lined ', he ' vows to read with Rosalind ', as Bassanio to her Portia.

Twelfth Night was also read, with Meredith as Malvolio. Alice had been encouraged to believe that she had the makings of an actress, and her account of the proceedings is worth quoting.

> My mother refused to let me take part in any private theatricals, and sternly refused to let us have anything but a Reading. Moreover, she declined to let me read any part with a young man as my lover. To her old-fashioned mind this was not seemly. She consented to Mr. Meredith's taking these parts, as she said ' he was always so good for Allie, as he understands girls so well '. All the parts were studied beforehand, and were more or less acted by the performers, while delightful incidental music was played by Mr. Edward Dannreuther. Mr. Meredith was an admirable coach. His comments and sarcastic imitations of our efforts were very amusing; everybody enjoyed his criticisms; they were pure fun, and nothing unkind was ever said. Most of the readers were very young, and we used in our ignorance to prance through the most awful passages; then Mr. Meredith would, without a smile, take the book, pencil out the objectionable passages, and say ' *Don't read that !* '

Edward Dannreuther was at that time becoming one of the most prominent musicians in London. He was a fine pianist, and conducted the first series of Wagner concerts, in 1873-4. For the next twenty years his chamber music concerts at his house in Bayswater were famous. Meredith and his wife used to go to them with the Brandreths, and at one of them they were introduced to Wagner. Browning and George Eliot were also to be seen there.

Alice Brandreth's reminiscences were written fifty years after her first meeting with Meredith; but she shows him as seen by a nice wholesome girl who wasn't afraid to make fun of him by imitating the way he tossed his head and shot his linen cuffs while reading Shakespeare. (She adds that ' he enjoyed the joke, though Mrs. Meredith didn't quite approve '.) Through her eyes he appears as an avuncular friend of the family, the distinguished author in his shirt sleeves, just beginning to be the grey-headed sage and picturesque celebrity of later years. She could even dare to tackle him about his style.

> I suggested that we should all enjoy his books much more if he would condescend to make the language less involved and difficult to follow, and the story more easy to understand; and I quoted to him the saying of another well-known writer: ' I am sure I should enjoy Meredith's novels, but I have no time to read *shorthand*.' In answer to this cool suggestion on my part, he replied: ' Yes, I know what you would like me to say: " She went upstairs, her heart was as heavy as lead," and so on with various other most conventional phrases.'

But she did not repeat to him a remark of her mother's—that she wished he would copy Miss Charlotte Yonge's method of telling a tale!

From these unpretentious and frequently trivial recordings one gathers quite a good impression of him at forty-five to fifty. The writer often stayed with her Gordon relations near Box Hill, and he was fond of going there for a talk with old Dr. Gordon, who was a well read man and a linguist, and in his youth had lived in Weimar and known Goethe. Fragmentary glimpses reveal Meredith visiting his wealthy neighbours, chaffing them genially about their orchid houses and French cooks, and asking them when they returned from their town mansions, ' Well, have you been going to many gabble gobble dinner parties? ' No longer the isolated literary man of his Esher years, one sees him mixing with conventional people who probably understand him very little. They think him a queer character, but he enlivens their tea-parties with his teasing, witty, restless talk, while Mrs. Meredith sits, demure and dependable, glad that her clever husband should be appreciated, and seldom saying anything with that ' pretty French accent ' of hers.

One day at a garden fête, a careless footman spilt a plate of strawberries and cream all over her new Paris gown. She laughed away sympathy, and said there were plenty more dresses to be had, but Mr. Meredith whispered to Mrs. Gordon: ' I can hear her give a fifty guinea sigh! '

No doubt he found Surrey society a pleasant contrast to Flint Cottage, which was small and overcrowded. (His daughter Marie had been born in June, 1871.) But in those days—and possibly in these—an author who was a notable figure in London could be considered unimportant by his country neighbours. Often may a lorgnette have been levelled at the loquacious gentleman with the bright red tie, when some county dowager inquired who he was—and was it true that he wrote books. Then it would be divulged that he was a friend of Admiral Maxse's—that notoriously eccentric Radical and Reformer—and no more explanations would be considered necessary. ' The Admiral's friends are always so extremely odd! But, really, my dear, the way he waves his hands about while talking! *Most* extraordinary! '

In Alice Brandreth's account of him he is either giving her serious advice—' he spoke of the opening out of Life's obliga-tions, and how earnestly I ought to guard against self-satis-faction '—or else pouring forth a spate of satirical and humorous inventions. She admits that it is beyond her powers to repro-duce his illuminating talk. But I doubt whether that has been done by anyone. Conversational feats which are an expression of irrepressible vitality and high spirits, even when adequately reported, lose most of their transparency and appropriateness. Pinned down on paper, they retain none of their magnetism. The best of Meredith's sayings went into his writings. And it is dangerous to embalm for posterity the badinage of a famous man trying to amuse his friends by flights of comic hyperbole or extemporised epigrams. I sometimes find these piously pre-served drolleries of Meredith embarrassing. It is as though he had been photographed playing the fool to amuse the children. And we know that snapshots of people wearing one another's hats, and facetious inscriptions in visitor's books, do not always look so good afterwards. In lighter moods, Meredith gave of himself generously, sometimes resorting to an almost meretricious smartness in repartee, though often genuinely wise and witty. He did not intend that people should go home and record the froth of his conversations for their reminiscences. In old age, deafness compelled him to become a monologuist, depriving him of what he most enjoyed in social intercourse— lively discussion and argument with ' the speechful, the reciprocating, the sunny and unpresumptuous, who speak from the healthy breast of that dear Mother of us, the Moment '.

To me, the astonishing thing about him is the high pitch of tension at which he seems to have lived. After working with concentrated energy for hours on end, he could emerge for a further exercise of nervous output, his fund of volubility undiminished. If there were no one to talk to, he would probably go striding away over the downs—a ten-mile walk was nothing to him. After thinking of him in his rôle of the vivid and provocative talker, one is conscious of the complexities of his nature. For in the solitudes of his inner self he was a profoundly serious man—serious even in his handling of the ludicrous aspects of human behaviour. Endowed with the tragic and comic instinct in equal degrees, to his friends he revealed a humour that could be fantastic, ironical, or Rabelaisian. He was a philosophic jester, a sage of mirth whose wit blew the mort over Folly. Nor was he above a bit of buffoonery, when it was evoked by kindred spirits such as Hardman and Sandys. Then one turns to his staid and thoughtful letters to Morley (no evoker of buffoonery he!). And in April, 1876, we find him sending, for *The Fortnightly*, a poem of three verses, which, he hopes, will be thought worthy of its pages.

I.

Last night returning from my twilight walk
I met the grey mist Death, whose eyeless brow
Was bent on me, and from his hand of chalk
He reached me flowers as from a withered bough:
O Death, what bitter nosegays givest thou!

II.

Death said, I gather, and pursued his way,
Another stood by me, a shape in stone,
Sword-hacked and iron-stained, with breasts of clay,
And metal veins that sometimes fiery shone:
O Life, how naked and how hard when known!

III.

Life said, As thou hast carved me, such am I.
Then memory, like the nightjar on the pine,
And sightless hope, a woodlark in night sky,
Joined notes of Death and Life till night's decline:
Of Death, of Life, those inwound notes are mine.

As an utterance of thought and emotion common to us all, *A Ballad of Past Meridian* needs no explanatory comment. In its ever-living, universal reality it is durable as though engraved on bronze. I have quoted it in this context because it means, to me, the essential Meredith.

2

Before reverting to the period when he had finished *Harry Richmond*, I must mention an event of some significance which belongs to the spring of 1877. This was the completion of the famous Chalet which for the next twenty years became his workshop, and has been so frequently described by his visitors. Standing on a terrace above the garden, its two rooms brought him much-needed detachment from the crowded interior of Flint Cottage. At the end of March he wrote of it to Morley:—

I think you will agree with me, that it is the prettiest to be found, the view is without a match in Surrey. The interior full of light, which can be moderated; and while surrounded by firs, I look over the slope of our green hill to the ridges of Leith, round to Ranmore, and the half of Norbury.

More important than the view from his study windows was the fact that he could now do his writing in seclusion. For more than eight years he had done it in a small-roomed house where quiet was impossible and a couple of children provided his thoughts with a perpetual accompaniment of distracting noises. Only a writer who has experienced such a contrast in conditions can realise what a mental luxury the change must have been to him. While the Chalet was still in process of edification he wrote to his old friend Bonaparte Wyse that he had a scheme for a long poem—'but as I see myself besieged by Butcher, Baker, and Grocer, I let it rest. Once let me be free, and I'll be aloft like the stars of a rocket benignantly brightening and dying in heaven.' Anyhow, it is certain that his Muse felt more at home up on the terrace, for some of his finest nature poems were written in the ensuing years, and his next long novel was *The Egoist*. Writing again to Morley early in April, he indicates the mental refreshment that he was enjoying.

> I work and sleep up in my cottage at present, and anything grander than the days and nights at my porch you will not find away from the Alps: for the dark line of my hill runs up to the stars, the valley below is a soundless gulf. There I pace like a shipman before turning in. In the day, with the S. West blowing, I have a brilliant universe rolling up to me. . . . I am very hard at work, writing a 5 Act Comedy in verse, besides tales, poems, touches of a novel, and helping my wife with a translation. But in this room of mine I should have no excuse for idleness. In truth work flows from me.

And now for *Beauchamp's Career*, begun in 1871 and finished early in 1874, rejected by *The Cornhill*, but accepted for *The Fortnightly* on condition that it must be cut down by almost a third of its length. This proved an agonising task, and for six months he was recasting, condensing, and discovering that much of it had to be almost redone, ' with shudders to think how much more there was to do '. The alterations and rewritings were, of course, structural; they were not caused by dissatisfaction with the novel as originally completed. But it must be remembered that Meredith was addicted to knocking his manuscripts about very drastically. One cannot help feeling that there must have been something amiss with a method which led to such savage excisions and reshapings. There is evidence that he would attack a new novel with daemonic energy, confident that it would be finished within a few months. A year or two later he is hacking it about and making no headway. Few novelists of his eminence can have been so

undeliberate in the progress of composition. Yet he wrote
every page with unrelaxing attention to style and detail. It is
difficult to understand how so fastidious a writer can have found
so much in his work that had to be discarded. The explanation, I suppose, is to be found in his turbulent temperament.
For there was nothing moderate about him. As a literary
artist he was forever engaged in overcoming an excess of
creative excitability. He could say, with Housman—

> Be still, be still, my soul; it is but for a season:
> Let us endure an hour and see injustice done.

But, as Housman did, he knew that ' the troubles of our proud
and angry dust ' were a ferment of impatience in him, and a
challenge to his ability to subdue them.

Meanwhile he wrote despondently about *Beauchamp's Career*
to Moncure Conway, who was negotiating for its American
publication. ' I feel bound to warn you of the nature of my
work. It is not likely to please the greater number of readers.
It is philosophical-political, with no powerful stream of adventure.' In April, 1873, he had told Jessopp that it would
only appeal to those who had a taste for him; it would not
catch the gudgeon world.

> I cannot go on with a story and not feel that to treat of flesh and
> blood is to touch the sacredest; and so it usually ends in my
> putting the destinies of the world about it—like an atmosphere,
> out of which it cannot subsist. So my work fails. I see it. But
> the pressure is on me with every new work. I fear that Beauchamp
> is worse than the foregoing in this respect.

And there is a passage in the book where he states his position
as an unpopular novelist.

> My way is like a Rhone island in the summer drought, stony,
> unattractive and difficult between two forceful streams of the
> real and the over-real, which delight mankind—honour the
> conjurors! My people conquer nothing, win none; they are
> actual, yet uncommon. It is the clockwork of the brain that they
> are directed to set in motion, and—poor troop of actors to vacant
> benches!—the conscience residing in thoughtfulness which they
> would appeal to; and if you are there impervious to them, we
> are lost: back I go to my wilderness, where, as you perceive, I
> have contracted the habit of listening to my own voice more than
> is good.

The case for and against *Beauchamp's Career* was stated by Swinburne in a letter to Morley.

> I have just been reading Meredith's book which I only tried by fits and starts as it was coming out in the *Fortnightly*. Full of power and beauty and fine truthfulness as it is, what a noble book it might and should have been, if he would but have foregone his lust of epigram and habit of trying to tell a story by means of riddles that hardly excite the curiosity they are certain to baffle! By dint of revulsion from Trollope on this hand and Braddon on that, he seems to have persuaded himself that limpidity of style must mean shallowness, lucidity of narrative must imply triviality, and simplicity of direct interest or positive incident must involve 'sensationalism'. It is a constant irritation to see a man of such rarely strong and subtle genius, such various and splendid forces of mind, do so much to justify the general neglect he provokes. But what noble powers there are visible in almost all parts of his work.

Published in 1876, it was more widely reviewed than the previous novels. Frederick Greenwood's *The Pall Mall Gazette* gave it two highly appreciative columns, by H. D. Traill, and although less successful commercially than *Harry Richmond*, it raised Meredith's reputation among percipient readers and was the turning point in his progress from neglect to recognition.

The most important review was one which must have passed almost unnoticed, since it appeared in an obscure journal, *The Secularist*. It was signed 'B.V.' This, of course, was James Thomson, author of that well-known, but seemingly underestimated poem *The City of Dreadful Night*. The article was a defiant championship of Meredith's work as a whole. Nothing finer had hitherto been written about him in eulogy.

> He loves to suggest by flying touches rather than slowly elaborate. To those who are quick to follow his suggestions he gives in a few winged words the very spirit of a scene, the inmost secret of a mood or passion. . . . He has a wonderful eye for form and colour, especially the latter; a masterly perception of character; a most subtle sense for spiritual mysteries. His dialogue is full of life and reality, flexile and rich in the genuine unexpected, marked with the keenest distinctions. . . . He has this sure mark of lofty genius, that he always rises with his theme,

growing more strenuous, more self-contained, more magistral, as the demands on his thought and imagination increase. His style is very various and flexible, flowing freely in whatever measures the subject and the mood may dictate. At its best it is so beautiful in simplest Saxon, so majestic in rhythm, so noble with noble imagery, so pregnant with meaning, so vital and intense, that it must be ranked among the supreme achievements of our literature.

How it warms the heart, to hear a man of genius praised by one of his peers! Thomson, whose career was ruined by hereditary intemperance, was reciprocally admired by Meredith. After reading *The City of Dreadful Night*, he wrote to him that ' there is a massive impressiveness in it that goes beyond Dürer's *Melancholia*, and takes it into upper regions where poetry is the sublimation of the mind of man, the voice of our highest '.

When Thomson died in 1882, Meredith was still unaware of the disastrously sordid circumstances of his private life. They only met twice, but Meredith did what he could to help him, and had a high opinion of his personal qualities. There was something in his poetry which appealed to him strongly and caused him to write that ' he was a man of big heart, of such entire sincereness that he wrote directly from the impressions carved in him by his desolate experience of life. Bright achievement was plucked out of the most tragic life in our literature.' Of Meredith, Thomson wrote, ' He is one of those personalities who need fear no comparison with their writings.'

3

And now for *Beauchamp's Career*—as I have already announced to the expectant reader. Now for yet another enormous novel which has been analysed, elucidated, and discussed by many a more competent pen than mine. And now—for some obscure reason—I feel the book a burden on me, and could almost wish that Meredith hadn't written quite so many enormous novels, all of which I have biographically covenanted to peruse— and proclaim as perusable—to a neglectful generation. For the fact is that Meredith as a whole is beyond the scope of my failing apprehension. My literary instinct has always been faithful to the beauty that flows from a full mind. When a volume of prose aims at being a work of art I profoundly prefer it to be compact and delicate in structure. By all means let a long-winded story lull me in my arm-chair with tracts of semi-dullness, as in Scott, deviseful diffuseness, as in Dickens, or in styleless style, as in Balzac. The disadvantage of Meredith— one may as well admit it—is that he makes too constant an appeal to thoughtfulness, and that his manner of narrating is too abrupt and allusive to allow the mind to listen comfortably. Often one feels out of step with him—and out of breath. He strides along, gesticulating vehemently; then he suddenly stops to insist on showing one the view across the valley or to explain the inner workings of a character. He is an uneasy companion in a pilgrimage of six hundred pages; and *Beauchamp's Career* is an extremely complicated pilgrimage in which romance and comedy are elaborately blended, country-house life is satirised, and a series of strongly drawn figures cross one another in intricate mazes of motive and action. When introducing the hero, he forewarned readers that there is no plot in his history, which is a romantic life-story amplified by a series of contrivances connected with the other characters. But why, I ask again, need there be so much of it? The apparent answer is that it had to be a three-volume novel. That answer does not satisfy me, because I regard the three-volume novel as a monstrosity, when imposed on an author who refuses to indulge in commonplace writing. Meredith conceded the demand for bulk because he had so much to say. He was, of course, along with George Eliot and Hardy, one of the makers of the modern novel of psychology, introspection, and ideas. The discomfort I have sometimes felt while reading *Beauchamp's Career* was due to his insistence on charging it with so many ideas and intellectual abstractions. The same can be said of his long poems. The following passage about Nevil Beauchamp might, conceivably, be applied to Meredith himself.

He had drunk of the *questioning* cup, that which denieth peace to us, and which projects us upon the missionary search of the How, the Wherefore, and the Why not, ever afterward. He questioned his justification, and yours, for gratifying tastes in an ill-regulated

world of wrong-doing, suffering, sin and bounties unrighteously
dispensed—not sufficiently dispensed. From his point of observation, and with the store of ideas and images his fiery yet reflective
youth had gathered, he presented himself as it were saddled to
that hard-riding force known as the logical impetus, which spying
its quarry over precipices, across oceans and deserts, and through
systems and webs, and into shops and cabinets of costliest china,
will come at it, will not be refused, let the distances and breakages
be what they may. He went like the meteoric man with the
mechanical legs in the song, too quick for a cry of protestation,
and reached results amazing to his instincts, his tastes, and his
training, not less rapidly and naturally than the tremendous Ergo
is shot forth from the clash of a syllogism.

Having got rid of my personal grumble against it, I must
hasten to express agreement with Swinburne about the manifold excellences of the book. In many ways it is an advance on
anything he had done before, provided that one accepts as
inevitable his refusal to proceed in an un-Meredithian manner
or to make any further attempt to please the general public.
It is full of delightful writing, such as the scenes in Normandy,
which he had absorbed while spending holidays with his wife's
relations at Nonancourt. And there is the superb passage
describing the Alps seen at dawn from the Adriatic.

He was awakened by light on his eyelids, and starting up beheld
the many pinnacles of grey and red rocks and shadowy high
white regions at the head of the gulf waiting for the sun; and the
sun struck them. One by one they came out in crimson flame,
till the vivid host appeared to have stepped forward. The
shadows on the snow-fields deepened to purple below an irradia-
tion of rose and pink and dazzling silver. There of all the world
you might imagine Gods to sit. A crowd of mountains endless in
range, erect, or flowing, shattered and arid, or leaning in smooth
lustre, hangs above the gulf. The mountains are sovereign Alps,
and the sea is beneath them. The whole gigantic body keeps the
sea, as with a hand, to right and left.

Beauchamp is Maxse. As early as Christmas, 1870, Meredith wrote to him that he had 'just finished the History of the
inextinguishable Sir Harry Firebrand of the Beacon, Knight
Errant of the 19th century', which seems to have been a
preliminary sketch with a different plot. At this time he had

also been writing *Celt and Saxon,* the less than half-completed
manuscript of which remained in his desk until published in
1910. Like his prototype, Beauchamp is an aristocratic
idealist, fanatical and impetuous, both dogmatic and emotional
in his crusade for democracy and the working man. Meredith
was fully conscious of his friend's dangerous tendency to
extremes and irrational eccentricities, and often referred to
them in letters to him. ' You must needs lay down positive
principles as if your existing state were the key of things.'
' Don't forget that mental arrogance is as a fiery wine to the
spirit—a little of it gives a proper pride: but you carry too
much.' But he had an immense admiration for him as ' one
who, by force of character, advancing in self-conquest, strikes
his impress right and left around him, because of his aim at
stars. He had faults; but where was he to be matched in
devotedness and gallantry? and what man of blood fiery as his
ever fought so to subject it? '

It is clear that Maxse afforded him splendid material,
and in using it he nowhere fails in lifelike and impressive
delineation. Beauchamp is one of the most splendid and
compelling failures in fiction. The ending of the book resembles
that of Richard Feverel in being almost impossible to accept
without protest. Beauchamp is drowned while saving the life
of a mudlarking urchin. The action was in accordance with
his character, but as a conclusion it makes one feel as if Meredith had lost patience with the tale and thrown it aside with a
savage gesture. The only explanation offered is that the
Comic Spirit demanded that his quixotic and frustrated
career should close with futile self-sacrifice. Apparently Meredith managed to convince himself that the tragedy was part of
his constructive plan. But even his most uncompromising
admirers seem to have been baffled by it.

With *Harry Richmond,* he liked it the best of his novels ' because
it was about Maxse ', and also because he thought the French
girl Renée one of his most attractive creations.

CHAPTER ELEVEN

1˙

In the autumn of 1876 he was working on a long essay, which he was induced to deliver as a lecture at the London Institution. This was *On the Idea of Comedy and the Uses of the Comic Spirit*, subsequently entitled *An Essay on Comedy*. He disliked lecturing, and it was his only appearance as a platform speaker. His own report of the occasion, which was on February 1st, 1877, is in a note to Morley.

> All went well. Morison in one of his enthusiasms—which makes one remember that one has word praise. Audience very attentive and indulgent. Time 1 h. 25 min. and no one left the hall, so that I may imagine there was interest in the lecture. Pace moderate: but Morison thinks I was intelligible chiefly by the distinctness of articulation.

One wishes that Cotter Morison had left us a written account, or that the young Edmund Gosse had been present, with his gift for penetrating and sensitive observation. It would also be interesting to know how much expression Meredith put into his reading and whether he controlled his tendency to gesture. I cannot imagine him subduing his vivid personality. (In private, his reading was magnificent.) I have searched diligently for a contemporary or reminiscent recorder of that memorable evening; but it seems that 'there ain't no sich person'. The Essay was printed in the April number of *The New Quarterly Magazine*, where it remained hidden for the next twenty years, 'cursed with misprints,' wrote Meredith, 'that make me dance gadfly-bitten; some, I am afraid, are attributable to me: I am the worst of correctors of my own writing.' (This was nothing new, for even the *Modern Love* volume had been peppered with misprints.)

When the Essay was at last published as a slim volume in brown buckram, it was welcomed by a fully representative chorus of dramatic critics, headed by Shaw in *The Saturday*

Review. He found it ' an excellent, even superfine, essay by perhaps the highest living English authority on its subject '. After that he spent the rest of his article in a brilliant exhibition of being ' G.B.S.', giving the Philistine Englishman a bit of his mind. Meredith, he said, knew more about plays than play-goers. He had suggested that the English public had the basis of the comedic spirit in them—an esteem for common sense.

But [says Shaw] I must tell Mr. Meredith that they are every-where united and made strong by the bond of their common nonsense, their invincible determination to tell and be told lies about everything, and their power of dealing acquisitively and successfully with facts while keeping them rigidly in their proper place: that is, outside the moral consciousness. The Englishman is successful because he values money and social precedence more than anything else, especially more than fine art, his attitude toward which, culture-affectation apart, is one of half diffident, half contemptuous curiosity, and of course more than clear-headedness, spiritual insight, truth, justice, and so forth. It is this unscrupulousness and singleness of purpose that constitutes the Englishman's pre-eminent ' common sense '; and this sort of common sense, I submit to Mr. Meredith, is not only not ' the basis of the comic ', but actually makes comedy impossible, because it would not seem like common sense at all if it were not self-satisfiedly unconscious of its moral and intellectual bluntness, whereas the function of comedy is to dispel such unconsciousness by turning the search-light of the keenest moral and intellectual analysis right on to it.

And so on, to his conclusion that ' the English playgoing public positively dislikes comedy ', leaving the present writer with a feeling that—unanswerably true though this Irish volu-bility may have been in 1897—he needs a pause to recover his mental equilibrium. What ' G.B.S.' omitted to mention, was modestly proclaimed by William Archer;—that ' *An Essay on Comedy* may without hesitation be set down as one of the subtlest, wittiest, and most luminous pieces of criticism in the English language '. Much has been written about it as an exposition of Meredith's philosophy of the ' Comic Spirit ', which G. M. Trevelyan has defined as

. . . the sane and thankful, but critically humourous, outlook on life commended to the world in his novels. . . . This Spirit believes in progress and evolution, but it knows the limits to the possible pace of advance. Those who would have the world stand still, and those who would have us fly through the air to Utopia, are both victims of its gentle shafts. . . .

The best cure for pessimism, as also for the optimism that denies facts, is laughter.

If the Comic idea prevailed with us, the vapours of unreason and sentimentalism would be blown away before they were productive. . . . It is not, he points out, the same as irony, or satire; and it is totally opposed to cynicism.

The Comic Spirit—'Sword of Common Sense! Our surest gift', he called it in his subsequent *Ode*—is a corrective and beneficent influence on civilised society. Applied to individuals, its service is to warn against taking the heart, instead of the brain, for guide.

> These are the children of the heart untaught
> By thy quick founts to beat abroad, by thee
> Untamed to tone its passions under thought,
> The rich humaneness reading in thy fun.

Elsewhere he has written that Earth is never misread by brain.

> Her children of the labouring brain,
> These are the champions of the race,
> True parents, and the sole humane,
> With understanding for their base.

The object of Comedy, he claims, is to awaken thoughtful laughter—the laughter of the mind. When brought to his test, very few Comedies survive it. Molière is the only playwright who satisfies him.

His laughter, in his purest comedies, is ethereal, as light to our nature, as colour to our thoughts. . . . The source of his wit is clear reason; it is a fountain of that soil, and it springs to vindicate reason, common sense, rightness and justice; for no vain purpose ever. . . . His art is a running brook, with innumerable fresh lights on it at every turn of the wood through which its business is to find a way. . . . Without effort, and with no dazzling flashes of achievement, it is full of healing, the wit of good breeding, the wit of wisdom. His characters quicken the mind through laughter, from coming out of the mind.

In Shakespeare and Cervantes, Meredith found ' the richer laugh of heart and mind in one; with much of the Aristophanic robustness, something of Molière's delicacy '. He admitted Congreve's *Way of the World*, with reservations; and singled out Fielding, Goldsmith, and Jane Austen as steeped in the comic spirit (though he was never a whole-hearted appreciator of Jane Austen). Addressed to an audience of seventy years ago, the lecture is now, I suppose, somewhat in the nature of a period piece. I am not capable of analysing its inappropriateness to the conditions of modern thought. The task was attempted in 1920, by a clever writer in *The New Statesman*, who acidly remarked that—

. . . as for the exposition of the uses of the comic spirit with which Meredith supported his claims, this arrant sophism can only be his ironical concession to the times. . . . The intellectualist method of Meredith was old fashioned enough to assume both the essential normality and the permanence of this civilisation now fluttering autumnal down, and so to reduce comedy to a quasi-logical repudiation of whatever was inconsistent with this normality and this permanence. To-day, from wealth of experience, not of wisdom, we see that assumption as itself stuff for comedy.

(Exit Meredith, with a gesture of ' fluttering autumnal ' discomfiture.) It remains for me to assert that, judged as a work of literary art, *An Essay on Comedy* is a performance of classic lucidity and grace. The outlook is large, the temper sane, and the style perfect. The whole thing is invigorating, keen, and yet bland. It acts on one—in his own words— ' like a renovating air—the South-west coming off the sea, or a cry in the Alps '. Intellectual atmospherics are variable, and literary fashions supersede one another. Prose such as this outlasts the touch of time.

If you believe that our civilization is founded in common-sense (and it is the first condition of sanity to believe it), you will, when contemplating men, discern a Spirit overhead; not more heavenly than the light flashed upwards from glassy surfaces, but luminous and watchful; never shooting beyond them nor lagging in the rear; so closely attached to them that it may be taken for a slavish reflex, until its features are studied. It has the sage's brows, and the sunny malice of a faun lurks at the corners of the half-closed lips drawn in an idle wariness of half tension. That slim feasting smile, shaped like the long-bow, was once a big round satyr's laugh, that flung up the brows like a fortress lifted by gunpowder. The laugh will come again, but it will be of the order of the smile, finely tempered, showing sunlight of the mind, mental richness rather than noisy enormity. Its common aspect is one of unsolicitous observation, as if surveying a full field and having leisure to dart on its chosen morsels, without any fluttering eagerness. Men's future upon earth does not attract it; their honesty and shapeliness in the present does; and whenever they wax out of proportion, overblown, affected, pretentious, bombastical, hypocritical, pedantic, fantastically delicate; whenever it sees them self-deceived or hoodwinked, given to run riot in idolatries, drifting into vanities, congregating in absurdities, planning short-sightedly, plotting dementedly; whenever they are at variance with their professions, and violate the unwritten but perceptible laws binding them in consideration one to another; whenever they offend sound reason, fair justice; are false in humility or mined with conceit, individually, or in the bulk—the Spirit overhead will look humanely malign and cast an oblique light on them, followed by volleys of silvery laughter. That is the Comic Spirit.

To an age which has destroyed so many of its civilised values, this poetic-philosophic presentment of an Idea is manifestly inapplicable. But this might now be said of almost everything except, possibly, the Wisdom of the Ages! In 1877 human consciousness was not disillusioned. The soul of man was not (as Meredith wrote of Alvan in *The Tragic Comedians*) like some great Cathedral organ foully handled in the night by demons. It is no part of my business to estimate Meredith's status as a thinker. I merely recommend him as a splendid and highly stimulating writer. And to those who have ears to hear I commend his Comic Spirit and its Uses.

2

The next number of *The New Quarterly* contained a long short-story, *The Case of General Ople and Lady Camper*, which richly deserved to be received with ' volleys of silvery laughter ', though General Ople is merely an inoffensive but obtuse gentleman involved in the dilemma of a matrimonial project with a lady whom he described as ' no common enigma '. The story

' The Case of General Ople and Lady Camper '

is a minor masterpiece, adroitly farcical and beautifully clear in execution. The writing of the opening chapters could almost be mistaken for Henry James in his middle period, though the action is treated with much more directness than he would have allowed himself. To re-write *The Case* as he might have done it would be an amusing exercise of ingenuity for someone with a talent for *jeux d'esprit*. The situation is one which would have suited him. Meredith made use of an affair which had occurred at Kingston, when a distinguished General was compelled to take action against his neighbour, Lady Eleanor Cathcart, an eccentric person who persisted in annoying him by sending caricatures of himself engaged in gardening and otherwise. General Ople's house is an accurate description of Kingston Lodge, and Lady Camper's is the one occupied by Hardman. Not that such details matter; for the tale is a delicious social comedy, and the absurdities of the General are disclosed with consistent delicacy and restraint, unmarred by exaggeration, yet broadly humorous in effect. One is at once struck by the neatness and economy of the narration. The eight chapters are short and perfectly proportioned; dialogue is condensed and explicit; descriptions and explanations are compact and informative. As a technical performance, the tale proves that Meredith could write with limpid concinnity when he chose to do so. The subject being little more than an anecdote, he instinctively adopted an appropriate method, restricting himself to a simplified scenario and discarding exuberances of epigram and allusion. The outline is as follows. Wilson Ople, a retired Brigadier-General, aged fifty-five, silver-haired and handsome, has taken a villa for himself and his young daughter. Next to this ' gentlemanly residence ', as he insists on calling it, is Douro Lodge, subsequently rented by Lady Camper, a widow, ' niece of an earl ', and forty-one. She is one of those ladies in whom Meredith undertook to show how an active brain and high spirit are compatible with middle age. The simple General, deferential and obsequious toward the aristocracy, is also shy and susceptible with women, and intensely sensitive to ridicule.

> Clever women alarmed and paralysed him. Their aptness to question and require immediate sparkling answers; their demand for fresh wit, of a kind which is not supplied by publications which

supply it wholesale; their power of ridicule, too; made them awful in his contemplation.

Self-satisfied, and rather vain, egoism is preventing him from realising that his daughter and Lady Camper's nephew, a cavalry officer, have fallen in love. Lady Camper, therefore, proceeds to weed him of his selfishness. Her aim is to rouse him to consideration for his daughter's happiness, but he is so hoodwinked by egoism that he interprets her remarks on marriage as advances to himself. To punish him, as well as to make a fresh attempt to stir his fatherly instincts, she leaves for the Continent, whence she sends him a series of merciless caricatures of himself, illustrating his selfishness and drawing attention to his habit of using such phrases as ' bijou ' and ' ladylike '. These drive him nearly distracted. In search of sympathy, he shows them to all his neighbours, thereby acting as agent to her efforts to make him ridiculous. But he is also fascinated by her cleverness, and his awful admiration of her abilities and indifference to conventional manners makes him desire to have the powers of his enemy widely appreciated. At last she returns and ends his torture by explaining the object of her cruel treatment, namely, a sense of his duty to the young people. Having thus induced him to settle half his money on his daughter, she marries him. She had found a husband who was ' likely ever to be a fund of amusement for her humour, good, impressible, and above all, very picturesque '. As for the General, he gloried in her ability to see through him.

> For as it was an extraordinary piece of insight to see him through, it struck him that in acknowledging the truth of it, he made a discovery of new powers in human nature.

Ludicrous, but likeable, he leaves an impression on one's mind of being a descendant of some character in *Tristram Shandy*. The solution of his ordeal by caricature has been objected to as an anti-climax. It is certainly a tame ending to such a brilliant and delightful farce. Possibly Meredith felt sorry for having been so unkind to the General. But I suspect that he became tired of the story, and huddled his characters off the stage by the easiest method.

3

Three tales appeared in *The New Quarterly*. *The House on the Beach* I have already mentioned as one of Meredith's least accomplished works. The third was *The Tale of Chloe*, which has been less admired than it deserves. The sub-title, *An Episode in the Life of Beau Beamish*, indicates that we are in Bath at the Beau Nash period, in the milieu of artificial manners and customs where a veneer of good breeding, elaborate courtesies and persiflage thinly covered the coarse passions of human nature. It is appropriately delicate and elegant in handling, but behind the Dresden China daintiness of it there is intimate analysis of character and a tragic motive. While never for a moment leaving its plane of comedy of manners, the story is managed with supreme skill and constructive suspense.

Beau Beamish, the suave but monarchical social arbiter of ' The Wells ', has undertaken the responsibility of controlling a youthful duchess, formerly a milkmaid, whose elderly and infatuated husband has allowed her a month's gaiety while he himself enjoys a respite from the fatigues of acting as her playfellow. The Beau assigns her the incognito title of ' Duchess of Dewlap ' and appoints as her chaperon a gentle, discreet, and distinguished lady who had spent her fortune to pay the debts of her handsome and spendthrift lover, Sir Martin Caseldy, who thereupon deserted her. For seven years she has lived in Bath, unreproachfully awaiting his return, keeping her faith in him, and maintaining her sprightly air and gay spirits. These qualities have won her the esteem and affection of the Beau. Duchess Susan is a warm thing of flesh and blood—a Kneller portrait—vulgar, ignorant, and beautiful. Chloe is most subtly drawn—too subtly for superficial description. She has affinities with Dahlia Fleming. Soon after the Duchess's arrival, Caseldy returns, ostensibly to reunite himself with Chloe, but really to make love to the Duchess. Chloe, while gradually growing aware of this, ' treated them both with a proud generosity surpassing gentleness. All that there was of selfishness in her bosom resolved to the enjoyment of her one month of strongly willed delusion '. At every fresh evidence of her lover's treachery, she ties a knot in a thick silken skein which she carries in her hands. She has her own plan for preventing mischief and saving her friend the Duchess, whose ' shepherdess in a hoop ' attractions have by now made her the toast of the town. The ladies thought that the odour of shepherdess could only be exorcised by powder for her auburn hair and dazzling red and white cheeks. They considered her blushing indecent. But the gentlemen ' behaved in a way to cause the blushes to swarm rosy as the troops of young Love round Cytherea in her sea-birth, when, some soaring, and sinking some, they flutter like her loosened zone, and breast the air thick as flower petals on the summer's breath, weaving her net for the world '. Matters are brought to a head by the lovers planning to elope at three o'clock one morning. Discovering this, Chloe puts her plan into execution. She hangs herself on the door of their sitting-room, and as the Duchess slips out she encounters this obstacle to her flight, and the elopement is prevented by the despairing self-sacrifice of—as the Beau describes her—' that most admirable of women, whose heart was broken by a faithless man ere she devoted her wreck of life to arrest one weaker than herself on the descent to perdition '.

The closing chapters have a strange beauty and tragic intensity, and one overlooks the improbability of Chloe's quixotic suicide. She is one of Meredith's finest and most convincing creations. From the first one feels her as a fated figure, and the delicacy of the setting assists the exquisite pathos of her history, which has the finest spirit of tragedy.

CHAPTER TWELVE

1

ONE gets a glimpse of him in a letter to Morley, headed *First ten minutes of 1878.* As most of us do when yet another last leaf is torn off the calendar, he was feeling a philosophic detachment from the ordinary run of affairs; but his look was forward, in contrast to our customary personal review of the past year, which in men of his age (he was all but fifty) seldom includes a strong desire to live it over again. And Morley, wise and helpful friend that he was, always offered an instinctive outlet for his graver meditations. It was needful to be serious when communicating with the man who instructed us that ' the great business of life is, to be, to do, to do without, and to depart '. Abstinence from frivolity has never been more wholesomely advocated—or more bleakly worded.

> I greet you [wrote Meredith] in the first hour of the New Year, after a look at the stars from my chalet door, and listening to the bells. We have just marked one of our full stops, at which Time, turning back as he goes, looks with his old-gentleman smile. To come from a gaze at the stars—Orion and shaking Sirius below him—is to catch a glance at the inscrutable face of him that hurries us on, as on a wheel, from dust to dust.—I thought of you and how it might be with you this year: hoped for good: saw beyond good and evil to great stillness, another form of moving for you and me. It seems to me that Spirit is,—how, where, and by what means involving us, none can say. But in this life there is no life save in spirit. The rest of life, and we may know it in love,—is an aching and a rotting. It is late. I have been writing all day. With all my heart I wish you well.

He was writing *The Egoist*—had been writing it since the previous summer—and the Comic Spirit of his Essay was the presiding presence above the chalet. The full-fledged Meredithian idiom was in process of being transmitted to an audience which, more than ever before, consisted of the author listening

139

to his own voice without expectation of being appreciated or understood even—as he afterwards wrote to Stevenson—by those who cared for his work.

Supposing he had—on that New Year's Eve—surveyed and recorded the circumstances of his existence, he would have been obliged to admit that he was an overworked and unpopular author with a young family and an income less than adequate for his needs. For ten years he had lived at Flint Cottage, drudging with mind and pen, but no rewarding prosperity was in sight. For more than six years he had not been abroad for a holiday, and his physical condition was showing signs of wear and tear. In the autumn of that New Year he was to write to Maxse:—

> I have been nowhere but on my weekly hack-cab-horse expeditions [as publisher's reader], and it is doubtful that I shall ever go anywhere but on that tramroad, until I proceed in mute accompaniment to my Last March. Life under these conditions is not so seductive as it appeared in youth, though in youth I looked out under a hail of blows. I don't complain, you see, of inconsistency in my career. If I could quit England, hold off from paper, and simply look on for the remainder of my term—mountains near— I would ask for no better.

But he had managed to build a spare bedroom on to the cottage, and the chalet must serve as substitute for Switzerland, supplemented by Leslie Stephen's prose poem *The Alps in Winter*, which had recently appeared in *The Cornhill*.

Fully as old as his age, he had reached the time of life when a man ceases to expect anything to happen which will be a springboard to fresh experience. Matured and permanent friendships remained—he could count them on his fingers (and anyone who can do that is lucky). But Hardman and the Jessopps were seen less often now; and in 1880 he would lose Tom Taylor, of whom he wrote so beautifully—

> When I remember, friend, whom lost I call,
> Because a man beloved is taken hence,
> The tender humour and the fire of sense
> In your good eyes; how full of heart for all,
> And chiefly for the weaker by the wall,
> You bore the lamp of sane benevolence;
> Then see I round you Death his shadows dense
> Divide, and at your feet his emblems fall,

Had he been a writer much praised by his contemporaries and admired by a large public, he would now have reached the stage where the younger generation advances to the attack. Delayed recognition had deprived him of this indication of eminence achieved; but it made him a suitable object for discovery and enthusiastic vindication by the enterprising, and we have already seen how James Thomson used his powers for this purpose. Anyhow, at the beginning of 1878 Meredith was greatly in need of encouragement and stimulation, not from a dull disciple's foolish face of praise, but from someone whose youthful appreciation he could respect, and—better still —reciprocate. In April of that year exactly the right person appeared. It was Robert Louis Stevenson, then in his twenty-eighth year, and just beginning to be observed by the literary world through a few essays (afterwards famous in *Virginibus Puerisque*) which had been published in *The Cornhill.* To Meredith he was quite unknown when he came to stay at the Burford Bridge Inn, with a letter to the Gordons from the publisher, Kegan Paul, who was about to bring out *An Inland Voyage.* His object, of course, was to obtain an introduction to Meredith, for whose work he had unbounded admiration. He seems to have stayed several weeks, for Alice Brandreth (who had just married her cousin Jim Gordon) naïvely records that

. . . they used to meet constantly in our garden. Mr. Meredith was much interested in Stevenson, and as they sat on the lawn would draw many confidences from the eager young author, who himself had the art of drawing out the best of Mr. Meredith's conversational powers. Their mutual liking was pleasant to see, yet I remember feeling somewhat surprised when he prophesied great things for Stevenson, and declared that some day we should all feel proud to have known him.

A variant version, by Edmund Gosse, can be quoted.

Stevenson threw himself with extreme enthusiasm into the acquaintance. I remember hearing at the time that the elder writer was not very responsive at first, that he was a little bewildered at being thus carried by storm. But one likes to fancy that this flush of generous juvenile admiration spread a certain additional lustre over the book which Meredith was then writing, and gave body to ' the human, red matter he contrived to plug and pack into that strange and admirable book, *The Egoist.*' (The words are Stevenson's.) Stevenson's influence in widening the circle of Meredith's admirers and in bringing him into his popular estate was greater than that of any other person. The pleasure which he received from such books as *Richard Feverel* and *Harry Richmond* was greater than was given him by the fiction of any other elder contemporary. The illuminating varieties of his humourous observation of mankind were full of exquisite pleasure for Stevenson, who, with a brain scarcely less rapid than Meredith's, could appreciate what the novelist was doing as he flashed, in a manner bewildering to common readers, from corner to corner of his glittering web.

Thus the Burford Bridge Inn added a page to its associations with literary history. For it was there that Keats stayed when finishing *Endymion*, at the end of 1817, and wrote: ' I like this place very much. There is Hill and Dale and a little river. I went up Box Hill this evening after the moon.' In another letter from the Inn, he says:—

I scarcely remember counting upon any happiness—I look not for it if it be not in the present hour,—nothing startles me beyond the moment. The Setting Sun will always set me to rights, *or if a Sparrow come before my Window, I take part in its existence and pick about the gravel.*

I have quoted this particular passage because the words italicised have a curious parallel in Meredith's *Ode to Youth in Memory*, where, speaking of Mother Nature, he counsels us that

> Who cheerfully the little bird becomes,
> Without a fall, and pipes for peck at crumbs,
> May have her dolings to the lightest touch. . . .
> And there the arrowy eagle of the height
> Becomes the little bird that hops to feed,
> Glad of a crumb, for tempered appetite
> To make it wholesome blood and fruitful seed.

I like to think of Keats and Meredith, though seventy-five years apart, when writing thus, being more or less of the same mind within half a mile of one another. In Stevenson's essay *A Gossip on Romance* there is a pleasant passage.

The inn at Burford Bridge with its arbours and green garden and silent eddying river—though it is known already as the place where Keats wrote some of his *Endymion* and Nelson parted from his Emma—still seems to wait the coming of the appropriate legend. Within these ivied walls, behind these old green shutters, some further business smoulders, waiting for its hour. . . . I have lived at Burford in a perpetual flutter, on the heels, as it seemed, of some adventure that should justify the place.

Early in June, when writing to Stevenson with warm appreciation and encouragement after reading *An Inland Voyage*, he mentioned that *The Egoist* was on the way to conclusion. It must have been during Stevenson's next visit, about a year later (after his return from wintering in California), that Meredith read him several chapters, which caused him to exclaim, ' Own up—you have drawn Sir Willoughby Patterne from *me*!' The reply was, ' No, no, my dear fellow, I've taken him from all of us, but principally from myself.'

Not long before that, he had written to Stevenson—

My *Egoist* has been out of my hands for a couple of months, but Kegan Paul does not wish to publish it before October. I don't think you will like it. . . . It is a Comedy, with only half of me in it, unlikely therefore to take either the public or my friends. I am about one quarter through *The Amazing Marriage*, which, I promise you, you shall like better.

(This work was put aside for fifteen years and completed in 1895. In the character of Gower Woodseer, it contained a portrait of Stevenson, who, by the way, was quite capable of criticising his hero, for some years later he wrote of him, to Henry James, ' He is not an easy man to be with—there is so much of him, and the veracity and high athletic intellectual humbug are so intermixed.')

The Egoist had been finished in February, after a three months bout of intensive work, much of it done at night. His health had suffered in consequence; and in the spring he wrote to Cotter Morison that he was ' lank, limp, and cavern-chapped ' and afflicted with what he called ' a sort of old man's cough '.

Not until some time after the cough had ceased to trouble him was it discovered that he had had whooping cough! The poor man tried to cure himself by what he called his unfailing specific of hard exercise. He still persisted in ' throwing the beetle ', but his physical strength was deteriorating, and

143

from this point he was never the same again. That desperate struggle with *The Egoist* marked the beginning of the spinal affection which ultimately crippled him. It was caused by overstrain of nervous energy. Even such a wiry frame as his could not withstand the demands he made of it. At this time his digestion also became deranged. In the abnormally wet summer of 1879 he had a short holiday with Morley in Westmoreland (it was of this summer that Tennyson wrote ' the cuckoo of a joyless June is calling out of doors '), and afterwards took his family to Normandy, leaving them there for a tour through central France. *The Egoist* was published in October, also appearing serially in *The Glasgow Herald* under the title *Sir Willoughby Patterne, The Egoist,* which caused him annoyance with Kegan Paul.

Without a word to me, he sold the right of issue to *The Glasgow Herald,* and allowed them to be guilty of a perversion of my title. I wrote to him my incredulous astonishment. He replied excusing himself with cool incompetency. He will have to learn (he is but young at it) that these things may be done once—not more.

2

Before calling to my aid the critical opinions of others, I will offer a few tentative suggestions about *The Egoist*; for the intuitions of an amateur can sometimes score a lucky hit or indicate something which has been overlooked by the experts. The operations of my mind, however, while approaching this *hors ligne* vintage from the Chateau Meredith vineyards, are not only tentative but positively pusillanimous. The subject itself is a formidable challenge to one's faculties of alertness in wit and acute response to intellectual virtuosity. And I am unable to believe that these requisite qualities have, so far, been conspicuous on my quotation-packed pages. In fact, when I contemplate myself squaring my elbows to discuss this astonishing compression of The Book of Egoism (which Meredith described as the biggest book on earth), I strongly suspect that an oblique light is being cast on me by the Comic Spirit, and can almost imagine that I am overhearing volleys of silvery laughter. For what Meredith put on paper up in his chalet

was something which can claim to be unique in our literature—
something so analytic of human nature that to analyse it seems
absurd—something so durably constructed, so ingeniously
contrived, that one's afterthoughts on it are like a festoon of
cobwebs, seen in the upward ray of the lamp and feebly oscillat-
ing in a faint draught of air from the inane.

Having thus thrown a rickety bridge over the gulf, I must
be bold and cross it. And there, in the Kingdom of Comedy,
I am met by the laughter of reason. 'And this laughter of
reason refreshed', says Meredith, 'is floriferous, like the
magical great gale of the shifty Spring deciding for Summer.'

There, in the famous Prelude * to the story, the Egoist is at
once revealed to us as one

> . . . who would desire to clothe himself at everybody's expense,
> and is of that desire condemned to strip himself stark naked. . . .
> You may as well know him out of hand, as a gentleman of our
> time and country, of wealth and station; a not flexile figure, do
> what we may with him; the humour of whom scarcely dimples
> the surface and is distinguishable but by very penetrative, very
> wicked imps, whose fits of roaring below at some generally
> imperceptible stroke of his quality, have first made the mild
> literary angels aware of something comic in him, when they were
> one and all about to describe the gentleman on the heading of the
> records baldly (where brevity is most complimentary) as a gentle-
> man of family and property, an idol of a decorous island that
> admires the concrete. Imps have their freakish wickedness
> in them to kindle detective vision: malignly do they love to
> uncover ridiculousness in imposing figures. Wherever they
> catch sight of Egoism they pitch their camps, they circle and squat,
> and forthwith they trim their lanterns, confident of the ludicrous
> to come.

Thus, with the author as Chief Imp, we are presented to the
imperishable Baronet with whose epitaph the Prelude ends.

> Through very love of self himself he slew.

But before going any further with him, it seems worth pointing out that Meredith's preparation for his masterpiece was the

---

* Henri Davray, the translator of *The Egoist*, was told by Meredith that
the preface is a series of imitations of various authors he knew. Meredith
read it aloud to Davray, vocally imitating each author, and Davray said
the effect was astounding.

writing of *An Essay on Comedy*. It can only have been through the thought he gave to the Idea of Comedy that he approached Sir Willoughby and resolved to make him the theme of a grand comic drama. Molière had been much in his mind, with his deeply conceived displaying of imposture, and it was on Molière that he was modelling his treatment of the Egoist, with Menander and Terence as a subsidiary influence. Had he been a dramatist, *The Egoist* would have come to us as a play—probably one of the most brilliant in the English language. In any case it has more of the unity of play-writing in it than any other of his novels. All the ingredients of a highly perfected comedy are there. I must admit to a feeling that I could do without many of the analytic disquisitions; for the action of the story is condensed, controlled, and self-explanatory. Also it has the sense of illusion, which he so often and so deliberately denied us, though it is an illusion of being in a world which has never existed outside of Meredith's mind. Soon after completing it, Meredith wrote :—

> I finished a 3 vol. work rapidly, and as it comes mainly from the head and has nothing to kindle imagination, I thirsted to be rid of it soon after conception, and it became a struggle in which health suffered.

I find this difficult to understand, because *The Egoist*, like all good books, gives a constant impression that the author was enjoying himself with his material. The atmosphere of it is comfortable,—more so, I think, than in his previous works. Patterne Hall itself, of course, is a background of palatial cosiness; all the amenities of affluence are there. But the writing is also comfortable and luxuriously leisurely.

One feels that in this book he really knew what he was setting out to do, and had his constructive outline clearly defined from the start. The actual narrative flows coherently along; there are no subservient plots to distract one from the central story; there are far fewer characters than was usual with him; and, owing to the grand comedy being enacted wholly in Patterne Hall and its neighbourhood, there is a pleasant sense of the action being well inside the frame of a stage setting. Above all, there is the ever-conspicuous figure of the Baronet to hold it all together. If I were asked to coin a key-word for the story, that

word would be *fondle*. For while the author performs his
relentless surgical operation on the psychology of Sir Willoughby
he somehow does it fondlingly—one is reminded of Walton's
instruction for baiting a hook with a frog, ' in so doing, use
him as though you loved him '. He tells us that the Egoist
inspires pity. But the streak of cruelty in Meredith is manifest
in his chuckling delight as he assiduously contrives the utter
discomfiture of the self-deluded gentleman.

Up to a point the Comedy is deliciously amusing. Not until
we are three parts of the way through does the deep seriousness
underlying it become apparent. The state of Sir Willoughby
then arrives at something like tragic intensity, comparable, one
feels, to the humiliation of Malvolio (though the latter is in a
different category of Egoism). We are shown the heart of the
Egoist, and it is not a spectacle for silvery laughter. It is the
climax of the comic drama of the suicide. ' Through very
love of self himself he slew.' For this is the tragedy of Egoism
in all its personifications. Egoists commit suicide by their
behaviour toward those whose love and admiration they
hungrily covet, and whom they desire to dominate. And
Meredith makes us fully aware of the purgatory they inflict on
themselves and others. Sir Willoughby is shown as ' Laocoon
of his own serpents, struggling in the muscular net of constric-
tions he flung around himself '. His pride is as a dagger in his
breast. He drinks self-pity like a poison. Rejected by the
girl he had appointed to be his bride, he turns to one whom he
had twice jilted, and is by her rejected. These women were
' expected to worship him and uphold him for whatsoever he
might be, without any estimation of qualities. . . . The
devouring male Egoist prefers them as inanimate pure-metal
precious vessels, fresh from the hands of the artificer, for him to
walk away with hugging, call his own, drink of, and fill and
drink of, and forget that he stole them '. ' Possession without
obligation to the object possessed ' is the felicity he demands.
And this, let it be said, is equally true of the female of the
Species, which is reputed to be deadlier than the male.

All of us are in some degree Egoists; but a measure of
redemption can be gained by admitting it, and by acting on that
admission.

To return to the literary aspects of the book; in style it is, of course, the first of the series which were written in the essentially Meredithian manner. And I suppose it to be generally regarded as the most masterly of his achievements. When comparing it with his previous novels, one finds that he has emerged from all his immaturities and acquired a mellowness which pervades both the material and his treatment of it. Rather to my surprise, I find myself discovering that it has affinities with *Richard Feverel*. For one thing, Sir Austin Feverel is an anticipation of Sir Willoughby Patterne. He is a study in Egoism, on a smaller scale, just as ' The Great Mel ' is an adumbration of the full-length flamboyancy of Richmond Roy. Sir Austin has an autocratic System for his son; Sir Willoughby was a System in himself—a walking and posturing System of self-love which planned to impose its will on everyone around him. But the main resemblance—though it may be a fanciful one—seems to be that one is breathing the same air at Raynham Abbey as at Patterne Hall. The two books are like different vintages of the same wine. They have the same flavour, though the '78 vintage is a more matured one than the '58. In *The Egoist*, of course, the writing is far more pointed and exquisite, the style has shed its occasional lumpiness, and there is a sustained air of ease and accomplishment. *Richard Feverel* is a young man's experiment, and therein lies a good deal of its attractiveness. In *The Egoist*, the maestro controls his orchestra with a life-learned ability to obtain his effects of tone and interpretation.

It is not my intention to discuss the characters of the book in detail—my main interest being the background of Meredith's mind and his art as a writer. In this connexion I cast an inquiring eye on Dr. Middleton, the father of Sir Willoughby's betrothed, Clara (who is one of the brightest and most beautiful figures of an English girl in our literature). He is described as follows:—

> The Rev. Doctor was a fine old picture; a specimen of art peculiarly English; combining in himself piety and epicurism, learning and gentlemanliness, with good room for each and a seat at one another's table: for the rest, a strong man, an athlete in his youth, a keen reader of facts and no reader of persons, genial, a giant at a task, a steady worker besides, but easily discomposed.

There, if one omits the piety and credits him with being a good reader of persons, is something not far from a representation of Thomas Love Peacock.

The leisurely promenade up and down the lawn in anticipation of the dinner-bell, was Dr. Middleton's evening pleasure. He walked as one who had formerly danced (in Apollo's time and the young God Cupid's), elastic on the muscles of the calf and foot, bearing his broad iron-grey head in grand elevation. The hard labour of the day approved the cooling exercise and the crowning refreshments of French cookery and wines of known vintages. He was happy at that hour in dispensing wisdom or nugae to his hearers, like the Western sun, whose habit it is, when he is fairly treated, to break out in quiet splendours, which by no means exhaust his treasury. . . . Dr. Middleton misdoubted the future as well as the past of the man who did not, in becoming gravity, exult to dine. That man he deemed unfit for this world and the next. An example of the good fruit of temperance, he had a comfortable pride in his digestion, and his political sentiments were attuned by his veneration of the Powers rewarding virtue.

One has only to compare this with the photograph of Peacock as an old man to be assured that Meredith had him clearly in mind. So little having been recorded of their relationship (one of the most significant in Meredith's literary career) one is grateful for this evidence that he remembered him with genial appreciativeness. Peacock, of course, was a complex character, and Dr. Middleton is only drawn from the outside as a simplified type. But Peacock, in his later years, was a great reader of Greek, and one of his biographers has stated that dinner was a ceremonious occasion with him and it was then that he talked most freely and displayed his quaint erudition. And like Dr. Middleton, he combined classical scholarship with a prodigious connoisseurship of vintages. It is the voice of Peacock that we hear in the Rev. Doctor's eulogy of great wines:—

Hocks, too, have compassed age. I have tasted senior Hocks. Their flavours are as a brook of many voices; they have depth also. Senatorial Port! we say. We cannot say that of any other wine. Port is deep-sea deep. It is in its flavour deep; mark the difference. It is like a classic tragedy, organic in conception. An ancient Hermitage has the light of the antique;

the merit that it can grow to an extreme age; a merit. Neither of Hermitage nor of Hock can you say that it is the blood of those long years, retaining the strength of youth with the wisdom of age. To Port for that! Port is our noblest legacy! Observe, I do not compare the wines; I distinguish their qualities. Let them live together for our enrichment; they are not rivals like the Idœan Three. Were they rivals, a fourth would challenge them. Burgundy has great genius. It does wonders within its period; it does all except to keep up in the race; it is short-lived. An aged Burgundy runs with a beardless Port. I cherish the fancy that Port speaks the sentences of wisdom, Burgundy sings the inspired Ode. Or put it, that Port is the Homeric hexameter, Burgundy the Pindaric dithyramb.

One could quote at greater length from this Chapter, which is one of Meredith's ripest exhibitions in the Pavonian vein. The extent of Peacock's influence on him is not easy to diagnose. One can say that it is occasionally observable,—less, perhaps, than that of Carlyle. But what made him significant was the contact of his mind with Meredith's when it was undeveloped and impressionable. He was the source and originator of what is known as Meredithian wit, though far below him as an intellectual force. The 'white headed old worldling', as Thackeray called him, was the sign-post which directed him to the road which led to *The Egoist*. And his definition of Sentiment as 'canting egotism in the mask of refined feeling' might well have come from Meredith's note-book for one of his novels. The price he paid for marrying the wrong woman in Peacock's daughter was a heavy one. Yet, through the mysterious workings of circumstance, his association with that family resulted in *Modern Love* and prompted him, in style and satiric outlook, to the right use of his powers. Nothing is gained by speculating on what would have happened had he never known them. But it is likely that we should have been the losers. That Meredith, at twenty-one, should have achieved a close relationship with Peacock must be regarded as one of those infrequent and felicitous occurrences which appear to have been arranged by some celestial Academic Committee.

3

The Egoist was reviewed three times by W. E. Henley, who had become—with his friend Stevenson, and James Thomson—one of Meredith's most active propagandists. After his death, Meredith wrote of Henley that ' as critic he had the rare combination of enthusiasm and wakeful judgment. He was one of the main supports of good literature in our time.' In 1879, at the age of thirty, he earned this tribute, for he wrote finely about *The Egoist* in *The Athenaeum*, *The Academy*, and *The Pall Mall Gazette*, qualifying his commendations with uncompromising criticisms, which were taken in good part by the author, who remarked, in a letter to Stevenson :—

His praise is high indeed, but happily he fetches me a good lusty clout o' the head now and again, by which I am surprisingly well braced and my balance is restored. Otherwise praise like that might operate as the strong waters do upon the lonely savage unused to such a rapture.

His trenchant statement of the obvious objections to Meredith as a novelist left very little for anyone else to say.

Like Shakespere, he is a man of genius who is a clever man as well; and he seems to prefer his cleverness to his genius. . . . It is a wilful hurly-burly of wit, wisdom, fancy, freakishness, irony, analysis, humour, and affectation; and you catch yourself wishing, as you might over Shakespere, that Mr. Meredith were merely a great artist, and not so diabolically ingenious and sympathetic and well-informed and intellectual as he is. . . . There is infinitely too much of statement and reflection, of aphorism and analysis, of epigram and fantasy, of humours germane and yet not called for; so that in the end the impression produced is not the impersonal impression that was to be desired, and the literary egoism of the author of Sir Willoughby Patterne appears to overshadow the amorous egoism of Sir Willoughby himself, and to become the predominating fact of the book. . . . His pages so teem with fine sayings, and magniloquent epigrams, and gorgeous images, and fantastic locutions, that the mind would welcome dulness as a glad relief. He is tediously amusing; he is brilliant to the point of being obscure; his helpfulness is so extravagant as to worry and confound. His ingenuity and intelligence are always misleading him into treating mere episodes as solemnly and elaborately as a main incident; he is ever ready to discuss, to ramble, to theorize, to dogmatize, to indulge himself in a little irony, or a little reflection, or a little artistic mis- demeanour of some sort. But other novelists have done these things before him, and have been none the less popular, and are actually none the less readable. None, however, has pushed the foppery of style and intellect to such a point as Mr. Meredith. Not unfrequently he writes page after page of English as ripe and sound and unaffected as heart could wish; and you can but impute to wantonness and recklessness the splendid impertinences that ensue elsewhere. To read him at the rate of two or three chapters a day is to have a sincere and hearty admiration for him, and a devout anxiety to forget his defects and make much of his merits. But they are few who can read a novel on such terms as these; and to read Mr. Meredith straight off is to have an indigestion of epigram, and to be incapable of distinguishing good from bad.

Henley's summary of Meredith's qualities and defects (afterward revised and printed in his volume of *Views and Reviews*) is a curious composite of panegyric and disparagement. With one hand he does what has just been quoted; with the other he proclaims his best work as worthy to rank with the greatest. One's final impression, however, is that Henley admired him too much to be able to forgive his faults. ' When we are clever enough ', he says, ' we are enchanted by his results ', which seems a poor compliment to one whom he has previously described as having a noble sense of the dignity of art and the responsibilities of the artist.

He will set down nothing that is to his mind unworthy to be recorded; his treatment of his material is distinguished by the presence of an intellectual passion (as it were) that makes what- ever he does considerable and deserving of attention and respect. But. . . . [All his praises lead to buts, and those buts are more like bludgeons than modifications.] The texture of his expression must be stiff with allusion, or he deems it ill spun; there must be something antic in his speech, or he cannot believe he is addressing himself to the Immortals; he has praised with perfect under- standing the lucidity, the elegance, the ease, of Molière, and yet his aim in art (it would appear) is to be Molière's antipodes, and to vanquish by congestion, clottedness, an anxious and determined dandyism of form and style.

And so on. All this is most unpalatable to me, who am no critic, but a tolerable appreciator. Incapable of pouring forth such penetrative comments, my answer to Henley would be nothing more illuminating than ' I must admit that I sometimes find Meredith rather heavy going ', or words to that effect.

At this point, however, some rejoinder is required, and I will conclude my orgy of quotation with the following extract from a masterly essay on *The Egoist* by Orlo Williams, written forty-five years later than Henley's.

To his readers of any particular moment, whether they be few or many, Meredith's reputation may safely be left. He demands of them education, the faculty of steady reflection, an interest in ideas rather than incidents and a somewhat abnormal promptitude in following metaphor. He gives them a great deal in return. If it be true that the psychological effect of great art is the organization of good impulses in the percipient, then Meredith's art is great, for the impulses which it organizes are those of liberty, enthusiasm, healthy-mindedness, alertness, self-discipline and wise laughter at folly. He was a penetrating reader of human motives and a keen critic of outworn dogmas. Tyranny, pedantry and sloth of mind or body were abhorrent to him, and it was to lashing these and encouraging their opposites that he united his analytical power and his poetic vision. In the name of Comedy he was a moralist, but he gave his morals the form of art. Many of the causes for which he fought have triumphed since his day; in fact, the state of society which excited his irony is as extinct as the Austrian domination of Italy. Yet the art remains, with its shining virtues and its obvious defects. His defects may repel, but there is surely enough, in his major works alone, to outweigh, if not to cancel, any just repulsion. His frequent over-emphasis and boisterous flights of a peculiar fancy, his exaggerated dislike for the obvious and the trite, his faulty ear for the cadences of English prose, an occasional grossness or want of fine taste, and a technique in dialogue which produces an effect of unreality, even, sometimes, of absurdity—these are the main heads of legitimate blame. We need not blink them if we remember that, like Carlyle, like Lamb and—one might truly say—like Shakespeare, he was so compounded as necessarily to be a mannerist. His mental progresses were abnormal, to an extent of which he, of course, was quite unconscious. He did not willingly torture our English tongue, nor deliberately intend to daze our minds with fantasies of elliptical imagery and irritate us with that somewhat garish verbal repartee which figured for him as ' wit,' preferably Celtic. The very gifts which gave him originality and an individual coign of critical vantage made him also, at times, volcanically obscure, bombastic and difficult of comprehension. However much we may regret his projection of his peculiar self into his work, it is of little use to protest against it or state it as a flat condemnation. It was inevitable. Moreover, if Meredith's prose is often involved, difficult and inharmonious, his thought is not obscure. A little patience will always find the thread, which is never trivial or unworthy. But he was a rhapsodist as well as a thinker, and one must hear and see the rhapsodist. The face and the voice of George Meredith, if we had known them, would have made many a rough place smooth.

For which I can only say ' Thank you ', wishing that I had written it myself.

CHAPTER THIRTEEN

In 1879 there appeared a book by Princess von Racowitza, giving an account of her love affair with Lassalle, the famous German Social Democrat, a stormy episode which had ended, fifteen years before, in his being killed in a duel with the man whom she afterwards married.

Out of this material, Meredith made a short novel which might almost be termed a free translation or transcript, for in the outline of the story and its main incidents he follows *Meine Beziehungen zu Ferdinand Lassalle* closely, accepting the accuracy of her apologia, although its reliability has since been questioned.

For the moment, however, I prefer to consider the book independently of its historical sources. I read *The Tragic Comedians* for the first time when I was about twenty-five and had no critical faculty whatever. After the manner of the young, I read it 'for the story', skating blithely over the reflective and analytical passages, though regardful of my responsibility to the whole as a piece of serious literature which would improve my mind. Never having been to Germany or Switzerland, I was unable to visualise the backgrounds or even dimly respond to the atmosphere of foreign society. I did not know that the story had been taken from 'real life', though Meredith informed me of it in a short Prelude (written in such enigmatic language that I failed to make head or tail of it). I had never heard of Lassalle, and should have been much surprised if I had been told that 'Ironsides' (with whom Alvan describes his having had an interview) was Bismarck. In fact, I knew nothing about anything, except that I felt it my duty to read as much of Meredith as I could, having recently bought the library edition of his complete works.

Had I been asked what I thought of it, I should probably have said that I hadn't enjoyed it at all, meaning that it was 'frightfully powerful and all that' but unpleasantly perturbing and full of bits I couldn't comprehend. The people didn't seem quite real; half-way through the book (I was thankful that there were only two hundred pages), the love affair began to go wrong; and Alvan's excruciating mental experiences in the second half were like a wild dream. No doubt it was all very magnificent and impressive and profound. But Meredith, I thought, must have got terribly wrought up when he wrote it. It wasn't my idea of Comedians, even if they *were* tragic ones! On the first page he compared Human Nature to a wandering ship with a drunken pilot, a mutinous crew, and an angry captain. I remembered that afterwards, because it made me *see* something (possibly *Treasure Island*). But my mind did not take the words in as having any significance except the visual image they evoked (almost certainly pirates).

Reading the book a second time for my present purpose, I find that my crude reactions to it were excusable. The story is finely told, and its painfulness was unavoidable. But it is presented in such a way as to batter and fatigue one's mind. There is no relaxation of the strained and strenuous style of narration. It is the equivalent of a gloomy and forcible play which contains no light relief. The effect is more than a sensitive reader can be expected to endure—an assault on the nervous system. After finishing it I felt that I needed an evening with *Cranford* or *Emma* to restore my serenity. The following fragments, from the second half of the book, may illustrate my meaning.

> She replied, in an anguish over the chilling riddle of his calmness: ' I will ', but sprang out of that obedient consent, fearful of over-acting her part of slave to him before her mother, in a ghastly apprehension of the part he was playing to the same audience.

> She became swayed about like a castaway in soul, until her distinguishing of his mad recklessness in the challenge of a power greater than his own grew present with her as his personal cruelty to the woman who had flung off everything, flung herself on the tempestuous deeps, on his behalf.

> He started himself into busy frenzies to reach to her, already indifferent to the means, and waxing increasingly reckless as he fed on his agitation. . . . Why, then, had he let her out of his grasp? The horrid echoed interrogation flashed a hideous view of the woman.

> He lost sight of her in the prodigious iniquity covering her sex with a cowl of night, and it was what women are, what women

will do, the one and all alike simpering simulacra that men find them to be, soulless, clogs on us, blood-suckers! until a feature of the particular sinner peeped out on him, and brought the fresh agony of a reminder of his great-heartedness.

She ran out to the shade of the garden walls to be by herself and in the air, and she read; and instantly her own letter to the baroness crashed sentence upon sentence, in retort, springing up with the combative instinct of a beast, to make discord of the stuff she read, and deride it. Twice she went over the lines with this defensive accompaniment; then they laid octopus-limbs on her. The writing struck chill as a glacier cave.

One cannot help wondering what Turgenev (that consummate artist in impersonal delineation of passion) would have thought of *The Tragic Comedians*, whose emotions exposed themselves with such violence through the medium of Meredith's mind when grappling with their fantastical and lurid catastrophe. Their acts, he wrote, were incredible. But he does not make them credible to me by all this convulsive vehemence. Biographically identified with him as I am, I feel moved to speculate on his mental condition as he sat up in the chalet with his imaginations of Lassalle and Helen von Dönniges. What possessed him to make this unrestrained—almost daemonic—demonstration about them? One explanation is that he needed a subject for another novel. And in the Racowitza autobiography he found one which needed no invention of plot or characters. But this does not explain the phenomenon of his paroxysmal writing and the clenched and overstrung quality which pervades the later chapters. He admired Lassalle and resented strongly, as many people did, his lamentable sacrifice for the sake of a shallow girl. And after the lighter comedy of *The Egoist* he may have felt that he needed a heroic figure and an elemental conflict of flesh and spirit. I suspect the book of having been a pot-boiler, for an abridged version of it began to appear in *The Fortnightly* in October, 1880, so it must have been finished in little more than six months. It shows no sign of hasty composition; the construction is clear, and the workmanship of the writing shows the usual concentrated effort. The earlier chapters, though overloaded with interpolations of the type to which Henley objected, make quite pleasant reading. It is when the climax begins to develop that the strain on one's nerves becomes distressing. But this overwrought effect, it will be said, was integral to the narrative. It was necessary for Meredith to work himself up to a savage frenzy while dramatising the havocked mind of Alvan. Nevertheless I am still wondering why the performance seems somehow abnormal, like a symphony scored with diabolic discords.

The most likely explanation which occurs to me is that it was a case where the family doctor should have been in consultation with Mrs. Meredith, urging a complete rest and change of scene. In these tormented pages I see a man whose health was beginning to fail him, a man driving his brain through haggard exertions to the limit of its powers of recuperation. A tired writer of fifty-two had no business to be wrecking his constitution like this. But Meredith was incapable of sparing himself, though he could tell one of his correspondents, ' you have youth; take my warning not to undermine it with the pick and blasting powder of pen and ink '. And so, in *The Tragic Comedians*, we see an artificial vitality superseding the rich impetus of his earlier work, and the spontaneous aliveness forsaking him. The brilliant brain was losing its sap. The mannerisms were becoming rigid. The sterility of expertly contrived writing was already apparent. Here and there one finds quotable passages, but they are not quite the real thing.

> Morning swam on the lake in her beautiful nakedness, a wedding of white and blue, of purest white and bluest blue. Alvan crossed the island bridges when the sun had sprung on his shivering fair prey, to make the young fresh Morning rosy, and was glittering along the smooth lake-waters. . . .
>
> Conjure up your vision of Italy. Remember the meaning of Italian light and colour: the clearness, the luminous fulness, the thoughtful shadows. Mountain and wooded headland are solid, deep to the eye, spirit-speaking to the mind. They throb. You carve shapes of Gods out of that sky, the sea, those peaks.

One must, however, allow for the fact that he was, in this book, editing as well as fictionising. His imagination was hampered by writing about people who had already invented themselves in a compelling and romantic love story. And, little as I like it, *The Tragic Comedians* will always find readers to admire its vivid intensity and emotional complexity.

CHAPTER FOURTEEN

THE TRAGIC COMEDIANS was published in December, 1880. His next book, which appeared in June, 1883, was *Poems and Lyrics of the Joy of Earth*. His letters during this period contain references to his bad state of health, which prevented him from making any progress with *Diana of the Crossways*, though he seems to have attempted work on it at the end of 1881. Poetry came easier than prose, and bedevilled him for it, he wrote. In March of that year he had written to Cotter Morison that the dreadful curse of Verse was on him, and had been for two months, and in July he told Maxse that he had been writing much verse. What he called ' the curse of Verse ' must have produced *The Lark Ascending*, which was in *The Fortnightly* for May, *Phoebus with Admetus* having appeared in *Macmillan's Magazine* in December, 1880.

The history of this volume, which can be called one of the landmarks of 19th-Century poetry, was peculiar. Twenty-one years had passed since *Modern Love*, which Browning considered a finer achievement than any of the novels. Yet Meredith was obliged to publish the new volume at his own expense, with full expectation of losing money on it. He did some grumbling about it in March, 1883, to Maxse, who was always strongly interested in his poetic productions. (The *Modern Love* volume was dedicated to him.)

I confess with shame that I am at work correcting preparatory to bringing out a volume of poems. . . . I ask myself why I should labour, and for the third time, pay to publish the result, with a certainty of being yelled at, and haply spat upon, for my pains. And still I do it. At heart, it is plain, I must have a remainder of esteem for our public; or I have now the habit of composition, which precipitates to publishing. I scorn myself for my folly. Where he can get no audience a spouting Homer would merit the Cap and Bells.

Ten days after publication he wrote again to Maxse:—

> I am informed that my little book is moving, yet expect a con-
> stricted bulk to be soon bellowing at me from stagnation that I
> was once more a fool to publish verse.

I have never seen a copy of the first issue of *Poems and Lyrics
of the Joy of Earth*, so cannot specify the defects which have made
it a collector's curiosity. As usual, there were some misprints,
but there must have been much else to complain of, and a
month later Meredith announces that ' Macmillan is printing
it again, at his cost, in disgust of the slipshod style of the first
issue '. This second issue ' satisfied the demand ' for another
eleven years. Its reception by the critics was respectful but
impercipient. Augustly anonymous, Watts-Dunton, in a long
and diffuse review in *The Athenaeum*, found many of the lines
rugged, harsh, and flinty, and summarised the qualities of the
volume as ' manliness and intellectual vigour, combined with
a remarkable picturesqueness '. He did not mention *Love in
the Valley*. It was left for Mark Pattison to describe it as
' one of the most remarkable of the volumes of verse which
have been put out during the last few years '. This eminent
man would have done better to have left it at that. But he
proceeded to refer to the previous *Modern Love* volume as ' a little
venture of the usual minor poetry class ', and followed this up
by remarking that ' *Love in the Valley* does not rise in general
conception and design above the average level of the minor
poet ', a comment which causes me to exclaim, like Archdeacon
Grantley after his first visit to Mrs. Proudie, when he raised his
hat with one hand and passed the other somewhat violently
over his now grizzled locks, ' Good heavens! ' One can only
add that Mark Pattison was in feeble health and died almost
exactly a year after his review adorned *The Academy*.

It was, by the way, the parrot of Mrs. Mark Pattison which
was heard exclaiming, after being plucked by the monkey,
' I've been having a devil of a time! '

Let us now put ourselves in Pattison's place—or rather in the
place of a methodical reader of that time who opens the book
at page one and is confronted by *The Woods of Westermain*.

I.

Enter these enchanted woods,
  You who dare.
Nothing harms beneath the leaves
More than waves a swimmer cleaves.
Toss your heart up with the lark,
Foot at peace with mouse and worm,
  Fair you fare.
Only at a dread of dark
Quaver, and they quit their form:
Thousand eyeballs under hoods
Have you by the hair.
Enter these enchanted woods,
  You who dare.

II.

Here the snake across your path
Stretches in his golden bath:
Mossy-footed squirrels leap
Soft as winnowing plumes of Sleep:
Yaffles on a chuckle skim
Low to laugh from branches dim:
Up the pine, where sits the star,
Rattles deep the moth-winged jar.
Each has business of his own;
But should you distrust a tone,
  Then beware.
Shudder all the haunted roods,
All the eyeballs under hoods
  Shroud you in their glare.
Enter these enchanted woods,
  You who dare.

Now what the reader might expect would be two or three
more stanzas of similar length, wherein the poet explains and
develops his theme, which is that human life—allegorically—
is a haunted forest, beautiful and homely to those who have no
fear, but madly terrible to those who ' quaver at a dread of
dark '. But Meredith was an athletic versifier; a stroll in
the fields was always liable to become a twenty-mile walk.
And his superabundance of intellectual energy needed an outlet.

The third section elaborates his idea in a hundred and fifty lines.

> You of any well that springs
> May unfold the heaven of things. . . .
> Drink the sense the notes infuse,
> You a larger self will find:
> Sweetest fellowship ensues
> With the creatures of your kind.

The thinker and the novelist are getting the upper hand of the poet in him. In a fourth section of three hundred lines they take charge. Ethical proverbs and precepts hurry on one another's heels. Shorthand metaphor becomes bewildering and breathless.

> Ended is begun, begun
> Ended, quick as torrents run.
> Young Impulsion spouts to sink;
> Luridness and lustre link;
> 'Tis your come and go of breath;
> Mirrored pants the Life, the Death;
> Each of either reaped and sown:
> Rosiest rosy waves to crone.

Here, indeed, is compactness of phrase. But the methodical reader finds the drift of it difficult to understand.

> Wisdom throbbing shall you see
> Central in complexity.

The rapid movement of the short lines rushes him off his mental legs. The tempo is *allegro vivace*; the congestion and concinnity of ideas compel him to play it bar by bar, with long intervals for reflection. He cannot say of it—

> Music have you there to feed
> Simplest and most soaring need.

All he can do is to admit that it is an astonishing feat of intellectual virtuosity. Personally I regard it as a Meredithian masterpiece, reserving the right to consider it redundant when judged by the standard of sustained lyricism of the highest order. But to complain of too much thought in Meredith is much the same as to demand more thought and less rhetoric and rhapsody in Swinburne. One can only wish that the thought had been more equally apportioned, and that Meredith had been endowed with a more sensitive awareness of his audience. In *The Woods of Westermain* he tells us many wonderful and memorable things, but the impact of his mind is, I think, somewhat overwhelming. It epitomises the main objection I have to his method, a wilful disregarding of the visualising capacity of the ordinary mortal, who protests against being pelted with an overplus of imagery and subjected to an immoderate exploitation of acrobatic metaphor. On the other hand, the pitch of intensity is amazingly well maintained, and description and allegory are superbly combined and interwoven throughout. To realise how remarkable in its strenuousness the poem is, one has only to compare it with some of Emerson's—for example, his *Woodnotes*. Meredith preferred Emerson's philosophy to Carlyle's, and there can be no doubt that *The Woods of Westermain* shows his influence, though the New Englander's muse was nursery-rhyme-like in comparison. (Meredith described Emerson's poetry as ' an Artesian well; the bore is narrow, but the water is pure and sweet '.)

> Laurel crowns cleave to deserts,
> And power to him who power exerts.
> Hast not thy share? On wingèd feet,
> Lo! it rushes thee to meet;
> And all that Nature made thy own,
> Floating in air or pent in stone,
> Will rive the hills and swim the sea,
> And like thy shadow, follow thee.

That, of course, is by Emerson. But the resemblance is perceptible. And I could quote many passages which show similarity to Meredith, though expressing a less systematic attitude to Nature. (Meredith subjects man to the law of things, whereas Emerson subjects the laws of things to the Universal Soul which speaks in man.)

> You must love the light so well
> That no darkness will seem fell

is an Emersonian percept, and there are others in *The Woods of Westermain*.

There are certain poems in the English language of which it can be said with conviction that they are matchless of their

kind.   To take a few examples—the first that occur to me—
it can be said of Andrew Marvell's *To His Coy Mistress*, Wordsworth's *Happy Warrior*, Tennyson's *Ulysses*, Browning's *Abt
Vogler*, and Christina Rossetti's *The Convent Threshold*.   I say
it now of *The Lark Ascending*, a sustained lyric of one hundred
and twenty lines which never for a moment falls short of the
effect aimed at, soars up and up with the song it imitates, and
unites inspired spontaneity with a demonstration of effortless
technical ingenuity.   At a first reading it may seem rather
breath-taking.   As usual, Meredith demanded a *tour de force*
of mental concentration.   But on this fortunate occasion he
was so completely successful that one has only to re-read the
poem a few times to become aware of its perfection.   The lark-
song, he says, is

> The song seraphically free
> From taint of personality,

and he himself, in the first eighty-four lines, comes as near as is
humanly possible to disproving his assertion that

> Was never voice of ours could say
> Our inmost in the sweetest way,
> Like yonder voice aloft, and link
> All hearers in the song they drink. . . .
> We want the key of his wild note
> Of truthful in a tuneful throat.

But to write of such a poem is to be reminded of its incomparable
aloofness from the ploddings of the journeyman critic, however
much he may be uplifted with the lark,

> As he to silence nearer soars,
> Extends the world at wings and dome,
> More spacious making more our home,
> Till lost on his aërial rings
> In light, and then the fancy sings.

Phoebus with Admetus offers itself more easily for exposition
because it is manifestly a metrical exercise—a piece of studied
versifying.   One's first impression is of something more
mannered than poetical.   Then one realises that the form fits
the subject, which is the legend of how Phoebus Apollo was
exiled by his father Zeus for having slain the Cyclops, and

condemned to serve a term on earth, tending the flocks of King Admetus of Thessaly, bringing to his land mighty yields of wool and corn and grapes. It is the tale of the shepherds and herdsmen who had known the divine guest and the season of plenty he created for them.

> When by Zeus relenting the mandate was revoked,
>   Sentencing to exile the bright Sun-God,
> Mindful were the ploughmen of who the steer had yoked,
>   Who: and what a track showed the upturned sod!
> Mindful were the shepherds, as now the noon severe
>   Bent a burning eyebrow to brown evetide,
> How the rustic flute drew the silver to the sphere,
>   Sister of his own, till her rays fell wide.

The effect of studied versifying or thought-out deliberation is produced by the triple hammer-beat in alternate lines. It is a master-stroke. Without it the poem would lose much of its character, though typically Meredithian in epithet and imagery. For me, *Phoebus with Admetus* has always had a magical quality of classic beauty (the words are trite but I can find no others). And one reason why I rank it so high among his poems is the absence of that didactic element which in the long run becomes too insistent. It is purified poetry, indirectly stimulating. His shepherds and herdsmen do not moralise about Apollo or about Mother Earth. They are magnificently content to conclude with

> You with shelly horns, rams! and, promontory goats,
>   You whose browsing beards dip in coldest dew!
> Bulls, that walk the pastures in kingly-flashing coats!
>   Laurel, ivy, vine, wreathed for feasts not few!
> You that build the shade-roof, and you that court the rays,
>   You that leap besprinkling the rock stream-rent:
> He has been our fellow, the morning of our days!
>   Us he chose for housemates, and this way went.

Austere, invigorating, and lit by poetic vision, it has the same indestructible originality as the *Ballad of Past Meridian*, which precedes it in the 1883 volume. It gives me the same sense of uniqueness as Browning's *A Grammarian's Funeral*. The two poems, of course, bear no resemblance to one another, except that both have a strong rhythmic beat. Browning's imagination was in Germany, ' shortly after the Revival of Learning '. He was, I think, the only other 19th Century poet who could conceivably have written *Phoebus with Admetus*, though one cannot put one's finger on any point where their minds and methods show similarity.

More exquisite, and suffused with an unwonted tenderness, is the companion-piece to *Phoebus*, the tale of *Melampus* the good physician to whom the woodland creatures in reward that he

> loving them all,
> Among them walk'd, as a scholar who reads a book,

taught their lore of medicine, and where to find the herbs of healing. The Greek legend that he obtained the power of understanding the language of birds, after his ears had been licked by some young snakes which he had preserved from death, is used to illustrate the proper relation of the highest human life to the life of animals and insects, and of nature in general.

The metre is a modified Swinburnian one, as may be seen when one compares

> Unknown sweet spirit, whose vesture is soft in spring,
> In summer splendid, in autumn pale as the wood

(from *A Nympholept*) with Meredith's

> Divinely thrilled was the man, exultingly full,
> As quick well-waters that come of the heart of the earth.

This line—which can be called a lilting Alexandrine—prompted him to an easeful style of expression which one finds more comfortable than the staccato emphasisings of *The Woods of Westermain*. Melampus moves, through fifteen eight-line stanzas, to a leisurely music. The poet has his surface intellect well under control; richness of thought is everywhere apparent, but it is transmuted thought, serving transmuted nature-observation. The poem is as gracious as its subject. We are in a sunlight-chequered woodland; silence is accompanied by a hum of insects, quickened by occasional bird notes, or the chuckle and gurgle of brook and runnel. Woodland smells are there, pungent from trodden plants that grow in marshy places. All this is implied in the substance of a poem which is as Wordsworthian in feeling as anything Meredith ever did, while exemplifying his divergence from Wordsworth's impassioned contemplation of nature to an acceptance of the view of nature offered by modern science—an eternal activity that overflows with individual life. The good physician Melampus is the outcome of Meredith the naturalist in the woods of Surrey, studying the lumped or antlered mosses, watching hedgehogs ' curl at a touch their snouts in a ball ' and spiders ' cast their web between bramble and thorny hook ', taking counsel of the growths of earth, seeing nature and song allied.

> For him the woods were a home and gave him the key
> Of knowledge, thirst for their treasures in herbs and flowers.
> The secrets held by the creatures nearer than we
> To earth he sought, and the link of their life with ours:
> And where alike we are, unlike where, and the veined
> Division, veined parallel, of a blood that flows
> In them, in us, from the source by man unattained
> Save marks he well what the mystical woods disclose.

Here we find, as elsewhere, ' that intimate interpenetration of earth and man which is the essence of Meredith's unique imaginative vision . . . a philosophy essentially terrestrial, but a philosophy of ascent '. (I am quoting from a fine appreciation by the American critic John Livingston Lowes.)

Earth and Man is the name of the next poem to be examined. It is a mind-testing one; its hundred and fifty-six lines are a formidable exercise in declaimed thinking; a pulpit poem, one might call it, delivered in a church of Free Thought, earnest, uncompromising and strenuous. It has the aspect of a ' great poem ', and Meredith must have intended it to be one of his most impressive. Certainly it is one of the important expressions of his philosophy. But to me, I must confess, it is less significant as poetry than those I have been discussing. He seems to be trying too hard; it is nobly versified, but oppressively didactic. The compression and abundance of thought prevent one's mind from being carried along. Each stanza commands one to halt and think it over. His Muse, after glancing in at the chalet window, became aware that her mysterious aids to imagination and verbal inspiration were being rebuffed by one of his big exhibitions of brain-power and domineering eloquence. He is straining to capture the mystery she holds, but the process of production is not instinctive. He is engaged in a warfare of words on behalf of Earth's ' great venture, Man '.

> And ever that old task
> Of reading what he is and whence he came,
> Whither to go, finds wilder letters flame
> Across her mask. . . .
>
> He builds the soaring spires,
> That sing his soul in stone : of her he draws,
> Though blind to her, by spelling at her laws,
> Her parent fires.
>
> Through him hath she exchanged,
> For the gold harvest-robes, the mural crown,
> Her haggard quarry-features and thick frown
> Where monsters ranged.

' Very fine,' murmurs the Muse, as she vanishes among the fir-trees behind the chalet.

> She hears him, and can hear
> With glory in his gains by work achieved :
> With grief for grief that is the unperceived
> In her so near.

For the Muse is his humanity, and these stanzas are on too abstract a plane for sensitive poetic results to emerge from them. I find myself remembering *Rabbi Ben Ezra*, where Browning humanises the relation of flesh and spirit, of youth and age, in Man.

> For note, when evening shuts,
> A certain moment cuts
> The deed off, calls the glory from the grey :
> A whisper from the west
> Shoots—' Add this to the rest,
> ' Take it and try its worth : here dies another day.'

From that I can get something visual and kindly. But somehow or other I am too weak a vessel for the massive admonitions of *Earth and Man*. I am told ' but that the senses still usurp the station of their issue mind, he would have burst the chrysalis of the blind : as yet he will '. Yes ; all will be well in the mutual relations of Earth and Man, whose genesis is of Earth and whose right temperament toward Life must be the reading of her.

> He, singularly doomed
> To what he execrates and writhes to shun,
> When fire has passed him vapour to the sun,
> And sun relumed,
>
> Then shall the horrid pall
> Be lifted, and a spirit nigh divine,
> ' Live in thy offspring as I live in mine,'
> Will hear her call.

In other and weaker words, I must believe in ' Evolution '. I do—to the best of my ability. But Meredith hasn't, in this poem, contrived to make the procedure palatable. I am acquiescent but browbeaten. His message is that through knowledge of Earth, our mother and instructress, we approach a fuller consciousness of the issues and meanings of life. We must discard 'fables of the Above', and faith in the Invisible of orthodox religion. In one of his sonnets he protests that—

> Our world which for its Babels wants a scourge,
> And for its wilds a husbandman, acclaims
> The crucifix that came of Nazareth.

In the '80s this must have been a startlingly unorthodox assertion. *Earth and Man*, one must add, was a splendidly courageous poem in its day, contradicting as it did the belief in survival after death which was held—and most beautifully expressed—by Tennyson, who ' found the idea of personal extinction unthinkable ', with Browning to back him up. Meredith had always been strongly anti-parsonic, a prejudice which was shared by Maxse. He felt more than tolerant of Bradlaugh, and toward the end of the '70s was in sympathetic communication with G. W. Foote, the propagandist of Free Thought, who, in 1883, was sentenced to a year's imprisonment for blasphemy—' a brave battle, for the best of causes ', he called it. Of ' immortality ', Meredith said, in old age, that he could not conceive it.

Which personality is it which endures? I was one man in youth, and another in middle age. I have never felt the unity of personality running through my life. I have been six different men: six at least.

Those who knew him, however, would have found difficulty in detecting these metamorphoses. He seems to have been consistently recognisable in his outward personality. Anyhow, that is what he said, and I have never seen him accused of saying what he did not mean. In *Earth and Man* he said, with immense emphasis, that the human race can rise to higher things by understanding its Mother Earth. Man must attain to the spiritual through the natural, not through the supernatural. He had said it before, in the 1862 volume, in his *Ode to the Spirit of Earth in Autumn*, had said it through an impassioned apostrophe.

> Great Mother! me inspire
> With faith that forward sets
> But feeds the living fire,
> Faith that never frets
> For vagueness in the form.
> In life, O keep me warm!
> For, what is human grief?
> And what do men desire?
> Teach me to feel myself the tree,
> And not the withered leaf.
> Fixed am I and await the dark to-be.
> And O, green bounteous Earth!
> Bacchante Mother! stern to those
> Who live not in thy heart of mirth;
> Death shall I shrink from, loving thee?
> Into the breast that gives the rose,
> Shall I with shuddering fall?
>
> Earth, the mother of all,
> Moves on her stedfast way,
> Gathering, flinging, sowing.
> Mortals, we live in her day,
> She in her children is growing.

But when he wrote that he could still take a hint from the great-hearted abruptness of Browning. For the *Ode*, though unequal in execution, has a glowing spontaneity and visual richness which cannot be found in *Earth and Man*. Nor can it be found in *The Day of the Daughter of Hades*, a long poem in which the subject is finely handled but the effect marred by

uncomfortable versification.   The metre is that which Matthew
Arnold used several times in unrhymed meditative elegies.

> Charm is the glory which makes
> Song of the poet divine,
> Love is the fountain of charm.
> How without charm wilt thou draw,
> Poet! the world to thy way?

I have chosen this example because it enables me to remark
that Meredith seldom allowed himself to conciliate the world
with charm.   The absence of it is perceptible in *The Day of the
Daughter of Hades,* though the story has poetic beauty and is
vigorously narrated.   It tells of how, in the flowery vale of
Enna, the youth Callistes witnesses the arrival of Persephone
from the underworld to visit her mother Demeter.   She brings
her daughter, Skiageneia, the child of Shadow, who spends her
day of freedom with the enamoured and bewildered Callistes
until her father Pluto comes angrily in his terrible chariot to
fetch her away.

The poem is notably unpauseful, which partly accounts for
one's inability to absorb it with enjoyment.   Not only does it
move at a helter-skelter speed, but the lines run on in long
breathless paragraphs.   And, as is often the case with Meredith, his brain works so rapidly that the words themselves
seem bustled along at a rate which does not allow them to
permeate one's mind with full effect.   Words resent being run
off their legs; Meredith often forgot this, and denied them the
slowness which enables them to do their proper service.   And I
cannot help feeling that an antique legend should be presented
with classic deliberation.   There is, surely, something to be
said for the Tennysonian method, as Meredith was fully aware.
One of his visitors has recorded how he quoted the following
lines as evidence of ' unequalled power of vignetting landscapes
in words '.

> The swimming vapour slopes athwart the glen,
> Puts forth an arm, and creeps from pine to pine,
> And loiters, slowly drawn.   On either hand
> The lawns and meadow-ledges, midway down
> Hang rich in flowers, and far below them roars
> The long brook falling through the clov'n ravine
> In cataract after cataract to the sea.

Controlled visualisation; perfection of word-music; and the flawless tone and texture of a Poussin landscape.

Skiageneia, however, was far quicker on her feet than the mournful Oenone, and the brook was no loiterer either.

> The steeps of the forest she crossed,
> On its dry red sheddings and cones
> Up the paths by roots green-mossed,
> Spotted amber, and old mossed stones.
> Then out where the brook-torrent starts
> To her leap, and from bend to curve
> A hurrying elbow darts
> For the instant-glancing swerve,
> Decisive, with violent will
> In the action formed, like hers,
> The maiden's, ascending; and still
> Ascending, the bud of the furze,
> The broom, and all blue-berried shoots
> Of stubborn and prickly kind,
> The juniper flat on its roots
> The dwarf rhododaphne, behind
> She left, and the mountain sheep
> Far behind, goat, herbage and flower.
> The island was hers, and the deep,
> All heaven, a golden hour.

This, as Charles Lamb remarked of an artist who had unsuccessfully depicted The Garden of the Hesperides, is not the way Poussin would have treated the subject. Even when two lines are read as one, the effect is restless, for the rhythm is jolting and awkward. There is too much energy and too little regard for delicacies of sound. The texture of the verse is hard and aggressive, and this passage is typical of the whole, which amounts to more than six hundred lines.

My opinion is that this metre, when rhymed, is only suited to short lyrics. It is worth pointing out that he used it in one of his short poems, *Change in Recurrence*, which has the charm of compactness, adroit alliteration, and controlled imagery. As a song of the joy of earth, *The Day of the Daughter of Hades* has been ranked among Meredith's finest achievements in verse by two of his most eminent admirers and expositors, Quiller-Couch and G. M. Trevelyan. He himself, as an old man, put it first among all his poems, because it expressed his conception of the right attitude toward the brevity and tragedy of life. This makes me wonder whether, after all, I am an appropriate person to write about him. For I have always preferred brevity to amplitude in poetry. If a poem must be long, I want it to be in the form of a dramatic monologue—subjective utterance rather than impersonal narrative. This one aimed at sustained lyrical and descriptive excitement; the subject demanded it. But I find the mental effort required too exacting.

The 1883 volume contains twenty-five sonnets—almost all that he composed.

> In his hands [wrote Trevelyan in 1906] the sonnet is the vessel always of original thought and pithy expression, and very often of the noblest beauty. Sometimes the eccentricity and carelessness of his powerful utterance seem uncongenial to the traditions of the sonnet, but often those traditions inspire him with the sense of order and of finished art, and force him to employ the weapons of construction and elucidation which it is his grave fault so often to leave in rust.

Very few of them satisfy Rossetti's injunction that the sonnet be ' of its own arduous fulness reverent '. Into most of them he tries to pack too much thought, and the effect is cumbersome. But they contain an epitome of his philosophy and ethics. Even the splendid *Spirit of Shakespeare* is addressed to Mother Earth, whence came ' the honeyed corner at his lips ', and the laugh ' broad as ten thousand beeves at pasture '. There is, however, one—*Lucifer in Starlight*—which holds a place among the greatest sonnets in the language. Miltonic in form, it has the hall-mark of his genius. None but he could have written it. Apart from this my preference is for the concluding lines of *My Theme*, which is otherwise unsatisfactory.

> I say but that this love of Earth reveals
> A soul beside our own to quicken, quell,
> Irradiate, and though ruinous floods uplift.

Those lines mean more to me than many of his longer poems, lock, stock, and barrel.

Of the other poems in this volume, the long and ingenious *Ballad of Fair Ladies in Revolt* should be examined in connexion with Meredith's Feminism. But not here. *The Orchard and*

173

the Heath, written in 1867, is one of his ' Roadside ' pieces, pleasant, but calling for no special comment.

Thus I arrive at *Love in the Valley*, which is one of the very greatest sustained love lyrics in English poetry. And when one has said that, it seems absurd to say any more. It was the supreme inspiration of Meredith's life. It is equally true that it was his supreme achievement in poetic art, for it is designed and executed with consummate artistry. In feeling, it is comparable to nothing else he wrote except the idyll of first love in *Richard Feverel*, with which it is inseparably associated in one's mind. This brings me to its literary history, which is a peculiar one. One might call it a poem which was evolved by felicitous fortuity. The 1851 version was directly suggested —or imitated—from George Darley's almost mawkish *Serenade of a Loyal Martyr*, to which it has a more than metrical resemblance, as may be seen from Darley's first verse.

> Sweet in her green cell the Flower of Beauty slumbers,
>   Lulled by the faint breezes sighing thro' her hair;
> Sleeps she, and hears not the melancholy numbers
>   Breathed to my sad lute amid the lonely air.

It is not known when he re-wrote the eleven immature stanzas, amplifying them to twenty-six, cutting out six, and leaving very few of the original lines unaltered. The poem appeared in *Macmillan's Magazine* in October, 1878, so it seems likely that the rewriting was done when he was busy with versifying up at the newly built chalet. But the interesting problem is—how did he recover the emotional enchantment of that first love—associated, moreover, with his bewitchment by Mary Peacock, who had brought him, ultimately, to ' vain regret scrawled over the blank wall ' ? Was it that he had become incapable of personal feeling about it and could contrive his poem with the cold-blooded detachment of literary art? In an earlier chapter I have suggested that there was something queer about the psychological process which produced *Modern Love*. Strange, indeed, would it seem if *Love in the Valley*, in its perfected state, were proved to have been a psychologically ruthless production, ' heartless as the shadow in the meadows flying to the hills on a blue and breezy noon '. But the most obvious and sensible explanation is that he had frequently been told that the boyish poem was 'one of the loveliest things he had ever written'. Tennyson's praises of it must have caused reverberations. One imagines him thinking 'Why not try to improve it?'—and then finding himself carried away on the wings of 'emotion remembered in tranquility'. For the miracle of it is that, while preserving the ecstatic youngness of his first conception, he brought to its rewriting all his fully developed technical mastery. It is a blending of love poetry with his nature poetry at its highest beauty and vitality of expression. Hence the unique combination of tenderness and strength which balances the exquisite intensity of

> Could I find a place to be alone with heaven
> I would speak my heart out: heaven is my need

with the wind-blown aliveness of

> Every woodland tree is flushing like the dogwood,
> Flashing like the whitebeam, swaying like the reed.

Wonderful, also, is the flexibility of the versification. The metre might easily be monotonous or jingling. But the rhythm of the lines is varied and broken, giving them the quality of passionate utterance. The Valley, described as an idyllic background, and the thoughts of the lover, alike have the cadence of sensitive speech.

> Lovely are the curves of the white owl sweeping
>   Wavy in the dusk lit by one large star.
> Lone on the fir-branch, his rattle-note unvaried,
>   Brooding o'er the gloom, spins the brown eve-jar.
> Darker grows the valley, more and more forgetting:
>   So were it with me if forgetting could be willed.
> Tell the grassy hollow that holds the bubbling well-spring,
>   Tell it to forget the source that keeps it filled.
>
> Yellow with birdfoot-trefoil are the grass-glades;
>   Yellow with cinquefoil of the dew-grey leaf:
> Yellow with stonecrop; the moss-mounds are yellow;
>   Blue-necked the wheat sways, yellowing to the sheaf.
> Green-yellow, bursts from the copse the laughing yaffle;
>   Sharp as a sickle is the edge of shade and shine:
> Earth in her heart laughs looking at the heavens,
>   Thinking of the harvest: I look and think of mine.

There are times when one suspects Meredith of having been somehow inhuman and insensitive. It has been written of him that ' his taste is for what is hard, ringing, showy, drenched with light; he does not leave any cool shadows to be a home for gentle sounds '. One cannot feel this after reading *Love in the Valley*, which is peerless among abundant evidences of the many-sidedness of his genius. In essence it is a pastoral, about a village maiden. A girl in a sun-bonnet, with a basket of wild flowers—yes. But also, in the words of her youthful lover,

> She is what my heart first awaking
> Whispered the world was; morning light is she.

In a landscape various with the seasons of the year, she stands —an adorable image of first love and its timeless transience—a daughter of earth with the light of living in her eyes.

CHAPTER FIFTEEN

1

FROM that other world of transfiguring thought wherein he sang the joy of earth revealed through ' blood, brain, and spirit ', one returns to his everyday existence. One returns to an overworked, underpaid, and as yet little appreciated author, struggling to support his ever more expensive family, discomforted by bradypepsia, and progressively deprived of exercise by his spinal affliction. This, and not much else, is what one finds in his letters of the early '80s. One thing which brought him pleasure was the institution, at the end of 1879, by Leslie Stephen, of the Sunday Tramps, a fellowship whose twenty-mile walks took them several times a year to the Box Hill country, where Meredith, though unable to share their exertions, delighted to join them for a beer-and-sausage lunch, and to entertain them at his home. In the list of members one finds the names of several of his most valued friends, Cotter Morison, Frederick Pollock, and R. B. Haldane among them. One also notes the names of Robert Bridges, W. Robinson, the famous gardener, and W. P. Ker, the eminent historian and dry wit. In the spring of 1882, he writes of them. ' They are men of distinction in science or Literature; tramping with them one has the world under review, as well as pretty scenery.' But at that time he was in no condition for tramping. ' The doctor interdicts writing. I just manage to do my morning's work. Any little in addition finishes me; for the seat of the malady is the pen.' In September of that year he wrote to Leslie Stephen that he was ' a bit stronger, less nerveshaken after holding the pen in earnest for a couple of hours '. He was trying to make progress with *Diana of the Crossways*, which, he hoped, would be serialised in *The Cornhill*.

If things go well I shall have the story ready by the Spring, but I dare not forecast hopefully. I begin rather to feel that I shall write when I try—that is, in a manner to please myself, which has not been in my power for several months of late, though curiously I found no difficulty in verse.

The story,' however, moved slowly, and was still uncompleted in June, 1884, when it began to appear in *The Fortnightly*, to be terminated abruptly in December, after twenty-six of its forty-three chapters, with the announcement that ' those who care for more of *Diana of the Crossways* will find it in the extended chronicle '. In October he wrote to Stevenson,

> My Diana is out of hand, leaving her mother rather inanimate. Should you see the Fortnightly, avoid the section under her title. Escott gives me but 18 pages in 8 numbers—so the poor girl has had to be mutilated horribly.

It seems odd that the editor (T. H. S. Escott, who had succeeded Morley in 1882) should have closed down the novel which proved to be Meredith's first real popular success. In an article published in 1898, Escott merely mentions *Diana* ' completing its appearance in *The Fortnightly* '.

When writing to Leslie Stephen in September, 1882, he was staying with his brother-in-law, Edouard Vulliamy, at Nonancourt, near Dreux, whither he had returned from a short holiday in North Italy, where he had been with his son Arthur. They met at Stresa, and after a week in drenching rain at Lugano, went to Milan, whence Arthur departed to Naples and spent the winter in Sicily. This, according to the evidence available, was the first time they had seen one another for seven or eight years. Arthur had remained away from England, his aloofness hardening to estrangement. He had a small income of his own, and had found employment in business at Havre, and afterwards in a linseed warehouse at Lille—the latter being obtained for him by Meredith's neighbours and friends, the music-loving Beneckes. It was obvious that Arthur preferred to be away from his father; but it must be remembered that for several years there was no room for him at Flint Cottage. It seems to have been a case where months of silence became years. When once people begin to drift apart, circumstances usually widen the gulf.

The silence between them had been broken by Meredith, in June, 1881. He had heard from Lionel Robinson that Arthur had become consumptive and had been in London to consult a doctor. There are four long letters, written between June 19th and August 5th, which effectively disprove any suggestion that his heart and mind were indifferent to Arthur's welfare. They show the deepest concern and anxiety, and breathe a spirit of reconciliation which seems to have created some warmth of response, although Arthur did not accept his father's offer of an indefinite stay at Flint Cottage, and remained abroad—obdurate as ever.

A few extracts from the letters should be sufficient evidence of the parental solicitude he received. After some inquiries and advice about his illness, and an offer of monetary assistance (which was persistently refused), he is told that the cottage can now supply a bedroom which is at his disposal for as long as he pleases.

> Your sister Mariette is a good, humane, intelligent girl; and Will, though not brilliant, is a kindly fellow, with wits of a slow sort. They will look forward to a glad time if you say you are coming. When informed of your wishing to throw up your situation at Lille that you might embrace the profession of Literature, I was alarmed. My own mischance in that walk I thought a sufficient warning. But if you come to me I will work with you in my chalet, and we will occupy your leisure to some good purpose. Assuming you to be under the obligation to rest, you might place yourself in my hands here with advantage; and leading a quiet life in good air, you would soon, I trust, feel strength return and discern the bent of your powers. Anything is preferable to that perilous alternation of cold market and hot café at Lille. I had no idea of what you were undergoing, or I would have written before. No one better than I from hard privation knows the value of money. But health should not be sacrificed to it. I long greatly to see you. You may rely on my wife's cordial anxiety to see you well and receive you here. . . .
>
> We have been long estranged, my dear boy, and I awake from it with a shock that wrings me. The elder should be the first to break through such divisions, for he knows best the tenure and the nature of life. But our last parting gave me the idea that you did not care for me; and further, I am so driven by work that I do not contend with misapprehension of me, or with disregard, but have the habit of taking it from all alike, as a cab-horse takes the whip. Part of me has become torpid. The quality of my work does not degenerate; I can say no more. Only in my branch of

the profession of letters the better the work the worse the pay, and also, it seems, the lower the esteem in which one is held for it. I shall hope to hear from you soon. Writing bent over a desk cannot be good for you, therefore do not write me long letters. A few lines of your state of health will be enough. My thoughts will follow you anxiously. It is a holiday to me to think of you having liberty.

Arthur had replied to the first letter, announcing his imminent departure from Lille to the Tyrolese mountains; he was also intending to visit Janet Ross at her villa near Florence. Meredith was urged by his wife to join him, but he was tied to his work. He will come, he writes, if he finds it prudently possible. He longs for Italian colour with mountain air, but could not enjoy it under pressure of work to finish. He has lost his old buoyancy. The only discoverable references to Arthur being with his father in England are in Lady Butcher's book. But her dates are vague and unreliable. She writes that she often used to see him when he came to stay with his father and stepmother at Box Hill.

I remember him as a bright-eyed and very intelligent youth, who talked easily and well on subjects that he was interested in. For reasons of health he was obliged to live a good deal abroad. . . . From time to time he made his appearance at the Cottage, when it was evident that his father enjoyed his company, and liked bringing him over to see his old friends.

This must have been some time after 1882. She also mentions his being with his father in October, 1885, and records that he was very fond of his half-sister Mariette. A year later Meredith is visiting him in St. Thomas's Hospital. After that his condition became worse. In 1889 he went to Australia, returning next year. He died on September 3rd, 1890. During his last years he was devotedly cared for by his half-sister, Edith Clarke, to whom Meredith wrote:—

I am relieved by your report of Arthur's end. To him it was, one has to say in the grief of things, a release. He has been, at least, rich above most in the two most devoted of friends, his sister and her husband. Until my breath goes I shall bless you both.

Thus ended a relationship which appears to have failed through incompatibility of temperament. Nothing that Meredith could do was able to win his son's confidence and affection. Arthur was proud and reserved. It is probable that, sooner or later, something was bound to be said which offended him. One assumes that he ' took after ' his mother, and had some of her liveliness and charm. But on the whole he emerges as a lonely and pathetic person, born to be unremarkable, to whom, after he grew up, his father must have seemed uncomfortably distinguished and dynamic. Both must have suffered. But Meredith, I think, was the one who was capable of suffering most deeply.

2

During the winter of 1883–4 he was steadily engaged on *Diana of the Crossways*, and by the end of March was able to tell Stevenson, who was at Hyéres, that although his spinal malady, at this time, prevented him walking much more than a mile, he was able to work passably well, and was finishing at a great pace a novel, partly modelled on Mrs. Norton. ' But this is between ourselves. I have had to endow her with brains and make them evidence to the discerning.' On the same day he wrote to Mrs. Leslie Stephen that his work prevented him coming to London to meet James Russell Lowell.

> Meanwhile I hope to finish with the delivery of the terrible woman afflicting me (a positive heroine with brains, with real blood, and demanding utterance of the former, tender direction of the latter) by the end of April.

Two months later he tells Mrs. Stephen:—

> Diana keeps me still on her sad last way to wedlock. I could have killed her merrily, with my compliments to the public. But the marrying of her sets me traversing feminine labyrinths, and you know that the why of it never can be accounted for.

Finally, at the end of August, *Diana* still holds him, only by the last chapter.

> She has no puppet-pliancy. The truth being, that she is a mother of Experience, and gives that dreadful baby suck to brains.

181

I have therefore a feeble hold of her; none of the novelist's winding-up arts avail; it is she who leads me. But my delay of the conclusion is owing to my inability to write of late.

The interruption of his work had been a grievous one, for in June Mrs. Meredith had undergone a severe operation in London. Under the stress of this experience he wrote to Maxse:—

> The soul's one road is forward. We go and are unmade. Yet it is quite certain that the best of us is in the state of survival. We live in what we have done—in the idea: which seems to me the parent fountain of life, as opposed to that of perishable blood. I see all round me how much Idea governs; and therein see the Creator; that other life to which we are drawn: not conscious, as our sensations demand, but possibly cognizant, as the brain may now sometimes, when the blood is not too forcefully pressing on it, dimly apprehend. . . . These are not words, they are my excruciated thoughts—out of bloody sweat of mind, and now peaceful, imaging life, accepting whatever is there.

In the following February there was a second operation for cancer. She had lost the power of speech. In June, after two months at Eastbourne, she was brought back to the Cottage, where she died on September 18th, having borne it all with noble fortitude. ' She was the Best of wives, truest among human creatures. I believe in Spirit, and have her with me here,' he wrote, soon after her death. But the loss, with its harrowing memories of her suffering, was shattering in effect, and on January 1st, 1886, he wrote to Morley:—

> I am still at my questions of death, and the many pictures of the dear soul's months of anguish. When the time was, and even shortly after, I was in arms, and had at least the practical philosophy given to us face to face with our enemy. Now I have sunk, am haunted. It causes me to write of her, which scorches the brand. I have need of all my powers. The thought often uppermost is in amazement at the importance we attach to our hold of sensation. So much grander, vaster, seems her realm of silence. She is in earth, our mother, and I soon shall follow.

The best tribute to Marie Meredith's qualities was written by Hyndman.

I have heard some of Meredith's friends speak of her as if she were intellectually quite unworthy of him. Genius has no mate. She was a charming, clever, tactful, and handsome Frenchwoman: a good musician, a pleasant conversationalist, a most considerate, attentive and patient wife and an excellent mother. Her care of her husband was always thoughtful but never obtrusive, and Meredith with all his high qualities was not an easy man to live with. At one time he would persist in turning vegetarian. It was well-nigh the death of him. But he had persuaded himself that that was the right sort of food to give the highest development to body and mind. So poor Mrs. Meredith saw him becoming every day more gaunt and hungry-eyed. It was useless for her or anyone else to suggest that this diet was unsuited to his habit of life and work, and that his increasing acerbity was caused by lack of sustenance and his energy sawing into his exposed nerves. She tried every conceivable device to arrest the nerve weakness she saw coming upon him—boiled his vegetables in strong broth, and introduced shredded meat into his bread by connivance with the baker. At last things got so bad that he recognized the truth, and was forced to admit that a man who does double duty as an athlete of mind and body needs meat. So he took to it again and all went well. I have always thought that this mistaken vegetable diet was responsible for the lesion which came later. For he was sound in every way up to that time.

3

Diana of the Crossways reached a third edition in three months. Public curiosity had been aroused by it, and for the first time a novel by Meredith was being talked about at dinner-tables and hastily skimmed through by society ladies who felt obliged to be able to claim acquaintance with it.

Mrs. Norton had died in 1877; but she had been so brilliant, beautiful, and well known that Society, which rarely retains a lively interest in the dead, decided that a book which was known to be ' all about her ' must be worthy of its patronage. Had the author been able to overhear the denizens of the great world asking one another ' whether he had written anything else', he might almost have exclaimed ' What honour I arrive at!' as Mr. Jorrocks did when offered a Mastership of Hounds.

And I imagine his sardonic smile when he thought of these materialists reading the famous first chapter, which artfully begins by conceding the clues to Mrs. Norton's career, and gradually develops into a prime specimen of Meredithian essay-writing on the necessity of brain-stuff in fiction.

> To demand of us truth to nature, excluding Philosophy, is really to bid a pumpkin caper. As much as legs are wanted for the dance, Philosophy is required to make our human nature credible and acceptable. Fiction implores you to heave a bigger breast and take her in with this heavenly preservative helpmate, her inspiration and her essence.

But it was not his philosophy which made Diana credible and acceptable to that London which he called 'say what you will of it, the largest broth-pot of brains anywhere simmering on the hob'. Much of her history must have been considered tedious and incomprehensible, though some may have believed that it was good for their minds. What won the novel readers was the fact that Diana, as heroine, was delightfully and vividly alive, ' a queenly comrade, and a spirit leaping and shining like mountain water'. It remains to be asked how far she and Mrs. Norton resembled each other.

To begin with, both were authoresses. Diana Warwick is presented as a successful novelist, writing with distinction, but urgently needing to earn money by her pen. Caroline Elizabeth Norton, as a young woman, made a considerable reputation as a poetess and became a popular writer for the literary annuals of the day. (She earned £1400 in a single year by such contributions.) She was also something of a pamphleteer on behalf of the rights of women, stimulated by her own matrimonial experiences, which amounted to persecution by her coarse and violent tempered husband. Diana represents one of Meredith's strongest efforts to forward the emancipation of Victorian womanhood from what she is made to describe as their being ' taken to be the second thoughts of the Creator; human nature's fringes, mere finishing touches, not a part of the texture '. The novels, *Stuart of Dunleath*, *Lost and Saved*, and *Old Sir Douglas*, written to earn money, showed that Mrs. Norton had no special gift for the form. During her later years, she wrote much anonymous literary and artistic criticism.

'Partly based on a real instance,' as he wrote of it, the story borrowed the main events of Mrs. Norton's early life. Her loveless marriage, followed by a compromising relationship with the Prime Minister, Lord Melbourne, from which she emerged with vindicated innocence after a *cause célebre* which collapsed; and the scandal which wrongly imputed to her the betrayal of a political secret. This incident, upon which the plot of *Diana* hinges, was the communication to the editor of *The Times* of Sir Robert Peel's resolve to repeal the Corn Laws, which she had been told of by one of her most ardent admirers, Sidney Herbert. By making Diana, in one of her incalculable moods, commit this offence, Meredith gave great offence to Mrs. Norton's friends. At the urgent insistence of her nephew, Lord Dufferin, a prefatory note was added to later editions—'A lady of high distinction for wit and beauty, the daughter of an illustrious Irish House, came under the shadow of a calumny. It has latterly been examined and exposed as baseless. The story of *Diana of the Crossways* is to be read as fiction.'

Meredith had known her when he was living at Copsham. She was an intimate friend of Lady Duff Gordon. She was then over fifty, and according to Janet Ross's account was not greatly impressed by him. It may have been a case of two brilliant conversationalists feeling the strain of competition.

Mrs. Norton was renowned for cleverness and charm, but we have seen that when modelling Diana on her he 'had to endow her with brains'. And there is evidence, in Mrs. Norton's verse, that this was needed. The Diarist in Chapter I. of the novel records a few of Diana's aphoristic utterances, which can appropriately be compared with some lines by Caroline Norton which appear in a Dictionary of Quotations.

Diana. (a) *Men may have rounded Seraglio Point : they have not yet doubled Cape Turk.* (b) (Of Romance.) *The young who avoid that region escape the title of Fool at the cost of a celestial crown.* (c) *To have the sense of the eternal in life is a short flight for the soul. To have had it is the soul's reality.*

Norton.
    (a) *I am listening for the voices*
       Which I heard in days of old.

(b) *God made all pleasures innocent.*

(c) *Love not ! love not ! ye hopeless sons of clay ;*
Hope's gayest wreaths are made of earthly flowers—
Things that are made to fade and fall away,
Ere they have blossomed for a few short hours.

Which settles the question of Diana's intellectual supremacy, though unfair to one whom Lockhart, in the *Quarterly*, justifiably described as the Byron of our poetesses.

Mrs. Norton was a grand-daughter of Sheridan. Diana was ' a daughter of the famous Dan Merion ', an iridescent Irishman. Her appearance is best described in the scene where Redworth, the man she ultimately marries, visits her in the middle of a frosty night, and she is lighting a fire for him in the old Crossways farm house.

The act of service was beautiful in gracefulness, and her simplicity in doing the work touched it spiritually. He thought, as she knelt there, that never had he seen how lovely and how charged with mystery her features were; the large dark eyes full on the brows; the proud line of a straight nose in right measure to the bow of the lips; reposeful red lips, shut, and their curve of the slumber-smile at the corners. Her forehead was broad; the chin of a sufficient firmness to sustain that noble square; the brows marked by a soft thick brush to the temples. The crackling flames reddened her whole person. Gazing, he remembered Lady Dunstane saying of her once, that in anger she had the nostrils of a war-horse. The nostrils now were faintly alive under some sensitive impression of her musings.

The head of Mrs. Norton by G. F. Watts, painted for Lady Duff Gordon in 1848, can be fitted to this description; but it does not express one's notion of Diana's character. In it one sees the matured Irish beauty, but one also sees the editress of Keepsake annuals and authoress of platitudinous poems. Impulsive and clever though she was, Mrs. Norton's portrait does not indicate the temperament of a war horse; nothing mysterious about *her*! Fanny Kemble, an acute observer, noted that she was ' extremely epigrammatic in her talk, and comically dramatic in her manner of narrating things '. It has been assumed that, when creating his brain-endowed heroine, Mere-

dith had Lady Duff Gordon in mind, though Diana's friend
Lady Dunstane seems also to have been drawn from her.
A novelist's material has to come from somewhere. All
that matters is the use he has made of it. In this case the result
was admirably summed up by Henley in *The Athenaeum*.

A great portrait is more persuasive and imposing than its
original. . . . It is the artist's function not to copy, but to
synthesize; to eliminate from that gross confusion of actuality
which is his raw material whatever is accidental, idle, irrelevant,
and select for perpetuation that only which is appropriate and
immortal. This is what Mr. Meredith has done in *Diana of the
Crossways*. It is said that she is studied from Mrs. Norton. Indeed,
in the first chapter it is confessed that she lived once, and was
famous in her day, and queened it in society, and was the bright
particular star of diarists and the dealers in anecdote. Here, with
a noble plea for philosophic fiction, and more wit and wisdom than
most men contrive to put off in three volumes, there are quotations
from the lady's works; also a subtle and authoritative analysis
of her intelligence and the quality of her wit. . . . Lord Melbourne's Egeria may well be her prototype. Whether this be or
be not the case is absolutely immaterial. As we know her Diana
is an original creation, and one of the loveliest in fiction. She
suggests Mrs. Norton, it is true, but she suggests Mr. George
Meredith still more, and Rosalind most of all. The comparison
is no doubt startling, but it is legitimate. For such a union as she
presents of capacity of heart and brain, of generous nature and
fine intelligence, of natural womanhood and more than womanly
wit and apprehensiveness, we know not where to look save among
Shakespeare's ladies, nor with whom to equal her save the genius
of Arden. . . . Diana's experiences are so much life taken in the
fact. She speaks, and it is from her very heart; she suffers and
rejoices, and it is in her own flesh and soul; she thinks, aspires,
labours, wins, loses, and wins again with an intensity of perception,
an emotional directness and completeness, that, so cunning is the
author's hand and so unerring his principle of selection, affect the
reader more powerfully than the spectacle of nature itself.

In his magisterial essay on this novel, A. W. Verrall, con-
fining himself to a single aspect of the work, asserted that ' the
reader who does not appreciate linguistic dexterity had much
better let Mr. Meredith alone. . . . What you have here is a
touchstone to ascertain whether you have the faculty of enjoying

dexterity in the manipulation of language '. His view was that the primary importance of Meredith consisted in his cultivation of the faculty of wit. An immediate answer came from G. M. Trevelyan, who pointed out that Verrall's appraisements were supremely well said and true, except that they made no mention of the poetic element, and by implication ruled it out. My own impression is that, in *Diana*, wit and poetry are attractively intermixed. The actual story is quite a simple one, and the style, quick as it is with imagination and brain-work, is singularly luminous and clear. The book contains some of his loveliest landscape pictures. Here is one of them.

Rain had fallen in the night. Here and there hung a milk-white cloud with folded sail. The South-West left it in its bay of blue, and breathed below. At moments the fresh scent of herb and mould swung richly in warmth. The young beech-leaves glittered, pools of rain-water made the road-ways laugh, the grass-banks under hedges rolled their interwoven weeds in cascades of many-shaded green to right and left of the pair of dappled ponies, and a squirrel crossed ahead, a lark went up a little way to ease his heart, closing his wings when the burst was over; startled blackbirds, darting with a clamour like a broken cock-crow, looped the wayside woods from hazel to oak-scrub; short flights, quick spirts everywhere, steady sunshine above. Diana held the reins. . . . Through an old gravel-cutting a gateway led to the turf of the down, springy turf bordered on a long line, clear as a racecourse, by golden gorse covers, and left-ward over the gorse the dark ridge of the fir and heath country ran companionably to the South-west, the valley between, with undulations of wood and meadow sunned or shaded, clumps, mounds, promontories, away to broad spaces of tillage banked by wooded hills, and dimmer beyond and farther, the faintest shadowiness of heights, as a veil to the illimitable. Yews, junipers, radiant beeches, and gleams of the service-tree or the white-beam spotted the semicircle of swelling green Down black and silver. The sun in the valley sharpened his beams on squares of buttercups, and made a pond a diamond.

Many a time had Meredith walked that way, going perhaps to the Maxses at Effingham Hill. Would he recognise the landscape now, I wonder, of which he wrote, in 1886, ' nowhere in England is richer foliage or wilder downs and fresher woodlands ' ?

CHAPTER SIXTEEN

1

THE resounding success of *Diana* resulted in a paragraph in *The Athenaeum* for May 30th, 1885, which announced that ' Messrs Chapman and Hall talk of publishing a uniform edition of Mr. George Meredith's novels, the great majority of which are quite out of print '. The publisher's formal announcement appeared in July, and the nine volumes, much revised, were issued within a year, at six shillings each. There is evidence that two thousand copies of each novel were printed. The volumes were sold separately and reprinted from time to time. From 1889 onwards the publishers issued them concurrently on thinner paper at 3*s.* 6*d.*

By the original agreement, Meredith received a lump sum of £100 for each volume, for a period of seven years copyright. Some interest attaches to this agreement.

> The secret history of the publishing of Meredith's earlier books is more than curious. I have heard some details of it. My only wonder is that human ingenuity did not invent literary agents sooner.

Thus wrote Arnold Bennett, in his *Books and Persons*. I had often wondered what these details were. I have now discovered some of them in a New York Auction Catalogue of 1911. In February, 1893, Meredith wrote two letters to Frederick Chapman, from which the following passages were quoted in this Catalogue. (One cannot help wondering how these letters came to be preserved and offered for sale!)

> You have not behaved openly and honourably in continuing to issue for a year and more the volumes of my works which had outrun your lease of the copyright. I wanted to correct the number of scandalous printer's errors. I requested the receipt for the money I paid into your hands for the copyright of *Evan Harrington*. I have asked for it numerous times close upon eight years.

And, in reply to Chapman's explanation :—

It is a pitiful tale that you reveal. I will not recall incidents which pluck from you the mask you choose to wear in decency. A gentleman will call on you to treat with regard to the use of my copyrights. . . . With regard to *Diana of the Crossways* the use of the copyright was for five years. You have therefore been entrenching on my rights for two years.

(The gentleman who called was W. M. Colles, one of the earliest of the literary agents.)

From this one can only infer that he had been very badly treated, and it is not surprising that the series of letters, about reading manuscripts, beginning ' Dear Fred ' were discontinued. Chapman was over seventy, and died three years later. It is to be hoped that he had been careless in the matter. But there is further evidence that 4000 copies of *Diana* had been printed after the expiration of copyright, and 2000 of *Richard Feverel*. One wonders what the Comic Spirit, ' born of our united social intelligences', thought about it. For in the previous autumn Meredith had been elected President of the Society of Authors in place of Tennyson.

In his history of Chapman and Hall, Arthur Waugh has stated that in 1880, when the firm became a limited company, ' it had two indisputable assets, in the persons of Meredith and Chapman, as literary adviser and managing director. Between them they worked in perfect harmony, and to excellent commercial purpose.' For thirty years Meredith received a salary of £250 a year. In 1894 he asked for an increase. It was refused, and he resigned. Such was his reward after the drudgery of reading manuscripts for a salary which, as Arthur Waugh admits, ' was certainly never commensurate with the work done '.

The uniform edition, however, definitely ended his thirty-five years struggle to obtain an adequate audience. Its appearance in America, where he had hitherto been almost unknown, caused him to become a literary celebrity, and it can be said that for two or three years his novels were more widely discussed and appreciated there than in England. This advance in his fame was expedited by an article in *The Princeton Review,* written by Flora Shaw, who had gained his friendship when staying near Box Hill, and had spent a night at the Cottage during Stevenson's last visit there, in August, 1886. At one time head of the Colonial Department of *The Times*, she was an able journalist; her well-written and illuminating article proved persuasive in influencing literary editors and university professors to discover and discuss the novels.

It was my good fortune [she wrote] to find myself in his company on the turf back of Box Hill one brilliant breezy morning. Our eyes travelled over the valley where park woods, russet with the changing leaf, clustered beneath the box and juniper of surrounding slopes, and threw into vivid contrast the yews of Norbury. West of the valley the greensand range rolled skyward, bearing a tower solitary upon its highest point. Southward the Weald of Sussex rolled under light October mists to Brighton downs and legendary glimpses of the sea. And while we mounted, with the horizon widening beneath us, we spoke of the share the intellect has had in human development. Mr. Meredith held the intellect to be the chief endowment of man. By intellectual courage, he said, we make progress. . . . When we consider what the earth is and what we are, whither we tend, and why, we perceive that reason is, and must be, the supreme guide of man. Perceive things intellectually. . . . I wish I could recall the vivacity, the keen vigor, the wealth of wit and illustration with which he sustained his theme. As we walked, with the southern landscape lying pearly beneath us, and a south-east wind singing through the reddening woods, he seemed to raise our spirits to corresponding heights. . . .

And so on. She was indeed one of those ladies who stimulated him to 'corresponding heights'. The article was what he had long awaited, and was entirely suitable to its purpose. One may add that in his later years he was destined to get more than enough of this sort of thing. Meanwhile, when inviting Maxse to meet her, he described her as 'unmatched in matters of abstract thought as well as in warm feeling, and quite as delightful to talk with as to look at'. And early in 1888, he wrote that he had received a startling cheque from his American publishers.

I had heard of large sales over there, and a man of experience tells me it is nothing to what it will be. But I confess the touch of American money has impressed me with concrete ideas of fame.

In a letter to Hilda de Longeuil, of whom there will be more
to say, he remarks that he has latterly been kept in employment
by Americans. He had been interviewed by an American
lady whose one object in England was to meet him. Articles
were sent, followed by the writer's request that he would inform
them whether they were in accord with his views of his work.
He complained that his time was taken up in replying to them,
but his letter to G. P. Baker, who had contributed an intelligent
article to *The Harvard Monthly*, is long, carefully composed, and
gratified.

> When you say that a change in public taste, should it come
> about, will be to some extent due to me, you hand me the flowering
> wreath I covet. For I think that all right use of life, and the
> one secret of life, is to pave ways for the firmer footing of those
> who succeed us; as to my works, I know them faulty, I think
> them of worth only when they point and aid to that end.

Hilda de Longeuil was a young cousin of Grant Allen, who
lived not far from Box Hill and was a friend of Meredith's.
He met her at the end of 1886, when she was unhappy and in
need of sympathetic guidance, which he gave in some remarkable letters after she returned to France. He was evidently in
love with her, though he expresses himself in a somewhat high-
flown style.

> Perceive that I embrace your whole existence, all that may or
> could in the chances have befallen you, and am, with this feeling
> of mine, barely of our world when I ally myself to your destinies
> and speculate on them, past and future. I ask to hear nothing
> that does not lead me to help you on to a healthier viewing and
> footing of the world. . . . Feel me in your soul's home. And
> believe that you have done more for me in so strangely making
> mine a habitation for you than I can ever repay by services.

Four months later she was still his 'friend and dearest'.
But his emotion was cooling off, and the last letter, though
'faithful and devoted', in September, 1887, is mainly an
account of his holiday at St. Ives, where he had taken a house
to be with the Leslie Stephens. Thus ended an episode which
had begun with some verses that might well be included in
his collected poems, as the following stanza shows.

Give Life to Life; in turn it gives.
Believe thy heart alive: it lives.
Know Love more heavenly than of old
Revealed, and Love will not be cold.

It is known that the young lady had distinction of mind and personality, combined with a French elegance and femininity. How copiously she responded to his strained intellectualism remains a mystery. Possibly she felt it rather overwhelming. For him, in his rôle of the sage enamoured, it was a luxury of sublimated emotion. And one may be forgiven for quoting, in comment of common sense on the situation, from a well-known ludicrous poem.

Will not a beauteous landscape bright—
  Or music's soothing sound,
Console the heart—afford delight,
  And throw sweet peace around?
They may; but never comfort lend,
Like an accomplished female friend.

He must have needed consolations. Deprivation of full bodily exercise meant more to him than to most men of his age, and at sixty he was already a physical wreck inhabited by a daemon of vitality and mental energy. (At this time, however, he was still able to walk to Leith Hill and back, a distance of ten miles, to visit Colonel Lewin, whose step-daughter, in 1892, became Mrs. Will Meredith.) Friends he had in his neighbourhood, and the human interest of his daughter Marie—his ' Dearie ' as he always called her—an interest which included the problem of finding suitable governesses for her. He was no longer driven by the necessity of earning money. (In 1888 he inherited a comfortable legacy from an aged aunt.) And there was, during the second half of the '80s, the gradual growth of literary prestige which resulted, as we have seen, in his being officially recognised as the head of English Letters. He was becoming a public figure, though of this invisible process the only outward signs seem to have been that in 1887 he attended an Eighty Club dinner and was introduced to Gladstone, and a year later was at a banquet in honour of Parnell, where he sat with Asquith, Haldane, A. J. Balfour and Morley. Through Morley and Haldane he was coming to be looked upon as one of the grand old men of Liberalism. But he was an independent Radical.

Frank Harris, that exuberant vulgarian of letters, has described his first meeting with Meredith, who was more tolerant of him, in subsequent years, than might have been expected. It was in 1887, at the office of *The Fortnightly*, of which Harris had recently been appointed editor. In his usual florid style he praises ' the King of contemporary writers ' for his sympathetic kindness to younger authors and his eagerness to champion any cause or person that seemed to him worthy or in need of help.

> As he got up to greet me, I was astonished by the Greek beauty of his face set off by wavy silver hair and the extraordinary vivacity of ever-changing expression, astonished, too, by the high, loud voice which he used in ordinary conversation, and by the quick-glancing eyes which never seemed to rest for a moment on any object, but flitted about curiously like a child's.

This restlessness of the eyes is a characteristic which I have not seen mentioned elsewhere. Possibly Harris exaggerated it in order to work in a passage about the bright quick eyes seeming to explain Meredith's style, ending, ' The style danced about for variety's sake to keep the eyes company.' It seems more than probable that he was somewhat self-conscious and uneasy in the presence of this terrific bounder.

In 1890 he first achieved the distinction of being parodied in *Punch*, which afterwards gave him several doses of laboured playfulness.

It has been said that he was indifferent to fame. We know that he never courted that fickle patron. Nevertheless one assumes that he relished his experience of the reversal of fortune, of whose buffetings he had every right to complain. The initial failure of *Richard Feverel* was a thing he never forgot or forgave. And the prolonged neglect of his poetry cannot have been easy to endure. A poet may persuade himself that he is writing for posterity, but he is bound to feel it a somewhat bleak occupation. A living audience is, humanly, preferable. Nor can it be denied that a modicum of official encouragement produces a pleasing effect on the literary artist who is too distinguished to win popular approval. Such praises are seldom presciently bestowed by persons prominent in public life. They are too busy with public affairs. They should, however, beware of how they award their infrequent laurels, as the following instance shows.

Had Meredith been present at the Royal Academy Banquet in 1888, his keen eyes would have watched W. E. H. Lecky, the eminent historian, rising to ' reply for Literature '. One pictures the delightful scene. Sir Frederick Leighton, the handsomest man of his time, presiding as only he, the melli- fluent, could preside. And Lecky, whom Carlyle called ' that willowy creature ', as in a *Vanity Fair* cartoon, tall, slim and impressive, with dome-shaped head, lofty brow, long nose, and side-whiskers meeting under the chin. One listens; and this, after sundry academic urbanities befitting the occasion, is what one hears.

I would venture to point to a Poem which has been but a few weeks in the world, but which is destined, or I am much mistaken, to take a prominent place in the literature of our time—a Poem which, among other beauties, contains pictures of the old Greek mythology, worthy to compare even with those with which you, Mr. President, have so often delighted us. [Pause; punctuated by an Olympian smile of acknowledgment from the P.R.A. and perfect host.] I refer to *The City of Dream*, by Robert Buchanan. While such works are produced in England, it cannot, I think, be said that the artistic spirit in English literature has very seriously decayed.

I have not read *The City of Dream*, and should be interested to know whether anyone else has done so. Replying to Lecky, for Posterity, I venture to quote the last line of *The Wandering Jew*, which was Buchanan's next magnum opus in verse.

God help the Christ, that Christ may help us all!

Meanwhile Meredith's *Ballads and Poems of Tragic Life*, which had been less than a year in the world, were lying unheeded in Macmillan's warehouse. The volume contained his *France, 1870*. It was to this that the tribute should have fallen from Lecky's lips and lofty brow. Buchanan is now remembered as the person who attacked the Pre-Raphaelites in a pamphlet called ' The Fleshly School of Poetry ', a piece of journalistic humbug which caused Rossetti inexpressible pain and annoyance, and afforded Swinburne an opportunity to join in the fray with indignant gusto.

Lecky, who was a valued friend of Tennyson, afterwards became M.P. for Dublin and a Privy Councillor, and was one of the first recipients of the Order of Merit. No doubt he deserved it; but not for his perceptiveness of distinction in contemporary poetry.

2

Apart from the 1870 Ode, which I have already discussed, there is very little in *Ballads and Poems of Tragic Life* that I wish to write about. Six of the poems, by the way, had been written between 1867 and 1876, and these make up almost half the book. Among them is the long *Nuptials of Attila*, a powerful dramatic ballad which Henley admired more than anything else in the volume, finding it ' informed by a strange and fierce intensity, and with touches of a weird and ghastly terror '. It illuminates the Dark Ages with historical imagination, ending—

> So the Empire built of scorn
> Agonized, dissolved, and sank—

(thereby anticipating a modern Barbarism which was also founded on scorn and disregard of others). But I must confess that the qualities which appealed to Henley sixty years ago are to me repellent. My soul craves for something gentler than ' arrow, javelin, spear, and sword '. The book contains several admirable short pieces, of which I would mention *The Two Masks*, with its memorable

> For this the Comic Muse exacts of creatures
> Appealing to the fount of tears: that they
> Strive never to outleap our human features,
> And do Right Reason's ordinance obey.

and *Bellerophon*, a most satisfactory classical picture, which somehow reminds one of Browning. There is also *Men and Man*, one of his few spontaneous lyrics—as will be seen from the first stanza.

Men the Angels eyed;
And here they were wild waves,
And there as marsh descried;
Men the Angels eyed,
And liked the picture best
Where they were greenly dressed
In brotherhood of graves.

A Reading of Earth, which appeared at the end of 1888, was
the culmination of his achievement as a philosophic nature poet.
The poetical style which he had invented is here employed with
consistent effectiveness, and although occasionally rugged and
over-compressed (particularly in *A Faith on Trial*), the obscurities are always fathomable and fruitful—a claim which cannot
confidently be made for some of his later verse. Here we find
' Sweet as Eden is the air ' and ' A wind sways the pines ', to
which I have already referred with unbounded admiration.
And here is one of his best loved poems, *The Thrush in February*.
Ever since I began this chronicle of his life and output it has
been at the back of my industrious cogitations. Following him
through his overworked and underpaid career, his failures and
frustrations, and the enigma of his unsuccessful domestic
relationships, I have thought—not of his ultimate and rever-
berant recognition as the most eminent of contemporary writers,
but of the musing, grey-haired man who in 1885 looked and
listened from his work-room and found utterance for this poem,
in which he speaks and is seen as though I heard and beheld
him. Once and for all he fixed and universalised a moment
of experience which he had long known and would know for
yet another twenty-four years, giving a self-portrait more
memorable and befriending than any other that he unconsciously created. And why I like it so well is because it shows
him at peace with life and his surroundings—he, whose mind
never found relaxation easy, whose temperament was unrestful,
and whose body was overcharged with nervous energy. I like
it also because I am myself an inveterate quietist and self-
corrector of inherent excitability, and because—in the unhalt-
able hither and thither of human occupations—I long for
something stilled and subdued to contemplation of experience.
For the keynote of *The Thrush in February* is serenity. It is a
twilight meditation, the expression of time-taught maturity,

and a summing-up of his whole nature philosophy. Its twilight
mood and setting are unusual from him, who was morning-
minded and loved to meet the sun upon the upland lawn.
Unlike Hardy, for whom day's ending was brooding and
crepuscular, he usually saw in his twilights a remnant of
brightness lingering above the earth. So, in this poem, the
evening star is seen ' a little south of coloured sky ', when a
rainy south-west wind has left the heavens clear. And—as
often happens when a poet's art is imbued by depth of feeling
and experience, it reads like a farewell. ' Darker grows the
valley, more and more forgetting' (one of the most heart-
holding lines ever written) while the star

> . . . seems a while the vale to hold
> In trance, and homelier makes the far.

In past decades, when Meredith's poetry was the subject of
numerous essays in the serious magazines, *The Thrush in February*
was frequently quoted as evidence of his ' Faith in enlightened
and fearless acceptance of reality and of its laws enjoined by
Reason ', and so on. Ploughing my way through a multitude of
these estimable essays, I have found no writer who showed that
he felt the poem as I do. All were earnestly preoccupied in
expounding the meanings of his thought, and none appeared
aware that poetry is the language of the heart as well as the
head. The main lesson of the poem, one of them pointed out,
is that Spirit blossoms from Brain—an idea which Meredith
has dinned into us again and again. Admittedly the poem
contains one of his most impressive homilies on the obligation
of our intellects to learn patiently the secret of Earth—

> For love we Earth, then serve we all;
> Her mystic secret then is ours.

But if he had written only the homilising stanzas (and the
import of some of them is not easy to grasp at a first reading)
the quintessence of the whole would be missing. ' Thought by
itself', as Leigh Hunt said, ' makes no poet at all. Feeling,
even destitute of conscious thought, stands a far better poetical
chance, being a sort of thought without the process of thinking,
—a grasper of the truth without seeing it.' It is the thrush that
makes the poem memorable, not the moralisings.

I know him, February's thrush,
And loud at eve he valentines
On sprays that paw the naked bush
Where soon will sprout the thorns and bines.

Now ere the foreign singer thrills
Our vale his plain-song pipe he pours,
A herald of the million bills;
And heed him not, the loss is yours.

My study, flanked with ivied fir
And budded beech with dry leaves curled,
Perched over yew and juniper,
He neighbours, piping to his world.

His Island voice you then shall hear,
Nor ever after separate
From such a twilight of the year
Advancing to the vernal gate.

He sings me, out of Winter's throat,
The young time with the life ahead. . . .

Is it Thought which causes that simple, concluding statement to touch one at the source of tears? ' The young time with the life ahead ' . . .

Why is it that, in that context, those ordinary words have a significance which vibrates, an urgency which appeals, a controlled passion which makes, as he elsewhere wrote:

The breast of us a sounded shell,
The blood of us a lighted dew.

Why is it so inexpressibly more satisfying to read those opening stanzas than to be told that

We breathe but to be sword or block?

The answer is that those two culminating lines have a double meaning. For he continues—not so felicitously—with—

And my young time his leaping note
Recalls to spirit-mirth from dead.

The bird foretells the spring. With rejoiceful notes he announces it. For Meredith, who

Keeps the youth of souls who pitch
Their joy in this old heart of things,

199

the song, the season, and the twilight of his familiar surroundings bring memory, the mother of the muses. In the winter of his oldness he can still feel the expectant thrill of juvenescence, but it is impassioned by unrevealed regret. Enough for him, it must be, that

> Full lasting is the song, though he,
> The singer, passes. . . .

He consoles himself with his belief in ' the rapture of the forward view '.

> Meanwhile, O twilight bird
> Of promise! bird of happy breath!
> I hear, I would the City heard.

And then, after a last look at Sirius—of whom he has written ' Be thou my star, and thou in me be seen '—he re-enters the chalet and lights the two candles on his work-table. And writes, perhaps, his noble poem.

In *A Faith on Trial*, which occupies almost a third of the volume, we have a biographical sequel. It describes how, on May Day morning of the same year, when he had lost all hope of his wife's recovery, he goes alone for one of their familiar walks in the woodlands of Box Hill. He mounts the hill with a lifeless and heavy heart, knowing only that his good companion and mate, ' who had shown fortitude quiet as earth at the shedding of leaves ', is dying. Unable to observe the loveliness of the day and the season, with inward sight he remembers happy times spent with her in the Normandy home of her birth. His private grief prevents him from taking in the wayside impressions which he now puts before us. As he continues his walk, he wishes only to observe the ' changeful visible face ' of Mother Earth, not to feel or to fancy. His observation of every detail of nature comes to him now at his need, because it has long ago become instinctive in him. His mind is an empty room, but he retains his ' disciplined habit to see '. Then the ' young apparition ' of a wild white cherry in bloom suddenly compels him not merely to observe but to feel, and restores his faith. He sees it as a white banner signifying ' victorious rays over death '; it teaches him to conquer despair, and not to divide his soul from his intellect, letting the intellect alone bear rule.

The second half of the poem is a discourse on his favourite theme, the human need to turn to Earth for wisdom and comfort.

> For the road to her soul is the Real:
> The root and the growth of man:
> And the senses must traverse it fresh
> With a love that no scourge shall abate,
> To reach the lone heights where we scan
> In the mind's rarer vision this flesh;
> In the charge of the Mother our fate;
> Her law as the one common weal.

The hopes of life beyond the grave are not reflected on the breast of Earth. If we ' strain to the farther shore ', it is ' flesh in revolt ' at Earth's laws—not Faith. If we crave for sure Permanence, we must learn to see it in the alternations of Life and Death by which the generations succeed each other. We must accept both Life and Death as being equally parts of the law of Reality, an altruistic idea of immortality originated by Comte. In the final hundred lines of the poem, Earth is allowed to speak for herself, telling ' how flesh unto spirit must grow '.

> Spirit [she says] raves not for a goal. Desires not; neither desires the sleep or the glory; it trusts; uses my gifts, yet aspires; dreams of a higher than it. The dream is Reason herself, tiptoe at the ultimate bound of her wit, on the verges of Night and Day.

Some of this, I must admit, is a little too much for me. The poem can be recommended to those who like poetry to be difficult. They will enjoy decoding such passages as:—

> Wisdom is won of its fight,
> The combat incessant; and dries
> To mummy wrap perching a height.
> It chews the contemplative cud
> In peril of isolate scorn,
> Unfed of the onward flood.

It is, in fact, fatiguing to read as a whole. The three-beat metre hurries one along, while the condensed and closely reasoned content demands concentrated attention. The writing is typical of Meredith's mind, leaping from image to image, piling metaphor on metaphor, regardless of the visualising faculty of the reader, who is likely to protest that one thing at a time is as much as he can manage. As a technical and intellectual performance it is extraordinary; as poetry it is ill-judged for its effect. And after reading it through several times for my present purpose, I begin to feel that, although it is my duty to be ' of her promptings wise ', I do not want to be lectured again about Earth, ' Mother of simple truth, relentless quencher of lies '. I prefer *The Question Whither*, a short poem which ends—

> Then let our trust be firm in Good,
>   Though we be of the fasting;
> Our questions are a mortal brood,
>   Our work is everlasting.
> We children of Beneficence
>   Are in its being sharers;
> And whither vainer sounds than Whence
>   For word with such wayfarers—

or the homely and beautiful elegy on Mrs. Meredith, *Change in Recurrence*, with its concluding—

> I gazed: 'twas the scene of the frame,
> With the face, the dear life for me, fled.
> No window a lute to my name,
> No watcher there plying the thread.
> But the blackbird hung pecking at will;
> The squirrel from cone hopped to cone;
> The thrush had a snail in his bill,
> And tap-tapped the shell hard on a stone.

The South-Wester is a characteristic specimen of his poetic idiom. He set himself to describe a day of cloud variations from dawn to sundown. It is, almost entirely, a series of sky pictures. I can imagine Shelley composing an ode on the same subject. The same effect of motion and magnificence would have been manifest. But, I must confess, the imaginary comparison is not to Meredith's advantage. Shelley would have read the first lines of this poem with an immediate response of delight—

> Day of the cloud in fleets! O day
> Of wedded white and blue, that sail
> Immingled, with a footing ray
> In shadow-sandals down our vale!—

And swift to ravish golden meads,
Swift up the run of turf it speeds,
Thy bright of head and dark of heel,
To where the hilltop flings on sky
As hawk from wrist or dust from wheel,
The tiptoe scalers tossed to fly.

But would not the continuation, which I transcribe as prose, have puzzled him?

Thee the last thunder's caverned peal delivered from a wailful night: all dusky round thy cradled light, those brine-born issues, now in bloom transfigured, wreathed as raven's plume and briony-leaf to watch thee lie: dark eyebrows o'er a dreamful eye nigh opening: till in the braid of purpled vapours thou wert rosed: till that new babe a Goddess maid appeared and vividly disclosed her beat of life.

This is a description of the eastern sky at break of day, accurately observed and uniquely worded. But it would not have seemed altogether lucid to that enchanting son of the muses, who called a cloud a cloud, and not a ' brine-born issue ', and used plain Wordsworthian language when telling us how

The everlasting universe of things
Flows through the mind, and rolls its rapid waves,
Now dark, now glittering, now reflected gloom,
Now lending splendour. . . .

Yet there is a Shelleyan essence in the poem, and a Turneresque vision, flawed though it be by strained use of metaphor and excess of far-fetched allusion. A master mind—if not quite a mastering hand—shows us the sublimity of Nature. And one is left asking—Meredith's idiom being what it was—how it could have been expressed otherwise, and how he could more superbly have suggested a day of weather when

. . . wonder with the splendour blent,
And passion for the beauty flown,
Make evanescence permanent,
The thing at heart our endless own.

One can only add that if Meredith had written like Shelley he wouldn't have been Meredith. Nevertheless *The South-*

Wester is in the direct line of descent from the *Ode to the West Wind*. And the oftener one reads it the clearer its complexities become.

Hard Weather is more didactic than descriptive. He tells us that when the wind has teeth and claws and ' Earth sits ebon in her gloom ', it is Nature's call to fortitude. ' Contention is the vital force.' The moral is that those who are strong in brain and prefer the sharpened life to easy drifting thereby find ' the station for the flight of soul '.

Once again we are being preached at in paragraphs of expert versifying. It is a frontal attack on one's poetic sensibilities. *Hard Weather* and its companion piece *The South-Wester*, run to more than 250 lines between them. And I am convinced that, as works of literary technique, they are inferior to the shorter poems in this volume. Read *Seed-Time* and *Outer and Inner*, and ask whether Meredith has not made his points more effectively than when taking three times as long to do it. And who can deny that precision of statement and shapeliness of design are more acceptable to posterity than diffuse declamation? Both these poems end with a Meredithian morality. In *Seed-Time* it is—

> Death is the word of a bovine day,
> Know you the breast of the springing To-be.

In *Outer and Inner*—

> . . . sure reward
> We have whom knowledge crowns;
> Who see in mould the rose unfold,
> The soul through blood and tears.

In both the conclusion is led up to with most delicate art and sensitive observation of Nature. And in *Earth and a Wedded Woman*, a favourite of mine which seems to have strayed out of the 1862 volume, there are touches which almost suggest Tennyson.

> The hall-clock holds the valley on the hour;
> Across an inner chamber thunder treads:
> The dead leaf trips, the tree-top swings, the floor
> Of dust whirls, dropping lumped.

But in most of his output one sees the antithesis of a mind which obstinately insisted on compressed utterance in phrase and statement while lacking the instinct for large-scale condensation.

In *Meditation Under Stars* he found an answer to Ann Taylor's ' how I wonder what you are '. Judged by Reason, the sight of the stars gives us the sense of brotherhood and lasting alliance with the infinite spiritual life scattered throughout space. It is an impressive philosophical exercise, rising at the end to poetic persuasiveness. The last two lines are a memorable inspiration.

> So may we read, and little find them cold:
> Not frosty lamps illumining dead space,
> Not distant aliens, not senseless Powers.
> The fire is in them whereof we are born;
> The music of their motion may be ours.
> Spirit shall deem them beckoning Earth. . . .
> Then at new flood of customary morn,
>   Look at her through her showers,
>   Her mists, her streaming gold,
> A wonder edges the familiar face:
> She wears no more that robe of printed hours;
> Half strange seems Earth, and sweeter than her flowers.

Some way back, when quoting *A Ballad of Past Meridian*, I remarked that for me it is the essential Meredith. And at that stage of my investigations I would have said that it is unlike anything else that he wrote, in cadence and expression. (The individuality of his poems is one of their merits.)

But I have now realised that the *Hymn to Colour*, written more than ten years later, is closely related to it, both in thought and form, though much longer. Anyone comparing the two will see the resemblance, though my own slow mind has only just become aware of it. The essential difference is that the *Ballad* is somehow homely and intimate, while the *Hymn*, until its final stanza, is mystical and sublime. And it differs from most of the verse in *A Reading of Earth*—verse which is undoubtedly great literature—in being great poetry. Thought is in it everywhere; but it is thought transmuted by imagination. The diction is musical and direct; the meaning not easy to divine at a first reading. Needless to say, one is all the better for knowing what it is all about, for the essence of it is profoundly spiritual. But it is one of those poems which can be enjoyed without being clearly understood. The vision that it brings is of mysterious beauty, of a world transfigured and immaterial, the world of summer dawn. And from the first one feels the breath of inspiration in it—that magical quality which causes the fortunate poet to wonder—afterwards—how on earth he did it! Therefore I feel disinclined to analyse and explain the *Hymn to Colour*—or even to quote from it. The thing is a perfect whole. I refuse to lay a finger on it. It is one of his grandest poems, and in some ways his greatest.

CHAPTER SEVENTEEN

1

THE publication of his next novel was an important literary event. For more than six years his reputation had been growing, and the successor to *Diana of the Crossways* was awaited with eagerness by a large number of people, very few of whom had troubled to inspect *A Reading on Earth* and its predecessor. *One of Our Conquerors* was serialised in *The Fortnightly* and—rather oddly—*The Australasian*. He received a thousand pounds for six years copyright. Reviewing it on the day of publication, *The Daily Telegraph* uttered a solemnly respectful warning to all who thought themselves likely to find it enjoyable reading. Meredith was given credit for being a singularly able psychologist. ' At the cost of infinite patience we appreciate that here we have the last word of triumphantly analytic science, dividing with merciless scalpel the living tissues of our common humanity.' *The Daily Chronicle* followed suit by saying that ' Mr. Meredith grows more and more trying. He seems to take a Satanic delight in wrapping simplicity in as many fantastic coverings as he can devise. Of course he doesn't mind your being cross; he enjoys it. You may take him or leave him; all's one to him.' A chorus of critics complained that he had put too great a strain on his readers. How right they were I have learnt by recent experience. Not until half-way through does one begin to be carried along by interest in the story. And, dutifully though I perused every word, there were pages and pages of analytic explanation which my mind refused to take in. The sense was so enwrapped in words that I could only unravel it by a special effort. Only when something was happening could I feel that the book had any grip on me. I was performing a task. At the end I asked myself whether the effort had been worth while. Of course it had; for there are at least three masterly character studies; and—for one who has learnt ' the language of Meredith '—a great deal of splendid writing. But the general effect is of a literary performance that lacks essential vitality. He is spinning a book out of his brain, and doing it with a certain gusto. He is a master of his own method, and his apparently loose construction is in reality a carefully contrived pattern. Nevertheless the style becomes, at times, almost intolerable. One can only say that such a style had never been invented before, and that it seems designed to demonstrate that the English language can be made into a monstrosity of affectations, counterfeit subtleties, pseudo-oracularisms, and forced and ornate phrases. Similar objections had been made to *The Egoist*, with less justification. There the phraseology is an artifice which seems appropriate. But *One of Our Conquerors* is encumbered by laboured locutions. In the first sentence of the book Victor Radnor, walking across London Bridge, treads on a piece of orange-peel and falls on his back. The orange-peel is described as ' some sly strip of slipperiness, abounding in that conduit of the markets '. Later on, a telegram is ' the brown-paper envelope of the wires '; a riding master is ' the hallowing squire of the stables '. What most people would call ' a grudging admission ' becomes ' he toned his assent to the diminishing thinness where a suspicion of the negative begins to wind upon a distant horn '. And when a man kissed his wife ' he performed his never-omitted lover's homage '. He had got into the habit of thinking and talking in this way. What had begun as lively conversational idiom and ingenious word-craft had become a preposterous mannerism, when used for the purposes of fiction. In a poem it was permissible to translate ' looking at the stars causes profound thought ' into

> To deeper than this ball of sight
> Appeal the lustrous people of the night.

In prose narrative simplicity is preferable. Fair dealing with the reader demands it of a writer. And in this particular novel he had a plot which needed no subtleties of treatment. Victor Radnor, a great City merchant and financier, is in the prime of life and success. At twenty-one he had married a wealthy woman, more than double his age, presumably for her money. When the story begins he has been living for twenty years with the beautiful Nataly Dreighton, an ideal happiness, but for the fact that his elderly wife has refused to divorce him. They have a grown-up and delightful daughter, Nesta, who is ignorant of her parent's position. (Nataly and Nesta are two of Meredith's finest creations.) The old woman is their skeleton in the cupboard while they live before the world. She is ill, but declines to die until the last chapter, when she makes her only appearance in the book with macabre effect. Meanwhile there have been inevitable complications about Nesta and the young aristocrat who wishes to marry her, but withdraws when Nataly tells him that her daughter is illegitimate. Nataly dies of heart-disease a few hours before the old woman; Victor loses his reason and dies a year later. Nesta marries the right man, Dartrey Fenellan, a handsome, athletic, and philosophic person of the type admired by Meredith. The background is filled in with several dozen supernumerary characters, most of whom fail to come to life. There is much arraignment of the place accorded to women by Society, and the clergy are handled with scant respect. The odd thing about it is that Meredith must have planned the book as being likely to arouse interest through its fearless discussion of contemporary problems. He was anticipating H. G. Wells in using the novel as a vehicle for conveying radically destructive criticisms of accepted and conventional ideas. He even ventilates his advocacy of conscription, and points to the unpreparedness of the Army to resist Invasion, bringing in ' the old generalissimo half-asleep on his horse ' while reviewing the troops, evidently a reference to the Duke of Cambridge, who was at that time Commander-in-Chief. And through the company-promoting activities of Radnor he indicts Mammon. But where a new novel by H. G. Wells was resistlessly readable and stimulating, this one fatigues by its inescapable aridity. To a 1906 admirer who had reluctantly described it as ' a sort of literary nightmare ', he wrote :—

It is a trying piece of work. I had to look at it recently, and remembered my annoyance in correcting proofs. But, strange to say, it held me. Also I found much in it that is now made manifest of the malady afflicting England.

The best that can be said for it has been written by Desmond

MacCarthy, who is far better qualified than I am to illuminate the subject.

The fact that he had been engaged during six years principally in writing verse accounts for the style of *One of Our Conquerors*, which proved so unpalatable that he almost lost the recognition which *Diana* had won for him. There were signs of a barometric fall in public favour. It is a style full of originality, picturesqueness, and vigour, but all cased and slated over in metaphor and trope. It is distracted into tortuosities, dislocations, crotchets, cramped terms, and quaintness. To those who prefer the regularity of the plough in a level field to a broken country with the swallows of fancy dipping overhead, it is impossible reading. It must be remembered in reading Meredith that half his touches are not intended to help you to realize the object so much as to put power into the form. Granted this style is far too self-conscious, over-informed with allusion, and that there is much wordy wilfulness in it; granted that he writes as a man who leaps continually beyond his subject, yet how admirably suited, nevertheless, is such a style to the novelist who would prepare us to rise at any moment from the high road of narrative into regions of poetry. . . . He is a poet using the novel as a means of expressing the beauty of life. He is too impatient to jump the dreary places which must be traversed if the novel is to be what it should be, a representation of life.

2

In spite of its unfavourable reception, *One of Our Conquerors* reached a second edition within a few months, for he had become the fashion with the serious-minded. This was further demonstrated in the autumn of 1892, when he published another volume of poems, *The Empty Purse*, of which several hundred copies were sold at once, though he had ceased to send out review copies of his books of verse. In this collection his diction has become desperately obscure. *The Empty Purse* is a social and political sermon, addressed ' To Our Later Prodigal Son '. Years afterwards he wrote of it, ' I regret that I have written didactic verse, such as *The Empty Purse*, which is not poetry. But I had to convey certain ideas that could not find a place in the novels.' Here is a specimen of how he did it.

> For the secret why demagogues fail,
> Though they carry hot mobs to the red extreme,
> And knock out or knock in the nail
> (We will rank them as flatly sincere,
> Devoutly detesting a wrong,
> Engines o'ercharged with our human steam),
> Question thee, seething amid the throng.
> And ask, whether Wisdom is born of blood-heat;
> Or of other than Wisdom comes victory here;—
> Aught more than the banquet and roundelay,
> That is closed with a terrible terminal wail,
> A retributive black ding-dong?
> And ask of thyself: This furious Yea
> Of a speech I thump to repeat,
> In the cause I would have prevail,
> For seed of a nourishing wheat,
> *Is it accepted of Song?*

Yet, among these turgid admonitions, there are fine passages where he repeats his warning that Age can only justify its existence by service to Youth.

> Thou under stress of the strife
> Shalt hear for sustainment supreme
> The cry of the conscience of Life:
> *Keep the young generation in hail,*
> *And bequeath them no tumbled house!*

Tragic words for the generations, old and young, of to-day, who have wrought and inherited ruin and ruin redoubled, in a world where belief in human progress has been replaced by stoical despair and the foundering of all philosophies which sustained the spiritual fortitude of homo sapiens, for whom omnipotent Science has provided knowledge which he cannot be trusted to use without destroying himself. The possibility of this climax to enlightened monkeydom was foreseen by Meredith when writing on Armaments.

> Since the discovery of the effect of the needle-gun, scientific men in all countries have been busying themselves with the invention of destructive engines that shall annihilate armies and fleets, and represent a fight of brains rather than animal force. We have heard philosophers of the old school declare that the end of all science was to polish man off the face of the

globe! Perhaps there cannot be much doubt that with man's consent the thing might be accomplished. With the rapid advance of the principle of destruction we are entitled to look forward all the more confidently to the advent of the millenium of peace.

Would his optimistic outlook withstand the present situation, I wonder?

Less difficult than *The Empty Purse*, because more rewarding, is the *Ode to Youth in Memory*. Here he expressed his philosophic attitude to the state of growing old. Read as a prose statement, it contains much that is both touching and impressive. We must accept the conditions, he says, and the compensations will come to us. Age should be content with the retrospect of a life well spent. Attempting to repeat the experiences and joy of youth, it wins only darkness. Among the compound compression of continuous metaphor one meets with occasional lines which are almost, if not quite, poetry, such as—

> . . . we win
> Clear hearing of the simple lute,
> Whereon, and not on other, Memory plays
> For them who can in quietness receive
> Her restorative airs: a ditty thin
> As note of hedgerow bird in ear of eve. . . .

Memorable, too, is his affirmation that—

> Did we stout battle with the Shade, Despair,
> Our cowardice, it blooms; or haply warred
> Against the primal beast in us, and flung;
> Or cleaving mists of Sorrow, left it starred
> Above self-pity slain. . . .

This, surely, is 'accepted of Song'. But deepest at the springs of Earth, he tells us, is an eye to love her young, whose glad companionship makes Elysian meadows for the mind.

> Blood of her blood, aim of her aim, are then
> The green-robed and grey-crested sons of men.
> She tributary to her aged restores
> The living in the dead. . . .
> But love we well the young, her road midway
> The darknesses runs consecrated clay.

Despite our feeble hold on this green home,
And the vast outer strangeness void of dome,
Shall we be with them, of them, taught to feel,
Up to the moment of our prostrate fall,
The life they deem voluptuously real
Is more than empty echo of a call,
Or shadow of a shade, or swing of tides. . . .

The *Ode to the Comic Spirit* is a four-hundred-line assault on one's bemused intelligence. It contains a few quotable sayings:

Ah, what a fruitless breeder is this heart

(a belated survivor of the poetic impulse which produced *Modern Love*).

Past thought of freedom we may come to know
The music of the meaning of Accord

(an emergence into lucidity with which he ends the Ode), and

The rich humaneness reading in thy fun—

(a reference to the Comic Spirit, reminding one of *An Essay on Comedy*, which is infinitely preferable, and nearer to poetry).

When describing it as an assault, I am not complaining so much of its component parts as of their cumulative effect. The verse paragraphs are often long, but not incomprehensible. What the mind recoils from is the effect of being shouted down by over-stressed images and ideas. Nothing could be more incompatible with the music of the meaning of Accord.

One turns with relief to *A Night of Frost in May*, which recovers the fine quality of *A Reading of Earth*, and gives us the nightingale's song as only Meredith could have rendered it. The strident jargonings of the didactic performances are forgotten; they move away like an arguing mob of social reformers. We are in the glade where—thirty years before— Sandra Belloni was set to sing against the nightingales ' under larches all with glittering sleeves, and among spiky brambles, with the purple leaf and the crimson frosted, and all the young green of the fresh season shining in white jewels '.

In this shrill hush of quietude,
The ear conceived a severing cry.
Almost it let the sound elude,
When chuckles three, a warble shy,

From hazels of the garden came,
Near by the crimson-windowed farm. . . .

Then soon was heard, not sooner heard
Than answered, doubled, trebled, more,
Voice of an Eden in the bird
Renewing with his pipe of four
The sob : a troubled Eden, rich
In throb of heart. . . .

3

Some attempt must now be made at a biographical outline
of the years up to 1896, when his working career may be said
to have ended and his physical disabilities restricted him almost
entirely to seclusion at Flint Cottage. By then his family life
had been simplified. In 1892, his son William married Miss
Daisy Elliot, whom he began by describing, to Mrs. Leslie
Stephen, as ' an accomplished musician, and an extremely sweet
good girl '—an opinion which he never found cause to change,
for there is every evidence that she was one of the blessings of
his old age. In 1894, his daughter Marie married Henry
Parkman Sturgis, whose pleasant house was only a few miles
from Box Hill. The sense of separation was thus mitigated,
and he subsequently had the pleasure of being often with his
grandchildren. It must also have been a relief to him, for at
the age of sixty-one he had found himself alone with a daughter
of eighteen whose interest in literature was—if perceptible at
all—quite superficial. She was a lively, pretty girl, and her
intention, as was only natural, aimed at ' being in Society '.
So he had to look about him for those who could launch her in
the ' whirl of gaieties ' for which she craved. This seems to
have been mainly effected by Mrs. Walter Palmer, who
appears on the scene early in 1889 with an invitation to take
Mariette to Bayreuth, where she had hired a house. ' Queen
Jean ', as Meredith called her, was the wife of a member of the
famous biscuit manufacturing family, and therefore extremely
affluent. A drawing of her by Sandys shows an attractively
handsome and vivacious countenance, and for several years
she reigned as Meredith's chief object of adoration. Through

her, he became rather more social than had been his habit. There is a photograph which shows him sitting with folded arms in a group, taken during one of her house-parties at Reading, in September, 1892. His beard has been neatly trimmed for the occasion, and he looks, as one would expect, as though he were feeling the strain of lionisation. Forbes-Robertson and H. B. Irving are there. Mrs. (afterwards Lady) Palmer, in a feathered hat, is leaning back in a negligent attitude, one hand behind her head. Sandys, in his drawing done four years later, must have idealised her, since here she strikes one as a typically resolute hostess. There is a world of evening parties in that face, and the eyelids are a little weary. I had almost added ' she is older than the rocks among which she sits ', but this is no Mona Lisa, for she is sitting on a sofa in a conservatory; and immediately behind Meredith, with one large hand on the corner of the sofa, stands Oscar Wilde, with lazy, amiable eyes, and an unuttered paradox hovering on his lips. Meredith wrote afterwards that he ' found him good company ', as well he might. Had he not written that Browning was great and that the only man who could touch the hem of his garment was Meredith, adding, ' Meredith is a prose Browning, and so is Browning ' ? (He had also described Meredith as ' an incomparable novelist '.)

About three months previous to this social *tour-de-force*, Meredith had been operated on for stone. The choice of surgeon was providential. Sir Buckston Browne, who died in 1945 at the age of ninety-four, was not only eminent in his profession and beloved by all who knew him, but a man of fine literary taste. He is remembered also for his benefactions, which included the gift and endowment, for the British Association, of Charles Darwin's house at Downe.

> I had for some years [he wrote in 1911] wished to see or know Mr. Meredith, and had often tried to imagine the personality of the author of *The Egoist* and *The Ordeal of Richard Feverel*, when one morning a letter came asking me to give him a professional appointment at my house. On June 20th, 1892, he plumped himself down in what has been called the victim's chair in my consulting room. He was then ataxic, and literally threw himself into chairs with alarming precipitancy. His first words were, ' Mr. Browne, I am a writer,' and I was able to say at once, ' Mr.

Meredith, you need no introduction here,' and opening a bookcase in front of him I showed a complete edition of his works. We became great friends. He gave me his entire confidence, and although exceedingly sensitive in every possible way, he proved an excellent patient. . . . I operated and removed a large stone on June 26. Owing to his ataxic condition, operation was again necessary in December, 1895, and again in March, 1899. . . . Although I saw him in all sorts and conditions of health, his welcome was always cheery and often rollicking, and I do not remember a single frown.

Lord Ormont and his Aminta is ' gratefully inscribed ' to him. Meredith had difficulty in getting him to take his fee.

Toward the end of this year he wrote to Mrs. Leslie Stephen that Watts had most generously offered to paint his head for the list among his gifts to the nation.

It is distressing, for I could not consent to absorb any of his precious time, or to sit for such a purpose. I am ashamed to say I have no ambition to provoke an English posterity's question, Who is he? and my grizzled mug may be left to vanish. To this effect I must write. It is really painful to meet the dear and noble fellow's offer in such a manner.

However, by the end of April, Mrs. Watts was able to write to Janet Ross—

You will be interested to hear that Signor has been painting a friend of yours and of Lady Duff Gordon, whose memory seems green and beautiful in his mind still. I mean Mr. George Meredith. Signor had long wished to have his portrait among the representative men he has painted. I think it will be fine. Mr. Meredith is very attractive to me. He is better than his work. He gives himself out more *simply* and with as fine a touch when he talks.

The portrait, which was finished in May, has been generally regarded as a failure. The beautiful face is there, but the daemon of genius has been tidied away. To me, it looks like a cross between a distinguished art-critic and a dilettante Ambassador. Tennyson had once asked Watts to describe his ideal of what a true portrait-painter should be, and had transmuted the reply in some lines in the ' Idylls '.

As when a painter, poring on a face,
Divinely, through all hindrance, finds the man
Behind it, and so paints him that his face,
The shape and colour of a mind and life,
Lives for his children, ever at its best. . . .

With Tennyson, Watts had been notably successful, both in 1859 and 1891. But Meredith was a more difficult subject than the statuesque and meditative Laureate. His face was a wind-blown sky of expressiveness and thought in action. In repose it may have been as Watts represented it. But I also suspect that Mrs. Watts, who ' had the delight to be sitting by when Signor painted ', made him feel prim and proper. One regrets that he refused to sit to Sandys, with whom he would have been exchanging ribald jokes. Sargent, who made two drawings of him in 1896, has caught the spirit of him (though Meredith himself surprisingly called it ' an amiable Shade '). Here he is not on his best behaviour. We see the proud old poet, time-ravaged, aggressive, indomitable, whose sword was common-sense and who could give as his gospel ' Fortitude is the one thing for which we may pray, because without it we are unable to bear the Truth '.

4

During the last twenty years of his life, an increasing number of people recorded their impressions of Meredith's personality and appearance, usually for immediate publication in magazines. The public was provided with a series of more or less stereotyped glimpses of him as the famous novelist in his home surroundings. Very few of them have any biographical value or interest. After his death the inevitable reminiscences cropped up, but even these were mostly lacking in candour and penetration. In 1933, however, unexpected revelations arrived in a volume called *Works and Days*. This was composed of extracts from the Journals of Michael Field. For the enlightenment of the uninitiated, I must explain that Michael Field was the pseudonym adopted by two ladies, Katherine Bradley and her niece Edith Cooper. United by a bond of passionate admiration for each other, they devoted their lives to a copious output of collaborative verse. In 1884 (Miss Bradley being

then thirty-nine and Miss Cooper twenty-four) they published
their first volume, containing two verse plays. This created
something of a stir in literary circles. They were greatly
encouraged by praise from Browning, whom they met about
half-a-dozen times, and who behaved to them with fatherly
benevolence, to which they responded with rapturous admiration and gratitude. From their notes about him, which are
touching and valuable, one infers that Miss Cooper somehow
reminded him of his wife and brought the past back to him.
The sequel was a sad one. When Miss Cooper died, in 1913,
they had published, at their own expense, twenty-eight unact-
able poetic dramas and eight volumes of verse. Of these
publications, Logan Pearsall Smith, in a delightfully feline
account of ' these intrepid ladies ', has written:—

> Full of grandiose passions, dreadful deeds of lust and horror,
> incest and assassination, hells of jealousy and great empires
> tottering to their fall, these sombre and fiery volumes fell, all of
> them, one after another, into oblivion; the British public took no
> notice of them, the literary journals gave them scanty considera-
> tion; only once, when they gave the world some paraphrases of
> Sappho's verse, their attempt to breathe once more the air of
> Lesbos was answered by a few brickbats, flung at them by the
> Press in a somewhat perfunctory manner.

Convinced that they were the victims of a conspiracy, they
published most of their later books anonymously. (In my
youth I bought one, *Borgia* by name.) When anonymity failed
to break the spell, non-appreciation only served to enhance
their belief that posterity would award the praise denied them
and that the name of Michael Field would rank with the
immortals.

Their work had distinction and some intensity of lyric feeling.
But it was unrelated to living experience—one might almost
call it counterfeit literature—and was permeated by the life-
lessness which makes such productions unreadable. Imitations
of Euripides, and of Elizabethans such as Webster and Tour-
neur, could not succeed when evolved by two maiden ladies
who, however Maenad-like their imaginations may have been,
knew nothing of the world beyond their small coterie of artistic
and literary acquaintances, and for whom the death of their

dog, a Chow, was such a crushing calamity that it evoked an impassioned sonnet-sequence. Miss Bradley was ruddy, vivacious, and full of small talk and mild gossip. Miss Cooper was shy, gentle, and fragile, with little conversation. Their journals reveal them as acute observers of the people they met, in spite of irritating preciosities of phrase. But what they reveal best is themselves—proud, touchy, self-occupied, and excessively tiresome. It was, in fact, almost impossible to know them without ultimately offending them beyond forgiveness. Anyone who failed to treat them with the utmost respect and subservience was excommunicated. Such were the portentous females who, one April day in 1892, alighted from a cab at the door of Flint Cottage, having been invited to luncheon. For several years they had admired, and longed to know, Meredith—not from afar, since they were living only a few miles away, at Reigate. They had sent him several of their books, and had received the courteous and appreciative replies which such offerings demanded of him. Like Browning, he found promise, and even ' classic concision ' in their verse, and was probably interested by the phenomenon of the double-personality poet who was still being talked about by literary people who had yet to become surfeited by an inexorable and unremitting output of tragedies derived from remote historical themes. About two years before this, they had travelled to London with him in the same compartment of a railway carriage, but had got no further than sharing his foot-warmer. This encounter had caused a great flutter of excitement. They noted, in their high-flown way, that his eyes were ' much the colour of nuts at Christmastide; yet, with all their rapidity, a certain profound languor emerges, and slow recluse smiles ', supplementing this with ' his eyes—dusk as bloom of purple grapes, yet generative of fire and at moments with the alert brilliancy of lighted wine at a festival '. Early in 1892 he had sent them the reprint of *Modern Love*. When thanking him, they asked whether they might call on him. He replied that he was in bad health (he was, in fact, too unwell to receive his Degree at St. Andrews in April), but hoped to invite them soon. This caused them, while strolling round their garden, to clench their fists toward Box Hill and ' will with power that he be moved to ask us to lunch ' ! He did; and a few days before the event they were

introduced to Miss Meredith at a picture gallery. ' She is
frank, cold, spoiled, shallow. Her complexion fair, her eyes
steel-blue, blonde hair in masses, deep lips with lovely curves.
She is elegant, bears herself haughtily, has no graciousness in
the eyes.' (After meeting her again they relented—' She is a
nice maiden after all—a little spoiled, and only distant through
awe, which soon melts away.') Anyhow, here they are at last,
observing every detail of the house. While they wait on the
threshold, ' suddenly a grey figure jerks out of the door—I
see a knot of vermilion under the throat, a grizzledness, brown
skin beaten by life; from the indistinct vision I am conscious
of disappointment, that is a sorrowing pain. " I must come
forth to bid you welcome," says a voice highly artificial,
measured in pronunciation and rather rigid in timbre.' This is
Edith Cooper. Already she is finding difficulty in forgiving
the great man for not being in perfect preservation! (She
coins an exasperating label for him—' the Novelist Greyness! ')
In the drawing-room which is described in detail, they are
introduced to Richard Le Gallienne and his wife, who is un-
flatteringly vignetted as ' a boneless heap of green Liberty
smocking—over her happy aestheticism she pokes her chin,
while Richard Le G. is charming, handsome, with a look of
being delicately set apart.' Meredith always had lunch at
three o'clock, so he earns disapproval by vanishing until ' we
are taking salad to the cold lamb. . . . He asks if I enjoy
old Hock. I say Yes. Then one of the oldest bottles in my
cellar shall be brought for you. There is a sense of fuss as host
and housemaid disappear.' He joins them again, and ' diverges
into a Dionsyic homily on the rich power in wine of improve-
ment '. The Le Galliennes depart for their train, and they
settle in the drawing-room for conversation. Miss Cooper has
now ' had time to get an impression of him '. Here is what her
merciless scrutiny gave him in return for his best Hock.

His eyes are worn hazel—there is a little nervous difference in
their focus—about them something of that piteous old-dog
decrepitude one sees in portraits of Carlyle. The hair is in tint
stone colour, what there is of it curls. The mouth is gaunt with
suffering, the nose fierce and withered, the brow rather narrow,
much lined, the laugh a brilliant contradiction to the features—
Tragic life written over them—a certain distinction in his look

and manner, that of county society: solitude looming above every other record on the face—solitude that has embittered. . . . No one has said the truth: that bodily he is a ruin, that deafness shuts him from the *nuances* of repartee, of allusiveness in others, and that his own wise, witty discourse, emblazoned with metaphor, crystallizes into formal sentences that take the warmth out of speech.

Unconscious that he was the subject of this expert literary vivisection, he conducts them round the garden and up to the Chalet, doing his social duty for all he is worth, poor man. His conversation at tea is reported. He gives his views on Women's Rights, and one feels that he has not said enough to them about the works of Michael Field.

While we finish our cups of tea, our sluggish cab darkens the drive and crawls towards us under the box-hedges, as if it were a vehicle of Fate—the Fate that severs. At the door I turn suddenly to say good-bye—with nervous thrills he ejaculates ' How do you do? ' Painfully checked, I enter the cab, lower the window, meet his eyes, and with a bow lose sight of them. . . . We had been in contact with greatness that astonishes, irritates, pursues—that has nothing of breadth, peace or geniality in it. Like his work, his character lacks ease. One wants to see him again—not when one is with him, but when one has left him for some time.

Thus had the egotistical poetess inspected him, rather as if he were something at the Zoo. Apparently she made no allowance for his state of health, and was unaware that he was entertaining his guests by a forced effort of gracious courtesy. Nevertheless Miss Cooper's impressions have most significant value. She was remarkably intelligent, and the whole thing is refreshingly ' drawn from the life '. Eighteen months later they went to dinner, and found him far more vigorous. He won approbation by talking a lot about their plays in which he seems to have been genuinely interested. Their next visit is in September, 1895. They are with him for two and a half hours, and Miss Cooper's perceptiveness is again actively employed in registering fastidious feelings. She was indeed a difficult person to please. He comes to the carriage window with ' I am delighted to welcome you, ladies,' but she considers his courtesy disconcerting and aggressive. ' It is not a breath, but an emphasis—not an encouragement, but a declaration of itself.' In vain he treats them as equals and fellow workers, talking tirelessly to give them of his best. ' One goes away chilled—one's being unexercised—the conversation one has heard is like marvellous conjuring.' And once again she anatomatises his appearance.

I watch him and listen with a notebook open in my brain. His head is of Elgin marble perfection. . . . The same perfection haunts the eyelids. . . . With these two features, nobility is at an end—the nose is shrewish, lacking in generosity, breadth of inspiration, flutter of sensitiveness—a not ill-shaped, but poor nose. The mouth is sunk, grim—the words form in the brain and are emitted; they do not rise fresh on the lips. . . . He sits by one, a Stranger—almost belonging to another planet, where the laws of life are reversed, and the head generates.

Finally, after observing that ' a smile makes the ruin of his face bland ', she decides that ' his great women, so completely of this earth, come from creative depths—inaccessible to Welsh wrong-headedness and Keltic antipathies, modern self-consciousness and sententious sterility '.

One infers that Miss Cooper found him unsympathetic. She seems to have overlooked the fact that he had a sense of humour, possibly because she had none herself, and was over-poweringly ' arty '. My private opinion is that he was profoundly bored by ' Michael Field ', and breathed a sigh of relief when ' the vehicle of Fate ' conveyed them away, leaving him ' a lank shadow against the hall-light, keeping the form of an arrested bow as we depart '.

But they returned; though it was not until toward the end of 1896 when, as he told them, he was working at great pressure on his three enormous *Odes in Contribution to the Song of French History*. Miss Cooper mentions that ' a cold east wind deadened sky and air and made the distant coppices look distressing '. Evidently the weather was affecting their tempers, for when the unfortunate man announces that he is expecting a lady journalist from London, whom he has been unable to put off, they are ' angered through every bristle at such an unhonoured guest being asked to share our few hours at Flint Cottage '. In the middle of lunch she arrives, and at once creates an unfavourable impression.

She has a fleshy face—all the features flesh, as an uncooked pie is paste—eyes that are points in the unmeaning knobbiness, a laugh that sibilantly flatters, stiff body and chestnut clothes. I begin to look at the clock—one hour and three-quarters before our cab comes!

After lunch, Meredith lights a cigar, and we are told that he ' looks remarkably fine with the delicate gyration of the smoke-circles round his sinuous face—not a prophet but a god of snarls and irony in Pythian comradeship '. They are now progressively becoming offended with him. The lady journalist has got into the chair nearest to him, and Miss Cooper is left in a corner with the dog. When he remarks that Sarah Grand, who has been to see him, ' will improve, for she has said she has begun to care for nothing but literature ', Miss Bradley flares up with ' And you think *that* a good sign? I should think a writer worth reading would care most of all for life.' To which he merely replies, ' Ah, well! ' Meanwhile the lady journalist had been causing a mild disturbance by drawing out of her string-bag a parcel containing ' a model of the Dresden bridal-cup '. ' Not a gift, I trust,' groans George. ' Only a little thing to amuse you,' she warbles. ' You see, dear friend, it is only a toy.' It is well known that Meredith disliked being given expensive presents. On this occasion an argument ensued, and the cup was refused. Miss Cooper considers that her humiliation is deserved—' the gift is indelicate from a widow to a widower.' Anyhow, by the time their cab arrives they are thoroughly huffy.

We leave the room to fetch our wraps. I hear George say as we go, ' I hope you are not vexed with me, Hortense.' When we return he is deep in his seat with the new edition of *Richard Feverel* on his knees, feverishly inscribing it. With the absorption of age he hardly notices Michael's hand with a touch—he says to me carelessly, ' You will excuse my rising.' I am silent and bow like a snow-laden tree, while Michael's voice rings out as if a challenge were thrown down, ' Good-bye, Mr. Meredith.' An alarmed, hurrying ' God bless you,' and we are in the cab with seething hearts.

And Good-bye it was. Never again did their cab darken his door. Friendship with him had become impossible. His conduct, like that of so many people they knew, had fallen below the standard they expected. In 1898 they went to live at Richmond. Meredith wrote them two more extremely gracious letters, which appear in *Works and Days*. These, their editor explains, were preserved without comment.

If I have dallied at disproportionate length on this episode, it is because I found it so refreshingly real in comparison with much of my material. One cannot exactly accuse Miss Cooper of caricaturing Meredith. She merely saw him with un-compassionate eyes, during a period when he was fighting a losing battle with his failing legs, and overstraining himself with the effort of completing his last two novels. It has been pointed out by those who knew him well that he was only at his best when he felt himself to be liked. Except with his intimates, he became self-conscious and uneasily brilliant. Had this lady seen him in the serenity and patient cheerfulness of his last ten years, her heart might have melted toward him. But I fear that he would still have been expected to discuss the latest tragedy by Michael Field as though it were a rediscovered masterpiece by Menander or Marlowe.

CHAPTER EIGHTEEN

1

LORD ORMONT AND HIS AMINTA was published on June 18th, 1894. Having ascertained this date, I fell to wondering how the world and his wife were—as the saying goes—wagging at the time. Whereupon I pulled out a ponderous volume of *The Illustrated London News,* and was rewarded by the following paragraph.

> Lord Edward Cecil's marriage to Miss Violet Maxse was the occasion of a pleasant mingling of political parties in the congregation which assembled at St. Saviour's Church, Chelsea, on June 18th. The signatories to the register included Lord Salisbury, Mr. Chamberlain, Mr. Balfour, Mr. John Morley, and Mr. Asquith, who so recently was himself a happy bridegroom. Mr. George Meredith, who is seldom present at such society functions, came with his daughter, and had as neighbours in the church other representatives of literature, including Mrs. Humphry Ward, Mr. Oscar Wilde, and Mr. Hall Caine.

Looking up the date in Wilfrid Blunt's *Diaries,* I discovered that he too was there. ' At the bride's house the crowd was immense, and I found myself flattened like a herring between Lord Salisbury and a tall Dutch clock.' Turning to the previous page I was again rewarded by finding that on June 11th, when staying with Mr. Evelyn at Wotton, he had driven his coach and four to Box Hill, to see Meredith.

> He is terribly deaf and afflicted with creeping paralysis, so that he staggers from time to time, and once today nearly fell. It does not, however, affect his mind, and he has a novel on hand which keeps him writing six hours a day. He is a queer, voluble creature, with a play-acting voice, and his conversation like one dictating to a secretary, constant search for epigrams. I took the bull by the horns at once about his novels, said I never read prose and looked upon him only as a poet. This pleased him, and he gave me two volumes, recommending especially the piece called ' Attila '.

Blunt was a profound admirer of *Modern Love*. Of his own sonnet sequence, *Esther*, when it appeared in 1892, Meredith had written him a letter of high approval, sending him *Modern Love*, which was even then unknown to him. The two were sympathetic in many political matters, and Meredith once said of him that he was one of the few honest men in public life. But his sudden advent that afternoon must have been somewhat perturbing. 'During our talk a luncheon was brought to him on a tray, as he said he was too busy to sit down to a regular meal, and could not write after (having it at) one o'clock, so I left him to his work and drove on.' The wording of this strikes me as insensitive. He had seen what he wanted; away he drove, rather as though he had inspected a ruined abbey. Meanwhile the object of pilgrimage, tired and over-excited by his volcanic visitor, returned to the concluding chapters of *The Amazing Marriage*, wherein, as he told someone, he 'had to drive two dozen characters as two, making all run together to one end'. One is glad to read a note by Morley, telling how he visited him on June 16th.

> I had not seen him for an age. His disabilities in movement were painful, and he is very deaf. Otherwise he was less altered than I had expected. One or two splendid expressions fell from him, but on the whole he was less turbulent and strained than he used to be. We sat in the garden for a couple of hours. A glorious summer day.

Here, anyhow, was the kindly approach of an old friend who had never found him anything but manly and valiant. In the middle of August, Marcel Schwob, a gifted young French *litterateur*, went to see him. In his charming and sympathetic account he noted that when Meredith, who was working in the Chalet, came down to meet him he showed physical traces of his mental efforts. 'Those wonderful eyes of his, in the first few seconds of our interview, were literally intoxicated with thought.' Conventional people who visit a man of genius, and depart to record his superficial mannerisms, would do well to remember that they have, possibly, been intruding on spiritual territory which is beyond their understanding. Those who found cause to criticise Meredith's behaviour should have been reminded that with a great creative gift we must be willing to bear greatly, because it has already greatly borne.

M. Schwob was accompanied by a son of Alphonse Daudet. Eight months later the Daudet family arrived, *en masse*, shepherded by Henry James. (Daudet himself seems to have remained in London, being crippled by paralysis of the legs. Meredith greatly admired some of his writings.) Madame Daudet, who was given a bouquet of lilies of the valley, described the afternoon visit in a piece of vivacious but commonplace journalism which she supplemented by an account of her second meeting with Meredith at the Piccadilly mansion of Mrs. Walter Palmer—' handsome and kindly, robed in black velvet, her dress cut low over an under-vest of old lace, which made her curl-crowned head like one from an old Italian picture. She paid great attention to Meredith, in a way that showed she was in full sympathy with this great man of genius.' (As far as I can make out, Mrs. Palmer's attentions to him became less noticeable when his condition made it impossible for him to appear at London parties. His last letter to her is in the spring of 1899, when he, significantly, wonders whether there is any hope of seeing her after her return from the Riviera.) That Madame Daudet knew next to nothing about his writings was manifested when, after remarking that ' his work is full of human observation expressed in the highest manner ', she informed her readers that he is ' the Mallarmé of England '—a comparison which must have surprised him. He saw them off at Victoria, and one who was there has related that when the train began to move he was almost pulled off his legs owing to the heartiness of his final handshake with Daudet and the mutual stiffness of their rheumatic fingers.

2

In a previous chapter I have mentioned the Burford Bridge Inn and its literary associations, created by Keats and Stevenson having stayed there. One hot Saturday afternoon in July, 1895, yet another page was added. A passer-by, observing thirty or forty men assembled on the lawn, would have been unaware that something unusual was taking place.

Literary history, however, records that among those present were the editors of *The Daily Chronicle*, *The Westminster Gazette*, *The Pall Mall Gazette*, *The British Weekly*, and *The Illustrated London News*, i.e., H. W. Massingham, E. T. Cook, H. Cust, W. Robertson Nicoll, and Clement Shorter. Also Theodore Watts-Dunton, William Sharp ('Fiona Macleod'), George Gissing, and Max Pemberton (a prolific popular novelist who had recently resigned the editorship of *Chums*). J. M. Barrie, who was playing cricket that day, had telegraphed facetiously regretting his absence. But Edmund Gosse was there, and had brought as his guest a rather reticent little gentleman named Thomas Hardy. These notabilities had arrived for the annual country dinner of the Omar Khayyám Club, a convivial organisation founded in 1892 by enthusiasts for the author of the *Rubáiyát* and—somewhat incongruously—its shy and reclusive translator. The President of the Club for that year was Edward Clodd. It was he who had arranged that the dinner should be held at Burford Bridge; and the occasion was to be made memorable by the presence of Meredith. Clodd had known him since 1884, when he met him at Cotter Morison's house. (He mentions in his *Memories* that they lunched at the Garrick Club after attending Morison's funeral in 1888.) As an occurrence in literary history, one may suggest that it was concocted rather than spontaneous and unpremeditated. For the whole affair had been contrived by Clodd, actively assisted by his friend and confederate Shorter. Success depended on whether 'the greatest figure among leading men of letters' could be induced to put in an appearance. This had been safely engineered by the persuasiveness of Clodd, a worthy and jovial man, in many ways admirable, whose wiliness caused Meredith to address him in subsequent letters as 'Sir Reynard'. For reasons of health he was unable to appear at the dinner, but he would come down and join them for an hour or two afterwards. The scene was described by Robertson Nicoll.

Dinner was just over when Mr. Meredith appeared. He was, of course, received by the company standing, and with unfeigned demonstrations of respect and goodwill, demonstrations which evidently touched him. Mr. Shorter conducted him to the seat of honour on the right hand of the chairman, and he made a striking figure against the sunshine streaming through a window half covered with green boughs. The serene and honoured evening of his life has brought an expression of peace and geniality to his features which one does not trace in current likenesses. He is somewhat infirm, but moves with much stateliness, and his voice is loud and cordial. As he came in he saluted his acquaintances at the table, exchanged hearty greetings with Mr. Hardy, and seemed specially gratified to meet Mr. Gissing.

All, in fact, went swimmingly. ' The old man ' (as Shorter may have remarked afterwards in the adenoidish voice which I have so often heard imitated) ' came up to the scratch like a Trojan.' Meanwhile some of the now well wined Omarians must have been wondering whether he would be jockeyed into saying a few words. Clodd welcomed him in a speech which ' combined graceful badinage with more than a trace of deep feeling '. In order to work in Omar Khayyám, he referred to the capacity Meredith had shown to understand the East in his *Shaving of Shagpat*, whereat the great novelist was heard to say, ' I had forgotten that '. The proceedings became unmistakably historic when he rose and told them that this was the first time he had ever made a speech. (He might have qualified this by admitting that he had been making them, sitting down, most of his life.) He spoke of Clodd as the most amiable of hosts and the most dastardly of deceivers, chaffingly alluding to the fox-like trick he had played on him. (Years afterwards he reminded Clodd, in a letter, of how he had pitchforked him over the table of the Omar Khayyámites.) Robertson Nicoll described his speech as exquisite in form and benignant in feeling of personal gratitude to everyone there. Nicoll, by the way, had in the earlier part of his article stated that in his poor opinion *Love in the Valley* had been very much destroyed by alteration from its original form, a critical judgment which seems strange from one who was subsequently knighted for his services to literature.

Thereafter [he continues] we had the scarcely smaller privilege of a speech from Mr. Hardy, who looked somewhat worn and pallid. He recalled how Mr. Meredith had read the manuscript of his first book, and went on to say that, if it had not been for the encouragement he then received from him, he would probably not have adopted the literary career.

229

(I imagine that Hardy would much have preferred to be alone, either with Meredith at Flint Cottage, or with his private musings on the Keatsian associations of Burford Bridge.) After this, Gissing related his similar experience of helpful advice from Meredith. The evening concluded with a rush to catch the train back to London, where a rival entertainment awaited them, for the streets were full of excited crowds receiving the first results of the General Election, Lord Rosebery's Government having recently resigned.

Disrespectfully though I have treated it, the episode was significant. The gathering was representative of the best literary journalism of the time, and its attitude to Meredith showed how strong his ascendancy had become. Few of them had ever found him easy to read, and some of them, I suspect, hadn't read him at all. But they liked the idea of his being such a great man, and were reassured by the fact that he certainly looked like one. I doubt whether anyone there, with the exception of Gosse—and possibly Massingham—was capable of foreseeing that Hardy would ultimately be ranked above Meredith as a novelist, apart from his poetry, which he did not begin to publish until 1898.

Anyhow, one can be sure that the demonstration of respect and affection afforded Meredith pleasure and satisfaction, even after he had warned himself that he had, to some extent, been exploited by Clodd and Shorter—the latter being the type of literary man who would print a famous writer's blotting-pad in a limited edition if he could get hold of it, though, according to his lights and limitations, he did his best to further the appreciation of good literature.

3

Having allowed myself a few pages of digressive relaxation, I must, like the Omarian editors at Burford Bridge, return to the office, where Mr. Meredith's twelfth novel is still waiting to be pronounced upon by my expository pen. Compared with its predecessor, I found it easy to read. For one thing, it is a hundred and fifty pages shorter, and there are fewer minor characters than usual. Also the style is less difficult. One feels that in *Lord Ormont and his Aminta* he was attempting to let his readers off lightly. It is a romantic story, based on the career of Charles Mordaunt, Earl of Peterborough (1658–1735), a brilliant general who at the age of sixty-four married Anastasia Robinson, a celebrated singer. But Lord Ormont has served in the Peninsular War, and the period seems to be about 1840. In treatment the book is related to *Harry Richmond*, and recaptures something of the charm of the early Meredith manner at its best. Signs of fatigue are observable, however, not in the actual writing, which is as highly finished as ever, but in the sketchiness of construction and the smaller scale on which it is planned. Nevertheless there are delightful things in it. Lionel Johnson, who had a poet's fine ear for prose, wrote of it :—

> He excels in the description of movement; there are two perfect passages, one a country journey, the other a swim in the sea, which have much of his richest art. His style in such places has the brilliance of rippling and sparkling waves, laughing and dancing shoreward, with a kind of delighted waywardness, a grace upon their strength. It is joyous writing, cordial and entrancing; it clears the air to an exulting serenity.

This is the country journey, in a chariot, of Aminta, to prove that Lionel Johnson knew what he was talking about.

> She had rocked in a swing between sensation and imagination, exultant, rich with the broad valley of the plain and the high green waves of the downs at their giant's bound in the flow of curves and sunny creases to the final fling-off of the dip on the sky. Here was a twisted hawthorn carved clean to the way of the wind; a sheltered clump of chestnuts holding their blossoms up, as with a thousand cresset-clasping hands; here were grasses that nodded swept from green to grey; flowers yellow, white, and blue, significant of a marvellous unknown through the gates of colour; and gorse-covers giving out the bird, squares of young wheat, a single fallow threaded by a hare, and cottage gardens, shadowy garths, wayside flint-heap, woods of the mounds and the dells, fluttering leaves, clouds : all were swallowed, all were the one unworded significance.

Who can deny that Meredith was a superb impressionist? I advise those writers of to-day who sniff and raise their eyebrows at the mention of his name to read that passage carefully and ask themselves whether it is masterly writing. But it will already have been sufficiently obvious to the reader that the main purpose of this book is to show that Meredith, although seldom perused by the present generation, was one whose words, as Hardy wrote of them, ' wing on—as live words will '. No such admonition was needed in 1894, when several dozen newspapers and journals greeted *Lord Ormont* with lengthy reviews. Think what they might of his style, the denizens of Fleet Street bowed before him. Down in Sussex, however, Henry James was reading it with distressful impatience.

> The unspeakable Lord Ormont [he wrote to someone] has roused me to critical rage. Not a difficulty met, not a figure presented, not a scene constituted—not a dim shadow condensing once into audible or visible reality—making you hear for an instant the tap of its feet on the earth.

From the point of view of Jacobean technique, these remarks were, of course, fully justifiable. To comment on them would require of me an essay on the difference between the two novelists—' the one cautious, intricate, and complete, the other standing outside his characters and throwing upon them the searchlight of his intelligence ', as an eminent critic has observed. It is pleasanter to remember that James also said of him, ' He harnesses winged horses to the heavy car of fiction ', and, at the time of his death, ' He did the best things best '. Pleasant, too, to remember that they were friends, though for James his periodic visits were more in the nature of witnessing a performance than occasions for reciprocal communication. For Meredith, whose manners could be a mixture of exquisite courtesy and boisterous humour, his formality of deportment and over-considered utterance must have produced a somewhat non-conductive effect. About a year before his death, he made the following comment to an American journalist.

> His books are hard reading, but I have to read one every year. You know the book which he calls *The American Scene*. The substance of it all is not a revisiting of America, but a tour of James's own inside. He doesn't tell about America, but how he felt when he saw this or that in America. Now and then, he goes so far as to lead you to a little window in his anatomy, and show

you a glimpse of landscape that he says is America. But taken all in all, it's very little one sees beyond the interior of my dear James,

Here is how H. J. would have replied to G. M.—and had indeed already replied in the Preface to *The American Scene*.

My cultivated sense of aspects and prospects affected me absolutely as an enrichment of my subject, and I was prepared to abide by the law of that sense—the appearance that it would react promptly in some presences only to remain imperturbably inert in others. There would be a thousand matters as to which I should have no sense whatever, and as to information about which my record would accordingly stand naked and unashamed. It should unfailingly be proved against me that my opportunity had found me incapable of information, incapable alike of receiving and of imparting it; for then, and then only, would it be clearly enough attested that I *had* cared and understood.

Attested it was, though the clarity of the performance— nearly five hundred pages long—can only be comprehended by those—myself among them—who have acquired a palate for the tortuosities of his final period.

4

When, at the end of 1895, *The Amazing Marriage* had been bestowed on the expectant reviewers, some of them—possibly the hastier ones—proclaimed with relief that it showed a return to the style and rich vitality of the earlier novels. 'The genius,' wrote one of them, 'which over thirty years ago gave masterpieces to an unappreciative world, displays in its age, to a world watching its every effort, all the vigour and freshness of youth.'

'*Lord Ormont*,' remarked another, 'had, to the sense of some of us, a touch of autumn. There were whispers that Mr. Meredith was growing old. But here is the dispelling of such doubts, a book fit to stand beside anything that he has ever written. Of his previous work it is most like *The Egoist*. It is as fine, and vigorous, and subtle as anything he has ever written.' Yet another found it 'a pleasant stride into a past whose fleeting we had feared irrevocable', adding that the first part of the book was perhaps the most satisfactory. Of course it was; because, as we already know, Meredith had written to Stevenson in April, 1879, that he was 'about one quarter through *The Amazing Marriage*'. There is also evidence that he was continuing it in the early '80s, when planning *Diana*. (He had a habit of working on two novels at once, by turns.) It is impossible to ascertain where he returned to it after finishing *Lord Ormont*. No doubt he touched up the earlier chapters, but they are full of gusto and freshness, which perceptibly diminishes as the story progresses. In Chapter 9 we find him saying 'language became a flushed Bacchanal in a ring of dancing similes', which suggests his later style. It seems likely that only the first eight chapters were written when he was in his best form, for they contain passages and qualities which surpass anything in *Diana*. It is significant also that when the manuscript was bought by Pierpont Morgan, those eight chapters were missing, and that Meredith had begun to number the pages from Chapter 9 onwards. But this is merely guess-work. It was at the instigation of his friend Frederick Jameson that he decided to complete the long-neglected manuscript. The book was dedicated to him. Conan Doyle, who visited him in 1894, and to whom he read the first two chapters, has also claimed credit for encouraging him to go on with it.

Among the reviewers, Gosse was prominent in expressing a candid protest against the peculiarity of style which so many people have since found vexatious.

> When he was young he was not content to shine; he desired to dazzle also, and adopted the deplorable habit of saying nothing simply or easily, but always in the oddest language possible, with the maximum of effort. When at the height of his power the images which flooded his mind were so brilliant, the flow of them so copious, that he constantly overruled this tendency and wrote— never, it is true, simply—yet often vehemently and nobly. But with the increasing and inevitable languor of years his imagination has grown less active, and he has allowed it—without conscious affectation, we are sure—to take refuge beneath the increasing extravagance of his artificial diction, which has now reached such a pitch that it is difficult to enjoy and sometimes impossible to understand what he writes.

The passage he quotes in support of these assertions describes a young man seeing green gaming tables for the first time. (It appears in Chapter 9.)

Philosophy withdrew him from his temporary interest in the tricks of a circling white marble ball. The chuck-farthing of street urchins has quite as much dignity. He compared the creatures dabbling over the board to summer flies on butcher's meat, periodically scared by a cloth. More in the abstract, they were snatching at a snapdragon bowl. It struck him, that the gamblers had thronged on an invitation to drink the round of seed-time and harvest in a gulp. Again they were desperate gleaners, hopping, skipping, bleeding, amid a whizz of scythe-blades, for small wisps of booty. Nor was it long before the presidency of an ancient hoary Goat-Satan might be perceived, with skew-eyes and pucker-mouth, nursing a hoof on a tree. Our mediaeval Enemy sat symbolical in his deformities, as in old Italian and Dutch thick-line engravings of him. He rolled a ball for souls, excited like kittens, to catch it, and tumbling into the dozens of vacant pits. So it seemed to Woodseer, whose perceptions were discoloured by hereditary antagonism.

This Woodseer, who plays the same kind of part in the story as Vernon Whitford in *The Egoist*, was drawn from Stevenson, whose Open Road philosophy is fully apparent in him. Captain Kirby, ' The Old Buccaneer ', father of the heroine Carinthia, was derived from the career of Thomas Cochrane, Earl of Dundonald (1775–1860), a famous Admiral. The main action of the plot can be assigned to 1840 or thereabouts. It is an extremely elaborate plot; a bare outline of it would occupy several pages. As in the two previous novels, he set out to champion the wrongs of Englishwomen unsuitably married and oppressed by constraint put upon their natural aptitudes and faculties. At the moment, however, I am more interested in the problem of his handling of the English language, which caused Gosse to exclaim, ' How clever—how deplorably clever and distressing! ' Had he been writing more discursively, I feel sure that Gosse would have applauded the three prelusive chapters, in which Dame Gossip acts as Chorus, providing us with the antecedents of the story. This is not only delightful writing but a supremely expert specimen of a novelist's technical device. He would then have pronounced the next two chapters to be among the very best examples of Meredith's art as a poet-novelist.

They are indeed a beautiful beginning. Brother and sister are leaving their old home in Carinthia. It is empty and dismantled. At daybreak they set out to walk across the mountains. It is all seen and felt through the girl—seen and felt when Meredith was writing with every nerve of his sensitivity. Almost at once we come to the famous passage, ' Dawn in the mountain-land is a meeting of many friends.' This, for its proper effect should be quoted in full, and is too long for this context. It is, of course, an incomparable piece of writing. The narrative continues satisfactory until the aforesaid ninth chapter, a large part of which pictures the gaming saloons at Baden, though the nearest we get to straightforward description is, ' The clustered lights at the corner of the vale under forest hills, the burst of music, the blazing windows of the saloons of the Furies.' The remainder is a mighty exhibition of Meredithian pyrotechnics. Now it may be said that the subject-matter required something of the sort; and he may have intended it as a contrast to the grave simplicity of the mountain journey. And, although seemingly a product of his completing effort, the chapters that follow it are quite easy reading and full of splendid passages—in fact his loss of vitality only becomes obvious after the seventeenth chapter. At this point the writing begins to resemble *One of Our Conquerors*. But I have been asking myself whether, in Chapter 9, he was not reduced to a display of elaborate faking. Had he any detailed remembrance of what the gaming saloons were like? Or was he covering up his hazy recollection of the scene, when spinning out stuff such as ' the Black Goddess Fortune, the pain of whose nip is mingled with the dream of her kiss; between the positive and the imagined of her we remain confused until the purse is an empty body on a gallows, honour too, perhaps '? I have sometimes suspected that, in the pages of his novels which afflict me most, he was in the dilemma—so well known to all writers—of not knowing how to fill a gap, with the result that he practically parodied himself. Prolonged passages of verbal affectation and over-elaboration of metaphor do not occur very often in *The Amazing Marriage*. But there are many pages of narrative and of psychological explanation wherein the staccato sentences exhaust one's mind. The concentration of thought is relentless, and the style a *moto perpetuo* of statements, like someone talking rapidly, never allowing time for reception of the ideas. In persuasive prose there should be *rallentando* and variations of vocal cadence.

While engaged on these tentative remarks I have come across an extreme example of the aesthetic attitude to the ' chaos illumined by flashes of lightning ' method of narration in Meredith. The writer—it was ' Vernon Lee ' in 1905— admits that, compared with the deliberate skill of the great French novelists, there is much blundering, and that the characters are often unreal and unconvincingly presented. Nevertheless she finds that this seems to bring out, by the sense of effort, our vivid perception of his genius. There is no illusion of reality to divert us from the passion and fancy of the author. The random words and sentences take shape into something too marvellous to be called a description.

> Think of *The Amazing Marriage* [she says]. Here one is tempted to imagine that the seeming imperfections are only part of the excellence. Are all our aesthetics mistaken, and is it possible that the greatest written things are just those which have least literary body, which are quickest dismembered and absorbed by the reader, turned into part of himself? This leads her to suspect that ' what we take for the recognition of reality, may be, in the higher walks of literature, the recognition of what our soul requires '.

In the higher walks of intellectualism, this was the correct way to talk about Meredith, before he went out of fashion. Personally, I don't believe a word of it. My soul requires that reality should be robust and recognisable.

Reading the first few chapters again, I have felt that his natural abilities were such as might have made him, unassailably, the greatest of our novelists. For he had certain quintessential qualities of intellectual and imaginative power which could have raised him above Fielding, Dickens, and Thackeray. (But Dickens was Dickens, and to compare him with anyone else is absurd. The same remark applies to Scott.)

To this I would add that one reason why Meredith failed to achieve supremacy was—as I have suggested in an earlier chapter—the tyranny of the three volume novel. He groaned under it, and so did Hardy. They knew quite well that a lot of what they wrote was rubble and fustian. But Hardy's fustian never makes one feel so uncomfortable as Meredith's. It should, however, be borne in mind that the beginning of *The Amazing Marriage* was the last work he did in prose before his health failed. At fifty his mind was in the plenitude of its powers. And then his body let him down.

My final impression of *The Amazing Marriage* is that in Carinthia he has once again created a magnificent woman. If one were to extract from the book every passage in which she is directly presented, it would be found that the writing is never laboured and always empowered by imagination. As in several of his novels, this one woman is the living heart of the story. Again and again, after traversing tracts of narrative that seem sunless in an east wind, one meets her like the warm south-wester that he loved so well. One of the later chapters begins with a description of her walking over the Welsh highlands on a rainy morning. The smell of the air makes her remember how, as a child, she walked with her father through a mountain forest in Austria, ' listening, storing his words, picturing the magnetic veined great gloom of an untasted world '. Writing such as that needs no comment.

5

Among the first notices of *The Amazing Marriage* there was one by the anonymous writer who was contributing to *The Pall Mall Gazette* a weekly column called ' The Wares of Autolycus '. Meredith had already been attracted by these little essays, with their grace of manner and sanity of thought. He was now delighted that this gifted critic should have found poetry to be the conspicuous secret of his book, realising at once that such sensitive appreciation could only come from someone of fine spirit and distinguished mind. The writer was Alice Meynell. A meeting between them was soon arranged, and this began a friendship which, for the next few years, brought him an almost rapturous experience of felicity. He had acquired an ideal Egeria. After one of their first conversations, he said that they had ' waltzed together on celestial heights '. Her talent was cloistered and fastidious—her expression of it characterised by a conscious femininity. She had the quality—now less often met with—of readiness to look up to masculine achievement and experience with tremulous admiration. A few years before, she had become the close associate of Coventry Patmore, and had thrilled reverently to his directive influence on her poetic art. With Meredith she liked to be a listener, but was never his disciple. What she brought him—apart from charm and distinction of personality and gaiety of spirit—was the strength and subtlety of a first-rate mind. He had found a woman who could think with originality and reason clearly. He was tired of people who only talked to him about his novels. Here was someone with whom he could discuss poetry, someone who was his equal in the art, and whose knowledge and judgment of it matched his own. ' I shall teach you nothing that can be new to such a mind as yours,' he wrote to her, ' but I shall be leaven to your deeper thoughts of earth and life.'

> Sunset worn to its last vermilion he;
> She that star overhead in slow descent:
> That white star with the front of angel she;
> He undone in his rays of glory spent.

Thus, in the twelve lines called *Union in Disseverance*, he expressed their relationship through sublimated thought.

One sees her best in Sargent's drawing, tall and graceful, with large, pensive and penetrating eyes—a figure which somehow suggests, not one of Meredith's heroines, but a lady who has stepped out of the pages of Henry James. Posterity will prefer to associate her memory with that lovely lyric *The Shepherdess*, with the spiritual and exquisite utterance of *A Thrush before Dawn*, and with the intellectual passion of *Christ in the Universe*.

Meanwhile Meredith, by the middle of 1896, was drudging at the revision of his novels for the uniform and complete edition of his works, which appeared, two volumes at a time, for sixteen months, beginning in November of that year. The portentous seriousness with which his novels were now regarded was shown by numerous articles, paragraphs, and letters to the Press, in which his alterations and omissions were exhaustively criticised and debated upon. These alterations were afterwards made accessible to the student in the collected editions.

Age and infirmity were now telling on him. In April he had stayed with Mrs. Palmer in London for an orchestral concert, and had gone with her to the Private View of the New Gallery

Exhibition, where the Sandys portrait of her was being exhibited. This was the last public function that he attended. In the autumn he made an expedition to Cromer, where he stayed with Lady Battersea, a member of the Rothschild family, much valued, by all who knew her, for intelligence and endearing character. It was on this occasion that he met Augustus Jessopp again. In her delightful *Reminiscences*, Lady Battersea wrote of them ' sitting cosily over the fire together indulging in recollections of past days. I had imagined that Canon Jessopp was a Conservative, and this error of mine caused much merriment on the part of the two elderly gentlemen, who kept on ejaculating, " Fancy such a thing! " between peals of laughter, in which I joined.' But, although the visit was repeated a year later, he was becoming too shaky for such efforts. Lady Butcher (Alice Brandreth) tells how, in the summer of 1897, he stayed at her house in London for the last time, and hurt himself rather badly by slipping on the stairs. Intellectually, he was indomitable. During the second half of 1896 he was taxing his faculties to the utmost while working at three enormous *Odes in Contribution to the Song of French History*. Early in December he had finished *The French Revolution* and was halfway through *Napoleon*. ' I make History sing while interpreting her,' he wrote, when inviting Frederick Greenwood to come and hear him read two of the Odes. He thought them almost his best work in poetry, and was disappointed that they did not excite greater interest when published in 1898. Apparently he had no idea how difficult he was, or how violently strained his verse had become. It has been asserted by distinguished authorities that these Odes are among the greatest political poetry ever written. ' It is doubtful ', wrote one of them, ' whether any prose writer has given the essence of Napoleon with such amazing insight. . . . He gives not the mere facts but the essential meaning, the spirit of the facts.' The Odes must therefore be recommended to the attention of historians. G. M. Trevelyan, while admitting that they are ' somewhat too like a chaos of half-completed images ', claims that ' out of the chaos, the ideas emerge with primitive strength when they emerge at all '. For me they are altogether too forceful. I am compelled to agree with a certain eminent writer who found them ' cryptic, jerky, and uncouth '. Meanwhile on his seventieth birthday he received the following address of congratulation.

You have attained the first rank in literature after many years of inadequate recognition. From first to last you have been true to yourself and have always aimed at the highest mark. We are rejoiced to know that merits once perceived by only a few are now appreciated by a wide and steadily growing circle. We wish you many years of life, during which you may continue to do good work, cheered by the consciousness of good work already achieved, and encouraged by the certainty of a hearty welcome from many sympathetic readers.

(Signed) :

J. M. Barrie.	F. W. Maitland.
Walter Besant.	Alice Meynell.
Augustine Birrell.	John Morley.
Austin Dobson.	F. W. H. Myers.
Conan Doyle.	J. Payn.
Edmund Gosse.	Frederick Pollock.
R. B. Haldane.	Anne Thackeray Ritchie.
Thomas Hardy.	Harry Sidgwick.
Frederic Harrison.	Leslie Stephen.
' John Oliver Hobbes '.	Algernon Charles Swinburne.
Henry James.	Mary A. Ward.
R. C. Jebb.	G. F. Watts.
Andrew Lang.	Theodore Watts-Dunton.
W. E. H. Lecky.	Wolseley.
M. London (Mandell Creighton).	

Acknowledging the scroll of parchment, he wrote to Leslie Stephen :—

The recognition that I have always worked honestly to my best, coming from men and women of highest distinction, touches me deeply. Pray, let it be known to them how much they encourage and support me.

To Edward Clodd he made the following facetious comment.

I know what they mean, kindly enough. Poor old devil, he *will* go on writing; let us cheer him up. The old fire isn't quite out; a stir of the poker may bring out a shoot of gas.

The absence of W. E. Henley's signature calls for a footnote. The active organisation of the address was undertaken by Gosse, toward whom Henley had been inexplicably hostile, though Gosse admired his powerful genius. One can only assume that Henley's signature was not asked for, or that he refused to give it. Even this is difficult to understand, since Leslie Stephen, as editor of *The Cornhill*, had been one of the first to befriend and encourage Henley.

CHAPTER NINETEEN

1

IT is not always easy to think of him in the guise of old age. There were times when, as he admitted in a letter to Greenwood, he began ' to feel old in bottle '. But his septuagenarian body contained an unconquerable energy of mind and spirit. ' I had a jump of the heart to be with you,' he wrote to Mrs. Sturgis, in June, 1898, when she was in Guernsey, remembering his yachting trip of 1862 with Cotter Morison and Hardman. About a year later his infirmity debarred him from receiving an Honorary Degree at Oxford. But he had another ' jump of the heart ' when he was almost seventy-two. Lady Granby sent him a reproduction of her delicate pencil portrait of Lady Ulrica Duncombe, to whom he subsequently wrote some very good letters in his role of Enamoured Sage. Lady Ulrica, who had been at Girton, and had studied philosophy with M'Taggart, became a society success in 1899. The portrait shows a type of beauty that suggests Aspasia rather than Juno. The features are refined and regular, affording evidence of an intention to exist on a high plane of serious-mindedness. She was a great admirer of Goethe. Young ladies who saw themselves as ' Meredith heroines ' were now liable to appear on his doorstep at any moment, and this was one of them. He gave her plenty of encouragement, and though it is unlikely that she saw him many times, could sign himself ' with all my heart, your most faithful ', and counsel her that he preached for the mind's acceptance of Reality in all its forms—' for so we come to benevolence and to a cheerful resignation; for there is no other road to wisdom '. She did not like his Diana Warwick, whose passionate, impulsive nature was unlike her own, which he found a little frigid. Sending her an analysis of Diana's character and activities, he ends—

> My Lady has Diana's brows,
> Diana's deer-like step is hers;

243

> A goddess she by every sign,
> Then wherefore is she not divine?
> She has no ear for lover's vows,
> For lover's vows she has no ears.

She has been by the sea; he has had the vision of her shining salt in the sea-breeze and inspiring a grey Triton with the passion to enfold and bear her to his domain.

A few months later she is robing herself to take part in the Coronation and he feels that it is not the moment to write on one of the deep themes of life. Then she goes to India for the Durbar, and offends him by writing that she will not bore him by descriptions of her experiences.

> It is a matter of surprise that she who was placed high as the celestial blue above the Smart Set should on her return from India have adopted their tone and style. . . . We have to suppose that the Lady's mind was a blank, her heart a mechanical beater, her indisposition to 'bore' a blind to such sad facts. And then we are dragged back into formalities with the question, will she be welcome here? The answer to which is in her heart and mind if they be still evident.

This was the end of his intimate inclination to set her on the road to wisdom. He used to say that she ought to marry a Bishop, but she became engaged to the Viceroy's military secretary, Everard Baring, and was married in 1904. Anyhow, she had provided Mr. Meredith with an afterglow of romantic feeling, for which we must be grateful to one whose distinctive beauty interested him more than her aspirations to be highly educated.

In the summer of 1900, the death of Admiral Maxse struck him a heavy blow.

> The loss to me is beyond all count [he wrote]. For I see him, hear him, have him sitting in the chair beside me, as on the day before he left for South Africa, promising to come here early on his return—and now I look at the hill that leads to Dunley, where is hollowness, a light gone out. But still it cannot be quite death for a man so good and true as he. The unsuffering part of him lives with those who knew him. Nobility was his characteristic, and always where that is required in life, I shall have him present.

In May, 1902, when he heard that Leslie Stephen had cancer (of which he died early in 1904)—he wrote to him—and surely these are noble words :—

> We two have looked at the world and through men, and to us the word consolation is but a common scribble, for there is none under a deep affliction that can come from without, not from the dearest of friends. What I most wish for you I know you to have, fortitude to meet a crisis, and its greater task, to endure. We have come to the time of life when the landscape surrounding ' haec data poena diu viventibus ', the tombstones of our beloved and the narrowing of our powers, throws a not unpleasant beam on the black gateway, as we take it to be in the earlier days. And those young ones, whom Nature smites with the loss of us, she will soon bring into her activities, if they are the healthy creatures we wish them to be. . . . So I see things in your mind as well.

Shortly before his death, Stephen wrote, ' My very dear friend. I cannot trust to anybody else to say how much I value your friendship, and I must send you a message, perhaps it may be my last, of my satisfaction and pride in thinking of your affection for me.' Of all Meredith's friends Maxse and Stephen were the two whose temperaments had most in common with his own. All three were spiritual pilgrims, made uneasy and impatient by sensitiveness to their surroundings and urgent awareness of unrighted wrongs. Meredith, of course, was endowed with a creative genius to which the other two made no pretentions. But it is significant of his character that he looked up to them, setting their human qualities above his own. Maxse, most gallant of men, was always his hero. In Stephen he found critical insight and equable integrity and something loveable which profoundly sustained him. Beyond all, perhaps, he valued in him the courage of the magnificent Alpine climber.

During the first years of the New Century he was habituating himself to inactivity. Reliant on the resources of his mind, he made the best he could of an existence which can have provided few outward events beyond the visits of friends and admirers. In the summer of 1903 he was ill, and a news agency announced that his condition was critical and that he was only partially conscious for short periods. This roused him to send for publication a caustic telegram :—

Report of me incorrect; though why my name should be blown about, whether I am well or ill, I do not know. The difficulty with me is to obtain unconsciousness; but sleep, on the whole, comes fairly. I am going on well enough. This for friends who will have been distressed by the report.

In the autumn he became seriously ill, and spent most of the winter recovering in his daughter's house. For five months he never held a pen except to sign his name.

When interviewed by W. T. Stead in the previous summer, he said, ' I do not feel old or lonely. I have my books and my thoughts, and the constant companionship of nature. My religion of life is always to be cheerful. Happiness is the absence of unhappiness.' And in January, 1903, when giving his views on Liberalism to *The Manchester Guardian*, he ended by remarking that he did not feel to be growing old either in heart or mind. ' I still look on life with a young man's eye. I have always hoped that I should not grow old as some do— with a palsied intellect, living backwards, regarding other people as anachronisms because they themselves have lived on into other times and left their sympathies behind them with their years.'

In June 1904 he gave another interview, which appeared in *The Daily Chronicle* and was copiously re-echoed and commented upon in other journals. The reporter was H. W. Nevinson, already a well-known war correspondent, who had obtained the privilege through the connivance of the artful Clodd, to whom, while the affair was being arranged, Meredith wrote, ' I am in the toils of Sir Reynard, and experience tells me that they relax not, struggle as one may. I fear much that your visit will give you but a wizened old hen instead of the plump pullet you look for whenever your sagacious nose is laid to earth.' He stipulated that there must be no shorthand, and Clodd brought Nevinson to lunch.

Meredith discoursed with vigour and occasional jocularity, on his attitude to old age and death, and ' the great issues of the day '. As usual he grumbled a little about the English people and their disapproval of his work. He put in his plea for conscription. ' Every manly nation submits to universal service. In the present state of the world it counts among the necessities for safety.' He gave his opinion on politics and the power of the Press, indulging in some provocative table-talk in the tone of an optimist in a pessimistic mood. Evidently he enjoyed letting off steam to the likeable and brilliant young Nevinson, and neither knew nor cared that his remarks would be the subject of numerous leading articles. The significant fact about these interviews was that they started a new phase in the public recognition of his eminence. Thenceforward the journalists adopted him as an oracle, and for the remainder of his life he was expected to concede them his views on contemporary questions, which, with some reluctance, he occasionally did. (His gardener, Frank Cole, who served him so faithfully for the last thirty years of his life, told someone that ' the guv'nor simply hated interviewers '.)

2

The septuagenarian Mr. Meredith has been described with beautiful precision by Desmond MacCarthy. One December afternoon in 1901 he paid his first visit to Flint Cottage. As he approached the quiet house, with its high box hedges, damp gravel drive, and black speckless windows, his mind was alight with hero-worshipping excitement.

The next moment we were in a narrow passage-hall hanging up our caps and coats, and through a thin door on the right I heard the resonant rumble of a voice. The great man was talking to his dog. He was sitting to one side of the fire, dressed in a soft quilted jacket, with a rug upon his knees. On a little rickety table by his side stood two candles and one of those old-fashioned eye-screens which flirt out green wings at a touch; a pile of lemon-coloured volumes lay beside it. (In his later years much of Meredith's reading was of French memoirs and novels.) His face beneath a tousled thatch of grey hair, soft as the finest wood-ash, and combed down into a fringe upon a high round forehead, had a noble, ravaged handsomeness . . . a noteworthy boldness. I guessed him to be one of those men who seem bigger seated than when on their legs. At this time he could not rise from his chair. That keen look in profile, as of an upward-pointing arrow, had gone. Old age had blurred his eyelids, and his eyes, once blue, were faded and full of ' the empty untragic sadness of old age '; but that vitality which had inspired many a packed page still vibrated in his powerful voice, and told in the impetuosity of his greeting. His talk was full of flourishes and his enunciation grandiose, as though he loved the sound of his own words. This characteristic, I remember, somewhat disconcerted me. It struck me that he talked with a kind of swagger, and I was not prepared for that. Copy-book biographies always insist upon modesty as a sign of true greatness. I had certainly found out that humility was not the invariable accompaniment of power and insight, but I still clung to the idea that great men were always as biographers say, ' simple '. Now ' simple ' Meredith was not, nor was he ' natural ', ' unaffected '; in fact none of the adjectives of obituary respect would apply to him. He was almost stone-deaf, which accounted for the exaggerated loudness of his voice, and the continuity of his discourse, which rolled elaborately along; but the eagerness with which he would now and again curve a hand round his ear and stoop forward to catch an interjection, showed that he was not a born monologist, and that he missed the give and take; though he was, I expect, one likely in any company to follow the sequence of his own thoughts. My Irish name set him off upon the theme of Celt and Saxon. The English were not in favour with him just then; the Boer War (he detested it) was dragging lamely on, and he belaboured the English with the vigour and bitterness of a disillusioned patriot: few men thought more often of their country, or felt more pride in her than Meredith. He accused the English of lack of imagination in statecraft and abused their manners and their unsociability, their oafish contempt of friendly liveliness and wit, the sluggish casual rudeness that passed among the wealthy for good form; mouthing out sentences he had used, I felt, before, and throwing himself back before a burst of laughter, with the air of one saying, ' There, what do you think of *that*? ' to watch upon our faces the effect of some fantastic, hammered phrase.

Then came the question of refreshments. What would we drink? Tea? Beer?—a list of wines ending with champagne (pronounced in French fashion, with a gusto that brought foam and sparkle before the eyes). I forget the beverage we drank, for, shouting like a boatswain in a gale, I was directing the chasing waters of his discourse to irrigate fresh subjects. I wanted to hear him talk of his famous contemporaries. . . .

By this time I had come to feel rather the zest behind his elaborate phraseology than its artificiality, and to marvel at and enjoy his determination to strike a spark from every topic, astounding in a paralysed old man, and in one to whom physical decay must have been the most depressing of all humiliations. Scraps of his talk I still remember. Speaking of Gladstone, he said he was ' a man of most marvellous aptitudes but no greatness of mind '; of Swinburne and his emotional mobility that ' he was a sea blown to a storm by a sigh '; of Dickens' face, when he laughed, that the surprise of it was like the change in a white-beam ' when a gust of wind shivers it to silver '—this spoken with a rapid gesticulation, which suggested the vehemence of his talk in youth. Indeed, there was still such a fund of invincible vitality in him, that it was incongruous to hear him bemoaning himself as one already dead and better buried: ' Nature cares not a pin for the individual; I am content to be shovelled into the ditch.' I remember how in the midst of such discourse, solemn as the wind in the pines, with a humourous growl in it, for an undernote, he looked toward the black uncurtained window, past which a few large snowflakes came wavering down, and that the animation of sudden interest was like a child's. It was a momentary interruption, on he went: yes, the angel Azrael was standing behind him, and he hoped he would touch him on the shoulder. It was, however, a nurse who appeared and stood over him, with a graduated glass containing some dismal fluid in her hand; and we, who had forgotten we had been listening for two hours to an old invalid, took our leave. I looked from the door. He had sunk back in his chair; and with a wave of his hand he sketched an oriental salaam. Had we tired him unconscionably, we asked ourselves anxiously outside the door. As I was hoisting on my coat, I heard again that resonant rumble. He was talking to his dog.

It was thus that he delighted to entertain himself and others, but it can be assumed that on that afternoon he was specially responsive to the good company of a gifted young man of letters. Several of the politicians were taken to see him when he had become a memoirable object of pilgrimage. Lord Haldane has recorded that at various times he was accompanied to Flint Cottage by Asquith, Grey, John Dillon, and Lloyd George. John Burns was another whom Meredith knew and liked. None of them have written their impressions of his personality, but Haldane has given an anecdote of the meeting with General French.

Author and general got into an argument about the disposition of troops at the battle of Magenta. French having said that no

one with any military knowledge could have imagined that at
that stage a whole division could have been brought up to the
point which Meredith thought, Meredith retorted ' General, I
have observed that cavalry leaders however distinguished are bad
judges of the operations of mixed troops.'

Whereupon Haldane hastily ordered the motor and took the
General back to Aldershot.   There is abundant evidence that
Meredith foresaw the military aggression of Germany as
inevitable.   In the last years of his life he wrote that ' those
who know the German mind are of opinion that there is an
intention to try conclusions with England when Germany has
ships to protect a landing '.   At the same time he published a
poem, *The Call*, in which he said :—

> It cannot be declared we are
> A nation till from end to end
> The land can show such front to war
> As bids the crouching foe expend
> His ire in air, and preferably be friend.

Haldane had for many years admired him immensely, and as
Secretary for War must have been considerably influenced by the
strong opinions which Meredith had shared with Maxse.   Had
he lived to see the 1914 Expeditionary Force which ' saved the
sum of things for pay ', Meredith could, perhaps, have claimed
to have been indirectly concerned in Haldane's achievement.

3

The last weeks of the summer of 1904 were spent in sea air at
Peacock Hall near Worthing, rented by him with Will Meredith
and his family, where he was enlivened by visits from congenial
friends, J. M. Barrie and Owen Seaman among them.   He no
longer felt equal to seeing many people at a time.   In July
he had made a final effort of the kind when he welcomed
in his garden about fifty members of the Whitefriars Club,
headed by T. P. O'Connor and Sarah Grand.   An address of
homage was read, in which the ' Friars '—who had already
lunched and made speeches at the Burford Bridge Inn—
assured him that they came ' with the reverence of pilgrims
visiting a hallowed shrine '.   Meredith was unable to rise from

his chair, but after shaking hands with them all, he said a few words in reply, talking in a conversational tone, with abrupt pauses, and now and then a great hearty laugh. ' Respect is a very great thing,' he remarked, ' but I think we are in the habit of falling into a kind of delirium in regard to men who after seventy years or more have made a name. We take them as brandy—it is better to make a kind of dilution, and therefor I mix a considerable amount of water with your compliments.' After that he chatted to two ' fair interlocutors ' while the rest of the disciples sat round and listened to ' this rare unfolding of the master's mind '. A visit was paid to the Chalet, ' where alas, it is to be feared his quills now lie idle ', a ' floral souvenir ' was presented to each lady member of the party, and then they trooped back to the Inn, where ' tea was partaken of '. And the object of veneration, possibly with a sigh of relief, was wheeled back to the house, to ask himself whether his work really was ' the highest blossom of the tree of civilization '. Anyhow, he had given these worthy folk an afternoon of memorable enjoyment, and could now return to the translation of ' The Frogs ' of Aristophanes, which he was reading with pleasure at the time.

His quills were indeed lying idle. He had tried dictating, but nothing came of it. He told someone that sometimes, by the fireside, when he closed his eyelids, whole chapters of new unwritten novels threaded their way before him.

When younger novelists came to see him he would offer them the plots he had thought of. He did this to H. G. Wells. And G. K. Chesterton was given an outline of about a dozen stories. Writers such as these had a tremendously stimulating effect on him. They were of his own mental calibre, and to them he spontaneously revealed the creative energy of his former output. Chesterton's account is extremely valuable as evidence of the extraordinary intellectual opulence which caused so many people to assert that he was much the most remarkable talker they had ever met.

I went through the garden and saw an old man sitting by a table, looking smallish in his big chair. His hair and beard were both white, not like snow, but like something feathery, or even fierce. I came up quite close to him; he looked at me as he put out his frail hand, and I saw of a sudden that his eyes were startlingly young. He was deaf and he talked like a torrent—not about the books he had written—he was far too much alive for that. He talked about the books he had not written. He asked me to write one of the stories for him, as he would have asked the milkman, if he had been talking to the milkman. It was a splendid and frantic story, a sort of astronomical farce, all about a man who was rushing up to The Royal Society with the only possible way of avoiding an earth-destroying comet; and it showed how even on this huge errand the man was tripped up by his own weaknesses and vanities; how he lost a train by trifling or was put in gaol for brawling. That is only one of them. I went out of that garden with a blurred sensation of the million possibilities of creative literature. I really had the feeling that I had seen the creative quality; which is supernatural.

Elsewhere, he wrote that Meredith was that great and powerful paradox, an optimistic reformer who said that the world is so good that it must be improved.

He combines with great primary jollity a great love of oddities, of eccentricities, even of affectations. He is Elizabethan in many things, but pre-eminently in this combination of masculinity and power with literary ingenuities and dandyisms. He is the type of a stronger generation, in his mountainous love of liberty, in his large and ambitious scheme of work; in his philosophic sense of human fraternity, and in his child-like gusto for complexities and vanities.

Up at the Chalet, or somewhere about the house, were the unfinished and long-since-discarded manuscripts of two novels, added to the collected works after his death.

Celt and Saxon is the less than half completed first draft of a full-length story, written between *Harry Richmond* and *Beauchamp's Career*. It contains one amusing and likeable character in the exuberant Irishman Captain Con; and the mysterious Adiante, who never actually appears, suggests that she might have emerged as one of his most alluring heroines. The book is interesting as a specimen of his work before revision and re-writing. The first twelve chapters average ten pages each, and show that, had he chosen, he could have been an excellent straightforward story-teller. These chapters are good novel-writing, putting in the background and laying the foundations of the plot in a distinct, delightful, and masterly manner. The second half of the fragment becomes more diffuse, and with the appearance of Rockney, the great journalist, drawn from Frederick Greenwood, we get some ultra-Meredithian pages in which John Bull is exhibited as a colossus of absurdity. ' He is our family goat, ancestral ghost, the genius of our comfortable sluggishness. At times he is a mad Bull; a foaming, lashing, trampling, horn-driving, excessive very parlous Bull. . . . Englishmen of feeling do not relish him.' It is an example of Meredith losing control of his artistic intention. After the unelaborated pictorial beauty of the earlier chapters, such out-pourings of rhetoric make one feel that the story is going to pieces. Of *The Gentleman of Fifty and the Damsel of Nineteen* there are only six short chapters, presumably written soon after his second marriage. Here the writing is consistently clear and descriptive, the story being told alternately by ' He ' and ' She '. The elements of a minor masterpiece are apparent, and one laments that he never finished this charming piece of Victorianism. His comedy *The Sentimentalists* was begun in 1862, put aside for fifteen years, and again abandoned. Some time after 1895 he worked on it again. After his death the fragments were collected by Barrie and it was produced by Granville Barker for a few performances. What there is of it is elegant and artificial. Written with no sense of the theatre, it reads like a weak imitation of classic French drama. *A Reading of Life*, published in 1901, contains two poems which could not be excluded from a representative selection of his verse. *A Night Walk* is an old man's imagination of ' the pride of legs in motion ', a recovery of some moonlight night when he walked with a friend, ' delighted with the world's embrace ', when Youth was ' rapacious to consume ' and ' cried to have its chaos shaped ' :

> Absorbing, little noting, still
> Enriched, and thinking it bestowed ;
> With wistful looks on each far hill
> For something hidden, something owed . . .
> So royal, unuttered, is youth's dream
> Of power within to strike without.
>
> To either then an untold tale
> Was life, and author, hero, we . . .

For we were armed of inner fires,
Unbled in us the ripe desires;
And passion rolled a quiet sea,
Whereon was love the phantom sail.

Song in the Songless is one of his shortest, and, at first sight, slightest lyrics. Yet I know of no other poem wherein an old man's spiritual music has been more movingly expressed. He is a dry reed, but the response to life is still in him. One sees his time-worn figure walking by the river in the dusk of a winter day. An epitome of what Hardy called 'the sad science of renunciation', it can also be interpreted as showing the survival of emotion in old age. The words are few, but what they leave unspoken is a universalisation of experience. They have the insubstantial vibrations of unforgettable poetry.

They have no song, the sedges dry,
    And still they sing.
It is within my breast they sing,
    As I pass by.
Within my breast they touch a string,
    They wake a sigh.
There is but sound of sedges dry;
    In me they sing.

CHAPTER TWENTY

1

In March, 1905, the offer of the Order of Merit was imparted to him by Morley, who had himself received it in 1902 when the distinction was created by Edward VII. Meredith replied:—

> Good Friend,—when the communication came I had a vision of an enormous misty mountain that had been in some odd way benevolent to me, and I was mystified until I detected the presence of an active mouse, assuring of a living agency in the strange matter—anything but a ridiculous birth. For evidently it had fretted at the ear of the Premier and caused A.B. to cast eye on a small a.b., long a workman in letters. Was I not right? A title would have sunk me. But I could not be churlish in this case. Besides, I am to be ranked with and near you.

The award was announced in June, producing ' a rain of telegrams ', followed by a command from the Lord Chamberlain to present himself at the Palace in levée dress. This being impracticable, the investiture was performed at Flint Cottage in December, by the King's private secretary. It can be assumed that Morley was mainly responsible; but the honour was generally recognised as due to one whose service to English literature had been so impressive. It added an aura to his renown, and gave deep satisfaction to his fellow writers.

The cause of the delayed investiture was that in October, while being helped into the house by Cole, he had slipped and broken his ankle, which took more than two months to mend, and for half that time was suspended in a cage. He did his best to win a smile through it, but found himself ' shipped by Tedium into the region of Doldrums, where all things droop, and Patience, like a trodden toad, hops and yawns in the endeavour to act up to her name '. In one of Gosse's delightful letters to Hardy there is a reference to the accident.

> George Meredith told me in the summer of your visit to him, which he enjoyed very much. Rather quaintly he said that your

' pessimism ' had grieved him. I wonder whether you were not saddened by his optimism? There is something almost flighty in his cheerfulness. You know he has broken his ankle? He appears to be quite cheerful about that too. What a very curious thing temperament is—there seems no reason at all why G. M. should be so happy, and in some irrational way one almost resents it.

Meredith, when thanking Gosse for his congratulations on the O.M., had written, ' Hardy was here some days back. I am always glad to see him, and have regrets at his going; for the double reason, that I like him, and am afflicted by his twilight view of life.' Gosse's comment need not be taken seriously, being written for the divertment of Hardy. The cheerfulness of Meredith was not temperamental, but a manifestation of stoic fortitude. He had never been urbane; and if he was sometimes bad-tempered there was every excuse for it in his last years, when he was often lonely, often in pain. Deafness all but deprived him of conversation and debarred him from hearing music, which he loved. And he had always lived predominantly in the present. Most old people find consolation in living their years over again. No doubt he had his moments of rich remembrance; but he had not the habit of mind which can make past experience a thesaurus of sustaining recollections. ' The worst of a long life,' he wrote, ' is the seeing our friends drop by the way, and leave in our minds the flickering rushlight of them in memory.' It is worth recording that when Cotter Morison died, Meredith burnt all the letters he had received from him. For him, as he said when almost seventy-five, there must be no ' backward living '. But the present must have taxed his philosophy of resignation; for he needed to be up and doing; and all he could now do was to read, smoke a cigar and go for the daily airing in his chair, drawn by the donkey ' Picnic ', led by Cole, the gardener, with his devoted nurse, Bessy Nicholls, in attendance, and the dog ' Sandie ' scampering among the bushes of Box Hill. It was Miss Nicholls, by the way, who remarked to Barrie—with an affectionate glance toward the unhearing invalid, ' They assure me that he has a wonderful knowledge of woman; all I can say is that I don't think he knows one little thing about women.' One indomitable expedition he made, in January, 1906, to register his liberal vote at the General Election. The donkey-chair went all the way to Leatherhead, about six miles each way, and he was carried in to the polling-booth, providing good copy for the Press photographers and some saddening pictures for those who had known him in his pedestrian heyday. In the previous July and August he had rented a cottage at Aldeburgh, where he was made much of by Clodd, who had a house there, and found ' no scenery, dead flat land, and a long line of shingly beach '. On the ancient quay, along which the poet Crabbe had rolled the barrels of salt which were under his father's charge as collector of duties, he would sit in his bath-chair, sniffing a bunch of bladder-weed from the sodden timbers, and watching the old ferryman, with whom he enjoyed conversing, describing it as his one intellectual amusement. He had, however, the lively society of Clodd and his friends, among whom was Clement Shorter with a camera which produced some photographs of the great man, more permanent than the products of his editorial pen. The air being beneficial, Meredith returned a year later. After that his only change of scene was when he stayed with the Will Merediths, who had a cottage at Fleet. One of his main pleasures after 1902 was an occasional motor drive with Lady Butcher, whose father had acquired a car. Toward the end of his life he sometimes hired one. In his last letters, there are several references to motoring expeditions, and in the autumn of 1908 he went for ' a spin of a hundred miles into Sussex '. Meanwhile his eightieth birthday had been made the occasion of an orgy of homage and adula-tion. From the King he received what was described as a ' cordial and almost affectionate ' message of congratulation, which gave him great gratification, although he must have been aware that the monarch, who seldom trifled with printed matter, could not be numbered among the perusers of his works. Anthony Hope, Israel Zangwill, and Herbert Trench arrived with an address from the Society of Authors. Clodd and Shorter delivered a memorial signed on vellum, and sump-tuously bound, by 250 names representative of art, science, literature, and public life. For a few days Flint Cottage was illuminated by the fickle glare of topical publicity. A blizzard of telegrams and letters descended, and every newspaper in the land—to say nothing of the United States and elsewhere—

had something to say about the Great Optimist, for whose influence as writer and thinker they confidently predicted a perpetuity of recognition by an appreciative posterity. Reporters came thick and fast and inquisitive. A select few were permitted to collect their personal impressions of the celebrated octogenarian, who went for his customary morning drive, appropriately accompanied by Maxse's daughter, Lady Edward Cecil, to whom he may have enjoyed making some caustic comments on the proceedings. For, heartened though he must have been by these demonstrations, he can hardly have failed to wish that a fraction of them had occurred when he was in his prime, and have surmised that the Comic Spirit was casting its oblique beam upon the swarm of temporary enthusiasts who were treating themselves to this ebullition of dotard-worship. ' When I was young,' he told Clodd, ' I had thoughts, ideas, ravishment, but all fell on frosty soil; and a little sunshine would have been so helpful to me.' And when Mrs. Will Meredith asked whether adversity had helped his work, he replied that the peach on the wall ripens best if it has *some* sunshine.

2

For about fifteen years, one of his best friends had been Dr. H. G. Plimmer, a distinguished scientist and fine amateur musician. (The association had begun through Buckston Browne.) He had a great affection for Dr. Plimmer and his wife, who was one of the few people from whom he accepted presents without protest. Her munificence in sending him creature comforts caused him to call her his cornucopia.

In the autumn of 1908 Dr. Plimmer was instrumental in persuading him to compose a poem to be read at the Milton Tercentenary celebrations organised by the British Academy. The forty-six blank verse lines which he produced gave splendid evidence of undiminished powers of mind. They also showed him capable of adapting style and utterance to an official occasion, for they are Miltonic in spirit and expression.

> Defender of the Commonwealth, he joined
> Our temporal fray, whereof is vital fruit,

> And choosing armoury of the Scholar, stood
> Beside his peers to raise the voice for Freedom:
> Nor has fair liberty a champion armed
> To meet on heights or plains the Sophister
> Throughout the ages, equal to this man,
> Whose spirit breathed high Heaven, and drew thence
> The ethereal sword to smite.

It was when he was meditating this—the last piece of verse to which he set his hand—that Constantin Photiadès paid him the visit which he recorded so admirably. On that showery September afternoon he was in good health. Photiadès duly noted

> . . . the noble and ruddy countenance, the large and mobile mouth, the nostrils indicating both delicacy and pride, and the hands which displayed an energy and a vigour surprising in a partly paralysed old man. The nervous and quick gestures which accompany his speech, denote a temperament certainly passionate if not irritable. So far from yielding to physical decadence, he struggles to deny it. . . . I notice that he speaks both clearly and distinctly, and that he articulates each syllable with a precision very remarkable in an Englishman.

The interview lasted several hours, and Photiadès admits that at the end he was acutely fatigued by the strain of conversing with the old Master whose pride would not allow him to use an ear-trumpet. The monologue had been copiously revealing, for he was always willing to open his mind to an intelligent visitor from his beloved France. He spoke of his delight in French art—Watteau, Chardin, and Fragonard were his favourites—and of Clemenceau, whose conversation had so captivated him when he ' had the pleasure of receiving this indefatigable fighter '. Anatole France and Mistral were also mentioned with admiration. It was, however, unfortunate that he inflicted on this sensitive foreigner one of his grumbles against critics and public—a grievance which he persistently and perversely exaggerated.

> The press has often treated me as a clown or a harlequin. And with such little respect that my fellow-citizens can scarcely put up with me. Certainly, at this late hour they accord me a little glory; my name is celebrated, but no one reads my books. As for Englishmen, I put them to flight because I bore them. . . .

No, my countrymen do not value me; at the most they will appreciate me after my death. As to solitude, I have been accustomed to it since my youth. And I am interested in so many things that I never feel lonely. Papers and books make up my society. They keep for me those precious and lofty illusions which are dissipated by contact with men.

It is difficult to decide how much significance should be attached to these complaints, which, in the last ten years of his life, were wholly unjustifiable. From the first, he had written for an audience of the *élite*, and by the time he was fifty his novels had won strong support from that audience. From 1896 onwards his publishers (of whom Will Meredith was a director) had issued three complete editions of his works, and four of the best known novels had appeared in sixpenny paper covers. The novels and poems had been exhaustively discussed in all the leading weeklies, monthlies, and quarterlies, by writers who insisted on his eminence as teacher and master of characterisation. The intellectual vogue of his novels was an indisputable fact. But his poetry had never found many readers, and it may have been this which irritated him. Meanwhile, poor M. Photiadès, who had expected his idolised author to be sagely serene, was compelled to confess disappointment at what he described as a wilful display of supercilious and bitter modesty. Meredith, as he perceived him, suffered continually and deeply from being misunderstood by his contemporaries. But it is certain that the clever young men of 1908 and thereabouts gloried in the elucidation of his obscurities, and if they failed to understand him, it wasn't for want of trying. Anyhow, he was unable to withdraw from his attitude of resentment against supposed neglect. The generation that had rejected him in the '50s and '60s was never forgotten or forgiven. Yet this was a man who proved himself consistently unenvious of the success of others, and who gave ungrudging encouragement wherever it was in his power to do so. In Meredith's mind were many mansions. From the best of them he could say that he did not dread competitors, but rather gave them hail.

> My betters are my masters: purely led
> By their sustainment I likewise shall scale
> Some rocky steps between the mount and vale.

3

In November, when Lady Butcher visited him for the last time, he was weary and spoke very little. She herself was crippled and unwell. The two old friends sat together in the failing autumn light while the fire flickered in the grate. Most of the time he was dozing, and when she departed he barely roused himself to give a farewell benediction.

But during that winter his interest in current events was maintained and his vitality appeared to be unimpaired. His eighty-first birthday was fine and sunny. He took his usual drive. In the evening his son and daughter and daughter-in-law dined with him, together with J. M. Barrie and his wife and the Plimmers. Morley and Haldane had also been with him a day or two before. To Morley he cheerfully remarked— ' Going down quickly; no belief in a future existence.' To him, death had become ' a friend without whom life would be impossible '.

On the 10th of April Swinburne died. This caused him a greater emotional shock than might have been expected. For thirty years their estrangement had been unbroken, until 1898, when Meredith's seventieth birthday reunited them, though only by letters. But Swinburne as he had known him in the '60s was a prodigious phenomenon, and the thought of ' that brain of the vivid illumination extinguished ' was something he could hardly realise. He felt the loss, so he wrote to Watts-Dunton, as part of his life torn away. He was profoundly shaken by it. His last public act was a letter to *The Times* in which he said, ' Those who follow this great poet to his grave may take to heart that the name of Swinburne is one to shine star-like in English literature, a peer among our noblest.'

In the first part of May there was a spell of wintry weather. On May 14th, while out for his drive, he caught a chill which was worsened by going out again next day. Conscious almost to the end, he died in the dawn hour of May 18th. It was characteristic of him that, a few hours before the action of his heart failed, he drank a bottle of beer and smoked a cigar. His death was honoured as a national event. His cremated ashes were buried beside his second wife, as he wished. The Dean of Westminster had denied him the Abbey as a resting-place, though this had been influentially urged. Innumerable columns of applausive print paid tribute to his achievements. But the only thing that mattered was the fact of his release from ' the soul's dark cottage, battered and decayed ', which had housed his invincible youthfulness of heart and clarity of mind. The thoughts and feelings of those who had known him found gracious expression in the words of J. M. Barrie when he wrote that Mr. Meredith was now no longer old. Restored to the plenitude of physical power, he was striding away to join his timeless equals, the immortals. While the funeral procession rumbled along the road to Dorking Cemetery, Meredith was up on Box Hill in the glory of early summer where

> A young apparition shone :
> Known, yet wonderful, white
> Surpassingly . . .
> O the pure wild cherry in bloom.

Freed the fret of thinking, he would revert to the semi-pagan self of his prime—pagan in acceptance of the life-giving and joy-giving power of Nature. And it may be that this is the essential part of him which survives. Most of his finest poems are inspired by the connection of human life and passion with the life of Nature, and it is only when they stand in direct contact with Nature that the characters in his novels put on their full grandeur and charm. The enduringness of his work depends on this rather than his interest in analysing character and conduct, his delight in linguistic dexterity and epigrammatic display, and his abounding humour. As a delineator of womanhood he stands alone in modern literature. But he has also given us a heightened consciousness of Nature which differs from other poets of the 19th Century, whose effects are, I think, mainly pictorial. The great moments in their writing seem held by an imperishable stillness. Meredith is unlike them through his association with movement. He is with us in the lark ascending, in the cloud shadow flying to the hills on a blue and breezy noon, in the flush and fervour of eastern clouds at daybreak, and when evening has brought the shepherd from the hill. In many a mutation of weather and landscape he has made ' the thing at heart our endless own '. Others have shown a sanctioning star above the troubled world of men. The star of Meredith burns and is alive with constant fire. He is the poet of Nature in action and the joy of earth. At any season of the year he stands the test of being thought about when one is out of doors. For the outdoor element in him has the oxygen of aliveness in it. I was once asked what I meant by saying that I liked the idea of Meredith though I couldn't always enjoy what he wrote. I was too young then to be able to frame the answer which has since become apparent to me. It is that the idea of Meredith means a sense of being fully alive. To be at one's best is to be Meredithian.

THE PRINCIPAL WORKS OF GEORGE MEREDITH

POEMS, 1851

THE SHAVING OF SHAGPAT, 1855

FARINA, 1857

THE ORDEAL OF RICHARD FEVEREL, 1859

EVAN HARRINGTON, 1860

MODERN LOVE, 1862

EMILIA IN ENGLAND, 1864

SANDRA BELLONI, 1886

RHODA FLEMING, 1865

VITTORIA, 1867

THE ADVENTURES OF HARRY RICHMOND, 1871

BEAUCHAMP'S CAREER, 1876

THE HOUSE ON THE BEACH, 1877

THE EGOIST, 1879

THE TRAGIC COMEDIANS, 1880

POEMS AND LYRICS OF THE JOY OF EARTH, 1883

DIANA OF THE CROSSWAYS, 1885

BALLADS AND POEMS OF TRAGIC LIFE, 1887

A READING OF EARTH, 1888

JUMP-TO-GLORY JANE, 1889

THE CASE OF GENERAL OPLE AND LADY CAMPER, 1890

THE TALE OF CHLOE, 1890

ONE OF OUR CONQUERORS, 1891

POEMS: THE EMPTY PURSE, ETC., 1892

LORD ORMONT AND HIS AMINTA, 1894

THE AMAZING MARRIAGE, 1895

AN ESSAY ON COMEDY, 1897

ODES IN CONTRIBUTION TO THE SONG OF FRENCH HISTORY, 1898

A READING OF LIFE, 1901

LAST POEMS, 1909

CELT AND SAXON, 1910

INDEX

Index

Index

Printed in Great Britain by
RICHARD CLAY AND COMPANY, LTD.
BUNGAY
Suffolk